La

La Perla Negra

• • •• •• • •• •• •• • • •• • •• •• • •• •• •• • ••

The Black Pearl

BY

ROCKY BARILLA

ROSQUETE PRESS

Book 1 of the Little Gems series

Book Art by Rocky Barilla © 2021

Library of Congress Control Number: 2020910550

ISBN: 978-0-9904851-8-6

OTHER WORKS BY ROCKY BARILLA

SHATTERED DREAMS
Honorable Mention Winner of the 2022 International Latino Book Awards for the Rodolfo Anaya Best Latino Focused Fiction Book

SANCTUARY
Honorable Mention Winner of the 2021 International Latino Book Awards for the Rodolfo Anaya Best Latino Focused Fiction Book

STARS
Honorable Mention Winner of the 2020 International Latino Book Awards for Best Novel - Romance

Esmeralda
First Place Winner of the 2019 International Latino Book Awards for Best Novel - Fantasy Fiction

Harmony of Colors
Second Place Winner of the 2018 International Latino Book Awards for Best Novel - Latino-Focused Fiction

Ay to Zi
Award Winner of the 2018 Latino Literary Now's Latino Books into Movies Awards for Romance
Second Place Winner of the 2017 International Latino Book Awards for Best Novel – Romance

The Devil's Disciple
Award Winner of the 2018 Latino Literary Now's Latino Books into Movies Awards for Suspense/Mystery
Second Place Winner of the 2016 International Latino Book Awards for Best Novel – Mystery

A Taste of Honey
First Place Winner of the 2015 Latino Literary Now's Latino Books into Movies Awards for Fantasy Fiction
Second Place Winner of the 2015 International Latino Book Awards for Best Novel - Fantasy Fiction

All works are published by Rosquete Press. All works are or will be available as Kindle or CreateSpace editions on Amazon.com

DEDICATION

This book is dedicated to my wonderful wife, Dolores, who has been my soulmate in life, writing, and love. I am very grateful and blessed for having her by my side. How she tolerates me, I don't understand. Many years ago, our best man toasted us with "¡Salud, amor, dinero, y tiempo para disfrutarlos!" and now the rest is history.

Sabor a Mí
by Álvaro Carrillo

Tanto tiempo disfrutamos de este amor
Nuestras almas se acercaron, tanto así
Que yo guardo tu sabor
Pero tú llevas también
Sabor a mí
Si negaras mi presencia en tu vivir
Bastaría con abrazarte y conversar
Tanta vida yo te di
Que por fuerza tienes ya
Sabor a mí
No pretendo ser tu dueño
No soy nada, yo no tengo vanidad
De mi vida doy lo bueno
Soy tan pobre, ¿qué otra cosa puedo dar?
Pasarán más de mil años, muchos más
Yo no sé si tenga amor la eternidad
Pero allá, tal como aquí
En la boca llevarás
Sabor a mí

TABLE OF CONTENTS

ACKNOWLEDGEMENTS

Several years ago, my wife Dolores and I were in Zihuatanejo, Mexico, where we live part of the year. Think "Shawshank Redemption." It was around the time of my birthday when my compadres, Yesenia and Hector, gifted me a book about an adventurous sixteenth-century sea voyage from Zihuatanejo to the Moluccas (the Spice Islands in Indonesia) at the behest of the El Conquistador Hernán Cortés. The purposes of this ambitious expedition, modeling Magellan and Loaísa, included proselytizing indigenous peoples and establishing trade with the East Indies. Or to be said succinctly, god and gold (or pearls and spices).

I had read about the attempts by the Jesuits to convert the Japanese and about other colonization efforts by various European powers. However, reading the voyage of Álvaro De Saavedra Cerón (a relative of Hernán Cortés) from Zihuatanejo to Tidore had me mesmerized. As a youngster, I had fantasized about going around the world aboard a sailing ship. I read travel adventures by Jack London, Joseph Conrad, Jules Verne, and Emilio Salgaro. I was hooked.

Then the Covid pandemic hit, and we stayed home. Since I had more than the usual amount of free time, I decided to write my next book. Another magical realism book inspired on the Spanish conquest of Mexico and Spain's desire to trade with the Pacific Islands. Through my research I found evidence that Mexican gold made its way as far west as Thailand.

Additionally, spices, silks, silver, opals, and pearls became the cornerstone of commerce between China, the Philippines, the Moluccas, and Mexico.

Five hundred years later we have a multicultural, global world.

A special thank you to all the chroniclers who have described their journeys in intricate detail so that the rest of us could vicariously tag along.

PROLOGUE

Thursday, January 6, 1527
Zacatula, New Spain (Mexico)

The cool pine-scented Pacific Ocean breeze wafted up the slope to the adobe Franciscan church, where the faithful Spanish residents and the local elite were listening to the ancient Fray Luis Reza tell the story of the three kings who brought the baby Jesus gifts. The diminutive man had less than a dozen thin strands of silver hair, was almost blind, limped, and could barely be heard by the congregation. He had come to New Spain during the time when Hernán Cortés conquered the Aztec Empire in 1521.

Today was the feast of the Epiphany and now a hymn was being sung by the local Spanish landowners and merchants. The altar was marked by a white lace cloth and vases of large crimson poinsettias. A young postulant swung the brass thurible that emitted a sweet-smelling incense that wafted throughout the house of worship. The church was very austere and had been recently built in 1525 with thick walls for its protection. The front entrance had a large atrium cornered by

four capillas posas "little chapels" and its four walls were
painted with the fourteen Stations of the Cross. The crosses did
not have figures of Christ on them. The friars did not want the
indigenous natives to equate the natives' former practice of
human sacrifice with Christianity and Crucifixion.

Friar Reza, who was so old that he was barely able to hold
the gold chalice upright, started to serve Holy Communion. His
assistant, Friar Lorenzo Moreno, was the second in charge of
the church and monastery. He looked after the older priest and
conducted most of the administrative functions of the parish.
Friar Moreno was of medium stature with a pot belly and
tonsured brown hair. He loved the natives whom he adamantly
wanted to convert to Christianity for the church. Friar Moreno
conducted a mass for the indigenous peoples at dawn every day
in the church atrium. This segregation of the church goers
allowed Friar Moreno to bond with the natives.

Friar Moreno, in turn, had a 20-year-old native postulant,
Diego Garcia, helping him. Diego had been brought to
Zacatula by Friar Reza, but he soon became more closely allied
with Friar Moreno. Unlike the friars who wore the ascetic
brown habits, young Diego wore only a leather string with a
Tau cross on it around his neck and a long tan-colored tunic to
distinguish himself as a novice of the Franciscan Capuchin
Order. Diego had been conscripted as a translator for the

Franciscan monastery in Cuernavaca after Cortés' blood bath at Tenochtitlán, in which Diego's family had been massacred. His father had been a royal scribe in the Aztec court and who had passed his language skills onto his son. Diego was therefore able to assist Friar Moreno to learn Nahuatl and later on, to proselytize other indigenous natives to Christianity. Friar Moreno was Diego's champion who saw this young convert as his possible successor. However, the very thought of a native becoming a friar in the Catholic Church went against the local policies of the Spanish rulers who did not even want the indigenous people to become educated for fear of inspiring an uprising. Moreover, the Church believed in separating the Spanish colonizers from the natives as much as possible.

Now, at the later mass for the Spanish elite, Diego was gently guiding Friar Reza by the elbow across the front of the church as the friar delivered the sanctified wafers to the believers. At the side altar, Diego suddenly noticed a young girl kneeling on a pew waiting for communion. He observed that she was not Spanish. Indigenous natives were severely discouraged from attending the nine o'clock mass. But this young woman was different. She wore an ivory-colored rebozo thrown over her head that shielded most of her dark-skinned face and ebony eyes. The clothing of this *cuēitl huīpīlli* (Aztec woman) seemed to be of the highest quality. Her multi-colored thread linen *huipil* (blouse) had dark pearls sewn onto it. A white *cuēitl* (skirt) flowed down to her leather *cactli* (sandals).

As Diego held the gold communion plate under her chin, she pulled her rebozo to the side to receive the host. The postulant could not stop staring at her. He was supposed to be concentrating on being pure of mind and spirit, but his body and all his senses tingled from within. *Please, Lord, help me control myself!* His hand lingered for an extra second. He did not want to leave her. *Please, Lord, deliver me from temptation!* Finally, he broke away. Father Reza continued with the mass, but Diego kept stealing glances to the side chapel where the young woman sat next to an older indigenous woman. The mass ended and Diego wanted to go immediately to Confession. Normally, he went on Saturdays. Could he wait another week? He went back to the monastery proper, with its cloistered area for the residents, that was located just south of the church. He entered the chapel to pray. *Should I just ask Friar Moreno why this is happening to me?! He will probably tell me that I am having impure thoughts. I am sinning! God Almighty will be furious with me!*

The rest of the day Diego alternated between doing his daily chores and praying in the monastery chapel. He was not hungry at dinner time, especially since the fare was very meager in the austere Franciscan tradition.

The next day he walked to his part-time secular job at the open-air warehouse and shipbuilding yard of Don José Alberto Romero, originally from Barcelona. Don José was a distant Habsburg relative of Carlos V, Emperor of the Holy Roman Empire (also known as King Carlos I of Spain). There was a weekly mule caravan from Mexico City and Vera Cruz that brought in Spanish provisions, like olive oil, wine, and dry-cured hams.

Diego was responsible for handling the inventory of the goods coming and going from Spain and recording the transactions in the Spanish language. At times he would have to deal with local indigenous suppliers who only spoke Nahuatl and delivered fish and other daily staples. Don Romero trusted Diego and allowed his young clerk to negotiate with the natives. This permitted Diego to benefit from the business bonus of the "pilón" (the equivalent of a baker's dozen). Diego was theoretically bound to follow the Franciscans' vow of poverty and not to indulge in eating sweets, so his entire earnings went to the monastery. But if the local merchants gave him an extra apple or a coconut confection as a favor, that could be excused as the "unfortunate" cost of doing business. He was not allowed to weigh goods under the law, so sometimes a wink and a smile concluded a deal. In the end, Diego would encourage the local suppliers to come to mass on

Sundays to sell some of their goods. They would be one step closer to God, he thought.

The six-day work routine went by quickly with Diego constantly juggling his secular duties with his religious ones. More often than not, a religious holiday would take precedent and he would have to be absent from the warehouse. Sunday arrived and again Diego assisted the elderly Father Reza at the nine o'clock mass. Diego tried mightily to avoid looking toward the side chapel to seek out the young woman. However, there she was with her loyal indigenous caretaker. He thought she was glowing. She wore similar clothing as the prior week, but this time she seemed to be praying with a special rosary. Father Reza said the mass. Later, as the maiden took communion, Diego had an uncontrollable desire to touch her shoulder. But he didn't.

The following Sunday at dawn, Diego went to the church to give his confession. Father Reza was listening to the pleas for forgiveness from the congregation. But he was not really hearing the confessions since he was almost stone deaf. Diego was given the pro forma ten Hail Marys and five Our Fathers as penance for his sins.

The same routine occurred over the next few weeks with Diego becoming more brazen in his stares at the young woman. *I want to touch her just once. That's all,* he told himself. These transgressions always culminated with the Sunday morning confession to old Friar Reza.

It was the second week in February and Ash Wednesday was quickly approaching. The Franciscan friars were getting ready for the daily Lenten masses. The parishioners were stockpiling exotic foods and wines for their celebrations before the Lenten fastening. Diego was at the public market purchasing a twenty-kilo bag of lentils for the monastery. Their fare would be Spartan for the forty-plus-days fasting period during this religious season. Even onions were "prohibidas". Diego spotted a woman by herself haggling with a purveyor of cacao beans. She looked familiar. Ya! She was the caretaker to the indigenous young woman. He approached her. He was simply dressed, but still wore his Tau cross.

"Good morning," Diego bowed before the woman. He addressed her in Spanish.

She looked at him harshly. She did not respond.

"I am Diego García," he took a step closer. "I am a postulant at the church. I see you at mass."

Still the woman remained silent.

"Who is that young woman I see you with?"

The woman seemed annoyed. She said something to him in Nahuatl which he understood. She wanted him to leave her alone and go away. Diego backed off.

The next several months were uneventful, except that the town's largest merchant, Don Romero, had been given a military decree by Hernán Cortés himself to make ready to supply three ships for a trans-Pacific journey. The work at the warehouse and shipyard doubled. The shipbuilders were working all day and all night. Natives were transporting local timber, hemp rigging, cotton sails, and sap for the ships.

Time was racing and it was now October 30, two days before El Día de Los Muertos. Father Reza warned his flock against celebrating the Day of the Dead which was a pagan rite. There was no afterlife for pagans. There was only heaven and hell.

This decree created a terrible conflict for the natives. The indigenous people were accustomed to celebrating El Día de Los Muertos from November 1 through November 2. Everyone honored their dead relatives by building multi-leveled altars, called ofrendas, and decorating them with candles, copal, marigolds, and the deceased's favorite items.

As Diego was cleaning up the church after mass, it occurred to him that the young woman and her companion were not at mass that day. That was a first, he thought.

Later that day, he went back to the monastery to do more chores. One of his fellow religious aspirants handed him a small cloth wrapped package. Getting some sort of present was a new experience for him.

He took the parcel to his ascetic room. He opened the packet and discovered a leather pouch filled with beautiful black pearls. It reminded him of something that he had seen before but couldn't recall. Also, inside the pouch was a wrinkled piece of paper that had a one-sentence message written in large, crooked letters. It was in Nahuatl. Diego's eyes dilated as he read it:

"I'm KIDNAPPED!"

CHAPTER 1 – 490 YEARS LATER

Tuesday, October 31, 2017
Stanford University

The tall, slender, olive-skinned professor was pacing back and forth in front of his Medieval and Early Modern Latin-American History class. He ran his fingers through his black spiked hair as he paced, deep in thought. Francisco Xavier Reynoso was a very popular professor at Stanford University and his classes were always over-enrolled. This was an upper division class with a few graduate students taking it as an elective.

The weather was cold and everyone was wearing sweaters and coats. The heating in the building left much to be desired. The students were taking notes on their laptops and tablets. Although most of the students seem to be Latino, there was diversity amongst them.

"Last week we ended the European Middle Ages part of the syllabus with Christopher Columbus coming to North America on a shipping expedition financed by Los Reyes Católicos Ferdinand and Isabella. But before we move on to the Early

Modern Ages section," Professor Reynoso stopped and did a half turn looking up to the higher rows, "who can tell me the nationality of Captain Columbus?"

Several hands were raised.

"Spanish!" said the brunette wearing a cardinal red sweater.

"Nice guess, Debbie, but no," Reynoso shook his head in disbelief. "You all should know this. This is really simple."

"Italian, of course," yelled out the John Travolta clone.

"Giovanni, you know that no matter what the Knights of Columbus proclaim, the kingdom of Italy did not become a country until 1861."

Another hand shot up. "He was Genovese," said the Eritrean exchange student sporting a Golden Warriors warmup suit.

"Good job, Assim!"

Reynoso loved to engage with the students, to challenge them, to keep them off-balance. They loved it. They were learning and their education was fun and interesting. His goal was to make them all lifelong learners, just as the nuns had encouraged him to be.

Francisco was born in the Mount Washington area of Los Angeles in 1971. After surviving twelve years of Catholic schools, he went over to the west side of town and earned his bachelor's degree in Spanish at UCLA. He was fortunate to do his junior year abroad in Barcelona where he fell in love with the Hispanic culture.

After graduating, he moved to South Central Los Angeles and enrolled at UCLA's cross-town rival, USC. It took him four grueling years to earn his doctorate in Latin American studies. His Ph.D. thesis was entitled "Mexico: Benito Juarez and French Imperialism.' This controversial work was printed by the California University Press, and it placed him in the limelight of academic debates and in the center of Latino community protests. Stanford University snatched up this gutsy academic and hired him in their Latino American Studies Department.

Since then, Professor Reynoso had done well on the academic circuit and had published works on "The Caste System in Spanish Colonies," "The History of Slavery in Vera Cruz," and "Remedios Varo Uranga Goes to Mexico." He liked to travel and took advantage of conferences in Central and South America. His notoriety was rewarded with visiting professorships at La Universidad de las Américas in Cholula/Puebla, Mexico in 2004, and the University of Texas at Austin in 2011. He currently was working on his sabbatical proposal for 2018-19. He was doing some preliminary research on the topic of "The Christianization of the Philippines."

• • •

"Okay, let's talk a little bit about the start of the Early Modern Age," Reynoso continued his peripatetic pacing. "Many scholars believe it started after Columbus, with at least part of Europe rediscovering classical cultures, the arts, politics, and global economics and commerce. Give me some names of famous people in the early 1500's."

Most of the students raised their hands. The exceptions were those in the back of the room.

"Henry VIII!" the Black Londoner Richard Freeman yelled out.

"Michelangelo and Da Vinci!" Giovanni was making a comeback.

"Martin Luther!" said Nancy Van Krupp with the pigtails.

"Copernicus!" "Machiavelli!"

"Good answers!" Reynoso praised them. "But how about Suleiman the Great?"

There was buzzing and confusion. *Who?*

The class finally ended and Professor Reynoso gave them the assignment to read about Pope Nicholas V and "Dum Diversas." In less than a minute the Wallenberg Hall classroom was empty. Reynoso hurried over to the monthly Stanford University Latinx Association luncheon at the Centro Chicano on campus. A group of the students were planning a "Día de

Los Muertos" event to commemorate family members who has passed away. They were going to assemble a giant oferta with such items as photos, favorite foods, and marigolds. It was to be held at the Holy Cross Cemetery in Colma, about 25 miles north of the university. Some of them would carpool, others would take Caltrain. Everybody was advised to bring jackets, blankets, and flashlights.

After the meeting, their 46-year-old faculty advisor, Professor Francisco Reynoso, followed the sloped pavement down to his departmental office back at the Quad. His right hand stroked the three-day old beard that was showing a few silver highlights. He was deep in thought. The Hoover Tower was casting an opaque dreary shadow over the campus buildings. There was still the scent of damp eucalyptus in the air. Reynoso had eaten only half of his bean and cheese burrito. He would have loved a Pepsi, but he had given up carbonated sugar drinks years back. Besides, a nice Corona cerveza would have been better.

At the faculty office, Professor Reynoso greeted the always cheery Mary Beth Smith, the secretary that he shared with Professor Hypakia "Patty" Papadakis. His office mate told everyone to call her Patty, because otherwise they would slaughter the pronunciation of her full name. She was a professor of Roman and Greek Classical History. To everyone's delight, she brought in kourabiedes that her mother baked on a monthly basis.

"Patty, when are you going to marry me" Francisco would tease.

"When my husband and two kids let me go," she would retort.

The kourabiedes reminded Francisco of his nana's Mexican wedding cookies which he was weaned on during his youth in Los Angeles. Lots of powdered sugar to dust up one's clothes. "My kingdom for a cookie!" he would yell as he helped himself to Patty's kourabiedes.

Francisco's ten-by-ten office had all four walls covered with plaques, photos, and prints. He had a framed certificate of his Ph.D. in Latin American Studies earned at the University of Southern California in 1997. There was also a group picture with a youthful, long haired, mustached version of himself with César Chávez and other UFW supporters during the table grape boycott. And then there were the small 8 by 10-inch print copies of artwork by Latino artists that included Alejandro Rangel Hidalgo, Remedios Varos, and Frida Kahlo.

His stellar research assistant, Tina Fang, was a doctoral student in the Romance Language discipline. The 5'8" stylish woman with long black hair, brown tortoise shell glasses that framed her marquis-cut emerald eyes, and thin scarlet red painted mouth, always surprised people meeting her for the first time not because of her appearance but because of her heavy English accent. The 24-year-old was born in the Macau/Hong Kong region. Tina's family migrated to Vancouver where she graduated with a degree in Spanish from the University of British Columbia. But she disliked the inclement weather of the Northwest. She preferred hot. During the summers of undergraduate school, she attended languages schools in Antigua, Guatemala; San José, Costa Rica; and Valparaiso, Chile. Tina's passion was learning new languages while continuing to improve her Spanish. She had fallen in love with the colors and trams of Valparaiso and returned there to earn her master's degree in Spanish in 2017.

In terms of a career path, Tina was torn between finding a profession where she could be financially successful (her parents' preference) and academia (her grandmother's first choice). She could hear her maa maa's admonitions: "You don't need a man. Too needy. You study hard. Go to college. Be professor. Fortune will find a woman with an education." With her parents' blessing, she enrolled in a doctoral program at Stanford University. It didn't hurt that her father had a third cousin who worked at the HSBC International Bank Centre in San Francisco. And, her parents would have an excuse to come and visit.

Her fate was sealed when upon arriving on campus she saw a university posting for a research assistant position in Latin American Studies working for a Professor Francisco Reynoso. Her language proficiencies in Cantonese, Portuguese, English, and Spanish made her a shoe-in. Reynoso thought he had experienced nirvana when she applied, and he subsequently brought her on as his RA.

It was now the middle of the 2017 fall semester, and Tina was trying to procure original documents or online copies from institutional and private sources about Christianity in the Orient. Ironically enough, it was difficult to gather information from the Catholic Church bureaucracy. There was always some bishop in the Holy See that had to approve such requests. *Thank God, they weren't trying to do a piece on Galileo*, Tina thought.

CHAPTER 2 – POWELL'S BOOKSTORE

Friday, November 3, 2017
Stanford University

On Friday, Professor Reynoso sat at his walnut desk scattered with wrinkled papers and stacked with dusty books. The lighting was uneven due to burned out bulbs in the moldy water-damaged ceiling. He was trying to catch up on his emails and academic committee work. Thank God the amount of paper had actually diminished over the years. However, the computer-generated correspondence could fill a small library.

He scrolled down his computer screen trying to triage his emails. There was a notice for the monthly Faculty Senate meeting. On its agenda was a proposed resolution addressing single-use takeaway food containers. Then, there was a short note from his ex-wife, Maureen Brady, who worked for the Los Angeles City Attorney. She was inquiring if Francisco wanted to join her and her live-in boyfriend in the City (San Francisco) on Saturday. The relationship between Mo and Paco (Maureen and Francisco) was cordial and friendly, but she was Type A and was always in full-speed ahead mode.

He replied that, unfortunately, he had a prior commitment. Francisco always had difficulty saying "no" straight away to his ex. The pair had been married for almost five years and had dated off and on for three years prior, but their personalities were too different and not compatible. Francisco's current girlfriend, Zoe Walters, whom he had met at a fellow faculty member's party in Silicon Valley, was completely different than Maureen. Zoe was someone's sister and had come with two other ladies. Francisco found the curly-haired brunette so laid back and relaxed. Her perfect million-dollar smile forced him to get her email address. A month later the two were dating. She worked as a systems analyst for Adobe Acrobat in San José where she lived. She was a project supervisor tasked with making its software more accessible to users with disabilities.

Reynoso grabbed a small expresso coffee and two stale black and orange glazed Halloween cookies from the table in the departmental kitchen. Tina was there drinking her green tea and talking with another graduate student.

His RA was ready to call it a day. "Goodbye, Professor Reynoso," Tina said, and continued with a Downton Abbey accented Spanish pronunciation of "hasta mañana."

"Be safe, Tina," Francisco shouted out. "Don't forget your committee needs to meet sooner than later." He was on her doctoral committee and needed to prod her about finalizing a dissertation topic. The professor knew that Tina's research would take her ten times longer than she planned for.

Francisco slipped back into his office. Mary Beth came in and handed him some phone messages and his afternoon mail. After she exited, he began to update his calendar. *Need to buy some football tickets.* A chime suddenly sounded on his computer. He typically received between 50 and 100 emails per day, not counting spam and junk. This new email had Powell's Bookstore in Portland, Oregon, as the sender. The name of the sender, Joel Brenner, was unfamiliar to Francisco. The professor rarely dealt with independent bookstores, except Kepler's which was located in nearby Menlo Park. The subscript under Joel's name had his title as the Assistant Manager of Antiquarian Collections. Reynoso collected primary authority works, not old books. The message read:

> Professor Reynoso, found 16th Century Mexican chronicles. Not in the best condition. Price negotiable. Contact me if interested. Joel.

Reynoso tried to go to the Powell's Bookstore website, but had trouble navigating the four hundred different book sections and departments. *This sounds like a good project for Tina*, he thought. *This will help her with her research skills. Mexican chronicles about what? The life of a Spanish hidalgo? The enslavement of the indigenous natives?* Maybe, if he was lucky, it would be a cookbook.

• • •

The dull light came in through his bedroom window. Francisco woke up Saturday morning at his normal seven a.m. He could never sleep in. The night before, he had gone to happy hour with two of his buddies from the gym. A few brewskies and a burger made for a great end of the week ritual. Ace was a financial advisor for Morgan Stanley who was hot on Apple stock that week. Miles was a probate attorney who wasted his two-hour gym workouts bullshitting most of the time. All three were divorcés. Francisco seemed to be the only disciplined one in terms of doing real physical exercise. His body was trim and he was fairly strong for his size and weight.

Francisco began his 45 minute run through the neighborhood after a quick breakfast. "Good morning!" Francisco said to his neighbor down the street who was raking leaves in the front yard. He had three alternate routes, depending on his mood. One was all hills, but today he took the easy route. After showering, he did his weekly grocery shopping at Trader Joe's, stocking up on Greek yogurt, blueberries, and nineteen cent bananas.

On Saturday night, Zoe and he went to Kabul's, an Afghan restaurant in nearby San Carlos. Zoe loved the kaddo, the sugar pumpkin with yogurt and tomato sauce over basmati rice. Francisco inhaled the grilled chicken skewers.

Sundays were kickback days for Francisco. He ran errands, went to movies at the Stanford Theatre, or prepared for his classes.

• • •

On Monday, he was back in his office editing his commentary on a colleague's academic article on the Ming Dynasty. Since he knew very little about the history of China or the Middle Kingdom, he made notations on form and style only.

He was on page three of the work when he heard a slight tap on his office door.

"Enter!"

"Good morning, Professor Reynoso."

"Morning, Tina," Francisco turned his head away from the computer. "How was your weekend?"

"Good," she replied. "Spent the weekend in San Francisco with Issa's cousin. Hung out in J-town and the Asian Art Museum. Very cool!" Issa was her boyfriend.

The rest of the day went by quickly. Francisco was just about to grab a cup of coffee when he received another email from Powell's bookstore. *Crap! I forgot to assign this to Tina!*

CHAPTER 3 – DUM DIVERSAS

Tuesday, November 7, 2017
Stanford University

Class days were serious business for Professor Reynoso. He hurried to his office on campus to review his class notes. On Tuesdays he taught his Medieval and Early Modern Age History class in the morning.

The class began with a student trying to sneak his German Shepherd into the back row.

"Joel, please take your pet outside," Reynoso shook his head. Every once in a while, one of his students would push the envelope. "You know the rules."

There was a small buzzing among the students.

Professor Reynoso starting his pacing. Class had begun. "Last week I told you we would be talking about Pope Nicholas V and his papal bull 'Dum Diversas.'. . . What was a papal bull?"

The question prompted a lot of chuckling amongst the class. After a few prompts by Professor Reynoso, the students became engaged in a discussion about the pope speaking *ex cathedra* or as the direct spokesperson of god. Some of the students who were not familiar with Catholicism were lost.

"When did the notion of White supremacy start?" There was a loud silence in the class. *Why was he asking this question?*

Joel made a fatal error by reentering the classroom at this time. "Joel, what do you think?" Reynoso asked him. The professor repeated the question.

"With the Egyptians?" Joel guessed.

"Someone else," Reynoso looked to his front row where usually the smartest students sat. They were usually well prepared.

There were a lot of answers but they were all shot down by Professor Reynoso.

"In 1452, Pope Nicholas V issued his papal bull, 'Dum Diversas,' which allowed European Christian rulers to seize the property of non-Christians. Although the concept of the "White Race" had not yet be formulated, Europeans unsurprisingly fell into this category. This allowed them to conquer, colonize, exploit, and enslave non-Christian lands and persons. Not surprising, was the fact that the conquered and enslaved people were usually non-white. Moreover, Spain took it one step further when it claimed the entire Pacific Ocean.

"In terms of International Law, totally misnamed because only Christian countries were signatories, Europeans were allowed to ignore the sovereignties and rights of indigenous people all over the world. Guess what?! The victims of the colonizations were people of color. This became the basis for the Doctrine of Discovery.

"In 1513 Spain issued its "Requerimiento" which gave it the divine right to seize properties of the New World and subjugate the indigenous people. The confiscated lands were then under the authority of the pope and the king of Spain. The other European countries used the same justification for slavery and land seizures."

The class discussion turned to slavery in the New World. A hand went up. "Professor, how did the United States justify killing the Native Americans and stripping them of their lands?"

"That's a great question, Toby," Reynoso kept walking back and forth as he spoke. "In 1823 the U.S. Supreme Court in *Johnson v. M'Intosh* held that the "discovery rights" of Europeans in the New World had been transferred to the United States. President Polk used this rationale in his Manifest Destiny approach to expand the U.S. territories to the Pacific Ocean with the extermination of the Native Americans. The

'Indians' were considered infidels, heathens and savages . . ."

The class ended, but the students wanted to continue the animated discussions. Finally, everyone exited and Francisco walked back to his office. He checked his computer and read his emails. He decided to try to call Joel at Powell's Bookstore. He dialed and got a voicemail message. "Hi, this is Joel. Your call is very important to us. Please leave your name, the time that you called, your phone number, and a brief message. We will call you back as soon as we are able."

Francisco grumbled and left a voice mail for Joel to call his assistant Tina Fang.

The next morning Tina promptly dialed Powell's and talked to a store clerk who told her that Joel didn't get into his office until ten. Tina went back to her cubicle and began studying for her afternoon Italian class. The class was taught by the Romance Language Professor, Vito Segreti, who was also on Tina's doctoral dissertation committee. She knew that she had to make everyone on the committee happy if she was to succeed.

The day's Italian lesson was going to center on whether or not William Shakespeare stole some of his stories from the Italians. They were going to discuss whether the Bard had purloined "Romeo and Juliet" from Luigi da Port (1530's).

There seemed to be many similarities with some of
Shakespeare's works! But, hey, there were no copyright laws
in those days. Ol' Willie probably stole some of the stories, fair
and square.

At 11:15 Tina's office phone rang. It was Joel from
Powell's. He apologized profusely for his delay in returning
her call. He explained that he had a collection of 16th century
chronicles and diaries from Mexico. They were on
consignment from a Mexican estate via a private book seller in
Mexico City. Tina wasn't sure what Joel was trying to peddle.

"Why don't you try to sell them to a university or museum"
she inquired.

"From what I gather, they tried," Joel answered. "but had
no success."

"Exactly what are these papers?"

"Well, the two main docs are naval chronicles from Captain
General Saavedra's ship, the 'Florida.' The other is the naval
chronicle of the ship 'Santiago,' and the third is the diary of
Diego García."

"I'm sorry, Joel, I'm lost," Tina was perplexed. "What is
their significance?"

"We think they chronicle a sea journey from Mexico to the
Moluccas."

"Sorry!" Tina clenched her lower jaw to elongate her question with an English accent twist. "Where are the Moluccas?"

"In Indonesia. West of the Philippines."

"Okay, I'm still confused."

"This would have been the first sea expedition westward from the Américas to the Spice Islands."

"And that is important, because?" her voice exhibited frustration. *Was this on par with Hernán Cortés slept here?* She wondered.

"They were trying to find Magellan's and Loaísa's convoys."

"Okay, I'll talk to Professor Reynoso," she wanted to end the conversation. "We'll get back to you."

CHAPTER 4 – PROVENANCE

Thursday, November 9, 2017
Stanford University

Tina spent the next day doing some preliminary research for Professor Reynoso. She had always been an overachiever. She liked Reynoso and wanted to be an excellent student. Besides, some letters of recommendation from him down the road would be great. She drafted a little memo to him regarding the background of the Powell documents and emailed him a copy.

November 9, 2017

To: Professor Reynoso
From: Tina Fang, RA
RE: Background on Magellan and De Loaisa Expeditions

In 1519, the Portuguese captain commonly known as Ferdinand Magellan left Spain with five ships and 270 men under the authority of Carlos I, King of Spain. The mission was to take a western route from Spain to Las Moluccas (the Spice Islands). The eastern route to the Spice Islands was controlled by the Portuguese, under the Treaty of Tordesillas. Magellan was killed in the Philippines at the Battle of Mactan. Only one ship of the five returned to Spain, under the Basque second-in-command, Juan Sebastián Elcano. This ship succeeded in circumnavigating the globe.

In 1525, the Basque captain, García Jofre de Loaísa was ordered by Carlos the First to colonize the East Indies. Specifically, he was charged with rescuing Magellan's ship, the "Trinidad," and finding the ancient region of Ophir, known from the biblical times of Solomon for its wealth. Loaísa and Elcano left La Coruña, Spain, with seven ships and 450 men. Only the "Santa María de la Victoria" reached the Moluccas. Unfortunately, Loaísa and Elcano died of scurvy during the journey. The survivors, including the Augustine friar Andrés de Urdaneta y Cerain, did not return to Spain until 1536. Another of Loaísa's ships, the "Santiago," reached Mexico in 1526 with Fortunio de Alango taking over command.

In the late afternoon Reynoso called Tina into his office. Today, Francisco was wearing casual attire, a red Stanford polo shirt and tan chinos. He was taking advantage of the fact that he had no meetings to attend. He was slowly sipping his tepid expresso.

"Thanks for the memo," he grinned at his RA. "As usual, it was succinct and informative." Tina smiled. *Have to make everybody happy*, her mother had drilled this into her. As a practical matter, Tina needed to learn how to gather and research primary sources for her doctoral dissertation. This would be good practice.

"Professor, I talked to Joel. It seems that these lost chronicles are on consignment to Powell's from the UNAM (Autonomous National University of Mexico). They were gifted to the university by a Roberto Gutierrez. Professor Elias Tobias at UNAM was put in charge of the documents but he unfortunately suffered a stroke. He was unable to start the project and nobody wanted to take over. UNAM is trying to dispose of the archives through a private Mexican bookstore that in turn is contacting large bookstores like Powell's."

"I wonder why the school doesn't give the collection to the University of Guadalajara or some other place," Reynoso was thinking out loud.

"One reason, professor," Tina responded assertively, "is that there may be some problems of provenance. The ownership and transfers of these old works have not been well-maintained. Joel has no evidence to vouch for their authenticity."

"Oh, great!" Reynoso was pondering his options. *Could this be a new project? Could he change his sabbatical assignment to research these documents? Is there a slight chance that there might be something relevant in these archives for Tina to use in her dissertation? If Tina did all the leg work, the two of them could write an academic article and he would give her co-authorship credit.* "What is your recommendation, Tina?" He was testing her.

"I think these materials are very speculative and high risk," she was prepared. "On the other hand, as they say in Mexico, 'quién no se arriesga, no pasa la mar' (nothing ventured, nothing gained)." Reynoso smiled. She was so bright.

"How much are they asking?" he inquired.

"Five thousand."

"Five thousand!!!"

• • •

The next day after her Friday morning research techniques seminar, Tina placed a phone call to Joel. She and the professor were going to reject the offer on the historical documents.

"Mr. Brenner is not here at the moment," a young female voice from Powell's Books answered the phone. "May I take a message?"

Tina didn't want to drop the bomb on poor Joel via a telephone message. That wasn't her style. She gave the person on the other end of the line her name and requested that Joel call her that afternoon.

Twenty minutes later Tina and Joel were talking.

"Sorry, Joel, but Professor Reynoso said five thousand is too much."

"Well, how much is he willing to pay?"

Tina had Macau blood in her veins. She knew how to negotiate. It sounded like Joel really needed to sell.

"Don't know. You really haven't given us an accurate description of what you have and what you are selling." *Make him play defense.*

"Well, we have two naval logs and two diaries plus a handful of handwritten notes from a ship that traveled from Mexico to Indonesia in 1527."

"Sorry, Joel, you lost me. Why is that important?"

"Well, this was the very first expedition ever from the Americas to Oceania," Joel was speaking quickly. He sounded like an amateur salesperson.

"We thought Magellan and Loaísa were the first," She was trying to find out how much Joel really knew.

"No! No! They came from Spain, not the Americas," he sighed. "The ships we're talking about left from Mexico."

They went back and forth for a few minutes.

"Joel, this is really difficult to discuss without seeing the actual documents."

"I could send you some PDF copies to give you a sample look," Joel was now taking control. "How about if I send you a copy of the Cédula from Emperor Carlos V of the Holy Roman Empire to Hernán Cortés?"

"What is a cédula?" Tina was now caught off balance.

"You know, a royal decree."

"Okay, fine," she capitulated. "But what about the provenance? Its authenticity?"

"Well, that's kind of a problem," the air was being let out of his voice. "These documents have not been well kept for the last four hundred years."

"How about if you send us twenty pages of your best samples?" Tina was pressing. "Originals. No copies. No PDFs."

"Don't know if I can do that," Joel responded.

"Joel, we are not going to make a purchase blindly."

"Well, I guess we could insure them," he hesitated. "Don't know how much for."

"You wanted five thousand for the total collection. I am assuming you have all the works in your possession. Let me see what I can do."

"Okay."

"Tina, I have your mailing address. I will send examples to your attention, is that all right?"

"Yes."

"And Tina, please inform Professor Reynoso that if he wants all the documents, we can let him have them for 4500 pesos."

Tina couldn't believe her ears. Not five thousand dollars! 4500 pesos! That was less than $250. *Wait until I tell the professor!*

On Monday, Tina had received both PDF files and original samples via express mail. She was overwhelmed. There was no semblance of order in the papers. Most of the examples were worm-eaten, torn, or water damaged papers. They smelled moldy and dusky. Moreover, the documents were in several languages: Castilian Spanish, Portuguese, Latin, Arabic, and Nahuatl. She scheduled a meeting with Professor Reynoso for the late afternoon.

The professor offered her a chocolate peanut butter protein bar. He had skipped lunch because of an informal meeting with the dean regarding his winter quarter teaching schedule and a potential committee assignment.

"No, thank you, professor," Tina politely declined.

"Tell me what you have," Reynoso began. "I know you have been working hard. Thank you for doing this. These things are never as simple as they look."

Tina dipped her head politely and started:

"The papers do not seem to be in the best of shape judging from the examples. They have been damaged by moisture, mold, worms, and other elements. I even think there were rat droppings in the materials. The quality is poor. The ink is faded, and the writings are barely decipherable. I have good reason to believe that large portions of the documents are missing."

Reynoso listened carefully, taking notes on a legal pad. He was impressed. When Tina was finished, he asked the crucial question:

"What it your recommendation on the purchase?"

"We should buy them, but at a lower price," she said confidently.

"Why?"

"I think there might be some valuable historical information in the papers," she leaned forward in her seat. "Also, the asking price is in pesos, not dollars. It might be affordable."

Reynoso's jaw dropped. He was overwhelmed. He quickly did the math and said, "Okay, then, offer the young man $150. U.S. dollars!" The professor smiled and then she reciprocated.

"Yes, professor."

"What are you and Izzy doing this weekend?" Reynoso asked. "I don't want to see you here."

The remainder of the week raced by. It was a quarter to five on Friday afternoon when Francisco left the office. Tonight, he was going to meet up with his colleague, Kenji Sato, at the Dutch Goose for happy hour and maybe some shuffleboard.

Sato had published several books on the efficacy of bilingual education in the public school system. He had done extensive research on the academic achievement of Mexican limited English proficient (LEP) immigrant students and this had been the basis of his friendship with Francisco.

• • •

A week and a half went by and Tina was still trying to resolve the Powell's Bookstore offer.
The first thing that Tina did on that November Monday morning was to call Joel at Powell's.

"Hey, Tina, how was your weekend?" Joel was trying to make nice.

"Lovely."

"Did you get a chance to check out the papers?"

"Yes."

"What do you think?"

"Honestly, Joel, the quality of the documents seems very poor. They're in horrible condition. Not even collated," Tina was ready to negotiate.

There was silence on the other end of the line.

"Joel, are you still there?"

There was a cough. "Maybe I could get the price down to $225."

Late that afternoon, Tina stuck her head into Professor Reynoso's office and told him that the deal was made.

"Great job!" Francisco beamed. One more thing off his plate. "How much are we paying?"

"$100 AS-IS," she replied.

His head snapped back in shock. "That's almost a Christmas present to us." Reynoso smiled.

"What are we going to do with the materials?"

"I think we have at least two options," the professor stated. "I can hire another person to digest these materials and write a preliminary report. Or I can hand the project over to you." The professor expected his RA to think it over.

"If it is acceptable to you, professor, I would like to do the initial research," she exuded confidence. "I think it will help me when I do my dissertation."

"As you wish," the professor was elated. "The project is now officially yours."

"Thank you."

• • •

The next day Professor Reynoso almost drowned as he rushed from this office to the Wallenberg Hall classroom. The rain was fierce and cold. His Stanford-logoed Gortex rain jacket was soaked and he had a challenge peeling it off.

The students piled in, leaving puddles of water everywhere. The smell of the hot coffees in front rows of the students seemed to perk him up, although there was a hint of mildew in the room.

The professor started his usual pacing. "Was Hernán Cortés a good guy or bad guy? That is what we are going to discuss today."

A few students straggled in late. Then there was a bark.

"Toby!"

Reynoso picked up his notes and began.

"Hernán Cortés was a child of the Reconquista," he stopped and made a U-turn in front of the class. A little sloshing squealed out of his wet Rockports. "Christian Spain had finally been victorious against the Islamic Moors in the southern part of the unified Spain. This was known as the Reconquista.

"The deepening religious fervor in the Spanish territories spawned the Spanish Inquisition which was established to identify heretics. Jews and Muslims quickly converted to Catholicism. Who were the Conversos?"

A few hands were raised.

"They were the Jews in Spain and Portugal who were forced to convert to Catholicism," the young man with the black frizzy hair answered.

"Good answer, Manny," the professor gave him a thumbs up. "What happened if they didn't convert?"

"I think they were expelled from the country," a heavy reddish-brown hair woman responded. "For sure, they were persecuted and lost all of their properties. And probably their lives."

The faces of the students displayed shock and irritation.

"Who were the Moriscos?" The professor continued with his questions.

"They were the Moors who converted to Catholicism," the black-eyed Fatima answered.

"Correct!" nodded the professor. "Interestingly enough, the Jews and the Moors and most of the Christians lived in harmony for several centuries before this. But what does all of this have to do with El Conquistador Cortés?

"His subjugation of the New World was to serve God and the Spanish king," the professor stopped and looked at the back row. "But what else?"

"To find new lands!"

"To get rich!"

"To become famous!"

"Hold on to that thought," Reynoso carried with his lecture. "In 1521, after Cortés had conquered the Aztec empire in Mexico, he was given the title of marquis by the king of Spain.

Spain sent over clergy, settlers, and of course, governmental officials. The clergy started to convert the indigenous people to Christianity. Aztec chiefs were allowed to keep their estates and status, if they converted. Sound familiar? Additionally, intermarriage between the newcomers and the indigenous people was allowed which led to the mixed race of mestizos.

"But Cortés had problems with the Governor of Cuba, Diego Velasquez. The latter was jealous and tried to turn the Spanish king against Cortés. But besides the conquest of Mexico, Cortés was famous for two other things. What were they?"

"His relationship with the Malinche?" Selena shouted out.

"Close."

"Stopping human sacrifice."

"Close.

"Finding gold.

"Closer," the professor shook his head. "He joined the unique group of explorers who first ventured into the Pacific. It is said that he may have discovered California. Okay, let's go back to his most famous contribution. What was it?"

There were a dozen guesses.

"Give up?" Reynoso stopped in front of the class and put his hands on his hips.

The total class nodded in resignation.

"On his fourth and last trip from the New World back to Spain, be brought back cacao beans to the king of Spain," the professor gave a slight smile. "And thus, chocolate was introduced to Europe, and the rest is history."

CHAPTER 5 – VA BENE

Wednesday, November 22, 2017
Stanford University

On Wednesday, the campus mail delivered three differently sized FedEx boxes from Powell's Bookstore to Tina. After lunch, she began carefully taking out the various stacks of the dusty and musty documents and pieces therein. Her first task would be to sort them out by language. At first glance, she recognized the Spanish, even though it was Castilian, and the Portuguese. She wasn't sure if the next language was Latin. She thought it was. For sure, the fourth language was Arabic. That was one she knew that she could not translate. But the last set of papers was very strange. They consisted of a combination of pictographs with Latin letters. *I may have bitten off more than I can chew,* she thought.

• • •

Thanksgiving was both a "hit or miss" event for Francisco. The "miss" was that Zoe was out of town. The professor hadn't wanted to accompany her to Orlando to have Thanksgiving dinner with her brother. The sibling was a redneck Southerner who was always railing against those liberal Democrats.

The "hit" came from one of Francisco's colleagues from the Stanford gym, Marty Gross, a Kinesiology professor and PE coach. She always invited "orphans" to her home for Thanksgiving. Her partner Heidi Kleinman was an excellent cook. One of Heidi's sons, Madison, and his 10 year-year-old son had driven over from Sacramento. Several women PE teachers from the area were also in attendance. They all seemed at least 6'2" or taller.

The food was insane. Marty had brined the 20-pound turkey and had started cooking it at 6 a.m. that morning. Francisco had felt ambitious and prepared a calabacitas a la mexicana casserole that he had learned from his mother. The wine flowed freely and he was almost too stuffed to try one of the half dozen desserts. The pumpkin pie was the winner. He had two slices. He waddled home.

The long weekend allowed him time to do two long runs. One was a ten-mile stretch at Half Moon Bay. When Zoe came home Sunday night. Francisco really didn't feel like going out to dinner with her. He was stuffed from all the leftovers he had brought home.

• • •

Tina worked on the documents all weekend. She made an appointment to see Professor Segreti after the Tuesday Italian class.

"Come stai, Tina?" the Romance Language professor greeted her in his tiny office that was covered with photos of cities from all over the world.

"Va bene."

"Are we going to talk about your dissertation?" Segreti asked.

"Mi scusi. Not quite there yet, professor," Tina gave him a disarming smile. She had thought that she would have had her dissertation proposal nailed down by now. She was falling behind, which was not her style.

He smiled and nodded. *She's the typical doctoral student. The hardest task of a dissertation is writing the initial proposal paragraph.*

"I am working for Professor Reynoso on some 16th century documents from Mexico that we have recently acquired," Tina explained. "And I am having some difficulties determining what languages they are written in."

Professor Segreti's eyebrows furrowed. "Do you have copies with you?" His interest was piqued.

"Yes, professor," she handed him several plastic protectors each housing a different individual document.

He took them and examined them one by one.

"Well, this one is Castilian Spanish," Segreti grinned. "I would have a challenge translating it."

Tina was jotting down notes and put a yellow sticky reminder on the sample he handed back to her.

Segreti performed these individual scrutinies several times. Indeed, the third language was Latin, he thought. "Reminds me of my days as an altar boy."

Tina was wondering if Romance Languages was really her calling. This was a lot of work. It was crazy.

"This is Arabic," he said confidently. "But this other one, I'm not sure."

Tina expected him to hand the last one back.

"Let me have it for a few days and let me see what I can do."

• • •

A week went by, and then on a Tuesday, Tina went into Reynoso's office. Her Italian final was finished, and she had turned in two term papers. She was here to give him a status report. "Professor, I sorted the documents by languages. There are at least five languages."

"Wow!" the professor was amazed. "You've done a great job!"

"I'm halfway finished with the Portuguese translation," she continued. "The language is archaic. It looks like a naval chronicle."

Reynoso blinked his eyes. This was way beyond what he was expecting.

"Professor, what do you think about me changing my dissertation topic to the linguistic interpretation of these documents?" Tina asked. If she was going to do all this work, she could combine the research project with her dissertation.

Professor Reynoso had contemplated using these documents for an academic article for the Stanford Press as part of his sabbatical. He thought about it for a minute. He could do the historical analysis and Tina could do the linguistic one. No problem with her doing this for her dissertation. However, he would have to think twice about letting her be a co-author on the article.

"I think it is a great idea," he said. "You could complete your dissertation sooner." *It will also help incentivize her to comprehensively devour this project*, he thought.

It will be a win-win. She will probably work the entire Christmas break on it. It's rough being a grad student.

CHAPTER 6 – TRANSLATIONS

Wednesday, January 10, 2018
Palo Alto, California

The noise level in the Faculty Lounge was moderately loud. It was after the Christmas break and everyone was wearing their new (but ugly) gifted sweaters. Francisco was running late and rushed in,

• • •

When Christmas break had begun in the middle of December, Francisco rushed to write his Christmas cards. They always had some sort of beautiful artwork, filled with lots of colors. He would inscribe a little note, like "Life is Good!" or something else philosophical. His parents had passed away years ago. He only had his older sister, Gabriela "Gabby" Jamieson who worked for the Pasadena Police Department in the Motor Vehicles Division. She was married to a really nice guy, Pat, who worked for San Gabriel Valley Water District. Francisco and he got always along great, always making fun of

Gabby behind her back. *What can I get them for Christmas? Probably another gift card. It's easier.*

His only other living relative was his nephew, Ray "Ramon" Jamison, who was a Marine stationed at the U.S. Embassy in Stockholm. He was only 26 and still single. In his latest email to his uncle, Ray hinted that he had just finished sub-zero arctic military training. It was classified, so Francisco didn't know for sure. Francisco had put $1000 into a trust fund every year for his nephew since his birth. This could help Ray purchase a house when or if he separated from the service.

On the home front, Francisco chilled with Zoe. A few days before Christmas, she decided to take a few days off from work because her office was half empty. She and Francisco then spent several days skiing at the Heavenly Ski Resort at South Lake Tahoe. The snow was perfect, but every joint in Francisco's body ached. Hot brandies by the fireplace brought him back to life. They spent Christmas together at her place in San José. Francisco bought her a sparkly green and red silk top. He received an Apple iPad from her. They had a special Christmas dinner at Il Fornaio and then she left to go to Orlando to see her brother for New Year's.

Fortunately for him, Francisco had been invited to numerous holiday parties and dinners. *Life was indeed good!*

• • •

January arrived and it was the third day of class for the winter quarter. Professorial conversations could be overheard discussing the new dean of the nanotechnology department, the campus policy on vaping, and the purchase of solar panels from China. Professor Vito Segreti was drinking a glass of Barbera wine when Professor Reynoso arrived. He stood up and gave Francisco a hug. They shook hands. Reynoso recalled meeting Vito at a departmental meeting years prior. A young woman had come up to Francisco Segreti and asked him in Italian if he was indeed Italian. He replied that no, he was Sicilian. After that Francisco and Vito became friends.

"We haven't talked in a long time, Francisco," Segreti gave him a big smile.

Reynoso nodded. He was hungry. His eyes dropped down to the menu.

A waitress came by and asked for his drink order. "A ginger beer, please." Reynoso usually didn't drink alcohol on campus.

"What's up, Vito?"

"First of all, I want to tell you that your RA Tina is delightful," the Romance Language professor began. "She is very bright. She told me yesterday that she was closing in on her dissertation topic."

Reynoso nodded. His street sense told him that Vito was up to something.

"She's the best," Reynoso corroborated Segreti's praise.

"As you know, she brought some papers recently for me to examine," Segreti leaned in. "I emailed scanned copies of them to a professor I know down in Guadalajara, Miranda Rios. She is a Linguistics professor at the university down there."

Reynoso thought it was interesting that his colleague had consulted this Mexican professor without consulting him first. Segreti must have had a special reason.

"She thinks that the language is Nahuatl," Segreti said. "The ancient language of the Aztecs."

"That sounds promising," Francisco looked closer at his colleague. His eyes moved back and forth. His mind started to race.

Vito blurted out, "If it is, it would be the oldest specimen of a Nahuatl document ever found!"

Reynoso's eyes widened.

• • •

Professors Reynoso and Segreti were both on Tina's doctoral committee. Several weeks later all five members of her committee approved Tina's dissertation topic, "A Linguistic History of Early 16th Century Mexico." She was advised that if she modified or refined her focus, she needed to bring any revised topic back to the committee. One of the members of the committee, Professor Ruth Horowitz, was concerned that the subject might be too narrow, but she left that up to Tina to decide.

At the same time, Reynoso went to his department head to get approval of the project. Although this was not necessary, departmental consent usually meant funding and support. Reynoso would also be using this as the basis for his sabbatical the following summer. He changed his travel location from the Mexican Cultural Institute in D.C. to the University of Guadalajara. Segreti was going to give him Professor Rios' contact information. Guadalajara was accessible to everything, not to mention great food. His favorite was the torta ahogada (drunken sandwich). Life is good!

When he got final approval for his project, he tried to get an additional stipend for Tina, but that was not approved. The better news was that he was approved to pay for translations of some of the papers. Specifically, for the Latin, Arabic, and the Castilian Spanish. The antiquated Spanish was problematic for anyone not from the mother country, Spain, but there were several graduate Madrileños who could do the work.

Tina would translate the Portuguese since she was fluent in this language. But the weak link was the Nahuatl writing. At least once a week Professor Reynoso began having conference calls with the Linguistics Professor, Miranda Rios, from the University of Guadalajara. She was making arrangements with an indigenous Purépecha teacher and part-time translator, Carlos Erandi, who spoke Tarascan, but who also was proficient in Nahuatl. Erandi was anxious to do the translations. Rios, through Reynoso, promised Erandi a sizable stipend (more than he would make in a year) and a dozen tablet computers for his high school students in Guanajuato.

For her part, Professor Rios began the paperwork for Professor Reynoso to become a visiting professor at the University of Guadalajara for the summer. This position would be in addition to his sabbatical stipend. Reynoso was ecstatic. Miranda Rios and her husband insisted that Francisco stay with them during his stay. They had a 17-year-old daughter, Mirasol, who was exploring colleges to enroll in. She was looking at the University of Salamanca in Spain, the University of Uppsala in Sweden, and the University of Bologna in Italy. She, like her mother, was proficient in five languages. Professor Rios hoped that Francisco could persuade her to apply to Stanford and maybe put in a good word for her.

Tina worked diligently on the project. Her regular schoolwork was stellar and earned her outstanding grades. She told Reynoso that she would work on their project first and then build her dissertation from her notes and from additional research sources.

Everybody was busy. In March Professor Reynoso received a well-wrapped package from the University of Guadalajara. It was from Professor Rios. Carlos Erandi had completed one Nahuatl translation into Spanish. Professor Rios had edited it and then translated the Spanish version into English.

Francisco made copies of the English translation from Nahuatl. He took Tina out for coffee (actually, she drank matcha tea) on campus and handed her a copy. She clapped her hands and bounced in her seat. They were both overwhelmed with joy. Now the real work could begin.

CHAPTER 7 – MAGELLAN & ELCANO EXPEDITIONS

Monday, March 26, 2018
Palo Alto, California

Time flew by and Tina was spending twice as much time on the ancient documents than on her own studies. The translations were coming together. Tina had finished the Portuguese; and the Nahuatl and Spanish documents seemed complete. The Spanish student from Granada spit out the Castilian translation in under two weeks, but the Latin counterparts were not completed. Tina had reviewed Professor Rios' memo and Erandi's translation of the Nahuatl pieces. They would suffice for Reynoso's article, but Tina would have to do more research for her own dissertation. She wondered if she would have to learn Nahuatl, or at least the basics. Going to Mexico might be interesting. Maybe she could tag along with Professor Reynoso during his sabbatical. Or would that be too crazy?

She had spent her weekend typing up the first draft of the proposed article. Tina needed to meet with Professor Reynoso with the initial installment. She had done several drafts. Even though technically it was Spring recess, Monday morning found Professor Reynoso and Tina meeting in his office. He was drinking a cappuccino and she had a chai latte.

"Professor, sections seem to be missing," Tina advised him in an apologetic manner as she handed him the initial draft of the Reynoso article. "I didn't want to delay the report. I hope this is all right."

"It's all good. One of the things that you will learn in preparing your dissertation," Francisco smiled, "is that the final draft is never final. You will always be making changes. Let me read it and we'll go on from there."

Professor Reynoso read Tina's revised version of the background leading up to the 1527 naval expedition from Mexico to the Moluccas (Spice Islands). He adjusted his glasses. *Hmm! This is really interesting.* He was elated.

March 25, 2018
To: Professor Francisco Reynoso
From: Tina Fang, RA
RE: Background of the Santiago (Loaisa) Expedition

The historical setting of the sailing of the ship Santiago to the Moluccas Islands begins with several key facts and figures:

The Treaty of Tordesillas

In 1492, Christopher Columbus reached the New World. When his sponsors, King Ferdinand and Queen Isabella of Spain, got word of his discoveries, they petitioned Pope Alexander VI (Spanish-born Rodrigo de Borja. Father of Lucrezia and Cesare Borgia) as to their royal claims. The pope issued a bull drawing a line of demarcation from the North Pole to the South Pole, 100 leagues (approximately 300 miles) west of the Cape Verde Islands. Spain was given the rights to discovered lands west of this line; Portugal was given the rights east of this line. This gave Spain control over all the Americas, except Brazil.

The Treaty of Tordesillas was signed in 1494 by the kings of both Spain and Portugal but revised the line of demarcation to 46°30′ W of Greenwich or 370 leagues (1185 miles) west of the Cape Verde Islands. This effectively gave the Portuguese the exclusive use of eastern sea routes to Oceania and eastern Asia. This forced the Spanish to explore western routes to the Americas and the Pacific.

Ferdinand Magellan
Ferdinand Magellan (aka Fernão de Magalhães) was born in Porto, Portugal, around 1480. In his mid-20's, Ferdinand joined the Portuguese navy and explored East Africa. In 1511, he participated in the capture of the Moluccas in Indonesia. In 1513, he served in Morocco where he was wounded. He was also charged with colluding with the Moors. He was then ostracized by the Portuguese king. In 1517, Magellan moved to Seville where he became an advisor to the Spanish court.

In 1519 Magellan pitched a plan to sail westward from Spain to the Moluccas Islands in Indonesia. Nicknamed the Spice Islands, there was a rich supply of cloves and nutmeg, which were literally worth their weight in gold. King Carlos I of Spain (later to be Charles V of the Holy Roman Empire) approved the proposal. On September 20, 1519, Magellan set out westward with five ships. After a mutiny and a shipwreck, only four ships continued down the eastern coast of South America to Patagonia.

By October 1520, Magellan and his men had entered what is now called the Strait of Magellan. It took them over a month to pass through the strait, during which time the master of one of the ships deserted and sailed back home. The remaining ships passed through the strait and into the Pacific Ocean. In March 1521, the fleet anchored in Guam.

Later in March of 1521, Magellan's fleet reached Homonhom Island on the edge of the Philippines with less than 150 of the 270 men who started the expedition. Magellan traded with Rajah Humabon, the island king, and a bond was quickly formed. The Spanish crew soon became involved in a war between Humabon and another rival leader. Magellan was killed in battle on April 27, 1521.

The remaining crew members escaped the Philippines and continued on toward the Spice Islands, arriving in November of 1521. Juan Sebastian Elcano, the Spanish (Basque) commander of the last ship, the Victoria, later set sail for home in December and reached Spain on September 8, 1522.

García Jofre de Loaísa
García Jofre de Loaísa was born in Ciudad Real, Spain, in 1490. He served King Carlos I of Spain and on June

25, 1525, was sent to find Magellan, colonize the Moluccas, and discover new territories for Spain. He left with seven ships, including the "Santiago." Sebastián Elcano (who was the first officer to circumnavigate the globe in the Magellan expedition) was second in command. Due to inclement weather, scurvy, and bad navigation, only the Santa María de la Victoria, a nao (a three mast sailing vessel) under the command of Andres de Urdaneta, succeeded in making it to the Spice Islands in September of 1526. Both García Jofre de Loaísa and his second-in-command Juan Sebastián Elcano had died at sea during the Pacific voyage. The patache Santiago, a two mast sailing boat, commanded by Raul Calderón, ended up sailing north and arrived in Mexico in July of 1526. Cortés took charge of the ship Santiago and had it escorted to Zacatula
.

Nota bene: Hans von Aachen, gunner for Magellan and Loaísa, returned to Spain, being the first person to circumnavigate the globe twice.

Hernán Cortés

Hernán Cortés was born in Medellin, Spain, in 1485. He is known as the Spanish conquistador who defeated the Aztec Empire with the aid of Doña Marina (aka Malinche) and other anti-Aztec indigenous peoples in 1521. He is also known for the Christianization of the indigenous people and his quest for gold and riches.

After conquering the Mexican territories, King Carlos I commanded Cortés, via a cédula (Royal Order) on June 20, 1526, to dispatch his newly constructed ships to the Moluccas to find Magellan and de Loaísa. Cortés, in turn, ordered his cousin Álvaro de Sayavedra Cerón to sail from Zihuatanejo in the province of Zacatula, to comply with the emperor's order.

• • •

Two days later Reynoso and Tina again met in his office. He was dressed in a light blue button-down shirt with tan chinos and cordovan loafers. She was wearing a black long sleeve blouse with black pants. He was sipping his expresso and she was drinking her matcha tea.

"That was a nice background piece," Professor Reynoso. "It was a good review for me. I had forgotten a lot of those historical details."

Tina smiled, but did not say anything.

"Your research was excellent, and the format was easy to read," Reynoso was softly advising her. "As you write your dissertation, it is important to understand that it not just what you write, but also how you write it. You will minimize negative critiques if you put your mindset into pleasing the five members of your dissertation committee. What does that mean? It may mean that you have to write for five different audiences."

Tina's eyes were bulging. She wanted to say something but was hesitant.

"Unfortunately, form sometimes gets in the way of substance," Reynoso continued. It was better that he prepares her now for the contentious realities of graduate school and departmental politics.

"But, professor, how will I know what pleases you and the other four committee members?" she finally asked. She had never been confronted with the harsh realities of being a doctoral student. She was afraid she had been too naïve up until now.

"You need to start writing your observations and feelings now," advised Reynoso. "An easy question: how do you see Professor Segreti and me?"

"I think you both as very smart professors who are good instructors. My linguistics professor Nora Pei is very similar to you and Professor Segreti, but she is very . . . emotive? I'm not sure that is the right word." She wanted to say "hyper," but knew she could not disrespect a faculty member. "I don't really know the other two that well. I will follow your advice and research them." She nodded as to acknowledge his counsel.

CHAPTER 8 – THE FRIAR'S TALE

Sunday, April 1, 2018
Palo Alto, California

Francisco spent the Easter holidays basically alone. Zoe and he had drifted apart since New Year's. Neither one of them made any plans to spend Easter together.

On Easter Sunday, Francisco took a long hike around Los Gatos. The weather was warm with a few puffy clouds scattered in the blue skies. He came home and showered.

His class preparation for the next day went along quickly, especially with a Corona in his hand. At about ten o'clock that night, he jumped into bed. He crawled under the covers that had a nice lavender scent. Per his usual routine, he sat up and read. Tonight, he had brought with him the manila envelope that contained the next research installment from Tina. He opened it. Curiosity got the better of him and he started to read the memo.

March 29, 2018
To: Professor Francisco Reynoso

From: Tina Fang, RA
RE: Friar Moreno's Records
Languages: Spanish and Latin

The following is a summary of some of the first documents that I have translated. A few are repetitive of the last memo I submitted to you, but they corroborate the information available from other sources:

After Cortés' defeat of the Aztecs in the Battle of Tenochtitlan in the middle of 1521, King Carlos issued a cédula to the Grand Conquistador.

One of the main charges that King Carlos I had bestowed upon Hernan Cortés, in addition to procuring more territories for Spain and securing the spice trade, was that the Spanish Conquistador convert the indigenous peoples to Christianity. Cortés requested that Franciscan and Dominican friars be sent to Mexico for this purpose. He did not want local diocesan priests because of their privileged nature. He wanted ministers of the Faith who could identify with the natives.

As a result of his plea to the emperor, a group of twelve Franciscan monks arrived in Mexico in May of 1524. They were nicknamed the Twelve Apostles of Mexico and were led by Friar Martin de Valencia. Cortés was known for his strong faith and was called "the new Moses" by the Franciscans . . .

Among the twelve Franciscans was Friar Lorenzo Moreno. This portly man of medium height and tonsured brown hair had been born in Córdoba, Spain in 1489. He had blue eyes and a jack o'lantern smile due to his missing teeth. Upon arriving in

New Spain in 1524, he began his quest to Christianize the natives. As a result of the Spanish battles against the Aztecs and subsequent efforts to reestablish peace, Friar Moreno was put in charge of a fourteen-year-old native princess from Texcoco. Yepyollotli was born in 1510 in Xalapa and was the daughter of the ruler Cacamatzin from Texcoco (25 miles south of Mexico City). After months of proselytizing, the girl was baptized with the name of María Del Rosario.

María Del Rosario had a caretaker from her Texcoco province, Cihuatl, a 32-year-old woman who had also been sent to Friar Moreno. The servant was also baptized and named "Inocente." María Del Rosario's father Cacamatzin had been killed by the Cortés invasion, and the girl and her servant were the spoils of war. To Cortés' credit, he spared the pair from being married off to some of his soldiers. He wanted to show the advantage of Christianity to the natives. Unfortunately for other captives, they were branded with the initial "G" and distributed to the soldiers and other native tribes loyal to Cortés. Nobody knew what the "G" stood for.

In 1525 Friar Moreno moved María Del Rosario, Inocente, and several other natives to the cathedral in Cholula. The neophytes led a very austere life that was filled with religious instruction and prayer.

The following year, Friar Moreno traveled to Zacatula on the Pacific coast with the girl and her servant. His new immediate superior, however, did not like women in his congregation. He cited immoral distraction to the other neophytes. Temptation. Temptation. Temptation. Friar Luis Reza was the superior of the church in Zacatula. The short, seventy-year-old elder had been born in Cadiz and was waning in health. He was almost blind, limped, and had blotched skin, but he remained steadfast in his dogmatic beliefs.

Despite his total commitment to the evangelization of the natives, Friar Moreno had a difficult time communicating with the natives. He spoke only Latin and Spanish, and the indigenous people spoke Nahuatl and Purépecha. Unfortunately, he did not have an ear for languages. Fortunately, Father Reza had a young assistant from Cuernavaca. The young man had been born in Tenochtitlán in 1507, the son of a royal Aztec scribe who was killed in the battles with the Spanish. In 1521 the youngster was sent to the Franciscan monastery in Cuernavaca to work as a translator for Friar Reza. He spoke Nahuatl, Purépecha, and was now learning Spanish and Latin. He was baptized with the name Diego García. In 1525 Friar Reza was assigned to Zacatula and brought Diego with him as a translator.

Diego García followed the strict discipline of the Franciscan Order and was a postulant. A one-year internship was required to qualify for the Capuchin religious life. Although Diego was a layman, he could join the other friars at mass, prayer, meditation, meals, and fraternity. Diego did not have to wear the habit, and just wore the "Tau" cross.

Because Diego was still a lay person, he worked at the shipyards for Don Romero, supervising native workers and managing the shipping accounts. Upon Friar Moreno's arrival, Diego was assigned to him. Friar Moreno showed a strong avuncular relationship with the young man and saw Diego as one day succeeding him as the local friar. The bond was further strengthened by Friar Moreno's overwhelming desire to learn the native linguae francae and Diego's ability to quickly learn Spanish. The synergy of the pair made the evangelization of the indigenous people easier.

The trusteeship of María Del Rosario and Inocente continued under the watch of Friar Moreno. He kept a tight rein on the pair. They were not allowed to leave the premises. María Del Rosario was always clad in native tunic dresses adorned with a necklace of black pearls. She also had a rosary of ebony pearls. Under her white rebozo she wore gold ear plugs. Inocente wore a simpler type of a tunic.

• • •

It was almost two o'clock in the morning when Francisco finished reading the Friar's story. *When did nuns start coming to New Spain? It seems that María Del Rosario was afforded special treatment. Why? Was Cortés a good guy or a bad guy?*

CHAPTER 9 – DURO'S LOGS

Wednesday, April 18, 2018
Palo Alto, California

Francisco had a hectic week and a half. He had to postpone the prior week's meeting with Tina because he was preparing a final examination for his Latin American history class. He then spent the whole weekend gathering up his receipts for his income tax returns. His printer wouldn't print, and he wasted time trying to troubleshoot it. Finally, he cleaned the printer heads and then everything was good to go. Francisco dropped off the newly printed tax documents at his CPA friend Tony's office in San Carlos. He signed a form requesting an extension to file a late tax return. *The pinche government takes out a lot of taxes.*

Tina came into this office wearing black jeans and a black Stanford-logoed sweater. Her hair was in pigtails. She had already grabbed her matcha tea from the faculty kitchen area.

"I liked the Friar Moreno piece," Professor Reynoso was showing his million-dollar white-toothed smile. "He seemed like a nice guy. Treated the indigenous folk well." *Well, after*

the Spaniards stole Mexico's gold and land, he grimaced. He
had read Bernal Diaz del Castillo's "The Discovery and
Conquest of Mexico" and Carey McWilliams "The Conquest
of Mexico" in graduate school. The foreign powers stole the
lands, and wealth, fair and square.

"In Hong Kong and Macau where I was born, there is the
history of the Jesuits," she allowed herself to share. "They were
very different than the Franciscans in Mexico. It seemed that
they were part of the mercantile class."

They discussed the Moreno piece for a while. It seemed to
be very vanilla. Then they began to review the translation of
the La Florida's naval log. Tina had submitted this to Professor
Reynoso the prior week, but he had not perused it.

"This was very difficult to decipher. The excerpts are from
the Captain Saavedra expedition ship's manifest," Tina began.

"These were Captain Saavedra's sea logs?"

"Yes, but actually written at least in part by Cesáreo
Fernández Duro, Saavedra's chronicler for the journey."

"Is this the mission from Mexico to the Moluccas?"

"Yes."

"Tina, can you give me a little background about the
Saavedra journey."

"I'll try," Tina began. "Many pages of the log were missing
or indecipherable."

"Is it Captain Saavedra or Sayavedra?" the professor inquired.

"According to the Spanish student who translated these pages, it's both. Sometimes it was spelled with a 'y' and at other times not," Tina tried to explain. "Juan Carlos and I have been talking. He's very good. He says that there are a lot of misspellings and grammatical errors in the original documents. He also thinks that at least two persons made entries into the ship's log," Professor Reynoso was not surprised. The ship's captain would quite often be semi-literate and would need others to assist him.

"Unfortunately, Tina, because we want to have this work published by an academic journal, our translations should be literal," Reynoso was beginning to fret over concerns if an editorial board rejected their work because of figurative interpretations or metaphorical opinions. The reviews wanted data and information in its rawest form.

Reynoso and Tina discussed the editorial challenges for the next twenty minutes. She was astounded at how picayunish the publishing criteria could be. In the end, they decided they would resolve nuances, corrections, and idiomatic meanings through footnotes (or endnotes). They would also have to notify the translators to flag areas of concern that had to be deciphered.

"Tina, are you hungry?" they had been talking for over an hour without even reviewing the latest translation. He felt that they needed a break.

"Sure," she smiled gratefully. Tina knew that they both had to unwind.

It was warm and sunny outside. The smell of Spring was in the air. They walked slowly up the inclined thoroughfare toward the Student Union. Students were zigzagging around them. Skateboards, razors, and motorized scooters were verboten on campus. Students of all shapes and colors passed them, speaking Spanish, Arabic, Mandarin, and a dozen other languages. Stanford University had the global reputation of drawing bright and accomplished individuals from all over the world.

Reynoso grabbed a veggie burger, and she ordered a Thai wrap. They sat at an outside table and made small talk while they ate.

An hour later Professor Reynoso and Tina were back in his office. Tina began an explanation of the expedition of Captain Saavedra from Mexico to Las Moluccas in 1527. For the next four hours they discussed multiple entries with just short breaks for coffee or to use the bathroom.

The sea logs of Álvaro De Saavedra Cerón from the flagship La Florida, were scribbled notes from his official chronicler, Cesáreo Fernández Duro. They were water damaged, worm eaten, and many pages were missing. Tina had written a memo summarizing these documents. She and Professor Reynoso began pouring over the information she provided.

April 10, 2018
To: Professor Francisco Reynoso
From: Tina Fang, RA
RE: Saavedra/Duro's Logs of La Florida - Overview
Languages: Spanish and Latin

In 1526, Emperor Carlos V sent a cédula (Royal Decree) to Hernán Cortés, the Conquistador of Mexico, ordering him to send his newly constructed ships to Las Moluccas (the Spice Islands) to find Magellan and de Loaísa. Additionally, it was to be a trading venture and new land discovery mission.

Cortés saw the procurement of wealth in his future. He chose his cousin, Álvaro De Saavedra Cerón, as captain general of the expedition. The Conquistador knew that the procurement of new lands and spices would please the emperor. Cortés also instructed Antonio Guiral, the fleet's accountant to record all trade transactions to ensure that Carlos V received the royal fifth of all wealth and gains.

Cortés had commissioned the construction of three ships (two three-masted caravels and one two-masted bergantín) in Zacatula (just north of Zihuatanejo on the Pacific Coast) for this expedition. Saavedra was in the fifty-ton flagship, La Florida, captained by Eduardo

Viurco and a fifty-man crew. The forty-five-ton caravel, the Santiago, with forty-five men, was commanded by Captain Luis de Cárdenas. Pedro Fuentes de Xérez captained the twenty-ton bergantín, Espiritu Santo, that had a crew of fifteen. Cortés spent sixty thousand gold coins outfitting the ships with food rations, trading commodities, weapons, building materials, medicines, and fishing gear. The crews included soldiers, sailors, smiths, masons, and friars.

The trading goods included multicolored beads, mirrors, Spanish and Mexican clothing, and Aztec feather work. The food provisions included biscuits, salt-cured pork, beans, dried fish, and wine. There was a partially illegible notation in the passenger manifest of a black pearl being part of the cargo of Espiritu Santo.

Francisco put down the papers for a moment and closed his eyes. This was tedious work and he felt a headache coming on. Finally, he resumed reading the ship logs of La Florida. It appeared that the author of the logs was Cesario Duro.

October 31, 1527 - Our three ships set sail today from Zihuatanejo, Mexico (17.6417° N 101.5517° W). Fortunately, Captain General Saavedra has charts of Magellan's expedition, plus those of the Portuguese pilot, Fortunio de Alango, who navigated the ship Santiago to Mexico from the Guevara/Loaísa expedition. A direct course from Zihuatanejo to Las Moluccas has been plotted.

November 13, 1527 - Our flagship Florida sprang a leak. Five tons of food had to be discarded to lighten the ship. The men are not happy to lose some of their provisions.

December 14, 1527 – Our convoy was caught in a storm. La Florida almost sank, and the Santiago and Espíritu Santo have been presumed lost at sea. We pray that we may still find them.

January 1, 1528 – We was anchored in Palau and procured fresh water. A few days later we resumed our journey. But soon disease broke out on La Florida and several men died. We buried them at sea. The men are grumbling more each day.

January 23, 1528 – Today the crew mutinied, and the ship's pilot died. Captain General Saavedra appointed Viurco to replace him. Many are still sick and hanging on to dear life by a thread.

February 1, 1527 - Our ship arrived in Mindanao, Philippines. Captain General Saavedra ordered La Florida repaired. It will take several weeks. Captain General Saavedra also made contact with the natives in order to procure food, establish trade, and inquire about other Spanish fleets. Captain General Saavedra presented letters from Cortés to the chieftains. They were written in Latin and pontificated about the grandeur of King Carlos V who wanted to Christianize them all. The natives were not receptive or friendly.

February 14, 1527 - A man was brought aboard who claims to be Sebastian de Puerta. He was on the Santa María de la Victoria from the Loaísa convoy. He had been shipwrecked on the coast. He was captured and enslaved by the local natives. He told Captain General Saavedra that he had heard rumors that eight of

Magellan's crew had been sold as slaves to the Chinese five years ago.

February 21, 1527 - Captain General Saavedra set sail and a few days later we landed at Sarangani in the southern part of the Philippines. Two more fugitives, Romay and Sánchez from Loaísa's expedition were discovered here. The natives here are friendly and furnished us with rice, pigs, goats, and chickens. Romay and Sánchez advised Captain General Saavedra that Captain Loaísa died on his expedition and that the Portuguese are building forts in Las Moluccas.

The fugitives also informed Captain General Saavedra that the Loaísa flagship, Santa María de la Victoria, with 120 men had reached the island of Tidore in Indonesia under Captain Hernando de Urdaneta. They were situated less than two miles from a Portuguese fort. The local natives were assisting the Spaniards because of their amiable dealings with Magellan. On March 30, 1528, La Florida landed at the Spanish fort in Tidore. Saavedra supplied the loyal Spaniards with arms, medicines, and supplies. Here La Florida was finally repaired and stocked with local provisions, except for pork because the locals were Muslim. There was a battle with a Portuguese ship in which the Spanish prevailed.

Francisco got up and went to the bathroom. He knew that the sea logs of La Florida were incomplete. Too many days had been skipped. He wondered why.

June 12, 1528 – Today La Florida set sail laden with eight tons of spices supplied by Captain De Urdaneta.

Due to the lack of wind, we made very little progress going eastward toward New Spain (Mexico).

June 30, 1528 – Today we landed in New Guinea and decided to stay until better winds prevail. Through treachery, Simon de Brito and several of the crew who are Portuguese stole the ship's rowboat and abandoned La Florida.

July 15, 1528 - La Florida headed northward and we were attacked by unfriendly natives in the Caroline Islands when we tried to land. Finally, we landed in another part of the Carolines and found much friendlier natives. Our ship had to be fully refurbished, including replacing and calking every plank. After the work was done and we were fully provisioned, we set sail eastward. For more than six weeks we had very little wind and finally landed in New Guinea in August of 1528. We then proceeded to the Marshall Islands.

September 15, 1528 - We finally retreated to Sarangani because of the unfavorable winds.

December 1, 1528 - We returned to Tidore. The natives were glad to see Captain General Saavedra and turned over the captured Portuguese fugitives to him, including Simon De Brito. Three days later these three scoundrels were executed.

October 8, 1529 - La Florida proceeded northeastward. The next day Captain General Saavedra died. He had been ill for several months. We conducted a very sad service for him before casting his holy body into the sea.

October 16, 1529 – Another unfortunate event. The successor captain Pedro Laso also died. We turned La Florida around. We need a captain who can sail our ship back home!

December 8, 1529 - Our ship returned to Tidore. Here we found out that the Spanish had turned over the island to the Portuguese. We were captured and are being held prisoners.

As he finished reading the logs, his head ached from eye strain. He was amazed at the adventures and hardships the early sailors endured

. He shuffled through some other research papers.   The sources stated that in 1534, five years later, La Florida's crew were sent back to Spain.

"Wow! That was some journey!" Professor Reynoso had been a Salgari and Sabatini swashbuckling aficionado as a young high school student. Pirates, evil lords, beautiful damsels, and treasure troves had filled his juvenile head while growing up.

Finally, Professor Reynoso and Tina decided to call it a day. They were both totally exhausted.

The next day Professor Reynoso and Tina resumed their meeting. "This was the fourth attempt at establishing a westward route to the Spice Islands," Tina remarked.

"It seems that Carlos V was talking out of both sides of his mouth," Professor Reynoso opined. "Christianity for the natives in exchange for wealth and territories. And not to mention the fact that spices were worth more than gold."

"I felt sorry for poor Captain Saavedra. He died on the trip," Tina added. "But at least there were some survivors."

"Do you want to call it quits?" the professor asked her.

"I think I don't want to stop," Tina was feeling a second wind although her mind seemed to be swirling. For the remainder of the meeting, they examined the levels of Spanish fluency in the chronicles.

"Professor, I think that the chronicles were initially written by Captain Saavedra," Tina posited. "But after the storm, according to our translator Juan Carlos, the Spanish version is more basic, and less, if I can be candid, learned."

"The captain's scribe, Duro, was probably just a poor clerk."

CHAPTER 10 – THE SUBSTITUTE

Friday, April 20, 2018
Palo Alto

The happy hour at the Dutch Goose bar with his Friday night colleague allowed Francisco to unwind after a hard week. He felt like going to bed early when he came home. He resumed reading an Emilio Salgari book, "The Lion of Damascus," as his escape. No word from Zoe.

Francisco hadn't been in bed more than ten minutes, when his cell phone buzzed. There was a text message. It was from Tina.

> Professor, need to meet asap. Juan Carlos sent me more translations. I am totally overwhelmed. You are not going to believe what they say!

Francisco texted Tina back. They agreed to meet at their usual time on Tuesday in his office. He was elated that she was taking this Saavedra expedition project so seriously.

• • •

Reynoso still had not heard from Zoe. On Tuesday he was wearing a pink button-down shirt under his Stanford V-neck sweater and was eating some Greek yogurt with granola when the doctoral student walked into his office. She sat down across from him.

"Tina, you're really doing an excellent job on this project," he gave her an avuncular smile. She was the best.

"I'm just trying to work hard, professor," she wore dangly blue turquoise earrings and was dressed all is black.

After going through some personal chitchat, Tina gave him a summary of a second and seemingly unofficial journal of Captain Saavedra's sea journey. It was chronicled by Vincenzo da Napoli. Juan Carlos had done the translation but had warned Tina that most of the diary was missing or in terrible condition. Less than ten pages were really salvageable but related an interesting counterpoint to the official journal. Reynoso was wondering if these new papers were worth anything.

"Juan Carlos did a great job interpreting these worm-infested papers," Tina continued. "There is one section about how one sailor had worms and how they tried to cure him. It was gross. Then there is an episode where a crew member stole a bottle of rum from the galley. Things did not go well for the thief.

"Then Juan Carlos said that he had problems with some of the Spanish nautical terms. Like the term 'bitacora'" Tina had a serious look on her face. "Or military terms like 'maestre.' He doesn't know anything about ships or navies."

"Neither do I. Tina, we'll have to follow up on this," the professor squinted. He was deep in thought.

"Professor, do you think that there would be someone in the Spanish navy who could help us out? The Spanish built a lot of ships."

"That's a great idea!" Reynoso was still thinking. "I need to make a note to myself to contact Professor Rios down in Guadalajara. She might know someone."

They continued onto other topics and other questions. So far, the documents that they had examined, analyzed, and essayed, had been less than high quality. Some of the pages were missing, adulterated, or illegible. Some writings were indecipherable. Juan Carlos sometimes gave alternative translations for the same passages.

"Professor, Juan Carlos noted that some of the pages seemed official. They had stamps and ink and wax," Tina pointed out. "Other papers looked like charcoal sketches."

"Shall we assume that the formal documents are the captain's? Or his clerk's?" Reynoso was thinking out loud. "Why would others want to chronicle the journey?"

"Boredom?" Tina said glibly. They looked at each and gave a little laugh.

They slowly continued from one topic to other. "I think da Napoli explains the mutinies as being caused by a curse on the fleet," Tina's face was scrunched up in thought.

"There is some mention of a woman being aboard one of Saavedra's ships," Tina said. "Supposedly, a Portuguese sailor complained about it and was subsequently flogged. In my culture, women on ships bring storms. But I have no answer for the flogging."

"Cortés and Saavedra certainly wanted spices and had a variety of items to trade," Reynoso was ruminating out loud. "We have a lot of unanswered questions, Tina."

"Including who this woman was and what happened to her?" Tina added.

• • •

The following Wednesday Francisco allowed himself the luxury of a five-mile jog around campus. Afterwards, his body tingled from the steaming hot shower. The Tiger Balm smelling faculty gym was small but provided a nice respite in the middle of the week for a little exercise. A few of the professors had been formidable jocks in their earlier years, but for the most part, this gym was a forum for wounded warriors recuperating from their latest medical operations. Today, Jake

Stern was giving an MSNBC news report on his arthroscopic surgery for the reconstruction of his deteriorated anterior cruciate ligament (ACL). In twelve weeks, he would be playing tennis again.

Not to be outdone, Randy White reported that he had had surgery on his left shoulder due to a torn rotator cuff injury. After five months of physical therapy and lap swimming, he had 75 percent mobility in his arm. He still was prohibited from playing golf.

The gym had a warm-up room, weight and cardio machines, and dumbbells. Francisco tried to lift weights two or three times a week. He ran on Wednesdays and Fridays and used the elliptical machine on other days or when there was inclement weather. But the real benefit at the fitness center was kibitzing about the Stanford athletic teams, the idiot U.S. president, or the rising Bay Area housing prices. A few stock tips, a recommendation for a good plumber, and the hottest new restaurant were added bonuses.

Francisco toweled himself dry. He trimmed his stubble beard prior to going to work. He finished dressing and grabbed his gym bag. It would take him approximately seven and a half minutes to walk to his office in the Quad, unless he wanted to grab a coffee first.

As Professor Reynoso entered his departmental office, his secretary Mary Beth had a very serious look on her face. Today she was wearing a white blouse with a rounded collar. Her tortoise-shell glasses looked like a tiara on top of her head.

"Professor, there is an urgent message from Dean Chandler," she said in an official tone. "She wants to see you as soon as possible."

"Thanks, Mary Beth." So much for sitting down and catching up on his emails. He dropped off his gym bag in the corner of his office and made his way down the hall to the other side of the department. Dean Chandler's secretary, Della Jackson, greeted him with her seductive ebony eyes.

"Hola, Francisco," her sweet voice rang. "I'll let the dean know that you are here."

Francisco was half-intimidated, half-intrigued with Della. He knew that she really ran the department. He always wanted to be on her good side.

A minute later he was sitting at the large walnut desk across from Dean Chandler who was wearing a navy business suit. Dorothea Chandler had earned her doctorate in International Studies from Bryn Mawr after being a Rhodes scholar. Her short brown hair framed her light blue eyes and ruddy cheeks.

"Thanks, Francisco, for coming on such short notice," she began in an even tone. "Congratulations on getting your sabbatical proposal approved. So, you're going to be in Mexico for a spell," she said more as a statement than a question.

"Yes, dean," he replied with a confident smile. "Got a visiting professor gig down there also."

"That's fantastic," she was sizing him up. "Francisco, let me just cut to the chase. I need a small favor."

Francisco's mind flew to high alert. Anytime she used the phrase "small favor" it usually involved ransoming one's first born or amputating a limb. He cleared his throat. "What do you need, dean?"

"Professor Ellison will be on a medical leave of absence for at least three months."

"Is he okay?" Francisco bit.

"He'll be fine. Just routine rest and recovery."

"Well," Francisco paused for a moment and asked, "What do you need from me?"

"I need you to take over one of his classes. You are a friend of LeRoy's, so I'm asking you to volunteer," she was being tactful. "I already have two of his other classes covered. This is the third one. He would approve of you covering for him."

"What if I can't do it?" Francisco was trying to retreat. *I can't teach another class just before my sabbatical!*

"Well, if I don't get a volunteer, I will just have to assign someone to the task," she was giving Francisco a serious look. "With your background, I think you can pull off a Caribbean history class. The quarter is half over. The class can do term papers for you. Maybe Ellison will be recuperated enough to grade them."

Francisco felt trapped. He couldn't say "no."

"In return, I think we can free up some more funds for your translation project," she smiled at him. *Welcome to academic politics.*

CHAPTER 11 – CUBA LIBRE

Wednesday, April 25, 2018
Palo Alto

Francisco was home by seven o'clock. He was overwhelmed. *Another class to teach?!* To provide himself a distraction, he picked up a thin book on the Taino Indians who had occupied Puerto Rico, Cuba, and other parts of the Caribbean prior to Christopher Columbus' arrival. The Tainos were always fighting with their fierce and savage neighbors, the Caribes and then were obliterated by the Spanish conquistadors. Later, African slaves were brought to the islands to harvest cotton and other crops. His eyes kept closing as he struggled to grasp the basics of Caribbean history.

The next day Professor Reynoso ambled over to the other side of the department where Professor Ellison had his office. He found a lanky, long-haired blonde with bangs and large hoop earrings behind a desk. She had a prominent mole on her neck. He knew that her name was Donna.

"Good morning, Donna," he smiled.

"Good morning, professor," her blue eyes burning a hole into his skin. *Ol' LeRoy really knows how to pick them,* he thought. "Dean Chandler told me that you would be coming by."

"Great," he was there to pick up the course materials for the Caribbean history class. "What do you have for me?"

"It's all on top of his desk," she started to stand up. She was at least 5'11" with long, slender legs. Her slinky black and gold dress clung to her like a glove. Donna sashayed as she led him into Professor Ellison's office. The small room was decorated with dozens of plaques and photos. There was a University of Miami Ph.D. certificate for Ellison, mounted prominently behind his desk.

Donna went behind Ellison's desk and grabbed a brownish accordion file folder, a five inch three-ring binder, and a box filled with books. "Here's his syllabus and class materials, professor."

"Thank you," *I think,* his mind cringed. *Was I a sucker to take this on?*

"Oh, I almost forgot," Donna opened the center drawer of the desk and pulled out a thumb drive to hand to Reynoso. "His class notes."

For the next ten minutes, Francisco and Donna went over the logistics of Ellison's class. It was scheduled to meet on

Mondays, Wednesdays, and Fridays at eleven o'clock. It was a three-unit undergraduate class. Reynoso knew he was going to assign term papers. He wouldn't know where to begin with trying to create a final exam. Dean Chandler had agreed that Donna would remain as a part-time secretary to Francisco for this class. Francisco got the impression that she was competent, but she was also very attractive. *Gotta stay far away from this.*

"I'll stop by tomorrow morning around ten thirty to see you before my first class starts," he said to Donna. "I know I will need something."

"No worries, professor," her smile was a killer.

Reynoso clumsily plopped the folder and binder on top of the box and started to exit. "Donna, is there a class roster or seating chart in here?" His head dipping toward the box of materials.

"Yes, professor," Donna replied. "It's in the sleeve of the binder. Twenty-six students."

"Thanks, again, Donna," Francisco smiled. He was staggering out the door, lugging twenty plus pounds of class materials. "Mañana."

• • •

Two long days later, Professor Reynoso dragged himself into his office with his second double expresso of the morning. He had spent the two prior nights (and early mornings) preparing for his first class. He had never taught Caribbean history before and had to rely heavily on Professor Ellison's notes which his colleague had written in an indecipherable shorthand. Reynoso had to make educated guesses about half the notations and deletions that he couldn't understand. He wanted to be prepared, but he didn't have Ellison's expertise. He would just do the best he could.

"Good morning, Mary Beth," Francisco gave his secretary a weak smile. They had talked briefly the day before and she said that she would coordinate with Donna to make the class a go. But Reynoso could tell from her quiet demeanor that she was not happy about the additional workload and having to deal with another secretary. He quickly checked his emails.

"I'll be back," Francisco shouted as raced over to the other side of the building to see Donna. It must have been "casual Friday" because the secretary was wearing tight black jeans with an off-the-shoulder red top. There was that mole on her neck again.

"Good morning, Donna," he plopped himself in front of her desk.

"Good morning, professor," her black eyeliner staring a second too long.

"I need a favor," he handed her a dozen pages. "Need twenty-five copies for my class."

"No problem."

Thirty minutes later Professor Reynoso was standing in front of two dozen students who could best be described as varying shades of black and brown.

"Good morning, I'm Professor Reynoso," Francisco knew that he had to take control of the class from the get-go. "Please sign the sign-in sheet. As you know, Professor Ellison is out on medical leave. He probably won't be coming back this quarter. I will be taking over."

Francisco's eyes scanned the room, arranged in simple classroom style. There was a very tall ebony-skinned young man wearing a basketball jersey seated in the back row. His long legs stretched over three places. He looked familiar.

"Here is your new syllabus," he had the students pass along the copies. "All assignments and class sessions will be posted online. Check it every day. I will have office hours on Thursday afternoons between 3 and 4, by appointment only. Check out the syllabus about how to schedule an appointment."

There was a low mumbling in class, but nothing rambunctious.

"Very quickly, let's go around the room. Give us your name and your major," he paced back and forth in front of the class. "And one interesting fact about yourself."

He pointed to the dark-skinned girl with a blonde Afro and hoop earrings in the first row. "Celia Sandoval. Spanish. My grandparents were Marielistas from Cuba."

Francisco nodded. He had a decent memory. It would take him about three classes before he would remember all their names. With rare exceptions, he knew that his seating chart was already in place. Students always gravitated toward the same seats.

"Tony LaPlana. Business," the blue-eyed guy with brown curly hair was next. "I develop apps for Latino small businesses."

Francisco's eyes slid over to the young woman who was directly in front of him. She had red-streaked black hair that contrasted with her dark brown, almost black, eyes. A seemingly innocent demeanor with lethal instincts.

"Monica Dumas. I'm a junior. My major is Fine Arts," her teeth were perfect. "I'm a fashion designer." *She does make quite an impression,* he thought. *Be very cautious.*

Over the next five minutes, each student introduced himself or herself. The tall guy in the back of the room that Francisco originally couldn't place was Ramón Rodriguez. He was the Puerto Rican who played power forward on the Stanford basketball team.

"Thank you, ladies and gentlemen," Reynoso continued. "Grades. Let's talk about grades. As you will see when you read your syllabus, there is no final. That's the good news. The bad news is that a twenty-page paper is due six weeks from today. June 8. No extensions! The really bad news is that your topic must be submitted to me via email no later than next Friday. The topic must be germane to this class." Reynoso was overwhelming the students. He wanted them to play defense. This was a class, not a democracy. "Any questions?"

No hands went up.

"Let's begin with some review," Reynoso moved from side to side in his customary peripatetic manner. "What geographic area does the Caribbean cover?"

Several hands went up.

"The Bahamas and Cuba."

"South Florida," that answer was met with several groans.

"The Antilles."

The students were engaged. Reynoso could tell that half the students in the class had Caribbean backgrounds.

"Well, for purposes of this class we are going to define the Caribbean as the thirteen sovereign nations plus foreign territories located in the Caribbean Sea, south of the U.S., east of Mexico and Central America, and north of South America. There is a map in the materials."

The students were silent.

"By the way, it includes the Florida Keys."

There was a loud hurrah from the third row.

Francisco walked back to his office after class. He was frazzled. He thought the class went fairly well. He always got energized teaching.

Back at his office, Mary Beth handed him an envelope. "This is from Tina."

CHAPTER 12 – FORTUNE COOKIE

Saturday, April 28, 2018
Palo Alto

Francisco slept in late that Saturday morning. The old-fashioned kitchen clock read eight o'clock. Francisco didn't have a dog, so he wasn't forced to get out of the house early. He took his time getting up, did a little stretching, and then went for a neighborhood jog. He listened to an audiobook that he had downloaded from the public library. He was hooked on Greg Iles' "Natchez Burning," that was about a civil rights-era murder in Mississippi. The first part of the run was uphill and wound its way through beautiful homes. Then he hit the bike path with walkers, dogs, and skateboards. It was a sunny day, and the flowers were in bloom. The air smelled fresh. Hopefully, allergy season would be mild.

A half hour later he was stepping into his shower. He concocted a berry-flavored electrolyte drink and made himself a grilled cheese sandwich with baby carrots and pine nut hummus on the side.

For the remainder of the afternoon he read, underlined, outlined, and annotated the materials for his Caribbean History class. He had to prepare for the entire week to be ahead of his students. Francisco perused the class notes. They put him in a foul mood. *Those damn Spaniards! They really screwed over the natives. Well, then came the British, Dutch, Portuguese, and French with more of the same.*

Sunday for Francisco was a repeat of Saturday. When Monday came around, he was well-prepared for class. He took roll. The students were seated in the same formation as the previous class meeting. Surprise! Ramon, the boricua basketball player, was wearing a loud red Adidas jersey.

"Okay, class, today we are going to discuss slavery in the Caribbean," the professor began. "Was it justified?"

"Heck, no," the light skinned Russell Baker shouted out. "It was inhumane."

"It was deemed legal under International Law," Reynoso said.

"That's just wrong, professor," responded Jason Byrd from the third row.

"I don't how it could really be International Law," the cappuccino-skinned Lourdes Sosa said defiantly. Reynoso remembered that this attractive student was pre-law. He knew that she was going to be formidable. "None of the Caribbeans were signatories to any documents or treaties. It was simply Europeans exploiting Africans."

"Were the slaves considered human beings?" there was silence that permeated the room when the professor asked this.

"Of course, all of us are humans," blurted out Rupert Jones who supported a big, black Afro that hid his thick glasses."

"Well, anyone who was not white was not considered a human being," the larger-than-life Ruby McVey remarked.

"If they weren't human beings, what were they?" the professor probed.

"Animals," James Lofton who was wearing a red Stanford polo shirt snickered. No one laughed. Everybody gave the blond-haired young black man some ugly stares.

"They were chattels. They were considered personal property of their owners," Lourdes was back in action.

The give and take made the hour fly by. The students were totally engaged. It was almost like they did not want the class to end.

"One last note," Reynoso was still in his professorial mode. "Why are some of these notions important for us to learn? Well, the concept of slaves as chattels carried over to the American Revolution. After the colonists had beat back the British, there was a peace treaty. George Washington had promised that slaves who had fought against the British would

be liberated after the conflict. However, Washington allowed
the British to reappropriate their slaves and take them back to
England."

"That sucks," someone yelled out.

"For next class, think about who sold the slaves to the slave
traders."

"You did a great job today, class," Reynoso was packing up
his class notes. "Don't forget that your term paper topics are
due this Friday." Groans were heard.

Reynoso grabbed a turkey and Havarti cheese sandwich on
whole wheat for lunch at the Student Union. He arranged to
meet with Tina the next day to discuss the latest translations.
Additionally, a copy of his upcoming airline reservations to
Mexico was in a file folder courtesy of Mary Beth. The
university had signed off on everything. He was excited.
Things were looking good.

• • •

A few days passed and Tuesday came around. Francisco
was in a great mood as he sauntered from the parking lot to his
office in the Quad. The morning sky was blue with a bright
yellow sun rising in the southeast. Students were happy or as
happy as students going to classes could be. He had grabbed a
90-octane smelling macchiato at a drive-thru coffee station on

El Camino. After his exhausting teaching day on Monday, he had crashed by eight o'clock.

His secretary, Mary Beth, was all smiles when he entered. She had a vase full of fragrant yellow roses on her desk. She had the habit of spending at least a half hour in her garden before coming to work. The departmental staff were grateful recipients of freshly picked snap peas, lemons, cherry tomatoes, and flowers.

Francisco was in his office beginning to clear emails on his computer. A student wanted an extension because of a death in the family. *Hmm?!* Another solicitation from the Stanford Wildlife Foundation. Free gym memberships, pizza deals, and exotic dating opportunities were unceremoniously deleted.

There was a tapping on his door. Tina had her hair in two braids with little red ribbons tied at the end. She was wearing a white blouse with a rounded collar under a denim jumper. Her shoes were powder blue Converse tennis shoes.

"Good morning, professor," Tina sang out as she took a seat in front of Reynoso.

"Morning, Tina," he returned the grin. "Sorry I haven't seen much of you lately. Two weeks? That new class of mine is a challenge. You will have the same pleasure if and when you start teaching. How's your dissertation topic going?"

"It's going well. I've been drafting an outline." She gave a slight smile. Her latest project was investigating the mysterious documents that were only partially translated. Some new documents that consisted of diary entries by Diego García whose name they had encountered in some earlier research.

"Sounds great," Reynoso said. "I only wish that you could join us down in Mexico this summer. Fresh mangoes, avocadoes and ceviche," he teased.

Tina, per her usual summer routine, was planning to attend a university somewhere abroad. She wanted to return to South America to attend the University of São Paulo in Brazil. She had cousins who had migrated there in the 1970's. Tina was taking classes to understand the Chinese emigration to Latin American and the Caribbean during the times of Manila galleons and Portuguese ships. She thought that this would give her greater breadth in terms of her dissertation research.

Reynoso was happy for her. São Paulo was a crazy megalopolis, but who could pass up such a great cultural experience. Reynoso loved Brazilian soccer and music. And of course, the food. *Move over Antônio Carlos Jobim!*

Professor Reynoso and Tina tediously went over some of Carlos Erandi's latest translations of Diego Garcia's diaries, line by line. These translations had recently arrived from Professor Rios at the University of Guadalajara. There was a lot of ambiguity in them. Francisco was hoping that these diaries would corroborate Fray Moreno's and Duro's notes.

"Tina, did we ever discover who the woman was on Saavedra's ship?" Francisco was trying to tie up a loose end.

"We're not sure yet, professor."

Reynoso knew that Tina had an Italian class to attend that afternoon. They decided to call it a day. They would meet again the next afternoon.

"Do you want to grab a sandwich, Tina?"

"No, thank you, professor," she smiled politely. "I'm good." She picked up her Hello Kitty backpack and left.

Reynoso was hungry. Going over the new Diego Garcia's translations had been tedious. He walked up to the Student Union. There was now a slight drizzle. One turkey breast and pepper jack cheese sandwich and a latte hit the spot. He strolled back to his office with beads of rain on his hair. *Lots to do!* He was swamped with teaching and getting ready for his sabbatical.

The rest of the afternoon flew by. He picked up some Chinese takeout on his way home. Back at the house he devoured his kung pao chicken and Szechuan eggplant while discarding his snail mail into the recyclables. All advertisements. He unwrapped the fortune cookie and read the little slip inside: "*A dream you have will come true.*" He wondered what the heck that meant. Chinese fortune cookies never seemed to make any sense.

Francisco turned on the television. Cable TV was a waste of money. He watched a little of a Giants game and then got ready for bed. He was set for the next day's Caribbean history class. Maybe he would continue to read Diego's diaries. He brushed his teeth and got ready for bed. He picked up the manuscript that he and Tina had been reviewing earlier in the day.

CHAPTER 13 – KIDNAPPED

Tuesday, May 1, 2018

Later that evening, Francisco began reading the last translation of Diego Garcia's notes just received from Professor Rios. The University of Guadalajara professor prefaced the version by stating that it had been paraphrased to incorporate the diaries of Diego García that were written in Spanish and Nahuatl. Carlos Erandi had been the main interpreter for the indigenous languages. Rios disclaimed that the translations were literal but instead were paraphrased due to the terrible conditions of the diaries and missing segments. Rios supplemented her report with additional historical and official information.

• • •

Diego García was the author of the diaries that were written in Nahuatl. He was born in Tenochtitlán in 1507, the son of a royal Mexica (Aztec) scribe. His family was killed in the battles with the Conquistador Hernán Cortés. As a young man, he was brought under the protection of Friar Moreno of the Franciscan Capuchin Order from Spain. The two had a symbiotic relationship, and Diego became a postulant. He assisted Friar Moreno in learning Nahuatl and Purépecha in the pursuit of proselytizing of the indigenous populations.

On October 30, 1527, Diego began his notes as follows:

• • •

I was given a mysterious note that said, "'I'm KIDNAPPED!"

Although it was forbidden for postulants to intrude into the friars' quarters, I rushed up the stairs and knocked on Friar Moreno's door.

The friar was kneeling by his bed praying before a plain wooden cross. He turned his head toward me in surprise.

"What is it, my son?" the friar asked me with a shocked expression.

I was embarrassed and bowed my head as I handed over the note to the friar that was from Inocente. "I'm sorry, padre. I didn't know what to do?"

"It's all right, my son," Friar Moreno read the note. It had only three words. It was in Nahuatl. "I've been kidnapped!"

"I don't know what this means, padre," I was at a loss.

"It means we've been betrayed!" Moreno jumped up. "We have to act immediately!"

The friar grabbed me under the arm and pulled me out of the room. We hurried down the dark hallway to the last door on the right. Moreno banged loudly on the door and barged into the ascetic setting.

Friar Luis Reza was laying under a modest cover, fast asleep with his mouth agape. He had his rosary resting in his hand. Despite the loud ruckus, Reza did not awake.

Moreno went over to the bed and shook the old man. Reza's eyes opened wide and he was frightened by the intrusion.

"It's all right, padre," Moreno said in a loud tone as he patted Reza on his frail chest. "It's only me. And Diego."

"What's happening?"

"They kidnapped Maria Del Rosario!"

"Who?"

"Cortés and his cousin Saavedra! We have to get them back," Moreno said. "That was our pledge."

The next day Friar Moreno and I went to mass and then rushed over to the local municipal palace in Zacatula. We found Don Rafael Aragonez behind his desk sipping a glass of red wine. The slender magistrate had long sideburns and was dressed in a black brocaded uniform.

"Friar, please be seated," Aragonez gracefully extended his right hand as he motioned us to sit in the brown leather and wooden chairs. The room smelled of stale cigars. "To what do I owe this pleasure?" He gave us an unctuous smile.

"Don Aragonez, thank you for seeing us," Friar Moreno bowed. Aragonez was a loyal parishioner who was a major contributor to the church. "This is Diego. He is a postulant in our Order. You probably have seen him assisting me at mass." Rafael Aragonez usually attended Friar Reza's Sunday services because the old priest catered to the wealthy Spaniards.

"A pleasure," Aragonez shook the young native's hand.

"Our ward at the monastery is missing. Along with her caretaker," Friar Moreno began an abbreviated version of what had occurred. "We suspect foul play."

"Are you sure that she didn't just run off?" the magistrate asked. "You said she was young. You know how these young girls are nowadays."

"No, Don Aragonez," Moreno countered. "She was under strict supervision at the monastery. She even had a caretaker to chaperone her. She simply disappeared last night. There were no witnesses." The friar did not want to share the note of her being kidnapped. Spanish officials were renowned for blaming the victims and not the perpetrators.

"I can assure you that there have been no major arrests recently," Aragonez shook his head apathetically. "Just some drunk natives."

I blushed. I knew that many Spaniards feel that way about the indigenous people. Friar Moreno is the exception.

"Have there been any special expeditions to Tenochtitlan (Mexico City)?" the friar inquired subtly.

"No, my friend," Aragonez replied. "I would have heard about it."

A quarter of an hour later, the friar and I left the municipal palace slightly discouraged. We sat down on a low stone wall around a yellow adobe building.

"It seems to me that whoever kidnapped Maria Del Rosario would have taken her someplace. Someplace out of town," Moreno surmised. "It had to be more than one person since Inocente was also taken."

"Why were they taken, friar?" I asked naively.

"That's a good question, my son. The girl is young and pretty. Maybe someone wanted her as his wife? That would point to a Spaniard. But they wouldn't want to marry her," he stopped. He did not want to think the worst. The enslavement of indigenous girls was commonplace. Their children would be mestizo bastards.

Father Moreno and I parted ways. The friar made his return to the monastery,
and I went to the commercial warehouse to begin my weekly work. The pale, middle-aged owner, Don José Alberto Romero greeted me with a pat on the back.

"How are you, Diego?"

"Fine, sir."

"You and I are going to lunch today," Romero said with a jovial laugh. "We are going to celebrate." I was bewildered. I did not dare ask why.

"Meet me in my office at two. We'll walk over to El Mesón," Romero was flying high. "This morning I need you to reorder a large amount of supplies from the commissary. We have to restock our inventory."

I remained puzzled. I braved a question. "Why do we have to resupply, sir?"

"I didn't tell you?!" Romero said gaily. "We supplied the royal fleet."

"I don't understand."

"Over the weekend, we delivered ten bales of corn . . ." Romero enumerated a mountain load of provisions. "And they paid us in gold!"

"Why did the royal fleet need so many supplies?" I inquired.

"Don't you know! The Commander General Hernán Cortés is sending a fleet to the Moluccas."

"What are the Moluccas?"

"The Spice Islands. There is a fortune to be made there! Spices are worth more than gold!"

"How will they get there?"

"They will sail west! The hell with the Portuguese! God forgive me!" Romero was animated. "We have a right to those islands."

"Where are the ships, Señor Romero?"

"They are down in Zihuatanejo," Romero smugly said. "The Commander General himself has paid for these ships."

Romero went on to explain that Cortés's cousin, Álvaro De Saavedra Cerón, was to command the fleet of three ships. A fourth ship, an old one, had been found not to be seaworthy.

"When are they departing?"

"Any day now."

Within the hour, even though I was out of breath, I began spewing the details of the Saavedra expedition to Friar Moreno.

"This is no surprise to me, my son," the friar had heard the confessions of Saavedra and knew that he was an ambitious adventurer. He would be the likely candidate for the abduction of Maria Del Rosario.

"Let me talk to Friar Reza," he said. "In the meantime, get the mules ready. Pack a little food, just in case. And water."

The sun was past noon, and the hot breeze was slight. Friar Moreno and I were on our way to Zihuatanejo. The path through the cactus and brush was dusty and uneven. We walked while pulling our mules cautiously. Franciscans are not permitted to ride horseback as part of their vows of poverty, chastity, and obedience, as symbolized by the three knots on Friar Moreno's rope belt. It would be slow traveling.

We trudged along for several hours, but it went quickly since we chatted most of the time. Friar Moreno was a gregarious sort and did not really adhere to his vow of silence. I had wanted to share some information that I knew about Maria Del Rosario but did not want to get anyone in trouble. Many months ago, when I was rebuffed by Inocente in the marketplace, I made it my mission to find out more about the two women wards. While, on occasion, I would see Inocente head into town to purchase supplies, I never saw Maria Del Rosario on the monastery premises or out and about. However, on several occasions I spied the cook, Alicia Aguas, delivering a tray of food to the chapter house on the eastern side of the cloister in the early afternoons. I was not permitted to go there.

Whenever, I tried to discuss the women wards with Fray Moreno, I was put off. "Father, why do *these women go to the nine o'clock mass and not the six o'clock mass like the other natives?"*

I was met with "Oh, it's too complicated to explain," or "I haven't got time right now." I decided to let it go. It really wasn't any of my business anyway.

However, on one occasions, I was dawdling in the kitchen. Alicia was scouring an old frying pan with her chronic cara mala. I handed her a little packet of chocolate nibs that Señor Romero had given me. She greedily took them and a creak of a smile sprang from her face.

"Alicia, thank you for all of your service," I began my ploy. "I appreciate how hard you work around here."

She nodded as she savored the chocolate.

"Do you also care for the women that Father Reza protects?"

The cook shrugged her shoulders and nodded yes.

"Who are they?"

"Trouble!" she became animated. "She is cursed by Coyolxauhqui!"

"Why?"

"Her father Cacamatzin promise the moon goddess his daughter as human sacrifice to please Coyolxauhqui. Did not happen! Coyolxauhqui

curse her. Aztec people all die or made slave. Moon goddess not happy!"

I did not understand. "Why are the women here?"

"People no like them. Everybody killed because of her. Need her sacrifice to Coyolxauhqui."

I could not share this conversation with Fray Moreno without getting Alicia in trouble. For the next few months, I simply observed. While I did not notice any open hostility by the local natives to María Del Rosario and Inocente, I did not see any evidence of friendliness either.

Late Tuesday afternoon, the first of November, Fray Moreno and I arrived at the port of Zihuatanejo. We had slept on a hillside during the night, suffering from the cold air. We had not brought blankets. After asking several indigenous persons, we found the stout port master who had a full scraggly beard.

"Señor," Friar Moreno approached the port master. "We are looking for the Saavedra expedition."

The stout man walked three paces to the right and without saying a word, pointed west toward the horizon of the ocean.

CHAPTER 14 – DIEGO'S JOURNALS

Wednesday, May 2, 2018
Palo Alto

Early the next day Francisco resumed reading Diego's diary where he had left off the night before. He had been inserting pink post-it notes on pages that he needed to discuss with Tina and yellow ones to signify important facts or events. *Was María Del Rosario the woman on one of Saavedra's ships? The woman that the ship's crew despised? Was she the cause of the curse?*

Francisco was intrigued by Diego's diary and sneaked a few more pages before having to rush off to class without breakfast. His Wednesday morning class was uneventful. Reynoso spent the whole class dialoguing with the students about Cuba. Nobody knew who Desi Arnaz was, but several loved Celia Cruz and her Afro-Cuban rhythms. Reynoso liked the students in this class. They were very laid back. By the end of class, everybody was shouting out "Azucar" with smiles and salsa moves.

"Last reminder, your topics are due on Friday. That's in two days!" he shouted out. "If you are having trouble choosing a subject, I have office hours tomorrow afternoon. You have to make an appointment! No exceptions!"

The rest of Professor Reynoso's day went by uneventfully. He was anxious to get back to the translated documents.

That evening Professor Reynoso settled into bed and pushed the pillows behind him. He should have been drowsy, but he wasn't. Reynoso resumed reading Diego's journal.

• • •

November 1527
Zacatula

Friar Moreno and I finally made it back to the monastery late the next day. It was now early November. Father Moreno was agitated. He didn't know what to do. His ward had been kidnapped right from under his care. He had made a pledge to safeguard her and he had failed.

We both were exhausted from all the travel and had a difficult time staying awake during the Vespers evening prayers. May God forgive us. We were even too tired to have supper. The next morning, we attended mass. Afterwards, Friar Moreno and I went into Father Reza's little room. Friar Moreno was seeking guidance on what to do.

Friar Moreno reported to Reza that Saavedra and his three ships had departed two days prior.

The expression on Reza's face seemed to pale. His wrinkly eyes just kept blinking. "I can't believe this, my son. We have been brought to New Spain to Christianize the natives. Our beloved Commander General would not do such a thing. He is a holy man."

"I believe you, Friar," Moreno realized that Reza was afraid of the political fallout. "But what shall we do?"

"Do? Do?" Reza was pacing back and forth. His head was bobbing. "There's nothing we can do! It's God's Will! They are savages anyway."

Fifteen minutes later Moreno dragged me back to the church. He was visibly shaken. "Diego, we need to pray. I don't know what we can do, but we pledged to take care of the natives. They are children of God. We have to at least try."

I agreed with him. We had to do something.

Later that morning I went to Don Romero's warehouse. I had to catch up on the ledgers I had neglected over the past several days. I started reordering supplies that Don Romero had been transferred to the Saavedra expedition. I went to see Don Romero in his little office in the corner of the warehouse.

"Diego, I put all the invoices and inventories over here at the end of the table," the owner smiled. "Take your time. I made quite a profit. We can have a nice lunch again if you want." He had a big smile on his face.

I had to fight the temptation. I try to follow the Franciscan vow of poverty. I have sworn an oath to live an ascetic lifestyle. I did not reply but walked over and sat down at the table. I opened up the large ledger laying there and grabbed an invoice. I started to read it. I made some notations in the ledger.

"If you need anything, Diego, just let me know." Romero started to turn around and walk away from me. "I have to finish the ship repairs."

I thought that I had misunderstood. "I thought the ships had departed!"

"Oh, yeah, the ones we built," Romero nodded. "But we still have to restore the Santiago."

"Don Romero, I thought Saavedra took her."

Romero laughed. "No, I'm talking about the old Santiago." He went on to tell me how the ship had been part of the Elcano expedition to the Moluccas, had gotten lost, and had fortuitously arrived in Mexico."

I have to admit that I was amazed. "Where is the ship now?" I asked.

"It's in dry dock in the port of Zihuatanejo," Romero continued. We had to replace all the wood. We are experimenting with some native resin to make sure it's in shipshape"

"What are you going to do with this ship now?" I asked.

"Don't know. Cortés only paid for the three that already sailed. Bad luck," Romero shook his head. "Could have made a bigger profit."

Later that evening after the vespers prayers back at the monastery, I shared the news about the ship under repair with Friar Moreno.

"If we only had some gold, we might be able to buy the ship," replied the friar.

"For what purpose?" I asked in bewilderment. What was the friar talking about? Buying a boat?!

"We could pursue the Saavedra expedition and rescue the girl."

"How?"

"I don't know how," Moreno was getting exasperated. "We just have to try. We must have faith and leave it up to God."

"Could this help?" I opened up my hand and showed Friar Moreno what I had. I was holding black pearls that had accompanied the abduction note.

The next day arrived and I accompanied Friar Moreno to Don Romero's warehouse. The owner was happy to see the friar and offered the holy pair some red wine. Friar Moreno was more than happy to indulge.
"Don Romero, we need to hire your ship," Friar Moreno began. He did not want to share too much information."

"And which ship would that be, padre?"

"I don't know," Moreno replied. "Do you have more than one?"

"Well, I just furnished Captain Saavedra with three ships. High quality. But, padre, if I may humbly ask, why do you need a ship?"

"We have to rescue some Christian souls. The Church has ordered it," the friar exaggerated the charge, but it was no more than a white lie.

"Padre, anything I can do to help, just let me know," Romero answered.

"The ship."

"Oh, we have been repairing the old 'Santiago.' It has sailed all over the world. She was in bad need of repair when she limped into New Spanish waters a few years ago."

Romero told us how the ship had been part of the Elcano expedition to the Moluccas and how by Divine Providence, it had found its way to Mexico. I had heard all of this before, but I kept quiet.

"So, who owns the ship now?" the friar asked.

"I would say that Commander General Cortés does," Romero's eyes slid sideways. His nose told him there was some money to be made. "We did extensive repairs on the ship. We were never paid.

We would have to settle up before we could consider parting with the vessel."

"Don Romero, how about making a charitable donation to the Holy Church?" the friar proffered.

"Friar, I wish that I could, but I have paid dearly for materials. My men still need to be compensated for their hard labor."

"How about if I paid you with one of these?" Friar Moreno held up his hand. In the open palm there was a black pearl.

Romero's mouth opened. He was stunned. "Mother of God! A black pearl! They are worth more than gold!"

"Do we have a deal then?" Moreno asked, knowing that Romero was a cunning business negotiator.

"My dear padre, if only I could. One of those beautiful beads would only compensate me for a minute portion of my expenses." Romero gave him a despondent look. "I would need at least five pearls at a minimum."

Moreno had heard Romero's confessions more than once and knew that the proprietor had often taken advantage of both sellers and buyers. "Don Romero, you will be given two pearls for the ship. If you furnish us with all the necessary supplies and a good sailing crew, you will be given another. We also need a good map."

"To where, padre?" Romero inquired.

"I'm thinking to the Moluccas."

After ten more minutes of negotiation and discussions, Romero held up his hands in feigned capitulation.

By the next morning Friar Moreno and Romero had found Raul Calderón who was the captain who brought in the Santiago to Mexico as part of the Loazia-Elcano expedition. He was the Basque brother-in-law of Elcano. He had arrived in port a few years earlier on the edge of death from scurvy and cirrhosis of the liver. Some cousins took him in and nursed him back to health.

"Captain, we are in need of your services," Friar Moreno began.

"I'm retired," the red-nosed salt stated in the midst of a coughing fit. "What are you offering?"

Moreno threw up his hands, not showing his cards.

"Where are you going?" Calderón's head leaned forward, his curiosity piqued by the strange request from the friar.

"To the Moluccas."

"Never got there the first time," the old sailor cursed. "Why should I try again now?"

"For the Church."

"I don't care about that! Look at where it's got me. I'm poor! I have no fortune!"

"We could pay you a modest amount."

"What are you offering?"

"A black pearl for you and a crew."

"I want two!"

"Okay, one now," Moreno was trying to close the deal. "and one when you return."

Calderón coughed and spit out a yellowish-green sputum. They all shook hands. Friar Moreno, Don Romero, and I left to walk back to the warehouse.

"When will the Santiago be able to sail?" asked Friar Moreno.

"In ten days, God willing" Romero said. "I will help Calderón secure a good crew. Probably a dozen or more men."

"And the supplies?" Moreno pursued.

"With your permission, I will work out the provisions with Diego."

CHAPTER 15 – THE LETTER R

Thursday, May 3, 2018
Palo Alto

On the following day, Reynoso's secretary, Mary Beth, informed the professor that he had five student appointments in the afternoon. The first student was Ramón Rodriquez, the Puerto Rican basketball player. He was wearing a purple and gold Kobe Bryant #8 jersey.

"Good afternoon, Ramón," Reynoso motioned for the student to sit down in front of his old wooden desk. "How's your day going?"

"Okay," the youth's head was bouncing up and down like a basketball. "Professor, I need your help. I can't think of a topic for the paper."

Reynoso was struck by how polite and well-mannered the young man was. "It happens to all of us, especially me," the professor said nonchalantly.

Ramón put his backpack on the floor in front of him. He looked sideways at Reynoso.

"Here is a trick I learned from an old professor of mine. He was probably younger than I am now," Reynoso chuckled. "What is your favorite letter of the alphabet?"

Ramon's face bunched up quizzically. He paused as if to think. "I think maybe 'R.' I don't really think I have one." He shrugged his shoulders.

"Okay, give me the first three words that start with R dealing with the Caribbean."

Ramón looked at the professor like he was crazy. "Ah . . . rum." He laughed. "Rice and beans." Another laugh. "Religion!"

"Problem solved!"

"Thanks, professor!" Ramón got up and left shaking his head and laughing to himself.

The next three students also couldn't think of topics, but finally were successful in conjuring some up.

Reynoso was on a roll. Dealing with students always energized him.

Ten minutes later, there was a knock on his door. His last appointment walked into his office. It was Lourdes Sosa. She was wearing a shiny, silvery blouse over black jeans. She had colorful, dangling earrings.

"Good afternoon, Lourdes," Reynoso gave her a look. She was probably the best student in his class. He would be surprised if she didn't have a topic yet.

"Hola, professor," she gave him a big smile.

"How can I help you?"

"Two things. The first, is to let you know that I was just elected President of the campus Latinx Club," she said proudly.

"¡Felicidades!"

"I just wanted to ask that you remain our faculty advisor for the club."

"No problem." Reynoso hadn't thought about continuing his current role, but he liked the students. He hoped that he was not stepping on anyone's toes.

"And we want you to be the moderator for the Latinx Club graduation ceremony. It's the same day as the regular graduation. About two hours earlier."

"No problem." Reynoso appreciated the fact that different groups on campus had their own unique ceremonies giving out special recognitions, like the LBGTQ and African American groups. Stanford was trying hard to recognize and appreciate diversity.

Lourdes made no attempt to leave. She looked at the professor without saying a word.

The professor then had to speak. "What's the other thing, Lourdes?"

"Professor, I know that you don't know me very well. I'm a junior and I want to go to law school when I graduate in a year. Would you write me a letter of recommendation?"

"It would be my pleasure." *Wow! She's already on top of her game. She's focused!* "What law schools are you looking at?"

• • •

Francisco was driving home, listening to the Oldies but Goodies Siri music station. "Go Away, Little Girl" by Steve Lawrence was playing. He was hungry. Need to grab some nourishment. More Chinese takeout? Naw! *I need some red meat! One cheeseburger coming up!*

CHAPTER 16 – STAMPS AND WAX

Friday, May 4, 2018
Palo Alto

It had been a busy week. Professor Reynoso began his morning Caribbean History class by passing out the attendance signup roster. He immediately noticed that there was an empty space in front of him. Monica was a no show. *Hmm!* He thought. Everyone else seemed to be present. Lourdes was wearing an indigenous flowered blouse. *Oaxacan?*

Today's session was on the subject of Jamaica. Several students tried to mimic the Kingston accent. Only one person knew who Harry Belafonte was. At the end of the class, the professor collected the term paper topics. "If you are going to email me your topic, it's due no later than 4 pm."

He walked back to his office. The temperature was starting to heat up. He was perspiring as he greeted his secretary. Mary Beth handed him papers, phone messages, and a few topics for the Caribbean History papers. He received copies of his airplane tickets for his Mexican sabbatical. He was happy. *Life is Good!* He emailed a copy of his itinerary to Professor

Miranda Rios at the University of Guadalajara, along with a polite note saying he was anxious to meet her and her faculty.

After lunch, Tina joined him to continue their debriefing on the last of the manuscripts. She had her black hair tied in a red ribbon that matched her lipstick. She wore a loose black chiffon blouse with three-quarter sleeves and white slacks. The emerald earring studs offset her eyes.

"How are you today, Tina?"

"Great!" Tina had a twinkle in her eye. "Professor, now that my dissertation thesis is officially sanctioned, I can start writing in the Fall. And my parents are coming down to visit me. They will stay with relatives in the City. But they actually prefer the Chinese food in Vancouver. They say it is fresher. And I am excited about going to Saõ Paolo and seeing more relatives."

"That sounds really interesting."

"Professor, one thing on these last manuscripts. It looks like they were written by two different people. One has a little Nahuatl mixed in and both have different styles of Castellano. One is at the educated level and the other is at a basic one. One must have been a Spaniard."

"Hmm, if one was a Spaniard, he must have been an official or a priest. The military men and sailors were not educated," Reynoso frowned. He was contemplating.

"The other thing. Professor, is that one has stamps and wax. The other doesn't."

"We're still not getting at why there are different versions of the same events, Tina. We need to research this to see if it was a common practice."

They ended their session in the late afternoon. Francisco wished Tina a good weekend and drove to his house to quickly shower and change clothes. He was ready for an early Cinco de Mayo happy hour at the Mezcal Restaurant, where he was going to join a few colleagues.

When he went home that evening, Francisco poured himself a shot of Partida añejo tequila and then got ready for bed. He was wound up and wasn't quite ready to go to sleep.

He picked up the Diego Garcia documents and rearranged his pillow so he could get comfortable in bed.

November, 1527
Zacatula

Friar Moreno and I had no idea what was needed to supply the ship. Since Don Romero could be trusted, he was put in charge. I just approved everything the owner suggested. As to the crew, Raul Calderón tried to round up some old friends. Most were too feeble, drunk, or lazy to be recruited. They did not seem to be holy men.

I was given the task of overseeing the delivery of our provisions that were set in a designated corner of Romero's warehouse. Everyday provisions were inventoried and put in their proper places. These included biscuits, Spanish wine, chickpeas, rice, olive oil, dried meats, salted cod, cheese, and barrels of fresh water.

Reynoso found a note stating there was a gap and there were missing pages.

During the second week of the voyage preparation, Friar Moreno approached me after vespers.

"My son, I wrote to the bishop to request a new friar to replace me while I go on the journey to rescue Maria Del Rosario and her guardian," he said breathing heavily. "However, His Holiness says that all the friars are committed and over extended. He said it would be very difficult to send one friar even at the expense of losing a thousand converts, let alone two."

"Shall I tell Señor Romero to cancel the voyage?" I asked naively.

"By no means, my son. You will take my place."

My head flew back. "I don't understand. I'm not a friar. I've never been at sea before. I won't know what to do."

"I have been praying on this," Moreno said in a solemn tone. "It is all very clear. This is God's will."

"What will I have to do, padre?" I was surprised with all of this.

"Just be the captain," Moreno released a laugh from his stomach.

"But I thought Señor Calderón was to be the captain? I've never been on a ship before. I don't understand. I don't want to jeopardize the journey."

"Relax, Diego, with God's assistance you will do fine," Moreno placed his hand on my shoulder. "Calderón will be skipper in charge of sailing the ship and commanding the crew. You will be the overall captain in charge of the expedition. You are acting under my authority and that of the Holy Church. You will be doing God's Will."

For the next half hour, we discussed the voyage. I had a thousand questions and trepidations.

"I will give you proper documents tomorrow," the friar ended our talk. "Don Romero will now be reporting to you, mi capitán." He laughed again.

For me, this was not funny. It was a very serious matter. I didn't want to fail. Why is God testing me?

The next day I walked over the warehouse where I found Don Romero. I handed Don Romero a piece of parchment that had been prepared by Friar Moreno. Romero slowly read the document, moving his lips as he did so.

"Congratulations, my boy!" Romero slapped me on my back. "This calls for a celebration. We will have a good meal today. I will miss you. You have been a faithful worker here."

Around two o'clock, Don Romero escorted me to his favorite dining place. A nice bottle of red Spanish wine was set before us. At first, I thought I should refrain, but then thought it really didn't matter.

"Salud, mi capitán!" Romero raised his glass and toasted. Two servers started the procession of food: Cured ham, cheese, olives, and herring in olive oil.

"Well, I think we have our crew. Some Spaniards. Some Basques. Some Portuguese," Don Romero then leaned forward toward me. "Be careful with these black hearts. You can't trust any of them. They will cut your throat and feed you to the sharks."

My brown eyes darted from side to side. I was very frightened. "But what can I do? I don't want to fail the Church."

"You will be fine, but I have some bad news, Diego," Romero tilted his head back and drank more wine. "The skipper, Calderón, has disappeared. They say he went back to Tenochtitlan. He wants to sail back to Spain."

I was saddened. "What am I going to do?"

"I'll find somebody to sail the ship for you," Romero said confidently. "In the meantime, drink up!"

That evening I informed Friar Moreno of the fugitive skipper.

"We paid that scoundrel with a valuable black pearl. God will strike him down dead!"

Friar Moreno instructed me to keep an exact inventory of every article purchased, traded, and sold. As the provisions for the journey came flowing in, I noticed that Don Romero would overstock us with certain items but would limit us on others. At first, I didn't understand, but then I figured that the owner was trying to get rid of old inventories. Romero was the consummate businessperson. But true to his word, Romero found a new skipper for the Santiago. His name was Samuel Bautista. He had been the first mate under fugitive captain Raul Calderón and was Spanish. Bautista and I spent many hours planning the voyage. My Spanish was not totally fluent so I had to struggle in order to communicate fully with Bautista.

Knowing that the crew was going to consist of Spanish, Basque, and Portuguese sailors, I was feeling tense about the communications aboard ship.

Every day I made reports to Friar Moreno who shared my concerns.

"Don't worry, my son," Moreno smiled. "The Lord works in mysterious ways."

A few days later, Moreno, Bautista, Romero, and I made the trek to Zihuatanejo to see the old ship,

Santiago, completely refurbished. The friar and I walked with burros. Bautista and Romero rode on horseback. At the port, Bautista recruited a few sailors and they sailed the refurbished Santiago around the bay for three hours. I had never been on a ship before and my face turned green. I got seasick.

Returning to the tiny dock, Bautista announced that the ship was seaworthy. He and Romero agreed to start retrieving the provisions from the warehouse to load onto the Santiago. Friar Moreno and I then started the journey back. I was still nauseous and had a headache.

"Pray, my son!" the friar yelled out.

I tried. I drank water out of a gourd after I had vomited twice. I had no appetite and I reeked. Near dusk we found a cleared-out area under a big pine. Moreno ate some old bread with hard cheese. I couldn't even look at food.

In the morning, however, I was miraculously cured.

"Friar, when are we setting sail?" I was now feeling human again.

"As soon as the ship is loaded. I have a few more documents to give you," Moreno added. "It is really up to Bautista. He knows about the tides and things."

"Do you know how long this journey will take, padre?"

"Not really, my son. But whatever God decides, it will be done."

Bautista and Romero had ridden ahead and were already at the warehouse when Friar Moreno and I came in. We had not yet stopped at the monastery to rest and recover.

"I am sending the first shipment of provisions this afternoon," Romero informed us. "Bautista is taking the crew down to Zihuatanejo to make preparations to get underway."

"What else is necessary for the trip?" I asked.

"Bautista has some old charts. He needs a real navigator."

"Can we find one?" Diego asked. How could one follow a trail in the seas?

"Let me see what I can do," offered Romero.

"Diego, let's go to the church and pray before we return to the monastery."

Two days later I was greeted by a dark-skinned man with a wrinkled face wearing a colorful cap. "Captain Garcia?" greeted the stranger with a slight bow. "Don Romero sent me. I am your navigator, interpreter, and assistant."

I didn't know what to make of this man. He was about to say something, when Romero rushed in. "I see that you have met Ismael Gavriel. Let's have some wine to formally make the introductions."

A few minutes later Don Romero and I were drinking some red wine. Ismael was drinking tea. I learned that Ismael had been born in Granada, Spain. His father was Jewish, and his mother was Moorish. He had been educated as a philosopher and spoke Spanish, Latin, Arabic, Hebrew, and Portuguese. He had gone to sea when the Inquisition started in Spain, on the advice of his parents who feared the cruel Christian persecution. I couldn't discern Ismael's age but knew that he was a man of the world and had much experience and language proficiencies. He was a God-sent.

Friar Moreno started to inundate me with more and more instructions. There was to be no priest or friar aboard the ship because it was so small. I could not say mass, but could lead the crew in prayer, once a day.

"But, padre," there was a sad look on my face. "How will I go to confession?"

Friar Moreno smiled. "In the first place, my son, don't sin!" he laughed. "God understands. Just say an act of contrition every day. Before you set sail, I will hear your last confession and absolve you of all of your sins until you come back."

The next few days flew by very quickly, and finally, Bautista announced that the sailing departure would be the early morning of November 24, 1527. This was almost four weeks after the Saavedra expedition had departed. Moreno knew that the possibility of tracking down the abducted girl was slim, but he had sworn an oath to protect her, and with God's Will she would be rescued.

Two days before the embarkation, Friar Moreno handed me still more documents.

"My son, here is a letter that I want you to read next week when you are at sea. It will explain everything. Your main objective is to rescue María Del Rosario. You have the black pearls. They are a last resort. I don't need to remind you to use them wisely. May God be with you."

"Yes, padre," I was overwhelmed. I had been given a herculean task. I would place my trust in God.

"Remember this: you must keep fastidious records of all transactions," the friar instructed. "Although this is an ecclesiastical endeavor, the king will want his royal fifth of all gains even so. Take these journals. They're blank. Bring them back filled."

"And what about Commander General Hernán Cortés?" I did not want to have any trouble with the authorities.

"Don't worry, my son," Friar Moreno blessed me. "I'll take care of everything. May God keep you."

Two hours later I was on the road pulling a donkey. Don Romero was accompanying me.

"I will miss you, Diego. You have been such a good and loyal worker," the owner said.

"Thank you, Don Romero."

"I need a small favor from you. All the preparations and provisions have cost me dearly. I need to recoup some of my expenses."

I was listening but was not understanding.

"I packed away some special packages for you aboard ship. They are stashed in the closet of the captain's quarters. They are bolts of beautiful cloth made by the natives. They are very valuable. You can use them as trade."

"Trade for what, Don Romero?"

"For spices. Nutmeg and cloves."

I wasn't sure, but I had heard that the Spanish were obsessed with spices from the Moluccas. I had been told that they were as valuable as gold and pearls. I didn't know the reason.

"I will give a generous donation to your monastery from my profits."

I wanted to object, but Romero put his hand on my shoulder.

"It's God's Will and the church will benefit."

CHAPTER 17 – DIM SUM

Tuesday, May 8, 2018
Palo Alto

Francisco spent the entire weekend in preparation for the upcoming week's Caribbean history classes. On Tuesday, Tina came into his office as usual. She was all smiles.

"It was great to see my parents. We went to Chinatown in San Francisco and ate a lot," she was jubilant. She wore a new jade bracelet on her left wrist. Tina noticed that the professor was staring at it. "Gift from my parents," she quickly responded.

They made social chitchat for a while. Her parents were going to stay in the Bay Area until Tina traveled off to Brazil. Since she did not have any finals, she thought she would leave right after the first of June. Tina would be staying with a host family in Saõ Paolo and wanted to get to know them and the city well in advance of classes starting.

"I'm torn about what to wear. The weather should be nice," Tina's eyes looked upwards and to the right. She was planning. "It's just like spring here."

"I like to travel light," Reynoso remarked. "Besides, you can always buy some new clothes down there."

"Great idea, professor. Thanks."

"You're a native-born Portuguese speaker. There shouldn't be any problems. Does your host family speak Cantonese?"

"The host family speaks several languages. My only concern is that Brazilian Portuguese is spoken softer. Not harsh like in Lisboa. They'll be able to hear the difference. I don't want to sound like a country bumpkin."

Reynoso gave a little laugh. *She is so fortunate!*

"That reminds me. I have to bring presents to the host family. I should also bring extra ones for other people I will meet," she added.

¡Demonios! Francisco gasped. *I have to buy presents for Professor Rios and her family and everyone else! I almost blew it!*

"Tina, what kind of presents were you thinking of," Reynoso was trying to pick Tina's brain for some ideas.

"I think the Changs have four kids. I'll probably buy a half dozen Stanford tee shirts from the bookstore. I know the ages and will have to guess at the sizes."

That's a great idea! Reynoso smiled to himself. Simple and inexpensive. He could walk up to the bookstore this week.

"For Mr. Chang, his wife told me that he wanted a Pebble Beach golf shirt."

"Does he play golf?"

"No, but it's a status thing."

"And for the wife?"

"I bought this really beautiful blouse with a San Francisco landscape on it. It's long and loose fitting. Buying a gift for a hostess is always a challenge. There can be cultural proscriptions."

¡Demonios! I can always get Señor Rios a golf shirt or a nice bottle of a Napa cabernet, and the daughter a Stanford sweatshirt, but what about Professor Rios? Don't want to ask Tina. If Zoe were still around, I could ask her. Maybe I can drive up to the City and find a woman's San Francisco logo top or something.

"Oh, professor, I almost forgot. My parents want to invite you for lunch next Saturday if you are available," her green eyes were glowing. "They are very grateful for everything you have done for me."

"I would be honored," he didn't want to offend her parents. He knew that her father was an architect in Vancouver. "Where?"

"They like the HL Peninsula Pearl in Burlingame. You do like dim sum, don't you?"

• • •

The next few weeks flew by. He finished his classes and was procrastinating on turning in the grades. He still had to pack and make final arrangements for his trip to Guadalajara.

Finally, the beginning of June arrived and he was as ready as he would ever be for his summer sabbatical. The Uber taxi ride to the SFO Airport was uneventful. He grabbed a latte and bagel by gate B18 before boarding. The Alaska Airlines flight left promptly at 8 a.m. There were no free movies, and the meals were for purchase. But at least there was Wi-Fi.

Fortunately, he had an aisle seat just behind the emergency row. The passenger next to him was already snoring. Francisco preferred not chitchatting with others, anyway.

One of the documents that Tina had left with him contained the notes of Vincenzo da Napoli. Da Napoli was La Florida's clerk assigned by Hernán Cortés to Saavedra to keep the records of the ship, especially its trade transactions. There was also an old torn and soiled map.

EXPLORACIONES TRANSPACÍFICAS
CON PUNTO DE PARTIDA EN NUEVA ESPAÑA

"Anything to drink, sir?" the striking flight attendant inquired.

"Coffee, please," Francisco had been fidgeting in his seat and knew that he was not going to be able to sleep. He needed a little caffeine jolt. "Just cream, please."

The coffee was strong, and it had powdered creamer loaded with dozens of strange chemicals. As a bonus, he was given a packet of faux biscotti cookies.

He began reading the Da Napoli records for Saavedra's ship, La Florida. He wondered why there were two sets of records for the same ship. He recalled reading the brief entries from the ship's logs written by either Captain Saavedra or his chronicler Duro.

As usual, Tina provided a concise introduction to the journal consisting of additional research that she had been conducting on her own.

• • •

May 6, 2018
To: Professor Francisco Reynoso
From: Tina Fang, RA
RE: Saavedra/Da Napoli's Logs of La Florida -
Overview
Languages: Spanish and Latin

In 1526, Emperor Carlos V sent a cédula (royal decree) to Hernán Cortés, the Conquistador of Mexico, ordering him to send his newly constructed ships to Las Moluccas (the Spice Islands) to find Magellan and de Loaísa. Additionally, it was to be a trading venture and new land discovery mission.

Cortés saw the procurement of wealth in his future. He chose his cousin, Álvaro De Saavedra Cerón, as captain general of the expedition. The Conquistador knew that the procurement of new lands and spices would please the emperor. Cortés also instructed Antonio Guiral, the fleet's accountant to record all trade transactions to ensure that Carlos V received the royal fifth of all wealth and gains.

Cortés had commissioned the construction of three ships (two three-masted caravels and one two-masted bergantín) in Zacatula (just north of Zihuatanejo on the Pacific Coast) for this expedition. Saavedra was in the fifty-ton flagship, La Florida, captained by Eduardo Viurco and a fifty-man crew. The forty-five-ton caravel, the Santiago, with forty-five men, was commanded by Captain Luis de Cárdenas. Pedro Fuentes de Xérez captained the twenty-ton bergantín, Espiritu Santo, that had a crew of fifteen. Cortés spent sixty thousand gold coins outfitting the ships with food rations, trading commodities, weapons, building materials, medicines, and fishing gear. The crews included soldiers, sailors, smiths, masons, and friars.

The trading goods included multicolored beads, mirrors, Spanish and Mexican clothing, and Aztec feather work. The food provisions included biscuits, salt-cured pork, beans, dried fish, and wine. There was a partially illegible notation in the passenger manifest of a black pearl being part of the cargo of Espiritu Santo.

Francisco put down the papers for a moment and closed his eyes. This was tedious work and he felt a headache coming on. Finally, he resumed reading the background of the ship logs of La Florida:

October 31, 1527

Our three ships set sail today from Zihuatanejo, Mexico (17.6417° N 101.5517° W).

Fortunately, Vincenzo Da Napoli was the accounting clerk on Captain Saavedra's ship, La Florida. He was born in Italy but later worked for the Spanish. His father had been an accounting clerk and taught Vincenzo how to read and write Italian, Spanish, and French. When Cortés had ordered Saavedra to Las Moluccas, Da Napoli was hired as a clerk under Antonio Guiral, the Saavedra fleet's accountant. He monitored all purchases, payments, and transactions. He kept his own set of records, apart from the chronicler Duro. King Carlos I was very adamant about adhering to strict accounting protocols, as was Cortés. Everybody was looking for the accumulation of Spanish *reales*, jewels, and spices.

Da Napoli had worked three days with Don Romero in Zihuatanejo overseeing the transference of food, provisions, and equipment prior to the sailing of the fleet. He also oversaw the passenger manifest which included the sailors, military personnel, friars, and other personnel. The expedition set sail in a southwesterly direction. According to Da Napoli's records, he believed that Captain Saavedra was transporting black pearls to trade with the Moluccans. It was detailed in the original inventories.

Saavedra's fleet was made up of three ships: the navio (cargo boat) flagship named La Florida; another navio, the Santiago; and the bergantín Espiritu Santo.

Da Napoli's diary of Saavedra's voyage aboard the La Florida were as follows:

October 31, 1527

On October 31, 1527, the trio set sail from Zihuatanejo in a west-southwest direction Our ships did not have favorable winds and progress was slow. Additionally, La Florida sprung a leak and the crew was continuously bailing out water. Food had to be discarded and fresh water was rationed. The crew members were tired and unhappy. They thought that our ships were cursed.

With food stores low and freshwater low, disease spread aboard La Florida. Several crewmen died.

A few days later, according to a report signaled by a crew man a league away on the brigantine, a Portuguese crewman was dragged up from below onto the deck of the Espiritu Santo with his hands chained behind him. The first mate ordered that the sailor receive a dozen lashes with the "cat." As he was flagellated, he kept crying out "La Perla! La Perla! Amaldiçoada! (cursed)".

The crewman's protestations earned him an additional twenty lashes. He later died. Some of the men aboard ship were agitated but were mollified with double rations of rum.

December 1527

The respite was short-lived. The middle of December brought several storms. The flagship *Florida* continued to take on water. The crew was overwhelmed trying to salvage the ship. The other two ships, the *Santiago* and the *Espiritu Santo* were thought to be lost at sea. When the foul weather subsided, and the winds were moderate, the course was changed to the northwest.

La Florida's crew members were angry and mutinied. Several crewmen were killed, including the ship's pilot. After a brief service, their bodies were thrown overboard. The first mate had to replace the pilot. Saavedra now had no control over his men. Some of the crew wanted to sail back because the new pilot didn't know the route to the Moluccas.

Others still believed that their fortunes were yet to be made. Finally, the ship limped into the port of Mindanao in the Philippines. The boat was repaired, and the men were fed. There seemed to be a truce between Saavedra and his men.

We sailed to Tidore in the Moluccas a few weeks later and joined forces with loyal Spaniards fighting against the Portuguese. The Portuguese crew on *La Florida* were not pleased about having to fight their own countrymen. The ship stayed in the area trading with the natives for spices.

All goods that were going out or were coming in were duly ledgered. It is well noted that Saavedra was trading beads, clothing, gold, and jewelry with the natives. Our records also show that no presence or disposition of any pearls was found.

The ship set sail back to New Spain, but there were no favorable winds. In October of 1529, Captain Saavedra died, and La Florida had to return to Tidore.

During their La Florida's absence, the Portuguese took control of Tidore. Upon their return, all La Florida's crewmen were imprisoned.

• • •

Tina had left yellow Post-It notes throughout the document. Reynoso was shaking his head and thinking that the Stanford student, Juan Carlos, had done a great job interpreting those worm-infested papers.

Looking at one of Tina's notes, it read, "I think Da Napoli claims that the mutinies were caused by a curse on the fleet. It seems to confirm that there might have been a woman aboard one of Saavedra's ships."

Another comment inquired, "And why was the Portuguese sailor flogged?"

Reynoso was pondering these questions and others. *Cortés and Saavedra certainly wanted spices and had a battery of items to trade. There are a lot of unanswered questions.*

Tina's last note asked, "Why was this woman taken? Why was she on board the Espiritu Santo?"

CHAPTER 18 – LOS TAPATIOS

Saturday, June 2, 2018
Guadalajara

Francisco's flight touched down at the Guadalajara Airport at 1:30 p.m. He set his watch ahead two hours. The remainder of his flight had been uneventful. He had a chance to review some papers and even took a little nap. The only other issue had been having to lend his pen to seatmates so they could complete their immigration and customs information forms upon landing. The passenger next to him, a Mexican man, had problems with the forms that were in English. The flight attendant who had passed out the travel forms didn't seem to speak Spanish and was oblivious to the non-English speaking passengers.

Going through Immigration was a breeze. The Mexican Immigration officer was very polite, although Francisco thought that she couldn't have been even 21 years old. Next, he encountered little children running around the baggage claim area with their mothers screaming after them. *Not my problem!* Francisco calmly picked up his duffel bag. *Ay! This and my*

backpack weigh a ton! He had to go through another baggage
security check and was passed through Customs (he had
pressed the button and it turned green, thereby avoiding an in-
depth inspection of his luggage).

One potty stop later and he was in the public area. A
medium-statured man with long black sideburns and slicked
down hair held up a sign with his name on it. Francisco walked
up to him.

"¿Señor Rios?" Francisco inquired in Spanish.

"Sí, Professor Reynoso," the man smiled and shook
Francisco's hand. He reached for the duffel bag. "Salomón
Rios at your service. Please call me 'Sol'."

Francisco shook his head indicating that he would handle
his own luggage, even though the backpack was a pain.

"How was your flight, professor?" asked the pencil-
mustached Sol as he started to lead Francisco away. Francisco
was struggling with the duffel and, finally, Sol succeeded in
taking the bag.

"Thanks, Sol," Francisco was breathing heavily. "And
please call me Francisco. The flight was fine."

An hour later Sol's white Ford SUV arrived at the Rios'
two-story house in the posh Chapultepec District of
Guadalajara. During the stop and go, circuitous drive,
Francisco learned that Sol was the owner of "Los Rayos de

Sol," a solar panel company. The conversation was light, and Francisco really enjoyed Sol's company. It reminded him of his family growing up in Los Angeles. Lots of laughing. Sol spoke a friendly version of Spanish, with a few slang words, exclamations, and palabrotas (swear words), especially when he was describing the recent loss of his favorite Chivas fútbol (soccer) team.

Sol told Francisco that he could leave his duffel bag and backpack in the SUV. *Thank God!* thought Francisco. Francisco quickly zipped open his duffel and pulled out a slightly scrunched red gift bag and brought it inside the house. Carmen, the ama de llaves (housekeeper), took his sport coat.

He was escorted to a large living room where a dark square wooden coffee table was flanked by a chocolate brown sofa and four matching chairs. There was a large terra cotta pot on top of the table with dozens of red roses. Their scent was sweet. Francisco sat on the couch and Sol took the chair next to him. Within a minute, Carmen returned from the kitchen with a tray of margaritas a las rocas and a bowl of chili-covered peanuts. Francisco felt his mouth water instantly.

"¡Salud!" Sol raised his glass and the two men toasted. The weather was hot and humid, and Francisco had to control himself from inhaling the cool drink.

"Those paintings and tapestries are beautiful, Sol," Francisco remarked as he scanned the living room.

"That one over there was my grandfather," Sol pointed to a six-foot oil painting in an obscure corner of the room. "He fought alongside Pancho Villa. So, we don't mention him in this house. *¿Tú sabes?"*

Francisco nodded. In his family, there were Republican sycophants and Democrat fanatics. They would yell and scream at one another, and then laugh over a couple of beers and tacos. *¡No importa!*

There was movement at the wooden double doorway that caught Francisco's eye. He immediately stood up. In walked an elegant woman with her black hair styled in a chignon. Her gold dangly earrings and turquoise necklace offset the flowered black dress.

"Professor Reynoso, it's a pleasure to finally meet you," said the stately woman in perfect English as she held out her hand. "Welcome to your new home."

Francisco smiled and shook her hand. "Professor Rios, the pleasure is all mine. You have a beautiful home." His head swiveled and then returned back to the hostess. "But please call me Francisco. Otherwise, I'll feel like I'm back in the classroom."

The two professors bowed and smiled. She replied, "You have already met my husband, Sol. Be careful of him. He'll want to take you to a Chivas game. By the way, please call me Miranda."

Francisco grinned. *And we would drink beer and yell. Sounds good to me.*

Carmen came into the room and offered Señora Rios a margarita and then gave the two men two more. Francisco had been overcome with ennui during the flight, and now he was energized.

The trio were making light conversation, when a tall, slender 17-year-old girl with long black hair bopped into the room. She was wearing a Hello Kitty white top with black jeans and black high-top Converse tennies.

"This is mija, Mirasol," the proud father introduced her.

Francisco shook hands with the youngster who had the world's whitest and straightest teeth. "You're the one who might be going to Stanford. Heard nothing but good things about you."

Mirasol turned her head toward her shoulder. Her face took a pinkish hue. "I hope so. Mom says it's a great school."

"And she earned all A's in English," remarked her mother proudly.

During the chitchat, Francisco brought forth the gift bag
and passed out the presents. Miranda gave him a "you
shouldn't have" smile, but quickly opened the tissue paper
packaging. It was a rainbow-colored San Francisco cityscape
silk scarf. She threw it over her shoulder for effect.

As for Sol, he stared at the sports jersey that said "San
Francisco Gigantes." Sol stared seriously at Francisco. The
latter wondered what was wrong.

"Amigo, you know I am a Dodger fan," Sol said with a
straight face, and then busted out laughing. Francisco had been
sweating bullets. "I love it, Francisco. I'm going to wear it to
the next Chivas game. And you're coming with me."

As for Mirasol, she was ecstatic about getting a red
Stanford polo shirt. She tried it on, and it was a little big on
her, but she didn't care.

Everybody was in good spirits. Francisco and Sol were on
their third margaritas. Carmen came into the room and
announced that dinner was ready. It was nine o'clock local
time which meant it was seven o'clock in San Francisco.
Francisco's stomach gurgled. He never ate this late. *But when
in Rome, do as the Romans do.*

They walked over to the dining room and sat at a huge
wooden table that seated twelve people. There were lit candles
and lots of silverware. The dinner started off with a tortilla

soup that smelled and tasted delicious. The main course was a filet mignon steak with vegetables. The dessert was flan. The meal was followed by coffee and a shot of brandy.

Francisco was trying not to fall asleep. It was almost midnight by the time Sol drove him to the University of Guadalajara's faculty housing in the Oblatos district, less than two miles from the Rios residence.

The only thing that Francisco could remember was that Sol was going to pick up him the next day for his comadre's birthday party.

CHAPTER 19 – THE RULES

Sunday, June 3, 2018
Guadalajara

The church bells in the distance had awoken him. Francisco's tongue licked his lips. His mouth was dry. *Too much alcohol last night.* His fuzzy brain tried to recall the events of the evening. It had been almost midnight when Sol had dropped him off at the three-story neoclassical faculty housing building. He had pressed the buzzer and was wearily greeted by Jorge, the night manager.

"Hi, I am Francisco Reynoso," the professor slurred his words. He just wanted to get to bed.

"Doña Prudencia was expecting you much earlier," Jorge replied in Spanish. "But you can come in. The room is ready for you. You can do the paperwork tomorrow."

Francisco didn't have to be asked twice. He walked up the two flights of steps schlepping his duffel bag and backpack. Jorge did not offer to help. Jorge opened the door and motioned Francisco into a small one-bedroom apartment.

In less than a half hour, Francisco was snoozing in the lumpy bed.

During the night, his head was swirling. He felt like he was rocking up and down in a boat in rough seas. His stomach regurgitated acid into his mouth. There was a slight odor of vomit. *What was he hearing? Waves against the sides of a ship? Howls of wind? It sounds more like a rhythmic chanting.*

Francisco had a hangover when he got up the next morning. He went into the black and white tiled bathroom and grabbed some aspirin from his toiletry bag. There was a bottle of water on the counter.

It was almost a quarter to ten when he staggered down to the mezzanine floor and walked down the hallway. The overhead sign read, "El Salon de Las Aguilas." He was met by a young, slightly built woman. Her long black hair was in coiled braids tied with red, white, and green ribbons. She wore a tan muslin dress with a colorful sash around her waist. She wore a plastic name tag that read "Carla."

"Buenos Días, señor," the woman addressed him with a friendly smile. "Please sit where you like. Coffee?"

"Descafeinado, por favor."

Francisco took a seat in the corner. There was a balding, elderly man sitting by an open window smoking. He was reading a Mexican newspaper. There were no other diners.

Carla brought Francisco a jar of Nescafe decaf coffee and a small, stainless steel carafe of steaming milk. There were two or three types of sweetener on the white tablecloth. He was already missing his soy milk. She pointed to a buffet table.

He prepared his java concoction and almost choked as he took a sip. *Ick! Tomorrow I will do the leaded version. When in Rome . . ..* The buffet consisted of bolillos, hard boiled eggs, and yogurt. There were also pads of butter, packets of strawberry jelly, and bottles of Cholula salsa. Francisco wasn't hungry but managed to stuff himself anyway. He finished and left a dollar tip on the table.

Francisco walked down the stairs to the small lobby. A stern looking woman in her fifties, dressed all in black gave him an unsmiling gaze.

"I am Doña Prudencia," she said without emotion. "We were expecting you last evening, Señor Reynoso."

"I ran into a delay," Francisco didn't want to lie, but felt that it was none of her business why he came in late.

"I need to see your passport, please."

He handed it to her and she took it to a little office. She didn't ask for his credit card. A minute later she was back with forms for him to fill out and a set of house rules. No smoking in the rooms. Breakfast: every day from 6 to 10 am.

Housecleaning: Wednesdays and Saturdays. No cooking in the rooms.

As he started up the stairs to his room, a young dark-skinned girl approached him. She had a piece of paper in her hand. She wore a beautiful indigenous dress that complimented her brown eyes.

"Excuse me, Professor Reynoso," she said in a soft voice, her head lowered. "A telephone message." She extended her hand and gave Francisco the note. Her name tag read "Albina."

Francisco was surprised for a moment and then uttered "thank you."

Back in his room, he read the note: "Change of plans. I'm picking you up at 3:30. Miranda and Mirasol are going to the 11 o'clock mass. They will meet us at the restaurant for Alexi's birthday."

¡Demonios! I had forgotten about that! I must have been bien pedo (drunk). Who is Alexi?

He brushed his teeth. *What am I going to wear? Can't wear the same clothes as last night. I was told it is supposed to be a casual affair, but you can't trust what is said. As his nana used to say, "Como te ven, te tratan." Sol was wearing a guayabera last night. They are always fashionable.*

Francisco plugged in his laptop with the 220-volt converter. He needed a password to get connected to the Wi-Fi. He grabbed the papers that Doña Prudencia had given him earlier. He finally found the elusive password and entered it. The internet connection was slow. He had only received a handful of emails, including three from Alaska Air stating that he had landed safely.

Next, he Googled: "Guadalajara Colonia Oblatos guayaberas."

An hour later he was walking out the door, headed toward the upscale Liverpool department store seven blocks away.

CHAPTER 20 – TLAQUEPAQUE

Sunday, June 3, 2018
Guadalajara

Francisco's shirt was soaking wet as he entered the department store. Although the department store was only seven blocks away, the humidity had made him melt. The white three-story building was crowded with shoppers of all shapes and sizes. Seeing the Tapatios (residents of Guadalajara) made Francisco realize that he may have packed the wrong clothes for this trip. This was not a beach resort where the dress was casual. Guadalajara was middle-class Mexico. Nobody wore jeans except the kids. Everybody was well-groomed.

The Liverpool department store had everything! As he entered the Men's clothing department, he was thinking about how his hosts were dressed. Last night Miranda had on simple, but stylish, clothes. Sol wore a guayabera. *That's it!* Francisco grinned to himself. *If I model Sol, I will be okay.* Guayaberas were also called Mexican wedding shirts and could be worn for any occasion. *That works!*

A very thin salesperson showed Francisco a wide array of guayaberas, running the gamut from white to black, cotton or a blend.

"What is your size, Señor?"

"Medium," Francisco replied. He was 5'11' and slender. *I better make sure I don't gain weight here. Don't want to become a macho luchador (Mexican wrestler).*

He had once owned a pale green guayabera, but it had long since disappeared. He selected a black one, a green one, a white one, and two others.

"Señor, the ones with the twelve pleats on each side are of excellent quality."

He went into a small fitting room to try them on. *Should I select light colored ones to keep me cool or darker ones to be more formal?* In the end, he picked a white four-pocketed long sleeved one, a burgundy two-pocked short sleeved one, and a black four-pocketed long sleeved one with gold embroidery. As he paid for his purchases, his stomach was tingling. He knew that he was not going to eat for several hours. Francisco did not want to go to the third-floor restaurant, and instead, took the escalator down to the basement level. He grabbed a pork torta ahogada sandwich and a mineral water from a lunch counter. As he was inhaling the spicy tomato-garlic salsa, onions, and lime juice, he saw a fresh flower stand. There were a million types of roses. He remembered that Guadalajara was nicknamed the "City of Roses."

I need to get a birthday present for the Rios' comadre. I don't remember her name. I can't buy her anything too personal. Definitely not red roses!

Finally, he settled on a crystal vase with white orchids tinged with purple.

Back at his apartment, he decided to shower again. Then he had a decision to make. He sported a three-days growth beard. From what he saw on the street, very few men had beards. *Should I shave it off?*

At half past three Francisco exited the faculty housing building. Sol was there waiting for him in his white Ford SUV. Sol was very friendly and asked how the accommodations were.

"Everything is fine," replied Francisco.

And then Sol went into a tirade about one of the Guadalajara Chivas' players getting injured.

"There goes their *pinche* middle field game!"

After twenty minutes of driving south, they arrived in the Tlaquepaque District. This was the vibrant artistic area of Guadalajara with a multitude of colorful artisan crafts. Sol parked in the private lot of the Abajeño Restaurant. They walked into a large open-air courtyard where two mariachi

groups were playing at opposite ends of the building. The pair
passed the seven-piece mariachi group dressed in chocolate
brown charro jackets and tight pants with silver braiding and
wide-brimmed sombreros.

Ay, ay, ay, ay,
Canta y no llores,
Porque cantando se alegran,
Cielito lindo, los corazones . . .

The smells of chile, garlic, and onions were driving
Francisco crazy. He and Sol soon found their party under a tile-
covered area in a corner. Besides Miranda and Mirasol, there
was another couple and a single middle-aged woman.
Introductions were made and Francisco was seated between Sol
and the single woman. A waitress wearing red, white, and
green ribbons in her black hair took their drink orders.

The couple were Gloria and Eloy Sifuentes. Gloria and
Miranda belonged to Guadalajara's professional women's
group. Gloria was a children's story writer. Her husband was a
dentist. The singlet was named Alejandra Mora and she was
the birthday girl. She was the godmother of Mirasol.

Alejandra put out her hand and Francisco shook it. "So,
you're the professor that Miranda has been talking about."

He blushed. Her black eyes shimmered against her red-
brown hair and gold dangly earrings. She was wearing a black

embroidered floral dress that accented her cinnamon skin. Her
ivory teeth smiled at him.

Francisco was saved from further embarrassment when the
chocolate brown outfitted mariachi group approached their
table. Sol requested that they play some of his favorite songs.

> *Soy puro mexicano*
> *Nacido en este suelo*
> *En esta hermosa tierra*
> *Que es mi linda nación*
> *Mi México querido*
> *Que linda es mi bandera*
> *Si alguno la mancilla*
> *Le parto el corazón*
> *¡Viva México! . . .*

Everybody at the table joined in the singing. After the
mariachis left, the waitress came back with their drink orders.
Francisco had ordered a cold Corona. After the night before, he
was staying away from tequila.

There was lots of chatter at the table. Sol and Eloy talked to
Francisco about soccer. Francisco was smiling and trying to be
polite, but he wasn't a big fan.

When the guacamole and chips came with the tamalitos and
queso fundido appetizers, Francisco turned to Alejandra as a
diversion. She was fluent in English and was very cultured. He
found out that she was an endocrinologist at the local medical
school hospital.

The entrees came before they could finish the botanas. Francisco was full already. *I definitely need an exercise routine while I'm down here. El Gordo here I come.*

The conversation ceased when everyone dived into their main dishes. The steak arrachera was flavorful and melted in his mouth. Sol had ordered the carnitas and Eloy had the fish huachinango. Francisco noticed that Alejandra didn't seem to be drinking much. She had ordered the gambas al ajillo (shrimp). Francisco wasn't able to converse with the other ladies because the table was so wide, and it would have been really rude to shout over the din of the restaurant.

An hour later, the dinner plates were removed. *Oh, my stomach! I'll never eat again. Wrong!!!*

The waitress, accompanied by two tall, handsome waiters strolled up to their table carrying a flan cake with one lit candle in the middle. The mariachis were right behind. The traditional birthday song, "Las Mañanitas" was sung.

> *Estas son las mañanitas*
> *Que cantaba el rey David*
> *Hoy por ser día de tu santo*
> *Te las cantamos aquí . . .*

Alejandra threw up her hands and profusely thanked the guests. Francisco guessed that she was in her late thirties or early forties but knew better than to go there.

Francisco forced himself (but not really) to have a slice of flan. He didn't want to be rude. *Huh!* With coffee. Oh, he wasn't going to sleep well tonight. He slipped the silver-haired violinist five dollars.

His eyes were drooping as Alejandra opened her presents. She made out like a bandit. She received a pair of tickets to Teatro Degollado from the Sifuentes and a pair of black pearl earrings from the Rios. Alejandra gave Francisco a look of gratitude for the white and purple orchids.

Another late night for Francisco. Sol drove him back to the faculty housing. Five minutes later he was snoring.

CHAPTER 21 – THE FIRST WEEK

Monday, June 4, 2018
Guadalajara

The Uber driver, Omar, dropped Francisco off at the main campus of the University of Guadalajara. All students roaming around looked like children. He had spent the morning doing an hour long walk around the faculty housing building that included getting Mexican pesos from an ATM machine. He had gone through an elegant residential neighborhood, seen six beautiful neoclassical churches, and walked through a park teeming with fragrant flowers.

Now, he was climbing the granite stone stairs to Professor Miranda Rios' office. The Linguistics Department secretary, Alma, escorted Francisco to the professor's office. The door was open. He knocked softly and Miranda motioned him in. The small room had dozens of plaques and certificates and three bookcases entirely full of various tomes. Francisco noticed ancient linguistics books by Chomsky, Hayakawa, and de Saussure. Situated on Rios' wooden desk there was a quinceañera photo of Mirasol.

The profesora got up and moved over to the little table by the window. He took a seat across from her.

"Well, how are things?" Miranda asked politely.

"Fine, thank you. Everything has been great. Thank you for inviting me to the party last night. I had a good time."

"You seemed right at home," she smiled mischievously. "Sol likes you. That's dangerous."

They both laughed.

She asked if he wanted coffee. He politely declined.

Then they got down to business. They started off chronologically with the different versions encapsulated in the logs, papers, and notes prior to the December storm of 1527. That seemed to be the event that differentiated the various accounts of the Saavedra expedition.

Francisco gave Miranda a brief overview of what he had learned so far about the two 1527 voyages from Zihuatanejo. He explained about the abduction of María Del Rosario and her caretaker, and how Diego was charged to retrieve them.

He also gave her a copy of a half dozen memos and a spreadsheet of the Mexico to Moluccas expeditions that Tina had diligently prepared based on the latest translations and with some additional notations.

THE PACIFIC EXPEDITIONS 1519-1527

Dates	Cmdr/Capt	Ships	Chron	Lang	Start	Destination
1519-22	Magellan	Victoria			Spain	Moluccas
		4 other ships			Spain	
1525	Loaisa & Elcano	4 other ships			Spain	
1525-26	Andres de Urdaneta	Santa María de la Victoria			Spain	Moluccas
		María Del Parral			Spain	Philippines
	Raul Calderón	Santiago			Spain	
1527	Saavedra/Viurco	Florida	Duro	Sp, Lat	Mexico	Moluccas
	De Xérez	Espiritu Santo		Sp	Mexico	Moluccas
	de Cárdenas	Santiago		Sp	Mexico	Moluccas
1527-34	Saavedra/Viurco	Florida	da Napoli	Sp, It	Mexico	Moluccas

The pair then discussed how they wanted to handle their meetings. They agreed to try to meet Mondays, Wednesdays, and Fridays for two to three hours. Miranda had a "Parataxis and Syntax" class to teach, a Faculty Senate assignment, and her women's foundation, Las Adelitas. The latter was a professional women's group that was dedicated to the education of all Mexicanas and to the protection against discrimination and sexism. Miranda was in charge of its fundraising for college scholarships.

"Francisco, I have found a retired admiral who might be able to assist us with our works, especially with all the navy jargon."

"That sounds good."

"He lives down in Zihuatanejo. If you want, I can try to get an appointment for you to see him. The problem is that I probably can't go with you. Too many commitments. You understand."

"That would be great," Francisco said. *Oh, my God! I hope I don't embarrass myself. My Spanish lack finesse and I don't know how to deal with Mexican VIPs. But I've heard that Zihuatanejo is beautiful. Well, I don't really have much to lose. Except maybe my pride.*

"I will have my secretary Alma contact Admiral Serafino Azueta," Miranda was writing a reminder to herself.

¡Ratas! An admiral! Oh, great!

"You probably don't want to fly," Miranda advised. "You would have to lay over in the capital. Unless, of course, you want to stop over in Mexico City. The other option is taking the bus. It's about an eight-hour ride. You should plan to spend two to three days down there. The fresh fish there is delicious."

It was getting to be late afternoon. As Francisco started to leave Miranda's office, she said, "Alejandra really liked the orchids you gave her."

Francisco smiled but did not say anything.

He caught an Uber back to the faculty housing. In the parlor there was hot water and he made himself tea. Doña Prudencia wandered in.

"Professor Reynoso, I assume everything is acceptable to you," her smile was painted on with a glue gun.

"Yes, thank you," Francisco knew better than to complain.

"If you need your laundry done, you can make arrangements with Sabina. She charges a reasonable amount and does a good job."

Sounds good to me. I probably need to keep records. Is this tax deductible?

He hadn't eaten lunch and was starving. After dropping off his things, he went out the door. He would try to find a snack place. If worse came to worse, he knew that he could eat at the Liverpool Department Store restaurant.

The week went by quickly with Francisco reviewing the documents between his meetings with Miranda. On Friday, Miranda dropped a bomb on Francisco. "I hope that you didn't have plans this weekend," she gave him a sheepish grin. "Sol has invited you to a Chivas' game on Sunday."

What could he say? He had no plans. He could do more research. That would be the best use of his time, but he could not be rude.

"Miranda, tell Sol thanks," Francisco looked at her. "I'm in." *What the heck! I need some diversion.*

"Okay, then you must come to dinner after the game," she graciously said.

When he returned to the faculty housing that late afternoon, he found his clothes folded neatly on his bed. They seemed to have a slight scent of lavender. Sabina had done an excellent job and she charged very modestly.

At the Saturday morning breakfast, he met two faculty members from Hungary. They were researching ways to increase commerce between Mexico and Hungary. They were both fluent in English and Spanish. They loved the spicy Mexican cuisine. Francisco had been to Budapest once and they talked about cultural and historical sites.

The takeaway from the informal conversation was that they recommended a local gym to him, not too far away. Francisco spent two hours doing a little cardio, weightlifting, and stretching. The club tried to talk him into purchasing a membership that included free Zumba instruction, but he passed. The Mexicans gym rats were short but beefy and had lots of tattoos. The females wore tight black outfits and full makeup. *If I'm going to eat everything in sight, I need to work out. What am I having for dinner tonight?*

CHAPTER 22 – ¿GOL?

Sunday, June 10, 2018
Guadalajara

He woke up with his shoulders aching from the prior day's workout. Francisco quickly showered and was waiting outside when Sol arrived to pick him up. Sol was wearing his San Francisco Gigantes shirt. With him was one of his foremen, Arturo, with his 25-year-old son, Victor. They had no problem parking at the Chivas' Estadio Akron in Zapopan. The seats were good, and the sun was shining. They were on their second beers after devouring some pork tortas. The Mexican national anthem played while the Chivas came out to the field accompanied by little kids. Next was the national anthem of Costa Rica, their "Friendly" opponents. The Chivas wore red and white vertical striped jerseys with blue shorts. The Ticos (Costa Ricans) had blue jerseys with red shorts.

The yelling was incessant. Drums pounded to the heart beats of the fifty thousand fans. Mexican flags, and red, white, and blue Costa Rican flags were flying all over the stadium. The starting whistle blew. The Costa Rican team played conservatively in the first half, using its defense to stifle the Chivas forward José Macias, or his right-wing Ernesto Vega. Similarly, the Chivas midfielders, Carlos Antuna and Jesús Molina, kept the ball in play and gave the local team the edge in time of possession.

More beers and food flowed.

"When is Almeyda (the Chivas coach) going to speed things up? He hasn't been the same since they won the CONCACAF," complained Sol.

"I heard that he may be leaving," replied Arturo.

Half time came and Sol plopped something into Francisco's lap. It was a Chivas souvenir jersey featuring Number 1, the goalie Raúl Gudiño.

In the second half, the Costa Ricans kicked their game into high gear. Gudiño made three spectacular saves. The game ended in a 0-0 tie. Nobody was happy. There was lots of grousing.

"¡Gracias a Dios! Mier stopped that fast break. The Ticos could have scored."

"But he got a yellow card," Arturo remarked. "It should probably have been a red."

"*No importa.*"

Francisco was almost asleep in the front seat of the SUV, when they dropped off Arturo and Victor. They arrived at the

Rios residence. In the daytime, Francisco realized how grand a place it was. Sol kissed his daughter Mirasol who was on the front porch waiting for him. The trio went into the living salon where Miranda and Alejandra were chatting, with the former drinking white wine.

Francisco gave Miranda a peck on the cheek and shook Alejandra's hand.

"How was the game, mi amor?" Miranda asked her husband.

"Same old. Bad coaching . . ."

Mirasol asked to be excused and left the adults. Alejandra leaned forward toward Francisco. "You've been here a week. You're almost a full-time resident."

"I really like it here. I could get used to this."

"Miranda tells me that your project is going along well."

"Well, thanks to her. She is very well organized," Francisco started to preach and then caught himself. *She doesn't want to hear this academic double talk.* "You know," Francisco said in a neutral tone, "I really don't know anything about you."

"There's not much to tell," she replied coyly. "I work at the hospital in the city. In the Endocrinology Department."

Two minutes later "dinner is ready" was announced by Carmen. The green salad had pine nuts, pumpkin seeds, pomegranate anils, and balls of queso fresco. The main dish was grilled beef skewers with bell peppers, tomatoes, and onions. The red wine was from one of Miranda's colleagues who owned a winery in the Guadalupe Valley in Baja California. Between bites, Francisco and Alejandra talked about the present day relationship between the United States and Mexico.

"On Friday, I am giving a lecture about some of the history of the United States and Mexico," Francisco looked over to Miranda who nodded in affirmation. "I hope they understand my Spanish," He knew that he should not have said that, but it just came out.

"I know you will do fine. Knowing two languages is a gift that takes a lot of effort to maintain," Miranda gently said to him. She had a manner that assuaged his nervousness. "I might even come to see you."

The party moved into the living salon where dessert was served. The orange cake was absolutely delicious. Against his better judgment, Francisco had coffee. Sol offered him an after-dinner liqueur, but he declined. Francisco observed that Alejandra had only a small bite of the cake and did not drink any coffee. *She takes good care of herself,* he thought.

Soon thereafter,

u Alejandra left the group, citing that she had early commitments the next day. She hugged Mirasol who had fallen asleep on the leather sofa and gave everyone pecks on the cheeks, including Francisco. She gave him a big smile. "Thanks again for the flowers. They are beautiful." *I guess I'm part of the family now!* Francisco smiled to himself.

Near midnight Sol drove Francisco back to his lodging. *How does he do it? I'm dragging.* The night was still warm, and the air was humid. The windows were rolled down. There still was a lot of traffic on the streets.

"Sol, what exactly does Alejandra do?" Francisco asked curiously.

"Oh, she's an endocrinologist. You know, the doctor that works with diabetes. She says I have to watch my sugar. My blood. Not too many sweets or alcohol."

"What about her family?"

"She is a widow. Her husband died many years ago. He was a doctor," Sol was starting to fade, and his driving showed it. "Her grandfather was a very famous Mexican singer here in town. I heard him sing when I was young."

They finally arrived at the faculty housing and Francisco thanked Sol for the shirt.

As Sol pulled away, he thought he heard Sol say, "Those pinche Chivas!"

CHAPTER 23 – TEXAS

Wednesday, June 13, 2018
Guadalajara

At her Wednesday meeting with Francisco, Miranda was all smiles.

"I have good news for you, Francisco, Alma has talked to Admiral Azueta's secretary. He and his wife are on vacation in Alentejo, Portugal. They will be there until the end of June," Miranda was very professional and efficient in her work. "Your appointment with him is on July 20. You probably need to spend two or three days down in Zihuatanejo. This does not include travel time. Unfortunately, as I said before, I can't accompany you."

"Well, that was fast," Francisco was already entering the dates on his iPhone.

"Don't thank me. You can thank Alma. She's the one who keeps this place in order," Miranda then started shuffling some papers on her desk.

They spent the next hour reviewing the logs of La Florida, commanded by Captain Saavedra.

"Professor Erandi is trying to track down some more Saavedra papers," Miranda added. Francisco had been impressed with Erandi's Nahuatl translations. They were going to meet with him the next time he was in Guadalajara.

When they were finished, Miranda asked, "Are you already for your first lecture on Friday?"

As part of his visiting professorship, Francisco had to deliver four lectures to the University students and the community. The first one was going to be on Friday. The topic was the history of U.S. and Mexican immigration policies.

"Let me or Alma know if you need anything."

Francisco had spent all his evenings this week preparing for his presentation. He had put together a short Power Point presentation. It was in Spanish and he had spent an inordinate amount of time on it. He had been given the choice of giving his lecture in English or Spanish. He chose the latter. He wrote his presentation bullets in Spanish. *This should help,* he thought. He practiced every night in front of a mirror.

Friday came and at 10:15 he was in a large auditorium. Francisco was wearing his sport coat with a tie. Dean Montoya greeted him. He was dean of the Social Sciences Department. It was his responsibility to introduce Francisco. The audiovisual technician talked with Francisco. Francisco gave him a thumb drive. They tried the Power Point program. It worked! The AV person attached a small microphone to Francisco's shirt pocket. They practiced speaking a few times and a few sound adjustments were made.

At just past 10:30 the doors to the auditorium were opened to the student body, faculty, and public. At first a few small groups of very young adults came in and were seated. They were noisy and goofing around. Then some faculty members took their places in the front rows. Miranda Rios sat next to Dean Montoya. By 11 a.m., the time of the presentation, there were approximately 120 people.

Five minutes later the dean was introducing Professor Francisco Reynoso from Stanford University.

Francisco was not nervous. He had lectured hundreds of times and had given dozens of speeches. Yet this presentation was different. It felt so personal. And he was doing it in Spanish, and he felt proud.

"Distinguished deans and faculty, students and leaders, members of the public . . ." Francisco knew that formality was required.

The students were taking notes with their tablets or taking photos with their phones. The faculty were nodding their heads in response to the salutations.

". . . And then the United States tried to buy Texas from Mexico. Mexico said no. The next thing you know, the United

States declared war on Mexico. Mexico did not have adequate resources to fight a war. Now the northern part of Mexico is the southwest part of the United States. I personally would be amenable to giving Texas back to Mexico."

There were chuckles and smiles from part of the audience.

"Nothing has changed much in the United States in terms of immigration policy. The U.S. repatriated thousands of Mexican-Americans back to Mexico in the 1930's . . ."

The audience had become more and more quiet. There was a lot of fidgeting in the chairs. Francisco paused and drank from a water bottle.

He was near the end of his presentation. "And when we thought things couldn't get worse, we elected the worst president since James Polk and Andrew Jackson. He hates everyone. He only wants to be emperor and makes lots of money.

"How can you trust a person who separates families? Who treats immigrants like hardened criminals? Who insults all people of color? . . ."

Francisco thought he could see some students raising their fists. His voice was straining. "But the Aztec blood lives on. On both sides of the border. Mexico will have to become more like the United States in order to survive economically. And the United States will have to become more like Mexico to order to protect family values, loyalty, and respect.

"Thank you, my friends, for your attention."

There was applause and cheers and the Mexican style of clapping that accelerates and ends in a crescendo.

Afterwards, Dean Montoya moderated the question-and-answer session that lasted almost twenty minutes.

Question: "Who does the United States want to win the Mexican presidency in our elections in three weeks?"

Answer: "I don't know."

Question: "Is there going to be a border wall? Who will pay for it?"

Answer: "According to former President Vincente Fox, if a border wall is to be built, it will not be Mexico who pays for it."

This brought applause and hooting.

"¡Viva México!"

Question: "If the United States withdraws from NAFTA, what will happen?"

Answer: "China and other countries will fill the void. They will show respect to Mexico. And maybe build more soccer fields."

Finally, the session ended. There were agua fresca and other refreshments. Several students and faculty members corralled Francisco and barraged him with even more questions.

That evening Francisco treated himself to several cold beers at a crowded cantina named "Frida" near his lodging. It was only then that he realized that Alejandra had not come to his presentation. *Oh, well! Not important!*

CHAPTER 24 – OUCH!

Wednesday, June 20, 2018
Guadalajara

June was speeding by and Francisco was not even a quarter of the way finished with his work. On Wednesday Miranda informed him that Professor Carlos Erandi would be coming into town and would meet with them the following Wednesday. Francisco had been very pleased with Erandi's Nahuatl translations of the diaries of Diego Garcia.

"I heard good reviews of your lecture last week," Miranda smiled.

"It was fun."

"What are you going to talk about next week?"

"Religion."

"¡Ay Dios Mio!" Miranda gasped. "You are crazy like my husband. Yesterday he was glad that the Chivas coach left. Today he's complaining about Obrador being elected president. Sol hates socialists. Hey, the PRI has been screwing things up for years. People wanted a change. They'll chose Obrador."

They chitchatted a while longer and then got down to business. Professor Erandi has sent a few more pages of translation in anticipation of their upcoming meeting. These were thought to be more pages from Diego Garcia's journal. They each had copies and began reading them

November 1527
Zacatula

After a brief mass, the refurbished Santiago set sail. I learned from Bautista that our ship was a bergantín, a two-masted ship with square rigging on the foremast and fore-and-aft rigging on the mainmast.

Our destination was the Moluccas (Indonesia) where Maria Del Rosario was thought to be taken. This ship had originally sailed with the Loaisa expedition from Spain and miraculously landed in Mexico. Now I am its captain and Samuel Bautista is the skipper or chief mate. The crew consists of six Spaniards, five Basques, three Portuguese, and one Italian.

We easily caught a southern equatorial current going west toward the Philippines. I had never been aboard a ship before and was throwing up daily into a bucket. Ismael gave me a weak tea with a little ginger root that eventually cured me. Ismael took me under his wing and we conversed on a variety of subjects on a daily basis. We were opposites in almost everything. While I was parochial in my upbringing and life experience, Ismael was worldly and loved everything and everybody. I let my chief mate Bautista do all the navigation. After the first week, I was back on deck, smelling the salty ocean air with a smile.

The course set for the ship tracked the equator, the same latitude as our destination, the Moluccas. There was a slight rain one night and the crew were able to replenish some of their water supply. The next day the sun seemed hotter, but the winds seemed weaker. By the third day, the winds were negligible. The Santiago was stuck in the doldrums. Bautista tried to explain everything to me, but I did not always understand.

"What should we do?" I asked Bautista.

"I think we can point the ship southward and see if we can pick up a little breeze."

"Okay, let's try that."

That maneuver didn't work. Ismael and I discussed the matter and came up with an unpopular scheme. I called the skipper to my cabin where Ismael and I were lodged together.

"Since your tactic did not work, Bautista," I was trying to assert myself as the captain. "then we may need a little assistance since the wind is not cooperating."

"Yes, captain. What do you suggest?"

"That we get out the oars and start rowing," I was repeating Ismael's advice. "In shifts of six men each."

Bautista was shocked. The men would hate it. "Are you sure, captain? The crew won't take kindly to this."

"Yes, I'm sure," I had to do whatever was necessary. I was charged with bringing back María Del Rosario to Father Moreno. "The alternative is to rot in the sun like old fish."

Bautista's order was met with grousing and cursing.

"The captain doesn't know a damn thing!"

"He'll kill us before we see land again!"

"Who in the hell does he think he is?"

For the remainder of the week, the men took turns rowing during the day. There was no activity at night so the men could rest.

On the morning of December 9, 1527, the ship suddenly stopped its forward motion. When Bautista went to see why they had stopped, he saw the crew surrounding a fallen Basque crewman named Blas who had grabbed his chest and fallen atop his oar. One of the men splashed water on him but to no avail. The man was dead. Bautista ran and knocked on my cabin to inform me. An hour later the man was laid to rest in a shroud. I sadly gave a brief funereal speech, and the corpse was buried at sea.

A husky red-bearded man rushed forward and shook his finger at me. I recognized him as one of the other Basque crewman named Iñigo Aguirre.

"See what you've done!" Iñigo cursed. "Why doesn't your God protect us?" He pointed to the Tau cross that I wore around my neck.

"Take this man and tie him to the mast!" Bautista commanded. "Gustavo, give him ten lashes for insubordination!"

• • •

Francisco and Miranda finished reading the excerpt almost simultaneously. They looked at each other wide-eyed.

"¡Dios mío!" Miranda exclaimed. "This is a very exciting narrative. Hopefully, we will be able to find out more about what happened on this journey."

"Yes!" concurred Francisco. "There must be more documents available somewhere."

They were both weary and decided to call it a day.

When Francisco returned to his lodging, he checked his email. There had been three messages from his secretary, Mary Beth, from Stanford. For the last two and a half weeks, there had been very little communication from his office, although he had received a selfie from Tina in São Paulo.

He read the messages:

#1 Professor, Joel Brenner from Powell's Bookstore in Portland called. He couldn't get a hold of Tina. May have something.

*Should I tell him that Tina is unavailable for the
summer?*
***

#2 Professor, Joel Brenner again. Wants to
know if he can talk to you directly. Has a lead
on something he thinks you might want.

*How do you want me to handle this? His tone
sounds like this is important.*
***

#3 Joel Brenner left you his email address and
phone number.

Should I call him back? What should I say?

Francisco immediately wrote back and informed Mary Beth
that he would handle it. He didn't want to interrupt Tina's
summer. He had not yet set up Mexican service for his cell
phone. He was trying to be frugal. He would email Joel and
have him call the lodging phone number. Five minutes later he
sent a small note to Brenner.

On Thursday, Brenner emailed Francisco back. Joel
Brenner would call him the following Monday morning, 11
a.m., Guadalajara time, which was two hours ahead of
Portland.

Finally, Friday came. Francisco and Miranda built a list of questions they would ask Professor Erandi at their meeting the following Wednesday.

Francisco went back to his room and spent a quiet evening doing some casual reading. He was enthralled with Denise Chavez's "Loving Pedro Infante." He had read a hundred pages before he called it quits.

It was eight that Saturday morning when his phone rang.

"Francisco, good morning!" the voice said. "This is Sol."

"Good morning to you," Francisco opened his mouth and yawned. He was not quite awake yet. "What's up?"

"I have some bad news, I'm afraid, It's about my wife, Miranda. She hurt her foot this morning, I have to take her to the doctor's right now."

"I'm sorry to hear that," Francisco's voice reflected his concern. "Is she going to be all right? What happened?"

Sol gave a three-minute narrative about how Miranda had banged the baby toe on the right foot going down the stairway that morning. The acute pain went straight up her right leg. She had to sit down. It took several minutes before Carmen found her and called out for Señor Rios. Miranda couldn't put any weight on her foot, and it was starting to swell. There was a slight discoloration that started to form.

Carmen called the family doctor while Sol carefully picked up Miranda and set her down on the couch. Socorro the cook was called over and told to bring ice. They put Miranda's feet up on a leather stool and applied a cloth, enclosing an ice pack.

The doctor told them to bring Miranda to the emergency room of the hospital and that he would meet them there.

"Is there anything I can do?" Francisco said in an automatic pro forma manner. *What could he possibly do?*

"No, thanks, mi amigo."

"When you have a chance, let me know what is happening. Does Miranda need me to do anything?" *I don't even know this city that well. How could I help?*

"No problem," Sol said. Then Francisco could hear an animated conversation between the spouses. "Miranda says she needs a big favor from you."

"Anything," Francisco's brain was at full attention.

"Our comadre, Alejandra, and Miranda were supposed to go to the Teatro Degollado tonight. Miranda knows that you would be a perfect gentleman and escort Alejandra to the performance. Can you do this?"

"No problem," what else could Francisco say. The Rios had been such gracious hosts. He owed them. Alejandra was very nice. *It could be fun!*

CHAPTER 25 – FOREVER TANGO

Saturday, June 23, 2018
Guadalajara

Francisco rushed down to breakfast. He barely chewed his food. Today there was fresh sliced papaya with yogurt. He slurped down his coffee. He was getting used to the caffeine buzz. On his way back up to his room, Francisco ran into Jorge, the night manager who seemed to work twenty-five hours per day.

"Good morning, señor," greeted Jorge with a big smile.

"Good morning, Jorge," Francisco had a thought. "Do you know where there is a barber around here?"

An hour later Francisco was sitting in a barber's chair at Chester's. It had been a fifteen-minute walk. Chester was the barber and owner of this tiny little spot. He was an ebony-skinned transposed Panamanian who had a thick Spanish-Caribbean accent.

"*¿Qué xopa, frin?* (what's up, dude?)" the young Chester threw the towel around Francisco's neck. Francisco spent the next two minutes trying to explain how he wanted his hair cut.

He didn't know what a #3 cut was. In the end it wasn't exactly how he wanted it. It was really short. But the price was right.

When he got back to his lodgings, there was an email message from Sol:

> Miranda is doing fine. She won't relax. She wants to do everything. The doctor told her to lay her foot in an elevated position and rest it.
>
> Alejandra will meet you at Teatro Degollado at seven o'clock. Good luck! Enjoy yourself, my friend.

In the late afternoon, Francisco debated whether to wear his sport coat or a guayabera. He finally decided on his new purple guayabera, with black slacks.

Hours later Francisco was standing nervously at the corner of Morelos and Degollado in front of a neo-classical building. Francisco took out his cell phone and took photos of the sixteen Corinthian columns and the nine Muses.

Alejandra was dropped off by a luxurious black Lexus SUV. Her black hair was up and revealed a beautiful black pearl necklace that offset the large gold dangly earrings. She wore a stunning, but subtle black A-line V-neck knee-length chiffon semi-formal dress. Her raspberry color lipstick offset Alejandra's white smile that greeted Francisco.

"I hope that we did not impose on you?" She said tentatively. *Who is "we" Francisco thought? Does she have a family?*

"No. Not at all," he answered. For some reason he was on the uneasy side. He turned his head from side to side, observing everyone as patrons started to arrive. Short, plump ladies in formal gowns. Silver haired gentlemen with pencil moustaches. Young girls in ballet-type garb. Francisco and Alejandra walked into the crowded main entry salon. Young men and women dressed in Argentinian tango costumes with swiveling hips strutted through.

Alejandra led Francisco to their seats which were in a private box on the first tier near stage left. Francisco was mesmerized by the large overhead chandelier that was brighter than the sun. He curiously picked up a program. While he and a former girlfriend had taken salsa lessons one year, this performance he was about to witness seemed to be a cross between gymnastics and sex. The male dancers wore dark suits with black shirts, black fedora hats, and two-tone shoes. The women glittered in their skintight dresses with exotic hair styles and bordello style makeup.

Francisco glanced at Alejandra as the performance started. She was all in. She leaned forward. She was absorbing the passion and the energy. Patrons were snapping cell photos even though there had been a formal request not to do so. *Así es la vida.*

They were so close to the stage that they could feel the heat. The dancer with a cigarette in his mouth slid his hand sensuously up the slit black skirt of the slender woman with the spit curls. Francisco's body was sweating. His tongue involuntarily licked his lower lips. His armpits were wet.

Alejandra was entranced. She leaned further forward.

For the second number, the bandoneon, an Argentinian accordion, dominated the eleven-piece orchestra. The platinum blonde arched her back like a bow. Her partner swooped on her like an eagle. Now Francisco was leaning forward.

For the next hour and a half there were innumerable lifts, twists, kicks, fancy footwork, and special effects. The finale challenged a Cirque du Soleil extravaganza. At the end of the event, Alejandra excused herself and they both used the facilities.

As they exited the theatre, Alejandra ran into a distinguished elderly couple.

"Doctor and Mrs. Tellez, I would like to introduce you to Professor Reynoso," Alejandra was very suave. "He's a visiting professor from Stanford. He's here to do conduct some research with Professor Rios."

Doctor Tellez shook Francisco's hand and told him how much his wife Gloria and he loved San Francisco. The conversation switched to English. Francisco noticed that Gloria wore more jewelry than the Taj Mahal. Dr. Tellez was a cardiologist.

As they were leaving the theater, Francisco was surprised to see a black Lexus SUV pull up in front. Alejandra said her goodbyes to the Tellez' and Francisco echoed the pleasantries.

Francisco instinctively followed Alejandra to the SUV.

"Are you ready for a little dinner?" she gave an inviting smile as he climbed into the vehicle and sat next to her.

CHAPTER 26 – LA FONDA

Saturday, June 23, 2018
Guadalajara

Francisco and Alejandra were dropped off in front of a rose colored building. They walked through the entrance of La Fonda Restaurant in the Zona Centro section of the city. The young hostess dressed in a traditional Jaliscense white blouse and sarape-patterned skirt escorted them to a table in a colonnaded gallery facing an open-air courtyard. The water fountain in the middle of the court was bursting with aquatic energy, and the tin star lights dazzled the patrons. A caged green parrot kept squawking, "hola."

The evening air was still warm, and Francisco was thirsty. The smell of grilled meat wafted through the restaurant. Before Francisco could put the white cloth napkin on his lap, a short waiter came over.

"Good evening, señores, welcome," he smiled with his curled up black moustache. "May I offer you something to drink?" He gazed at Alejandra first.

"I'll have a sparkling mineral water with lime please," Alejandra said in a soft but stately manner. She looked at Francisco and put her hand on top of his. "Order what you want. I don't drink alcohol."

Francisco didn't want to do margaritas again. They would put him in harm's way if he drank too many. He really wanted some very cold beer. "I will have a michelada (beer with lime juice and salted glass) with Negra Modelo please."

The waiter thanked the pair and left.

The noise level was high with a combination of the restaurant patrons' voices, and the singer with his musical trio at one end of the courtyard. The customers were dressed in everything from torn jeans to elegant attire and every type of footwear imaginable.

"This is a beautiful place," Francisco looked at Alejandra.

"It was once a Carmelite convent," she said. "This restaurant serves traditional food from Jalisco. It's a little bit different than the types you get in the States."

Francisco nodded. He really didn't know why he was acting so shy around Alejandra. "I really enjoyed the performance this evening. Thank you for inviting me."

"Well, I'm glad you enjoyed it. But it was actually Miranda who invited you after she broke her toe."

Francisco felt stupid, but Miranda continued. "I loved the choreography. The movements were exquisite. And having young bodies helps." She smiled slyly.

Well, yeah. Some of those women were really hot! Francisco thought to himself. "In the States we don't see much tango. It's more salsa."

A young girl with bouquets of red roses came up to the table and asked Francisco if he wanted to give some to his lady friend. He said no. *I don't want to be presumptuous and give Alejandra the wrong impression. On the other hand, it would have been a nice gesture. Damned if I do, damned if I don't.*

The waiter came and gave them their drinks. He handed them menus. Alejandra ordered some guacamole to go along with the complimentary totopos (chips).

"Francisco, tell me a little about yourself," Alejandra looked him in the eyes. "I know that you are a professor at Stanford. In what field?"

"In Latin American Studies." Francisco then proceeded to tell her about his bachelor's degree in Spanish from UCLA and his Ph.D. from USC in Romance Languages. "I have been doing research in the post-Columbian history of Mexico. That's why I came down here."

"Well, I hope we can give you some assistance," she said seriously.

Francisco suddenly remembered. "Oh, I brought you this," he pulled out a small black hardback bound book. It was "El Tulipán Negro."

"Oh, thank you. I love Alejandro Dumas. He's my tocayo (namesake)," She turned her face slightly as to blush.

"I thought you might like it."

The waiter came back, and they ordered. She ordered the shrimp mole while he ordered the chicken mole.

"Have you been married?" she asked boldly.

Francisco explained that he had been once married, and then divorced. "As I said, I'm concentrating on my research project with Professor Rios." He tried to change the subject.

They chatted lightly and the waiter came over for more drink orders. They ordered another round. Then it was Francisco's turn to be inquisitive. "Do you not drink for health reasons or religious ones?"

"My father died of leukemia. I may have a predisposition for this disease. So, I am careful of what I eat and drink. I am also an endocrinologist. I have to set a good example for my patients."

Francisco noticed that she did not wear a wedding band. Just a large black pearl ring to match her necklace. "Do you have a family?"

"I was born in La Paz, in Southern Baja, Mexico. I moved to Guadalajara to become a nurse. I met my husband, and we were married. He was a doctor. We were married three years. He died falling down some stairs. We didn't have any children. Then I decided to go to medical school. And here I am. And I still have family back in La Paz."

"I'm sorry," Francisco felt bad about asking such personal questions.

The food came. The smells were intoxicating.

"Here, Francisco, try this." Alejandra took one of her shrimp and reached over and put it on his plate.

"Oh, my God! This is sinful!" The tastes exploded in his mouth. He reciprocated and cut a slight portion of the chicken mole for her.

There were pauses of conversation between bites. They talked about their backgrounds and Mexico.

A five-year-old indigenous girl came up to their table and placed several little brightly painted animals on it. Francisco selected a reddish-orange striped and spotted doglike figurine with a bobbing head. He gave it to Alejandra.

She laughed as she took it.

The waiter came back after they had finished their dinners.

"Any desserts? Coffees? Kahluas?" he asked.

"Bring us a piece of the chocolate cake to share please," Alejandra ordered before Francisco could say a word. "Two forks."

Francisco had coffee. She didn't. They laughed. When all was said and done, the waiter asked if there was anything else. Both shook their heads no.

The waiter brought the check and placed it directly in front of Francisco. Francisco smiled gracefully. He had forgotten a basic Latin American cultural custom. The man always pays. *Así es la vida.*

They left the restaurant.

"Francisco, would you like to take a little walk? The cathedral is only about four blocks away from here."

CHAPTER 27 – THE PHONE CALL

Monday, June 25, 2018
Guadalajara

Francisco was having his breakfast in the lodging's lounge
that Monday morning. He liked the healthy continental fare but
would prefer some huevos rancheros every once in a while.
The night before he reviewed his notes preparing for the eleven
o'clock phone with Joel Brenner from Powell's Bookstore. He
already felt hyper but still dared have a second cup of coffee.
Miranda had called him the day before and said that she had
another doctor's appointment today and that she probably
would not make it into the office all week. She confided that
she was wearing a medical walking boot and wouldn't be
caught dead on campus with it. *Ah, vanity!* Francisco thought.
They would play out the week, day by day. Francisco was
flexible, so there was no problem.

However, Francisco was scheduled to give his second
lecture on Friday. This would give him more time to prepare
for his presentation on the Catholic religion and its
colonization of Mexico. Miranda had reminded him that they

had a meeting with Professor Erandi on Wednesday. She suggested that they have a luncheon meeting at her house. *No hay problema.*

"Oh, Francisco, I am so sorry that I am setting us back on our work schedule," Miranda apologized. "We'll make it up to you."

"Miranda, don't worry about it. I'm not concerned about our schedule. By the way, thank you for inviting me to the Teatro Degollado performance. It was great," Francisco hadn't wanted her to feel bad. "I really enjoy Alejandra's company. She's an independent soul."

"She likes you too," Miranda had said a bit over enthusiastically. "Unfortunately, she has hospital duty this next weekend."

Was that a hint? He wondered. Miranda was cool. *Maybe I should call Alejandra.*

"Miranda, can you please email me Alejandra's phone number?" Francisco asked.

Francisco finished his breakfast and it was now 10:30. Francisco walked up to his room and brushed his teeth. At precisely 11 a.m. the phone rang.

"Professor Reynoso?"

To his surprise, the reception was good. "Yes, Joel, this is Professor Reynoso. How are you? Is it raining up in Oregon?"

"I'm fine, and yes it's always raining up here," Joel Brenner responded. "Thanks for making this happen. I really haven't gotten to know you but working with Tina has been great."

Francisco remembered that she had negotiated the price of the 1527 papers to their advantage.

"How can I help you today, Joel?"

"Well, some original Saavedra notes and logs have become available through a private seller," Joel started to explain. "I did a little bit of digging. These materials were offered to several other private libraries and public institutions. I have talked to a couple of my colleagues who were contacted by a Roberto Gutierrez from Cuernavaca, Mexico . . ."

Francisco knew Cuernavaca. He loved it. It was called "the land of eternal spring." He listened intently to the amazing background of some new papers that were being offered for sale. Joel explained that he had found out that Roberto Gutierrez was the grandson of the infamous Arturo Durazo Moreno, commonly known as "El Negro." Durazo, as he was more commonly known, had been a childhood friend of Mexican president José López Portillo and became the Chief of Police for Mexico City. He turned his police force into a right-wing paramilitary group that was involved in corruption, extortion, smuggling illegal weapons, and cocaine. He did dirty work for the U.S., CIA, and the Russians. He criminalized everything, and victimized, tortured, and killed hundreds of people.

Durazo funneled his ill-gotten gains into vintage cars, expensive properties in North America, and rare art and books. He had palatial mansions in Mexico City, Cuernavaca, and Zihuatanejo (the latter modeled after the Greek Parthenon). In 1986 he was arrested, convicted of numerous crimes, and incarcerated. The federal and local governments tried to confiscate all his properties. Durazo's children and grandchildren had all the properties tied up in court proceedings. The family was trying to liquidate all his personal property assets. Roberto Gutierrez was in charge of selling off the art pieces and literary works from the Cuernavaca and Zihuatanejo mansions.

"Last month Roberto emailed me. He said that he had more old documents," Joel continued. "He didn't know if they were authentic records or fiction. There is no provenance (chain of possession). We talked and he offered lots of books and records. One work called 'Milo's Story' looked promising."

Joel went on to explain that there were no guarantees of authenticity. The question of selling price came up. Joel explained that Roberto was very motivated to sell because the

Mexican government was closing in on the Durazo estate and most buyers were not interested without chains of title."

"Well, Joel, what is your advice?"

"I think we can offer him $50 U.S. But the real problem is transportation and delivery," Joel was used to dealing in impossible logistics. "If we buy, he could ship it to me up here in Portland. That would be expensive and very time consuming. There would be no guarantees."

Francisco thought it over and knew that would not work. *How about Roberto shipping it straight to me in Guadalajara or to Stanford?* He mulled it over and feared that there would still be problems.

"Joel, you've done a great job," Francisco was serious. "Tina really enjoyed working with you," he exaggerated a little. "But let's hold off for a few days. I need to talk with my colleague here in Guadalajara and ask her opinion. I would trust her judgement."

"Sound good, Professor."

They hung up. *I know we can make this work. I just don't know how yet. Tina, where are you when I need you?*

He got up from his desk and grabbed his water bottle off the coffee table. Then he returned to check his email. He would write Tina to apprise of her of what was going on.

As he was checking his email, one from Miranda appeared. It was a one liner with Alejandra's cell number and email address.

CHAPTER 28 – PYRAMID OF THE MOON

Wednesday, June 27, 2018
Guadalajara

There had been an early morning rain and the streets smelled fresh. Francisco was taking an Uber ride driven by a middle-aged man named Raúl in a tiny white Kia. Francisco was meeting Professor Carlos Erandi at Professor Rios' house. Miranda's doctor did not want her to put weight on the foot with the broken toe for the first week. As a consolation, she agreed to host the consultation with Carlos Erandi and Francisco at her house, promising a nice lunch.

Earlier that morning Francisco had emailed Alejandra notifying her that he was giving a presentation on Friday entitled, "God and Gold," that dealt with Spain's religious practices in Mexico and other parts of its empire.

At the Rios residence he was greeted by Jorge and escorted to the salon where Miranda was sitting with her foot propped up on a leather stool. Their visitor, Carlos Erandi, was shuffling through reams of papers strewn on the coffee table.

Francisco and Miranda exchanged salutary pecks. The slender, shaggy haired Carlos shook Francisco's hand.

"It is a pleasure to meet you, Professor Reynoso," the bronze-skinned Carlos spoke Spanish with an odd accent.

"The pleasure is mine, Professor Erandi," Francisco reciprocated. "But please call me Francisco. The translation work you did was excellent. Thank you."

"Oh, it was nothing. Just call me Carlos," he seemed bashful "I am not even a real professor."

The threesome chatted amiably. Carlos was an indigenous Purépecha bilingual high school teacher in Guanajuato. He also worked as a part-time translator in Tarascan and Nahuatl.

Alma came over with coffee and pan dulce. The two men were not shy about helping themselves to the Mexican pastries.

Francisco gave a brief overview of the project and its potential future publication in an academic journal. It would be the property of Stanford University with the three of them as collaborators. Professors Rios and Erandi would be granted licenses to use the publication and research for academic purposes.

Carlos Erandi poured himself another cup of coffee and added three sugars. And for good measure, he took a rosquete pastry. He had thanked Miranda and Francisco a thousand times for the money and tablets for his students.

"I just have to make sure that they are not using the tablets to play games," Carlos gave a nervous laugh.

They talked about various aspects of the translations.

"The ones in Spanish are okay since they were not water damaged," Carlos said. "Others were written on parchment paper. Some were moldy. Lots of missing pages."

Miranda concurred. Francisco was taking notes. Since he was the manager of the project, he had to ensure its academic integrity.

"The documents in Nahuatl are very problematic. Written by two or three different people," Carlos continued. "Not great quality."

Francisco raised some of the questions that had plagued him about the Saavedra journey and the mysterious women aboard the ship.

"So far, we know that a woman named María Del Rosario and her maid were on one of the Saavedra ships, but we don't know why. And we know that a young apprentice cleric was ordered to set sail on a ship named the Santiago to retrieve her."

Miranda jumped into the conversation. "We also know that the Saavedra expedition was ordered by Hernán Cortés to sail to the Molucca Islands for the purpose of trading Spanish goods for spices. The secondary objective was to proselytize and gain converts for the Catholic Church. But where do the women fit in?"

The discussion went on for another hour. Socorro came into the room and announced that lunch was ready. They all meandered into the dining room. On the table was a mini buffet with platters of fresh fruit, greens, guacamole, carne asada, and black beans. Miranda carefully hobbled to the table by herself. *Was it self-determination, inner strength, or vanity?* Francisco wondered. Miranda sat down and Socorro brought her a plate. There was iced tea and water to drink.

"So, Carlos, what are you teaching this summer?" Francisco was trying to be friendly with his new colleague.

"Unfortunately, my friend, teachers here are not valued like in many other countries," Carlos' dark brown eyes looked sad. "We have to take extra jobs. I am a tour guide in Mexico City."

"Where?" Miranda was suddenly interested.

"Actually, a little bit outside the city. In Teotihuacan."

"I've been there," Miranda said. This was echoed by Francisco. They were both fascinated by Carlos' new revelation.

Carlos and his family lived in Guanajuato but in the summer, he had to go to where the work was. This summer he was assigned to do tours of the Pyramid of the Moon.

"I should have studied the pyramids more when I was down there years ago. I know very little about them," Francisco commented.

Carlos went on to explain that the pyramids in Teotihuacan were not actually built by the Aztecs. The sites were already abandoned when the Aztecs arrived here. The Pyramid of the Moon was at the northern end of the Avenue of the Dead. It was the second largest structure and situated at the highest point of the city. Nearby was a plaza that had an altar in the middle. This is where sacrificial rituals were carried out.

"Here's a question that everyone asks: Why the human sacrifice?" Francisco queried.

"It was used to keep order among the people and to give the rulers and priests power over their subjects."

"Who was sacrificed?" Miranda joined in the questioning.

"It could be captured enemies. It could be brave Aztecs to appease the gods or to recompense the gods for a blasphemy."

Socorro came to the table with coffee and cups of mango sorbet. Francisco and Carlos inhaled theirs.

Francisco and Carlos started back to the salon, followed by Miranda who was walking slowly with her boot. The trio resumed their discussions.

It was near the end of the meeting that Francisco mentioned his conversation with Joel Brenner about some documents in

Cuernavaca. He wanted their opinion about whether or not they should purchase the materials.

Miranda had no opinion.

"Milo's Story is legendary," Carlos was talking quickly. "I have never seen a copy, but it is supposed to be half-fiction, half-fact."

They talked over the pros and cons of acquiring the papers. Francisco mentioned the logistical problem of having the materials delivered to them.

"I can pick them up," Carlos said. The other two looked surprised. "I have to drive back to Mexico City tonight. Cuernavaca is just over an hour away."

In the end they all agreed that Francisco should contact Brenner and make the deal. Carlos would pick up the materials in Cuernavaca at a mutually convenient time for him and Roberto Gutierrez. Francisco then told Carlos that he would pay him $100 for this service, over the latter's protests. Francisco knew that Carlos probably didn't even make twenty dollars a day as a guide. Carlos needed money and Francisco wouldn't have to worry about the delivery. Miranda stepped in and said that it was only fair. Two against one.

It was just after four when the meeting ended. They agreed that they had to meet again, with the date and time to be determined. Carlos gave Francisco a ride home in his ancient caramel-colored Volkswagen bug with its dozens of dents and scrapes.

Back in his room, Francisco checked his emails. One was from Mary Beth about Fall class schedules, and then there was one from Alejandra.

Thank you for the invitation to your lecture. Sorry, I am scheduled the entire weekend at the hospital. Call me.

CHAPTER 29 – GOD AND GOLD

Friday, June 29, 2018
Guadalajara

Francisco was reviewing his lecture at the back of the university auditorium for his 11 a.m. presentation on "God and Gold." He was going to deliver the presentation in English to appease his comfort level. He paced back and forth in the small enclosed space.

Francisco knew that Alejandra Mora would not be present at his lecture. Francisco had called her twice on Wednesday night, but there was no answer. On Thursday morning he found a voicemail message on his cellphone asking if he would like to get together for lunch or a coffee the following Tuesday. It was her new day off. He texted her "yes." *He didn't understand why he was so jumpy dealing with her. She was very nice. Intelligent. Attractive. She knew what she was doing. Was he afraid of strong women?*

Unfortunately, Miranda Rios would not be in attendance either. She was told by her doctor that she had to be extra careful the first week after her fracture. Plus, she said that she would not be caught dead wearing a boot on campus. The good news was that as a consolation prize, Sol was taking Francisco out that evening for libations.

Francisco was ready. Moments later Dean Montoya was introducing Francisco to the crowd. The two gave each other warm abrazos.

Francisco did the usual honorifics for the deans and faculty and then he began.

"What is gold?" he began in a peripatetic manner pointing to the image displayed on the screen.

The audience looked puzzled by the question. "The simple answer is that it is an element, . . . a rock, that is turned into a metal. It's been around for millennia. It has been deemed one of the most valuable things we have. How many of you are wearing gold rings, gold earrings, or other gold jewelry? Raise your hands." About 90% of the room complied, looking from side to side to observe other responders.

"Why is it so valuable?" There were a lot blank stares. "The answer is because people say it is. Can you eat it? No. Can you drink it? Of course, not . . ."

Francisco had definitely gotten their attention. He talked about the history of gold and its uses. Monetary systems, art and jewelry, and industrial production.

"Here in Mexico, Meso-America, and the Americas, gold was one of the main reasons for European exploration, colonization, and subjugation. Our Aztec ancestors called gold, 'teocuitlatl'." There were a few chuckles among the visitors. "Yes, it means god feces." There was a mixed commotion of laughter and shock. "The Spaniards killed Moctezuma and sent the Aztec gold back to Spain to adorn their churches. The Aztecs weren't too concerned. They valued obsidian and flint more. The legend of the lost City of El Dorado . . ."

About twenty minutes into his presentation, Francisco started to get tired. He stopped and drank a half bottle of water before he resumed.

"Now where does God come fit into the picture? If we ask who or what God is, each one of us will have a different answer. And we all think that our version of God is the only real one. True or not true?'

Most heads nodded affirmatively. Francisco was sweating profusely. He grabbed another drink of water.

"Now let's tie gold to God," Francisco continued. "Well, each religion placed a different importance on gold. We know that in the Book of Exodus in the Old Testament of the Bible, God was not happy that the Israelites were worshiping the Golden Calf. The Muslims had their holy gold-covered Dome of the Rock in Jerusalem. And the Catholics tried to convert the

American indigenous people into Christianity while at the same time appropriating their gold. The Spaniards killed for it and enslaved indigenous people to mine gold . . ."

Francisco went through his slides on the Crusades, the Inquisition, the persecution of the Jews, and the Spanish caste system throughout its colonies. Finally, he concluded. The crowd applauded him, but there were a few hecklers.

And then the fun began. Dean Montoya facilitated the question-and-answer period. A young female student with dark hair and big glasses presented the first question.

"Professor Rios, do you believe in God?"

"I believe in a Creator," he assumed that she was rigorously religious. "I'm still striving to solve the puzzle. But to anticipate the next question. I do not believe in the biblical version or versions of God."

Another hand immediately shot up from the back. A tall male with a round ruddy face asked, "Do you believe that the Bible is the written Word of God?"

"No, the Bible is a book that was written by several people. It is a compilation of the early history of Jews, poetry, moral standards, and fiction." There was an undercurrent of mumbling in the audience. "Is it credible to believe that a fisherman or a thief could read and write in those days? The Bible is what the Council of Nicaea compromised on."

Another question: "Do you believe that God made man?"

Francisco responded, "I don't know. But I do know that man-made God." Hands flew up. People were stirred.

The flurry of questions continued. Some were hostile. Finally, Dean Montoya stated that there was only time for one more question.

"Professor Rios, it seems that you probably wouldn't invest your money in gold," a faculty member suggested.

"That's an excellent point," Francisco surmised that the questioner was in the university's Business Department. "I would invest in intrinsically valuable things. Clean air. Potable water. Sustainable and healthy food. Probably none of these things would make anyone rich. One more thing. I would invest in people. Fellow human beings. Investment in your brothers and sisters is a good thing. Thank you for your indulgence. It's been a pleasure."

There was a little reception with aguas frescas and pan dulce. Dean Montoya did his best to shield Francisco from the students who wanted to argue religion.

Francisco was totally exhausted when he went back to his room at the faculty lodging. He plopped into bed and took a nap. He woke up at four, took a quick shower, and put on clean clothes. A polo shirt and chinos. Sol picked him up at 6 p.m.

After a wild ride through town, they landed at Tía Chucha's Taqueria. It was crowded. It was loud. Everybody was drinking.

"Miranda told me to take you out tonight," Sol was dipping chips into the green salsa. "She felt bad about not coming to your presentation. She thinks that she is a bad hostess."

"Hey, no problems," Francisco replied. "I think if I talked ten more minutes, I would have been burned at the stake like a heretic."

They both laughed.

"I brought you here because this is one of my favorite places. Miranda doesn't like it. Too common. Let's order some tacos de birria and pork carnitas.

"Sol, brother, now you're talking my language."

Sol talked about his family and how he was concerned about his daughter, Mirasol. He knew that he could not protect her forever. Francisco shared about his divorce and recent breakup with his girlfriend Zoe.

"By the way, thanks for talking Alejandra to that tango thing. If you hadn't said yes, I probably would have been stuck going. I don't like that kind of stuff."

"I had fun," Francisco reflected. "Alejandra is quite a person. Very intelligent and very intimidating."

"You should ask her out. She doesn't bite," Sol took another sip of beer.

CHAPTER 30 – CAFECITO

Monday, July 2, 2018
Guadalajara

It was 8 a.m. Monday morning and Francisco was just minutes away from going downstairs to breakfast when his cell phone rang. Alejandra wanted to get together for coffee. She apologized for not being able to meet sooner, but she had had to perform two major surgeries.

"How about tomorrow? Very informal," she said over the phone. "I just need a break. One of my partners is on vacation and I have had to cover for him."

"No problem," Francisco had a smile on his face. She was nice and not demanding. "Where shall we meet?"

"Let's make it convenient for you," Alejandra seemed to be thinking. "You're in the Oblatos District, right?"

"Yes."

"How about the Café Shalom?" she suggested. "It's one of my favorite places when I want to get away," "It's across the street from the temple."

"Sure. Why not? What time?"

"How about 4 p.m.?"

He was really glad that she hadn't chosen a Starbucks.

Later in the morning Francisco went on a walk and came back to do his computer work. Tina had emailed him and said that she was doing fine. She had met a Brazilian guy and hinted that he was hot.

Francisco's afternoon was free. Miranda had notified him the day before that she had a doctor's appointment for her toe today and would be unable to meet. But Wednesday they would get together with Professor Erandi at her office.

• • •

Francisco arrived twenty minutes early at the brightly colored cafe. He sat at an aqua blue round table outdoors. The smell of the roasted coffee beans coming from inside made his chest hair grow. The place was relatively close to his lodging, and it had only taken him a half hour to walk there. He thought about bringing her a gift but thought twice about it.

Café Shalom had free Wi-Fi, so Francisco checked his phone to see if Alejandra had texted. A short, dark-skinned waitress came over to take his order, but he told her that he was waiting for his someone. Just as he said that, Alejandra arrived.

"Francisco! How good to see you again," Alejandra was bubbly and kissed him on both cheeks"

"Me, too!" Francisco's face was getting hot. He was almost blushing.

"Did you have fun the other night?" she asked with a curious smile. "You can be honest with me."

"Yes," he said shyly.

"What was your favorite part?"

"Sharing the chocolate cake with you."

Without missing a beat, she laughed, "That was good. It was almost as good as the shrimp in mole sauce."

"Alejandra, I am curious," he tried to regain his composure. "I thought that you said that you don't eat desserts. I've been trying to remember exactly what you said. Am I imaging things?"

"Well, professor, the truth of the matter is that I try not to eat a lot of sugar," she started to explain. She was interrupted when the waitress came back.

"What can I get for you today?" the food server inquired.

"I will have a dark chocolate mocha please," Alejandra said.

"What size?"

"Large, please."

"And for you, sir?"

Normally, back home he would have had a half decaf soy latte. But now in Mexico he was living dangerously. "I'll have the same, please."

"Large?"

"Yes, please."

"Anything to eat? Today's special is a banana Nutella crepe."

"Give us a minute, please," Alejandra took over.

"Good. I'll be right back with your drinks." The waitress left.

"As I was saying, I limit my sugar. For example, Nutella's main ingredient is sugar. It also has palm oil and fake vanilla," she explained. "Bad stuff!"

"But what about chocolate?" Francisco's forehead was furrowed.

"Well, that's a different story," she leaned toward him. "Is chocolate a fruit or a vegetable or a legume?"

Francisco had never really thought about it. "I'm guessing it's a fruit since it grows on trees. Is that right?"

"It's really all of the above," she laughed. "The cocoa tree is both a fruit and vegetable, but its pods are legumes. It's a controversial subject."

Francisco realized that she had been teasing him. He had been too serious. *Just be yourself! She's fun.*

"Okay, you got me. But that doesn't explain why you eat chocolate."

"First of all, I like it. Secondly, it doesn't have that much sugar. You noticed that we are having a dark chocolate mocha. It's mostly cacao beans that are very healthy for you," it seemed like she was giving him a friendly tutorial. "And it is culturally mandated to consume. The Greeks had their theobromine, and the Aztecs had their xocolatl."

The waitress came over and served their drinks. Alejandra ordered an Oaxaca cheese and tomato salad, and Francisco asked for the arrachera baguette.

"This drink is great!" he seemed surprised.

"And good for you!"

"Alejandra, you're too much!" He laughed. He was letting go. Francisco wanted to grab her hand but fought the urge. He could see why she was probably a good doctor and interacted well with patients.

"Please call me Alexi. My friends call me Alexi."

"Well, you don't want to know what my friends call me," he gave her a big grin.

After a bumpy start, the two started to connect and were getting to know each other.

Alejandra shared her experiences in med school. There were very few women in the program. She felt that she had to work twice as hard. But being a nurse had given her a distinct advantage in the practice of medicine. She could give an injection. She could touch any part of a person's anatomy, male or female. She could empathize with patients.

Once or twice while they were eating, their hands brushed against each other. There was no retraction.

Francisco shared that he was going through an existential crisis. "I really don't know what I want to do when I grow up." He tried to joke about it. "What am I doing? You're a doctor. You heal people. I just talk to a bunch of young people."

"Are you a good teacher?"

"I try to be."

"Besides the subject matter, do you teach them critical thinking? Do you teach them how to think and analyze?"

"Yes." They talked about him for a little while longer. He was feeling relieved. She made him feel good. She gave him confidence.

The cafecito had lasted over two hours. Francisco paid the check.

Francisco wanted to ask her out, but he hesitated a few seconds too long. Her black Lexus SUV pulled up in front of them. He opened the back door for her. As they started to shake hands. Alejandra leaned close to him and kissed him partially on the lips. Electricity went through his body.

"Why don't you come over to my house for dinner on Saturday?" she said in a sultry tone.

CHAPTER 31 – MILO'S DIARIES

Wednesday, July 4, 2018
Guadalajara

To accommodate Miranda, the meeting with Carlos Erandi had to be rescheduled to 1 p.m. on Wednesday. The good news was that Miranda was now able to use a lighter boot on her right foot. It was more of a precautionary measure to protect her broken toe and she was allowed to walk short distances. Today was her second day back in the office.

Francisco arrived early, and they chatted about how Sol had been the model host. He had kept Francisco entertained while Miranda was unavailable. The Rios couple seemed very concerned with keeping Francisco entertained. If Francisco didn't know better, he even would have sworn that the "dates" with Alexi had been planned by Miranda and Sol. He was waiting for Miranda to ask about her comadre. He didn't know what he should share.

"Hey, I hear you created quite a stir with your anti-religion presentation last Friday," Miranda said with a straight face.

"The diocese has sent a formal protest and several religious students groups are sending the administration nasty emails."

"I just spoke the truth," he tried to justify himself. She put a hand on his forearm.

"Just teasing. Dean Montoya loved it," she began to snicker. "He was kicked out of altar boys when he was a youngster. He would love for you to join our faculty. He says we need more professors . . . or heretics who can stimulate the students. We have too many tapados (bores)."

Carlos Erandi arrived just after one. Miranda had ordered some carne asada tortas for their lunch. She knew that Carlos had just driven six plus hours from Mexico City. He was bedraggled and spent ten minutes in the bathroom trying to recover.

There were the usual greetings and pleasantries.

"How was Cuernavaca?" Miranda began.

"Fantastic!" Carlos gushed. "You're not going to believe it!" He handed Miranda a stack of papers about an inch thick. "We're going to need three copies."

Miranda called her secretary Alma and asked for copies to be made. At the same time Francisco handed her a thumb drive and also asked for three copies of the "CarlosErandiInvoice7.3.18."

"Mr. Gutierrez was very friendly," Carlos continued. "He lives in a palace halfway, between the capital and Cuernavaca. It has a racetrack, a helicopter landing strip, two swimming pools, and even a full-sized gym. Roberto gave me a tour. The place is filled with boxes and crates packed with paintings, vases, sculptures, and other furnishings. He told me that he has to liquidate everything because the government is going to confiscate all the property due to Mr. Durazo's crimes and the corruption."

Alma reentered the room and gave the copies to Miranda and the thumb drive to Francisco.

Carlos continued, "These documents look like a personal journal of the cabin boy Milo, who described the journey of the Espiritu Santo that was believed lost in the Saavedra expedition. The original notes were in Nahuatl on the ship captain's parchment paper. It is high quality. Milo was not thought to be an official recorder of the ship's journal. How Mr. Gutierrez obtained these is unknown."

"Carlos, please eat," Miranda beckoned. "You must be starved." They all grabbed tortas. The carne asada was complemented by sliced tomatoes, cotija cheese, guacamole, onions, and refried beans.

After they ate, Carlos gave Francisco and Miranda an overview of some of the pages that he had had a chance to translate.

"Milo was born in Barcelona around the beginning of the sixteenth century. Unfortunately, his mother died when he was young. His father was a nobleman and remarried a distant cousin who had two children. You can imagine the jealousy. Milo was sent to a private boarding school. Milo and his stepmother got on rather badly. The boy was forced to join the military. He was shipped off to Cuba where he served under the Command of Hernán Cortés. He was part of the squadron that captured Mexico City, formerly known as Teotihuacan. There was a lot of bloodshed and the city was in flames. Milo was trapped in a burning hut. He was discovered by Aztec warriors and taken to their village outside of Teotihuacan. Eighty percent of his body had been burned, including his left arm, the left side of his face, and his manhood. He also could no longer speak. For some unknow reason, perhaps they felt sorry for him, the natives nursed him back to health and after nine months he returned to his military unit. The Spanish captain called him a deserter and sentenced him to be confined in the stockade. One of the Franciscan monks, Fray Nicolás Nadal, felt that this poor boy had suffered enough and asked for mercy. It happened that at this time Cortés was sending Captain Saavedra on a trade mission. The commander needed men and Milo was recruited as a cabin boy on the ship Espiritu Santo.

"According to his notes, the three-ship convoy left Zihuatanejo Bay on October 31, 1527. Milo reported directly to Pedro Fuentes de Xérez who captained the twenty-ton bergantín that had a crew of fifteen. But on the first day at sea, Fray Nadal gave Milo secret instructions that only he and the captain knew about. He had to covertly take care of two passengers who were lodged in a cabin next to the captain, in the aft of the ship. He was also instructed to wear a handkerchief over his face to cover his repulsive appearance.

"For the first few days, he just had to knock on the passengers' door and leave food or fresh water in front of it. He didn't know who his passengers were until one day he spied a middle-aged indigenous woman putting out an empty tray. She saw him. He was frightened and started to run off."

At this point Carlos took a sip of water and began reading directly from the journal:

November 1527
Espiritu Santo

"'Wait!' the woman cried out in Nahuatl. 'Do not be afraid. We will not hurt you."

I think Inocente felt sorry for me because of my disfigurement. She began inviting me into their cabin when I brought their breakfast tray that included breads and fresh water. I noticed that there was a young girl dressed in formal Aztec clothing praying in the corner of the cabin in front of a black pearl rosary nailed to the cabin wall. She looked familiar from the back, but I couldn't place her. Inocente, on the other hand, was very talkative. I had picked up some Nahuatl when I was recuperating from my burns in the Aztec village. Inocente and Maria Del Rosario had been abducted by Saavedra's men and forced onto the ship.

Gradually, I lost my fear of the two women and came into their cabin regularly. This saved me from beatings from the crew. Inocente shared that she was called "Cihuatlamacazqui" and was a devotee to Coyolxāuqui, the Goddess of the Moon. She was assigned to be the protectress of the Princess Yepyollotli (called "Yepy" by Inocente), the 17-year-old daughter of the tribal leader, Cacamatzin.

Over a series of days, Inocente revealed that Yepyollotli had been scheduled to be sacrificed in a sacred ceremony to pay tribute to the moon goddess, Coyolxauhqui in August of 1524 when a full moon and lunar eclipse were to coincide.

However, the tribute never took place because the girl was unexpectedly captured by the Conquistador Hernán Cortés and his army. The princess' family was slaughtered by Cortés' men, but she and Inocente were sent to live with some Spanish nuns in a convent in Zacatula. Yepy was forced to learn Spanish and to convert to the Catholic religion. Her name became Maria Del Rosario. And Cihuatlamacazqui pretended to become Catholic in order to protect her mistress. She was renamed Inocente.

Yepy had a cache of black pearls that had been converted into a rosary, a necklace, and other jewelry. Her father, Cacamatzin, had been a village chieftain in Baja California. Yepy was adamant about praying the rosary every day to Incocente's dismay. Inocente did not join her, but instead chanted to her Aztec goddess. The protectress knew that Coyolxāuqui would not be happy about losing one of her Aztec princesses to the Catholic god. Fray Nadal came to their cabin once when he was not seasick. They all prayed together.

I found Inocente's stories fascinating. She had also told me how the local natives hated Yepy and her, and blamed them for La Conquista. Since I only served the captain, Fray Nadal, and the two women, I had a lot of free time. I avoided the crew who called me a cursed monster and would push and kick me. Fray Nadal and I slept in a small closet near the crew's quarters. I took (borrowed or stole) paper and pen from the captain's cabin and created a daily journal. I kept my diary in Inocente's cabin for safekeeping and away from prying eyes. I wrote it in Nahuatl so none of the crew could decipher it, and I knew that Inocente was illiterate so she would not be able to read it either.

Most nights the salty sea winds howled and soft sounds could not be heard. This was exacerbated by the waves pounding on the bergantin. The Espiritu Santo always maintained a course within eyesight of Saavedra's other two ships. The ships communicated by flags, lights, or loud horns.

It was early December when I overheard three crewmen in an animated conversation with the cook. They were all speaking Portuguese. I could partially understand because it was closely related to Spanish and the banter was fairly simple.

"I tell ya, Rodrigo, somethin' ain't right," the emaciated cook Gonçalo Silveira said to the Rodrigo Alves, the boatswain. "I only send over some water and breads. Nothing much more. Oh, beans and rice, for sure. Nothing more. But the cups come back with a dark brown scum. It looks like Aztec hot peppers."

"Nothing wrong with that," barked the short, bearded boatswain who smelled like a hundred dead fish.

"But we don't see 'em. We don't hear them. Who is the captain hiding?"

"We won't have to worry about him much longer," Rodrigo sneered. "At the first opportunity, we'll get rid of him and get ourselves rich in the Moluccas!"

"But when?" persisted the cook.

"It will happen when it happens," Rodrigo turned his face toward them and gave them an evil smile. "In the meantime, Rubén, keep a lookout on the cabin. Don't get caught. Have a tool or something in your hand."

The three professors discussed the fantastic story line. Pieces of the puzzle were being to fall into place. Perhaps the answer to the mystery of the abducted women would be found in the rest of the documents.

It was now getting late. Poor Carlos was exhausted. The group was ready to call it quits for the day.

"Carlos, are you staying overnight?" Miranda asked. Maybe they could meet again the following morning.

"Sorry, profesora," Carlos blew out a breath. "I have a tour scheduled tomorrow. A group from the University of Perugia."

"Are you driving back tonight?" Francisco asked incredulously.

"Sí, claro."

Francisco wanted to offer him his lodging for the night, but there was no way Carlos could drive six hours tomorrow morning.

As they were saying their goodbyes, Francisco handed Carlos an envelope and an invoice form. "Carlos, I need you to sign the invoice for the project's records." The statement was in English and Carlos read it slowly.

"But, professor, this is for two hundred dollars!" Carlos was concerned. "We had agreed on one hundred."

Francisco did not want to offend his colleague, so he cleverly said, "Sure, one hundred for the services and one hundred for expenses." He winked at Miranda. "Isn't that correct, Miranda?"

She nodded affirmatively. Carlos left.

"I guess we now know what the sailors were complaining about. The two women on their ship were María Del Rosario and Inocente," she said, as she put her copy of Milo's journal into her oversized dark brown leather purse. "It makes sense."

"And this led to the mutiny," added Francisco nodding his head.

"We have a lot of reading to do," Miranda added. "By the way, I just called Sol and he is picking us up in ten minutes. He wants to take us out for a drink for your Fourth of July."

They waited for Sol in front of the Language Arts building. He had forgotten about the Independence Day holiday. A few beers with Sol would solve that.

"Thank you giving Carlos the extra money," Miranda looked seriously at him.

"No problem," Francisco tipped his head, but became a bit somber. "But there may be a problem with the journal article. The Milo journal is a translation. It's an interpretation, not a primary document, and Carlos says there are sections missing. We may not be able to establish provenance."

"That may be true, but let's see where all of this leads us," Miranda said cautiously. "Oh, by the way, I hear you are having dinner at Alexi's house on Saturday."

CHAPTER 32 – THE ASSAULT

Thursday, July 5, 2018
Guadalajara

The next morning Francisco reviewed an academic journal standards manual. There were always exceptions, such as best evidence, but events in Milo's journal could not be authenticated. He emailed Professor Segreti at Stanford and asked for his advice. An hour later the Romance Language professor suggested that they continue with the article and in the end, the journal editorial board could either accept or reject any documents.

Francisco decided to play it safe, and emailed his Dean, Dorothea Chandler, and asked her to please call him. The phone in his room rang twenty minutes later.

"Well, Francisco, I'm impressed," she greeted him. "I thought you would be at one of those beautiful Mexican beaches sipping a margarita."

The teasing went on for a few more minutes and then she asked him what he needed. He explained all the progress that had been made on the project but was concerned with the issues of authenticity. His reputation and that of the university were on the line.

"Francisco, you sure know how to pick them," Dean Chandler inhaled. "But I think you have two options. The first and most obvious one is to eliminate any non-corroborated sources. The other is to state that authenticity of some secondary sources cannot be certified. You will probably want to include a disclaimer in the beginning of the manuscript."

"Thank you, dean," Francisco was relieved. She had given him hope and guidance. She would also be the final judge in the submission of the article. "I can work with this. Okay, now I owe you. What kind of souvenir do you want?"

"Now, we're getting down to business," she laughed.

An hour later Francisco had a slight headache. He decided to do his daily walk. *His mind raced over to Alejandra. She mesmerizes me. She captures my attention.*

That evening after a little dinner of street tacos and Corona beers, Francisco began to read more of the journals of Milo.

December 1527
Espíritu Santo

Inocente and I became friends. She told me stories about this and that. Since I could not talk, I just listened and took notes. I kept my journal under a shelf in the two women's cabin.

I observed that Inocente was indigenous, not young and not old. She was short in stature and had wide shoulders. Her black hair was cut in bangs. She was simply dressed. She wore an off-color white cotton huīpīlli (blouse) and a long cuētl (skirt) held up by a red sash. Inocente always walked around the cabin barefoot.

Yepyollotli was the complete opposite. I knew that she was some type of Aztec princess, but wondered why she was on this ship. She wore the clothing of nobility. A multi-colored linen tunic over a long skirt. A white rebozo hid her black hair highlighted with purple streaks and her gold plug earrings. At times she wore some type of black beaded necklace. She wore leather sandals.

It was now early December, and a new moon was invisible in the sky. Customarily, I brought them some soup just before sunset. I made my way through the murky passageway and knocked on the door. The door opened and I took a step forward.

No sooner had I done that, when I was shoved forward from behind, spilling the tray of food and causing me to land harshly on the floor. It hurt!

"Alas! What do you we have here?" shouted Rubén in Portuguese. He had decided to make his move. "A woman! Wait, two of them!" He started to move forward. I tried to grab the sailor's raggedy pant leg but received a powerful kick to my face for the effort. I was stunned.

Inocente rushed the sailor. "You can't touch her!" she yelled in Nahuatl. Nobody understood her.

"She is sacred." She grabbed at Rubén's hairy left arm. He twisted around and brandished a small dagger in this right hand. He gave her a leering stare that could stop a ferocious lion. He knew that he had nothing to lose. He stepped closer and closer to Yepyollotli. The black eyes of the girl grew large, but she did not cry out. Between the roar of the seas crashing on the boat and the howling of the winds, nobody would have heard her anyway.

"Wait! Wait!" Inocente yelled out in broken Spanish. "I give you treasure. Leave her alone!"

Rubén stopped and turned to her.

She opened her hand. In her palm were three black pearls. Rubén's tongue licked his moustache that drooped over his upper lip.

"Aw right!" he howled. "I won't kill ya. I'll make it quick." He moved back toward the young girl. He wanted to grab her but had his knife in his right hand and the pearls in his left. His clothes were rags, and he had no decent pockets. He decided to swallow the pearls. He could recover them the next day, he laughed to himself.

He grabbed Yepy's right arm in a vicelike grip. She stifled a cry. Then he noticed the black pearl necklace around her neck. Just like the pearls he now had! He released her arm and started to fondle the pearls. He slowly pulled on them, drawing her closer and closer to him. His body filled with passion. He took a deep breath.

Rubén noticed out of the corner of his right eye that the black pearl rosary mounted on the wall had started to glow. It was pulsating! Was it on fire? There were flashes of light! Then he saw sparks flying from the girl's necklace. He jumped back. What is going on?

He turned around and saw Inocente several feet away from him and me lying flat on the ground. He felt a sharp pain in his side. Had he been stabbed? He saw no wound. His body started to shake. He had terrible abdominal pains. His back arched and his eyes rolled back in his head. His arms started to flop, and he dropped the knife. A black liquid started seeping from his mouth. Rubén fell to the floor in an epileptic fit. It took almost five minutes before he became totally motionless.

Yepy looked at Inocente with widened eyes.

"He's dead!" the protectress bellowed.

The princess was silent. I was writhing in pain.

"We need to get this beast out of here," Inocente immediately took charge. She looked around and picked up the fallen knife. She went over to the porthole and threw the knife out. There were two trails of ocean foam that tracked the Espiritu Santo. She paused and thought.

"Get up, Milo!" she commanded me. "Help me get this atlaca (sailor) up!"

My left shoulder ached and my left arm was glued to my side. Nevertheless, I struggled to get up and started pulling the corpse toward the porthole. The opening was small but Rubén was scrawny. Inocente used her superior strength to force the body through the porthole, hearing bones crack as she did so. Yepy stood staring at the spectacle.

"We can't let anybody know about this!" Inocente cried out to me. "More of them will come and attack us. We have a duty to keep Yepyollotli safe."

After several minutes of lifting and shifting, the dead body of Rubén Gomes was shoved out the porthole. María Del Rosario (Yepyollotli) crossed herself.

"We can't even tell Fray Nadal," Inocente was anticipating that María Del Rosario would want to confess this unfortunate event.

María Del Rosario cupped her face into her palms. She started to cry. Droplets of dark gray liquid fell into her hands.

María looked into her palms. The tears started to crystalize. In a few moments, she was holding a dozen black pearls.

Inocente looked at her ward. "Your gift is still with you. I fear that the Moon Goddess still wants your blood. Her curse on you will continue until she gets her due."

CHAPTER 33 – ANTOJITOS

Friday, July 6, 2018
Guadalajara

The telephone in Francisco's room rang loudly and he woke with a start. It was nine o'clock. He had overslept. Miranda was on the phone.

"Francisco, good morning," she sounded cheerful, but spoke at a quick pace. "I hate to do this to you, but we can't meet today. My foot is swollen. I think I overdid it the other day during our meeting with Carlos. Too much moving around."

"No problem," Francisco was actually relieved. Now he wouldn't have to rush out the door without eating breakfast. "By the way, I contacted my university. They think we can use the Milo materials under certain circumstances and with a lot of disclaimers."

She said that she understood and would rely on his judgment.

"I have continued reading Milo's journal," Francisco said in an enthusiastic tone. "This is great stuff."

"Did you reach the part about the curse yet?" Miranda inquired.

"Yes," he paused. "But I didn't understand it."

"Me neither," she agreed.

"And about the tears turning into pearls!" Francisco said excitedly. "This must be the creative writing part by Milo."

"It's all very confusing. I will contact Carlos and see what he knows. By the way, he really appreciated the money. Pobrecito."

They talked more about the materials, and then Francisco was ready to sign off.

"Oh, Francisco, before I forget," she was back to talking quickly again. "We've changed the venue for your presentation scheduled for next Wednesday."

Francisco was scheduled for his third of four lectures on July 11. He hadn't started his preparation yet. *Maybe I should start getting ready for it today since I'm having dinner with Alexi tomorrow.*

"I hope you don't mind, but we moved it to the banquet room at the Hotel Riu Plaza," she said matter-of-factly. "It is a very nice hotel. Our group, Las Adelitas, have our monthly meetings there. They will be cosponsoring the event along with the university."

"It shouldn't make any difference," Francisco replied indifferently. *No importa.*

"It was Dean Montoya's suggestion," she said glibly. "There have been rumors about an organized protest by some of the religious student groups on campus. This venue will ensure a well-behaved group."

Francisco remembered some of the angry participants at his last presentation. And then there had been formal protests from religious organizations accusing the university of having invited the antichrist to campus.

"Don't worry," she laughed. "Montoya . . . he likes to . . . how do you say? Stick it to them."

Friday afternoon Francisco reluctantly began the preparation for his Las Adelitas' presentation. The weather was hot and humid, and he took a lot of breaks. Beads of sweat were rolling down his forehead and his clothes clung to him. He had gone through almost three bottles of water.

The next day found him scrambling around. He resumed work on his presentation in the morning, went to the gym in the early afternoon, and spent the late afternoon getting ready for his Saturday night dinner with Alejandra. He decided to wear his white guayabera with black pants. He took an Uber to her residence. He probably could have walked, but he didn't want to arrive sweaty.

"Prado 128, Colonia Americana, please," Francisco directed his driver. Five minutes later he was dropped off in front of a two-story, yellow Moorish mansion surrounded by a tall black wrought iron fence.

At the gate he pressed a button. A slender white-haired man around sixty approached and let him in.

"I'm here to see Señora Alejandra, please," Francisco said not knowing if he should use her first name or not.

"Welcome, Professor Reynoso," the butler replied in Spanish. "My name is Esteban. I am at your service."

They walked up a semicircular driveway that had a garden fountain gushing with clear water. The steps leading up to the house were adobe bricks with blue arabesque tiles embedded in the risers. Esteban escorted him to a casual, but lavishly decorated salon. There were dozens of portraits in all shapes and sizes mounted on the walls. Light came in from the interior courtyard of the building.

A middle-aged woman came into the room and offered Francisco a tall glass of iced jamaica tea with mint leaves. "Welcome, señor," the native-featured woman gave him a big smile. "La señora will join you shortly."

Francisco took the drink. It refreshed him. He started walking around the salon admiring the paintings. A few minutes later, he felt her presence as she entered. What a transformation from the other night! Alejandra wore a fuchsia-colored silk dress on her 5'6" medium frame.

"So nice of you to come, Francisco," Alexi gave him a warm kiss and hug.

"So nice of you to invite me," he said with a wide smile. "You have a beautiful home. It's a museum."

The ama de casa came into the room and offered Alexi some jamaica tea. "No, thank you, Gloria. Not right now."

Gloria curtsied and left the room.

"Would you like a little guided tour?" Alexi asked her guest.

"Sure."

They strolled from room to room on the first floor and then went out to the nicely fragranced garden. A large black wrought iron cage housed two canaries that were resting on a wooden perch singing away.

"Those are Chiquita and Manguito," Alexi said with a happy smile.

They finally went back inside to the salon. There were different kinds and colors of tile and marble throughout. "This is like going to a museum. Thank you," they stopped in front of a large oil portrait of a beautiful woman. "Who is she?"

"That is my grand-aunt Gloria Marín. She was my nana. My real grandmother died when I was very young. So, my grandaunt stepped in. I always called her nana," Alexi raised her head slightly. "And Jorge Negrete was the love of her life until he died."

"I thought that he was married to María Felíx." Francisco recalled going to the Million Dollar Theatre in downtown Los Angeles with his parents who absolutely worshipped Jorge Negrete and La Doña María Felíx.

"Ay, Francisco! You can never speak her name in this house!" Alejandra grimaced. "Jorge and that other woman had a fake Hollywood marriage. But he really only loved my Nana Gloria."

"Señora, we have some antojitos ready for you," Vera informed the two.

CHAPTER 34 – EL PLATO FUERTE

Saturday, July 7, 2018
Guadalajara

"Vera has been with me for over ten years," Alejandra explained. "She received her diploma from the Cordon Bleu Cooking School in Mexico City."

Francisco was impressed. *I'd settle for a bean and cheese burrito with a few ice cold beers.* He looked at the fare in front of him. Vera had prepared virgin margaritas for Alejandra and Francisco. *No buzz there!* He started by taking some totopos and spooning some type of salsa onto a small cobalt blue ceramic plate. He also took a small appetizer. "Oh, my God!" Francisco's eyes lit up as he took a little bite of the appetizer. "The tastes are amazing. The flavors are exploding in my mouth!"

"This is Vera's signature dish," Alejandra was pleased. "Shrimp and sweet corn tamalito. For sweetness, she uses agave syrup rather than white sugar."

For the next half hour Francisco had to restrain himself from inhaling all the appetizers. Alejandra ate very little. She shared with him how she grew up in La Paz, Mexico, in Baja California, as an only child. When she was little, her great-aunt Gloria Marín whom she called "Nana" would visit with her there during the summers. It had been rumored that her nana could not bear children. Alejandra considered Jorge Negrete her "Tata" or grandfather. The couple treated Alejandra as their own child. The three traveled all over Mexico and sometimes to the States for concerts and movie promotions.

Sadly, her mother died when Alexi was only fifteen. Her mom was short in stature and weighed close to two hundred pounds. She had suffered from diabetes and high blood pressure which caused her to have severe cardiac episodes. Alexi's father was a fisherman who died a year later from leukemia. Then Gloria and Jorge began having relationship problems and Alejandra was ignored by them for a long period. Fortunately, she was raised by another aunt in Guadalajara who was a nurse and helped Alexi enter the medical profession. At the local hospital where she worked, Alejandra met a doctor and they got married.

"My husband died. He was a good man. We didn't have any children," Alejandra continued. "After he passed away, I went to medical school and you know the rest," she shrugged. "When my nana died, she left me this house for which I am eternally grateful."

As if on cue, Vera informed them that dinner was ready. They stepped into the dining room that had formal décor. The table was made out of mahogany and could have seated twelve people easily. Francisco sat across from Alexi at one end. A pair of chandeliers complemented by six candelabras lit up the room.

"We're going to eat American style," she grinned. "Everything on one plate at the same time. I know you must be hungry."

Francisco could have smelled the tantalizing food miles away. Vera brought him a large white floral-designed plate that was hot to the touch. There was sliced grilled porterhouse steak accompanied by chayote squash and quinoa. The steak knives had ivory handles with the initials, "G.M." engraved on them. The cutlery was heavy and looked like old silver.

"Francisco, may Vera bring you anything else?" Alexi solicited like the perfect hostess. *I need a few doggy bags to take some leftovers back with me,* he thought.

"Salsa picante, perhaps?" she added.

"No, thank you. This is great."

"Oh, I should have offered you some wine," she hesitated.

"No, thanks. I'm good."

"More mineral water?"

"Yes, please." He added another slice of lime into his drink.

Over dinner they talked about food. She took small bites and ate very little. Francisco, on the other hand, was not shy about eating.

"I should show you some different Mexican cuisines," her dark brown eyes narrowed. She was thinking. "When are you going back home?"

"I'm tentatively scheduled to return around August 4th." For some reason he was hedging on his departure date.

"Maybe we could visit some places here in the State of Jalisco," she beamed. "The food is exquisite!"

Francisco nodded his head in agreement.

Vera came into the room and approached Alejandra. "Señora, are you having dessert this evening?"

"Of course, Vera," Alexi turned to face Francisco. "She makes the best jericalla. Have you had it before?"

"I don't know."

"It's basically flan without the burnt caramel sauce," she said. "Not that sweet. More like a custard."

"Sounds good to me."

"Coffee?"

"Yes, please," *I'm never going to sleep tonight.*

"Vera, we'll take our dessert in the library."

"Sí, señora," the cook bowed.

Five minutes later Alejandra and Francisco were sitting on an overstuffed cordovan leather couch with red and black square cushions. Around them were thousands of literary tomes and musical works, neatly organized on bookshelves, stacked floor to ceiling. On a small coffee table sat two little vermillion plates with little squares of jericalla on them. There were also two matching demitasse cups of coffee with a creamer and sugar bowl next to them.

"Don't worry!" Alexi grinned. "It's decaf."

Francisco gave a weak smile.

They started to eat the dessert. *It's small but tastes great!* he said to himself.

She turned on her iPod that was plugged into a state-of-the-art entertainment center. "Any special requests?"

"No, not really," Francisco was in a mellow space. "Wait! Yes. My mother used to play the Trio Los Panchos every day when I was growing up in L.A."

"Excellent choice," Alejandra gave Francisco a million-dollar smile. "My nana used to hang around them. They were all good friends." The music began to play.

Que se quede el infinito sin estrellas
O que pierda el ancho mar su inmensidad
Pero el negro de tus ojos que no muera

Y el canela de tu piel se quede igual . . .

"Speaking of cinnamon," Francisco reached into his pocket and pulled out a small paper bag. He handed it to Alejandra. "I almost forgot. No books this time."

Alejandra's brow furrowed as she pulled out a small bottle wrapped in gold leaf. "What is this?" After pulling off the top part of the wrapper, she noticed it was some type of chocolate sauce.

"No sugar! No alcohol!" Francisco quickly added.

"That's fantastic!" Alexi was happy.

Vera came into the room.

"Anything else, señora?" the cook asked.

"No, gracias," Alejandra replied.

"Then I will go home now. Good night. Hasta mañana."

Vera was picking up the dishes and putting them on a silver tray. The music continued.

Escúchame
Aunque me duele el alma
Yo necesito hablarte
Y así lo hare

Nosotros
Que fuimos tan sinceros
Que desde que nos vimos
Amándonos estamos . . .

"Francisco, is there anything special that you want for breakfast tomorrow morning?"

CHAPTER 35 – MIDNIGHT DELIGHT

Sunday, July 8, 2018
Guadalajara

Vera left the room, leaving Francisco and Alexi alone. Francisco had not noticed that the lights had been dimmed. Alexi was sitting next to him. He could smell the fragrance of gardenias emanating from her body. The floral scent put him on high alert.

> *Es la historia de un amor como no hay otro igual*
> *Que me hizo comprender todo el bien, todo el mal*
> *Que le dio luz a mi vida*
> *Apagándola, después*
> *¡Ay, qué vida tan oscura!*
> *Sin tu amor, yo viviré*
> *Es la historia de un . . .*

Alexi twisted off the top of the bottle of chocolate sauce. She put it up to her nose and sniffed it. "Wow! It's smells great!" Alexi was happy. Energy was flowing from her body. She looked radiant. She dipped her index finger into the liquid in order to get a sample. She raised it to her mouth. "Ecstasy!" She closed her eyes and deeply exhaled.

She repeated the maneuver, but this time she put her chocolate-tipped finger up to Francisco's mouth. He hesitated and then leaned forward to lick the chocolate. *OMG! This is sinful!* He was in heaven. She withdrew her finger from his mouth.

Alexi did the move again but this time she rubbed the chocolate onto her lips. Then gently grabbed Francisco and pulled him forward. Her head tilted to the right. Her mouth gently touched his. He began to lightly lick her lips. The chocolate sauce started to boil as the heat generated between the two.

Minutes later she stood up and took him by the hand. "Let's go upstairs," she said in a sultry tone. "Don't forget the chocolate sauce."

"*¡Ay Dios mío!*" Francisco's brain snapped.

• • •

Morning found the two new lovers sitting at a little table overlooking the inner courtyard of the mansion. They were surrounded by the gurgling water fountain and the intricate garden of colorful flowers, whose scent permeated the open air. The couple could hear the canaries, Chiquitita and Manguito, serenading them.

Vera had placed two small glasses of a clear liquid in front of the pair. She had looked at the couple non-judgmentally. "Francisco, as you know, I try to stay healthy," Alexi put on a professional air. "This is a little concoction I drink each morning to hydrate my body and stimulate my appetite."

Francisco's mind went into another dimension as he listened to her. *Last night was one of the best times in my life! Alexi is fantastic. She is so intelligent and so together. She's beautiful! I want more of her!* "I'll give it a try. It looks harmless enough," he responded.

"It's a little warm water with a splash of lime juice, and a few flakes of chipotle pepper," she counted the ingredients on the fingers of her right hand. "A few leaves of cilantro . . . and how do you call bicarbonate of soda?"

"Baking soda?" Francisco frowned. "What's that for?"

"To balance my pH levels."

Okay?! He was still in the dark.

Vera brought over a wooden tray with large white cups, a small coffee pot, a creamer, and two white bowls circled in blue and orange. They each contained a mixture of yogurt, diced mangos, sliced bananas, and toasted almonds.

"Francisco, would you like an egg or toast?" Alexi asked.

"No, thank you," he replied. He really wanted some soy milk for his coffee but was hesitant to ask. "Alexi, do you drink soy milk or eat tofu?"

"No, there have been some medical studies that have linked breast cancer to the estrogen found in soy products," she replied clinically.

Okay! He thought.

They enjoyed their light breakfast. She asked him about his project with Miranda. He told her about the Spanish expeditions to the Moluccas aka Spice Islands. Francisco explained the challenges of the work in terms of missing, incomplete, or damaged materials, the various languages of the papers, and the provenance or chain of possession.

"And not to mention inhaling centuries of old mold," he added. She laughed.

Alexi, in turn, shared that she had both public and private patients in her practice. Currently, the wife of the mayor of Acapulco was suffering from acute pancreatitis. Alexi would have to fly down there soon to do a follow-up examination.

The chit-chat was nice, but Francisco realized there was an elephant in the room. *What now? So awkward! Do I go back to the faculty apartments? Do I ask to see her again? Was this a one-night stand?* He decided to man up and bite the bullet.

"Alexi, do you want to go out for lunch this afternoon?" This seemed fairly innocuous, but it was Sunday and restaurants would be crowded.

"Sounds nice," Alejandra replied. "But here's an alternative plan. We could go for a walk in the park. I like to do this on my days off. It keeps me in touch with nature."

An hour later, after Francisco had showered and put on the same clothes that were sorely wrinkled, the black Lexus SUV stopped in front of the faculty housing per his request. Francisco needed to change into clean clothes and bring an overnight bag. He was thinking big.

"I'll be back in ten minutes," Francisco rushed out of the SUV, leaving Alexi with her driver, Esteban.

"Don't forget your toothbrush!" she called after him.

The two spent the late morning and early afternoon walking through the Botanical Gardens near the hospital were Alejandra worked. He held her hand as they walked down the paths surrounded by dozens of species of colorful flowers. They sat on one of the bright red stone benches and looked at the large fountain with three spouts in the shape of fish.

"Seeing all these flowers, reminds me that I finished 'The Black Tulip.' It was very good. I loved it!" she said. "Dumas was such a romantic."

"Hey, there are more beautiful flowers over there!" she pointed.

Francisco looked and responded, "Remember what Dumas said, "to despise flowers is to offend God.""

"Well, how about this," Alexi countered, "to despise chocolate is to offend God. Are you ready to go back to bed?"

CHAPTER 36 – LUNACY

Monday, July 9, 2018
Guadalajara

Miranda was walking better now. The pain was gone from her toe. She told Francisco that she had to tape her last two toes together for the next four weeks, but she still couldn't travel. Today she insisted on coming to the office to catch up on her paperwork and resume her scheduled meetings with Francisco.

It was Monday and Francisco needed to prepare for his Wednesday presentation of Las Adelitas. His weekend with Alexi was the best thing that had happened to him in the last ten years. He was already regretting having to return home the following month. Alexi was stoic about the whole thing. But now he had to buckle down and get down to work.

"Qué será, será," Alejandra recited when they separated early that morning.

Francisco brought two coffees to Miranda's office. He had found a café nearby that had soy milk. He was so spoiled back home. He refrained from buying any pan dulce or other pastries. He knew that Miranda had to watch her diet carefully because she was unable to do any exercise. It would help him also since he had been eating everything in sight since he arrived in Mexico.

"I didn't read much more of the Milo journals," he confessed, looking at Miranda to see if she knew that he had spent the weekend with Alexi.

"Well, I had lots of time," she complained a little. "Since I can't move around much."

"How's your daughter?" Francisco tried to deflect the conversation.

"Mirasol is busy looking at colleges to attend. I think she will apply to Stanford. She was also talking about Bryn Mawr."

"Great! If I can help in any way, please let me know," he was sincere. "Have you heard from Carlos?"

"Yes, he found out a little more about the supposed curse on María Del Rosario," Miranda began. "Since Carlos works at the Pyramid of the Moon in Teotihuacán near Mexico City, he has access to the museum there, plus all of their private records. Several of the staff are pre-Colombian archaeologists and are helping him. He sent me a pdf copy of their pamphlet. I made a copy for you. He is working a lot and won't be able to drive over for a while."

Francisco nodded. She began explaining the curse: According to the Pyramid of the Moon brochure, Huitzilpochtli was the fifth Aztec god of Sun and War. His mother Coatlicue became pregnant with Huitzilopochtli when she was touched by feathers falling from the heavens.

Huitzilopochtli's siblings thought their mother had dishonored them with this unusual pregnancy. Coyolxāuqui, one of the sisters, encouraged her 400 siblings to kill their mother, Coatlicue. However, Huitzilopochtli flew out of his mother's womb and cut off Coyolxāuqui's head and threw it up to the sky. A lunar eclipse occurred, and she became the Moon.

From then on Huitzilopochtli demanded human sacrifices to secure rain and harvest.

Carlos had some handwritten some notes on the brochure:

The sun becomes red when it feasts on a sacrificial victim. <u>The same is true for the moon who also demands blood!!!</u>

Francisco shook his head. "Wow, I had forgotten most of this."

"Carlos also said that he thinks that Yepollotli, or María Del Rosario as she was later called, was supposed to be sacrificed to Coyolxāuqui, the Moon Goddess.

"Carlos confirms that Yepollotli was the daughter of the Aztec tribal chief, Cacamatzin, from Texcoco. The chief had promised his daughter as a human sacrifice to the Moon

Goddess. Yepollotli "Yepy" was supposed to sacrifice herself to the moon goddess, Coyolxāuqui, in order to protect her people. However, right before the sacred Aztec ceremony, Cortés attacked the natives and her father was killed. She was taken prisoner along with her protectress Cihuatlamacazqui. Yepy thought the Spaniards would kill her also. But instead, the Spaniards wanted to use her to control her people."

"So, she converted to Catholicism?"

"Yes, to further protect her people, she became a Catholic. She was christened 'María Del Rosario' because she carried a black pearl rosary. Her protectress, Cihuatlamacazqui, took on the Christian name 'Inocente.' Inocente was a devotee of the Moon Goddess and was responsible for the protection of her charge."

"Did Inocente convert to Catholicism?"

"Carlos doesn't think so. He says that she probably did just enough not to provoke the fanatics of the Spanish Inquisition."

"But what exactly is the curse on Yepollotli?"

"Carlos isn't quite sure yet," Miranda paused. "He is still in the process of researching it with his colleagues."

• • •

On Wednesday Mirasol was nervous as she drove her mother and Professor Reynoso to the meeting of Las Adelitas. She was a fairly new driver and the morning traffic always intimidated her. They drove over the magnificent Matute Remos Bridge and passed by the famous "La Estampida" sculpture depicting several running horses. Behind this sculpture stood the thirty-story luxury Hotel Riu Plaza in the Chapalita District. Mirasol handed the car keys to the valet. They casually walked to the ballroom where Miranda shook every third hand and kissed every fourth cheek. Mirasol and Francisco trailed behind.

There were two dozen round tables with white table clothes and red-rose center pieces. Mirasol sat in the front next to her godmother, Alexi, who was already there. Francisco and Miranda sat at the elongated front tables. The presentation was scheduled to start at eleven with a business luncheon meeting to follow. Since Alexi was a member of Las Adelitas, she was in attendance. She and Francisco planned to meet after the event.

Las Adelitas was an organization of professional women dedicated to building a highly educated, highly skilled female presence as an integral part of the Mexican economy and culture. It was women helping women.

"Ladies and gentlemen," Miranda was the hostess because of her position with the women's professional group and the fact that the university was a co-sponsor of the event. There were only a few men scattered in the audience. "I would like to introduce Professor Francisco Reynoso from Stanford University . . ."

The audience politely clapped. Francisco took a swig of water and smiled as he saw Alexi. She gave him a good luck wink.

"I feel so privileged to be discussing a very important topic dear to your hearts," Francisco began. "Thank you for inviting me."

Francisco had actually worn his sport coat and tie. He looked very professorial, at least by Stanford standards. *Como te ven, te tratan.*

"What is the feminization of poverty? Why do women earn less than their male counterparts?" he began. "Lower paying jobs? Discrimination? Domestic responsibilities?" He didn't have a PowerPoint presentation. He felt that people did not want to be overwhelmed by statistics. He continued on this point for about five more minutes. "The answer is 'all of the above.' "

"So how does this relate to the increase of female migration globally?" He paused and took another drink of water. The audience was quiet and attentive. "In the last two centuries, the migrants have been mainly male. Women followed as colonies grew, but the numbers were still skewed in favor of male workers because of the backbreaking skills required in such industries, such as manufacturing. But as wages increased and the competition among men for jobs rose, women were needed as maids, nurses, garment workers, nannies, . . . and I will say it, prostitutes." There was an undertone of shock throughout the audience.

He discussed in depth the fluctuations of wages for men and for women across several countries, both industrial and third world. "What effect did female migration have on marriage stability and the upbringing of children?"

Hands from the audience would go up, but Francisco had told them that he would take questions at the end. They were listening to him.

"The effect of female migration has been an increase in single mother poverty," he went on.

After about a half hour of lecturing, Francisco began running out of steam. Sweat beaded up on his forehead. "This feminization of poverty. This feminization of migration. This gender inequality will only worsen if the government and corporations don't start to care about women and do something about it . . ."

A few minutes later Francisco concluded and thanked the audience for their attention. Professor Rios then moderated a brief question and answer session.

"Professor, you have shared with us what the problems are," said a short, full-bodied woman in a stylish emerald green pantsuit. "But can you give us some solutions?"

"One thing that can be done is to focus on the education of mothers. Mothers are the role models for their children. Education gives them options. Education provides a path out of poverty and powerlessness . . ."

After several more questions, it was over. The audience took a break before lunch. As Francisco was walking over to Alexi's table, a blonde woman in her 80's, wearing tons of makeup stopped him.

"Professor, do you have a book you can sign for me?" her perfume overwhelmed him.

"Sorry, I don't."

"If you want to come over to my home tonight, I'm giving a little party. You could maybe bring one."

Francisco politely declined and finally found Alexi and Mirasol. They congratulated him and Mirasol went off to find her mother.

"Francisco, I can't have lunch with you today," Alexi apologized.

Is this the beginning of the end? he wondered.

"I'm sorry to hear that."

"I'm not feeling well."

Francisco started to panic. "Is there anything I can do?!"

"No. I am just having my menstrual cycle. I didn't realize that last night was a new moon. That's when I usually have my moon," she tried to explain.

"It's okay," he faked it. *He really did not completely understand.* "Can you take anything for it?"

"I drink chamomile tea to relax and hydrate."

"If that doesn't work, try hot chocolate with chocolate sauce," he suggested.

"Ay, Francisco, you're so evil!" she gave him a slight slap on the shoulder and pressed tight against him. "But I like it."

CHAPTER 37 – THE TEMPEST

Thursday, July 12, 2018
Guadalajara

The weather outside was hot and humid. The fan in his room produced little relief. Francisco wanted to take his third shower of the day. He had been exhausted from the prior day's presentation. Miranda was pleased, so he was pleased. He felt that the two of them made a good academic team. He was now reading the Milo papers. He would discuss them at his Friday meeting with Miranda. On the plus side, Alexi was excited about the coming weekend. He would have dinner with her on Friday at her place and the rest was open.

Miranda had called him earlier in the morning and confirmed that his meeting with retired Admiral Serafino Azueta was slated for the following week, July 20. It would be at La Academia de Los Marinos. She was busy making his travel arrangements. Miranda said that she could not accompany him because of her doctor's orders, and that Sol couldn't take that much time off. They both agreed that he should fly since there was travel money in the budget. Miranda said that her secretary Alma would arrange his travel.

Francisco sat on his bed. Papers were strewn all over. He took a sip a coffee, put the cup back on the bed stand, and continued reading Milo's diaries.

December 14, 1527
Espíritu Santo

The Espíritu Santo was sailing smoothly under clear skies. I was still with María Del Rosario and Innocente. In the cabin, I could hear María Del Rosario sniffling, "Why is the curse still upon me?"

Inocente grabbed Yepyollotli by both shoulders, "Because Coyolxāuqui wants her blood sacrifice. Your father promised you to Coyolxāuqui. Now the Spanish god has stolen you from her. She is angry and will not be denied. She has already forsaken your people and let the Spaniards conquer them."

"But Inocente, I now belong to the Spanish god. I even changed my name," Yepy stared at her protectress with a plaintive look. She took the black pearl rosary off the wall and put it over her own neck. She replaced the other black pearl necklace on the vacant peg.

"She must have her blood sacrifice, my child."

Inocente then turned to me and started to tend to my injuries. She applied a foul-smelling paste to my shoulder and back. I staggered slowly out of the cabin a few minutes later, writhing in pain after the brutal attack by Rubén.

Meanwhile up on the deck, the Spanish captain was ordering the crew to press forward under full sail. Even though there was no moon, he was using the stars in the cloudless sky to guide them. The sextant was useless tonight. He saw the lights of Saavedra's two ships on both sides of him. They were on their way to the Moluccas with the speed of a falcon.

By morning the winds started to pick up from the west. The color of the ocean was changing from jade green to dark grey. It was the season of fluctuating weather. The sun seemed more red than usual as it lifted itself up through the skies. I was slow in tending to my duties. I noticed a foul odor but could not determine what the source was.

As the day wore on, the skies began to cloud up. On the western horizon a black cloud was expanding. The winds began to pick up and howl. The sails were being pushed and pulled like an accordion.

A typhoon seemed to be forming in the distance. The bow of the Espiritu Santo started to rise and fall. The seas seemed to be getting angrier and angrier. The mizzen mast began to shutter. Lightning appeared several miles in front of the ship with cackling sounds. Throughout the day the clouds grew bigger and blacker.

By nightfall the skies were black and the lightning continuous. Sheets of rain showered the deck. The lanterns on the ship were swinging from side to side. The first mate, Gustavo Rodriguez, called all hands-on deck to batten down the hatches and to secure the riggings.

The ship began to quiver with the winds pulling it askew. The rains grew in intensity.

"Take down the main sail!" the Spanish captain barked. Some of the crew obeyed. The three Portuguese sailors did not. The first mate Rodriguez struck one of the shirkers with a cudgel to motivate him.

The strong pull of the ocean required another crewman to assist the helmsman. The waves smashed heavily on the starboard side of the ship. The lightning was getting closer and closer and the thunder louder.
Captain Fuentes instructed me to stay with Maria Del Rosario and Inocente, and to bring Fray Nadal into their cabin. They were all to be ready to come on deck, if necessary.

Crack! The trinquete (front mast) was struck by lightning. Sparks began to fly. Tongues of fire licked up the pole. Two of the sailors started to chop down the burning rigging. The wind gusts continued without quarter. The decks were becoming flooded. Water was seeping below deck. The first mate called out for pumps to begin. The bare foremast now looked like a burning torch.

In their cabin, Maria Del Rosario screamed, "What is happening?" The black pearl necklace on the wall seemed to spark. Yepy was frightened.

"It is the curse!" cried out Inocente.

The first mate ordered the crew to abandon the pumps in favor of securing the third (mizzen) mast. The torrential rains began to attenuate the fire.

The lights of Saavedra's other two ships could not be seen. Crack! The mizzen mast was also struck by lightning. Men flew in the air screaming. The mast fell on the deck crushing one sailor and throwing another overboard.

More water inundated the ship. The surface of the deck looked like a glass floor with foam swirling every which way. Cables were added to support the remaining main mast.

The captain called for me to bring the two women out of their cabin and have them ready to be put in a lifeboat.

The ship lifted and dropped. The course of the ship was indeterminate. The crew was wet, cold, and exhausted. We were all cursed.

CHAPTER 38 – THE BATH

Saturday, July 14, 2018
Guadalajara

Waves foamed as they splashed against the sides. The sloshing kicked up thousands of bubbles.

"Alexi, hand me the soap please," Francisco was rubbing her right foot with his hands. They were enjoying a hot bath that Saturday afternoon after a nice walk around the botanical gardens. There was the fragrance of lavender that permeated the open-air bathroom. Francisco closed his eyes. He was relaxed. His head rested on a large pink Egyptian cotton towel at the back of the tub. Their bodies faced each other while he massaged her foot.

Alexi slid the soap into his hand, and he reopened his eyes. He began to wash the bottom of her foot, moving in circles.

The prior night had consisted of a light dinner. The dorado fish fillet was perfectly grilled. It was accompanied by a mango salsa and sliced avocado and totopos. Francisco was getting used to the absence of wine with his meals. He compensated during the week by drinking a lot of cold beer.

The pink egg-shaped soap had a No. 5 embossed on it and had a mild scent. He lathered his hands and started rubbing her feet again.

"Francisco, you are spoiling me," Alexi said in a sensual tone.

"Well, mi querida," he replied. "You deserve it."

Friday night ended up with another chocolate dessert. They were quickly running out of the chocolate sauce.

They now seemed to be behaving as a couple. He had brought her a bouquet of red roses which was rewarded with a flurry of passionate kisses.

"Francisco, I'm sorry for the other day," Alexi was referring to their scheduled date after his Las Adelitas presentation that she missed when she didn't feel well.

"Hey, I had a sister," he shrugged it off. *Plus, a wife who was the queen of mean during her menstrual cycles.* "No problem."

She had definitely made up for it the night before.

"I get terrible cramps in my lower abdomen," she pointed underneath the water. "What's worse are the nightmares. My period always occurs around the new moon, but I see a full moon in my dreams. The moon turns into an Aztec goddess. With nose rings and pendants. She speaks to me in a different language. I think it is Nahuatl. But instead of words coming out of her mouth, it is blood. Black blood."

"But you did say that hot chocolate makes you feel better," Francisco was trying to assuage her worries.

"I am not superstitious," she withdrew her right foot so he could wash the other one. "But I don't know what to make of it."

"I think you need more chocolate sauce therapy," Francisco smiled.

On Sunday, they had been invited to Miranda's house for a late afternoon lunch. By then, Miranda (and the rest of the world) knew about Alexi and Francisco. Miranda didn't want to interrupt any of their plans but was simply offering some casual company and conversation.

"I feel I should go. I need to see my goddaughter, Mirasol," Alexi mildly asserted. "I haven't spent much time with her. Somebody has been keeping me busy."

Francisco smiled. He was flexible. "Sounds good," he reacted. "I can chat with Sol. I wonder how he is going to react about us. I'm sure Miranda warned him about being too nosey. But that probably hasn't stopped him before."

"One thing, Francisco," Alexi started to get out of the tub. She grabbed a towel that was close by. "I have to fly down to

Acapulco this week. I am performing an operation. I'll be down there for a few days."

"Mi querida, how far is Acapulco from Zihuatanejo?" Francisco perked up and he too started to get out of the tub.

"I think about 250 kilometers, more or less. It's about a three-hour drive depending on the time of day and traffic."

Francisco took his towel and started to dry Alexi off. She wiped her face dry and reciprocated with Francisco.

"Now what should we do?"

• • •

Chiquitita and Manguito happily sang for the lovebirds the next morning in the garden where the two took their coffee. After a light breakfast, Esteban drove them to a shopping area where they looked around for men's clothing. After going to several shops, Francisco ended up buying himself some cordovan loafers, tan pants, and two more guayaberas.

"Now you really look like a Mexican," Alexi teased.

Alexi had selected the clothes. She had excellent taste. She had expensive tastes. But Francisco didn't care. He was in heaven being with Alexi.

At around three in the afternoon, they were driven to the Rios' home. Hugs and kisses were exchanged. Miranda was walking around rather well. Margaritas were the drink of the day with a special virgin version for Alexi. Five minutes later,

Alexi went off with Miranda and Mirasol. Sol and Francisco moved to the back lawn. They found a couple of lawn chairs to relax on.

"Those pinche Chivas!" Sol was complaining. "Their midfield is worthless. I thought that when they got rid of the coach things would get better. Not so!"

Francisco was waiting for Sol to drop the bomb on him about being with Alexi. Nothing so far.

The maid, in her prim manner, informed the parties that dinner was served. Everyone gathered in the dining room. Francisco sat next to Alexi. He surreptitiously held her hand under the table.

The first course was a spinach salad with pomegranate arils and queso fresco.

"I must warn you that Mirasol is going through her vegetarian stage," Miranda cautioned her guests.

"Oh, mom," the daughter raised her eyes. "It's healthier. We should not eat innocent animals or their babies."

Francisco appreciated the fact that Miranda rarely talked shop in front of her family. Dinner was for family communication, not for business. Family came first.

The main course came. It was huachinango, a classical red snapper dish from Veracruz.

"Oh, let me correct myself," Miranda explained. "She is a pescatarian also. Eats only fish!"

"Oh, mom, it's no big deal. There are other kids that do it."

Sol invited Francisco for drinks the following week, but Francisco informed him that he would be in Zihuatanejo.

"Make sure to try the tiritas," Sol suggested. "We'll have to take our mija down there one of these days. She can eat fish for days."

"Oh, dad," Mirasol rolled her eyes.

Dessert finally came. It was coconut ice cream with berries. Alexi passed. Sol and Francisco had coffee. They all decided to retire to the salon. Mirasol held Alexi's arm as they entered. She looked up at her godmother and asked, her big brown eyes shining, "Madrina, are you two hanging out?"

CHAPTER 39 – THE AFTERMATH

Monday, July 16, 2018
Guadalajara

Francisco could barely make it into Miranda's office on Monday. He was exhausted from the weekend. "Thank you, Miranda, for last evening," Francisco said. "We had a great time." Miranda caught the inclusive language. Her comadre and Francisco were an item. *That is a good thing, at least for the moment,* she thought.

"Francisco, I want to apologize for my daughter being impolite last night," Miranda blew out a breath of air. "She wanted to streak her hair purple last month! ¡Ay Dios Mio!"

"No problem," he snickered. "I live in San Francisco. Anything goes." He leaned forward and lowered his voice. "Even walking desnudo on the streets used to be legal."

"¡De veras!" her eyes grew as big as melons. She had unconsciously switched to Spanish.

Francisco left Miranda's office earlier than usual that day and went straight to his apartment. He decided to skip lunch. He went instead to his bedroom and crashed. He napped for over an hour and was famished when he woke up. He left his lodging and went to the local taco stand, "Pancho Villa's," which now was one of his favorites. He inhaled a chicken taco and a carnitas one. Their salsa was killer. And then he returned to his apartment.

He checked his emails from Stanford and sent the latest copy of his report to Mary Beth, as a backup. He didn't want to lose any documents if something happened to his laptop. Francisco sent a check-in text to Tina and then called Alexi.

"Hola, querida," Francisco said sweetly.

They chatted for a few minutes trying to finalize their upcoming rendezvous in Zihuatanejo for the upcoming weekend.

"Francisco, I am flying out early tomorrow morning," Alexi informed him. I am performing the operation on Wednesday and doing the post-op on Thursday. And then spending the rest of the weekend with you!"

Francisco was flying to Zihuatanejo on Thursday and staying at the Hotel Las Vegas. The next day he would have his meeting with Admiral Azueta. Then he and Alexi would get together Friday evening in Zihuatanejo.

"I made us a reservation at the Casa Que Canta Hotel for the weekend," she smiled as she spoke over the phone. "Plus, I have the most perfect place for dinner on Saturday. And as you say, it's to die for."

For the rest of the afternoon, Francisco forced himself to get his head back into his work. He picked up the Milo papers and started reading where he had left off.

December 17, 1527
Espíritu Santo

Two days after the disastrous storm, the sun climbed slowly up the skies behind the crippled Espíritu Santo.

During the storm we totally lost contact with our mother ship, La Florida. We assumed that she had sunk during the tempest. The crew was totally exhausted from the ordeal. Three of the sailors had gone missing including the Portuguese sailor Rubén Gomes and the first mate Gustavo Rodríguez. Fray Nadal was deadly ill and was taken into the cabin of María Del Rosario, who looked after him. Inocente refused to acknowledge the Catholic religious brother, but instead fussed over me. She indulged me like a long-lost child when I visited.

Our ship was wrecked from stem to stern. Two of the masts were gone and the main mast was tenuous. Only one set of sails weakly propelled the vessel. The original crew had been composed only of sailors since the ship was a small bergantín. There were no craftsmen. Neither were there proper tools. There were no saws. Everything had to be cut with broad swords, knives, or two small hatchets. It took forever to clear the deck. Below, gallons and gallons of water had seeped in, causing untold damage. Two crewmen worked the pumps in a trancelike state. Half the merchandise was damaged. Anything broken or damaged was thrown overboard.

The crew was staggering around the ship bleary-eyed. Captain Fuentes ordered everyone to take two-hour naps. He and second mate, Arturo Narciso, would tend to the ship. The skies were now clear, and the winds were weak. The boat was not at full sail anyway and was probably only making three knots per hour at best.

During the respite, the renegade boatswain, Rodrigo Alves, and the cook, Gonçalo Silveira, were in close proximity, quietly conversing in Portuguese. I was less than ten feet away hidden underneath a stairwell.

"I aim to take over the ship, I do," said Rodrigo in an angry tone. "I am tired of these ignorant Spaniards pushing us around."

"How are you going to do that?" asked his compatriot.

"I am not going to do anything. The crew is going to make me captain. Fuentes has messed everything up."

"What did he do?"

"He brought two women aboard. There is an evil spell on this ship. The men already know about them. They are angry."

"Is that enough? What else can be done?"

"I want you to start a rumor that the merchandise is ruined and that we will be lucky to get a half share. Maybe only a quarter share for risking our lives for the captain."

"But why don't you do it? The crew would believe you before a lowly cook."

"Two reasons. First, you already talk to everyone. They all like you and will listen to you, even if they don't believe you. But the second reason is that I am going to side with the captain. I want to be first mate, since Gustavo has left us." Rodrigo gave an evil laugh. "That will put me in a better position to take over."

Within the next few days, Rodrigo's words had materialized. The crew was grousing about the terrible condition of the ship. Half of them wanted to turn back. The captain was having a difficult time appeasing them. He couldn't make any solid promises. And the conditions aboard the ship were getting worse. Fresh water and food were rationed. The captain was at his wit's end. Finally, he promoted Rodrigo to first mate and the Basque, Monixo Gharsiya, became the boatswain since Arturo Naciso had taken ill. For the time being the crew was placated.

However, conditions aboard the ship worsened. Two more of the sailors died, leaving only a handful of men to run the ship. A few ocean squalls helped with the supply of fresh water, but the food was nearly gone.

A note from Carlos Erandi state that the narration had abysmally ended at this point. There was a gap of at least a month until the final entry.

CHAPTER 40 – RESTORATION

Tuesday, July 17, 2018
Guadalajara

It was dawn on Tuesday when Alexi called Francisco from
the Guadalajara airport. She was on her way to Acapulco,
connecting in Mexico City. In a few days they would be
spending quality time together in Zihuatanejo.

At breakfast he talked to two new visiting faculty from
Algeria at the faculty housing. Their Spanish was impeccable.
They were petroleum engineering professors from the
University of Algiers. They were there to collaborate on a new
offshore drilling joint project with Petróleos Mexicanos,
PEMEX.

The Wednesday morning meeting with Miranda was short
and sweet. They had drawn up a list of questions that Francisco
would ask Admiral Azueta during Friday's interview.
Francisco scurried back to his apartment after grabbing a quick
lunch snack.

He began reading the last pages of Milo's journal. He
wanted to finish it so he could be better prepared to chat with

Admiral Azueta. After perusing only a few pages, Francisco could see that Captain Pedro Fuentes de Jérez was almost literally up the creek without a paddle.

January 26, 1528
Unknown Island

It was late January of 1528 when a flock of pelagic birds flew overhead.

"Land ahoy!" By Divine Providence, we had sighted land.

By the late afternoon, two rowboats from the Espiritu Santo landed, with all but two crew members onto the white sandy shore. Fray Nadal and I sat with Maria Del Rosario and Inocente under the shade of a coconut grove.

The captain put Rodrigo Alves in charge of procuring fruit, meat, and fresh water. The new first mate was assigned two crewmen and given a dozen water skins. Likewise, the boatswain Monixo Gharsiya was tasked with finding materials to replace the two demolished masts and the rigging. The second mate, Arturo Narciso, who was still recuperating, was ordered with three other men to build shelters. The cook, Gonçalo Silveira, was told to build a fire and to keep it going continuously.

Captain Fuentes and two of his trusted crewmen rowed back to the ship. They conducted another thorough inspection, noting what repairs and replacements had to be made. The captain went into his cabin and took his treasury box, navigational charts, and sextant. They loaded a few other items on the rowboat and returned to board at dusk. A deluge now begun. Gonçalo had put out pans to catch the rainwater.

Fortunately, Narciso had completed one lean-to shelter, and he and his men were working furiously on the second. Maria Del Rosario, Inocente, and Fray Nadal were all huddled together. I was close by. Silveira was hustling to keep the fire going. By nightfall the rest of the crew were soaked. However, there was a sufficient supply of fresh water. Rodrigo came back with a sack of fruits and two dead birds. The cook Gonçalo Silveira prepared the meager dinner, but it was a great improvement from the prior weeks. No guard duty was deemed necessary. The entire crew slept soundly that night except for the two officers.

By ten o'clock that night the clouds had parted, and the stars sparkled in the black sky. Captain Fuentes and his navigator Arturo Narciso walked from the sandy crescent beach to a high lava mound at the end. They took readings on the sextant after referencing the sliver of the moon. They calculated that our latitude was between 20 and 25 degrees north, and the longitude was approximately 160 degrees west.

The following morning found the crew eating fruit. I brought an armful of fruit to the lean-to of Maria Del Rosario, Inocente, and Fray Nadal. The entire day was filled with everyone doing tasks. Rodrigo and his crew decided to wade in the shallow waters. One of the men got severely cut on the razor-sharp coral, but they were successful in harvesting some mollusks and a few fish.

Nasciso and his men continued to build more lean-tos. The captain directed them to put up siding on Maria Del Rosario's lean-to by utilizing the damaged textiles. That led to the idea of using the rowboats to transfer the marred cloth from the ship. The materials were cleaned and hung out to dry on the bushes that aligned the beach.

By late afternoon, the primitive shelters were taking shape and the men were being fed. The crew laughed and smiled for the first time in over a month.

The next week was more of the same. Most of the lean-tos had cloth sidings. Rodrigo would alternate between foraging in the palm tree forest and harvesting shellfish in the waters. On at least two occasions, they caught tortoises that made an excellent soup. The highlight for the crew, however, was the grilled octopus.

Fray Nadal was making a full recovery with the care he received from Maria Del Rosario. The two prayed the rosary every day, sometimes in the palm tree forest. He with his wooden beaded rosary, and she with her black pearl one. Inocente stayed away, preferring to interact with me.

The captain and the boatswain discussed which of the trees in the jungle forest could be used as replacements for the two destroyed masts. The problems were twofold. Firstly, no one knew what the heights of the masts should be. Secondly and *more importantly, was the fact that the crewmen were sailors, not craftsmen.*

Fuentes knew that refurbishing the ship would be a herculean task. He met with his boatswain and held many discussions about the next steps. Nobody wanted to stay on the island. That meant that they had to make our Espiritu Santo seaworthy. The ship needed two new masts, several sets of sails, and repairs to the hull and rudder. Two days later, a handful of the crew was ordered back on board the ship. The anchors were raised, and the ship was pointed to a clear portion of the beach. After back-and-forth maneuvers, the ship was positioned parallel to the beach. With the assistance of high tide and low tide, the ship was beached several hours later. The crew secured the ship to the palm trees by sixty cables made from native vines.

"More!" barked Rodrigo. The crew pulled on the ropes. The ship was now leaning five degrees toward the trees. "More!" Now it was ten degrees. Slowly, the ship was tipped to a 45-degree angle. The captain knew that any attempt to repair the ship while she was still in water would have been futile. He had decided, therefore, to dry dock the vessel. It also gave him an opportunity to unload everything and take inventory.

The real work began the next day when the crew were assigned to refurbish the ship. The boatswain Monixo Gharsiya had found certain trees that oozed sticky saps and became sticky tars after being boiled. These would be used for the repairs and the masts.

Little by little, Maria Del Rosario and Fray Nadal began taking daily walks within the palm tree forest that was teeming with brilliantly colored birds that were constantly squawking. She would pick the bright, perfumed flowers or talk to the colorful birds. Inocente and I remained back at the beach washing the princess's garments. Maria and the friar would stop in front of a large black lava rock and pray.

Little by little huts made of large banana leaves, branches, and mud began replacing the lean-tos. More and different types of food were being gathered. Tortoise eggs were a treat.

It took several days to figure out how to mount the masts. The crew had cut, dragged, and dried out four seemingly suitable trunks. They had chopped two extra, just in case. Finally, by driving these latter two trunks into the sand and attaching a series of pulleys and levers, the first mast was successfully put in place and secured with tar and wooden pegs.

However, that same night a typhoon hit and razed half the huts. The shelter of Maria Del Rosario was spared. The storm finally subsided and after two days, food and water were replenished.

By the end of the week, the second mast was firmly in place. The captain and his boatswain inspected the ship from fore to aft. Everything looked to be ship shape. The captain then gave the order to gradually cut the supporting cables, one by one, in order to slowly bring the ship upright. After that, another visual inspection was made and minor repairs were made. Barnacles and scum were scraped from the hull. The next day, makeshift sails made from the damaged textiles were loaded onto the deck. They were not perfect, but they seemed functional.

Three days later, the captain called all the men together after breakfast.

"Men, I want to commend you all for the great work you've done for God and Crown. Weeks ago, we were like rats on a sinking ship. But through God's intervention and your courage, we now have a ship again."

Some of the men looked down. A few grumbled.

Fray Nadal approached from the side. "He will lead us in a prayer of thanks," Fuentes calmly said.

All the sailors fell to their knees and prayed with Fray Nadal.

During the prior week, the captain had finished conducting an inspection of the ship's inventory. More than half of it was damaged or missing. He never did find the black pearls listed on the register. Captain Fuentes then faced the crew again. "Men, you all swore an oath to deliver this ship and its goods to the Molucca islands. For God and Crown, you have risked your lives. But now, we are not sure where we are. We're not sure how to sail to the Moluccas or if we can even make it. We now have a choice to make. Try to go to the Moluccas and bring back cloves and other spices *that are worth more than gold or return to Zihuatanejo. The choice is yours."*

The crew looked at each other dumbfounded. They grumbled. Fuentes was the captain. He made all the decisions. The men began talking to each other.

"What am I going to do in Zihuatanejo? I'll just have to find another ship and sail someplace else."

"I still need to make my fortune."

"I don't really care."

After ten minutes, the captain called for a vote. "The majority decides," he declared. "Raise your hands if you want to sail back to Zihuatanejo." Monixo and two other Basque sailors raised their hands.

"Raise your hands if you are ready to go to the Moluccas," the captain shouted, as he took a step forward. Rodrigo and Silveira were with the majority in setting sail for the Moluccas.

"The second part of my plan is now in play," Rodrigo whispered into Silveira's ear.

A few days later, with a series of cut down tree trunks and with the use of ropes, the ship was moved closer to the water's edge. Then they waited until there was a full moon and a high tide to slowly and carefully position the ship into the water. After a long night of pushing and pulling, the ship was proudly afloat.

The following week everybody was busy reloading the ship with fresh water, fruits, dried fish, and other viands. The salvageable textiles were brought back on board.

On Sunday, Fray Nadal said a series of prayers. The Espiritu Santo then set sail once again in search of the Moluccas.

Francisco had just read the last page of the Milo journals. He realized that the remainder of the journey to the Moluccas was missing!

What happened?! He wondered.

CHAPTER 41 – TIRITAS

Wednesday, July 18, 2018
Guadalajara

Francisco woke up early Wednesday morning. He was beside himself. He had had a difficult time falling asleep. This fiasco with the Milo papers was frustrating. The documents were incomplete, and it presented a major problem to the whole project.

He fired up his computer and immediately sent off an email to Joel Brenner at Powell's Bookstore in Portland.

Joel, things didn't quite work out with the Milo journals. The ones that you obtained from Roberto Gutierrez. The records are incomplete. We only have half the journey of the Espiritu Santo to the Moluccas. Is there any way you can check with him and see if there are any more documents? Thanks.

Francisco only had coffee for breakfast. His stomach was acidy. He still had to pack for his meeting with Admiral Azueta on Friday (and the weekend with Alexi). But he could do that tonight.

"We need to reassess where we are," Francisco began talking with Miranda in her office. He had arrived earlier than usual to discuss the issue with the Milo journals. Miranda had finished reading her copy of the records and was of the same opinion. "Can we publish our article without further corroboration?" he asked.

"Francisco, I think there are several options. The simplest one is to only utilize the documentation on La Florida, the flagship of Saavedra's expedition. Which of those versions will we use? Saavedra/Duro's, DaNapoli's, or both? We'll have to discuss and decide. We also know that the Santiago was lost at sea and we have no records," Miranda was very methodical.

"That means we will have to eliminate the Espiritu Santo, if we don't find the rest of Milo's journal," Francisco exhaled a breath of resignation. "Ah, the fun of research," he said facetiously.

"As we say in here in Mexico, *algo es mejor que nada,* something is better than nothing," she added. "Do we know where the Espiritu Santo made its repairs?"

"According to the reported latitude and longitude," Francisco had Googled the coordinates that morning. "I think they were in Hawaii. Probably on the island of Oahu."

"I have never been," Miranda said. "But one day, Sol and I will go there."

They debriefed for a little while longer.

"I will contact Carlos Erandi and have him follow up with Roberto Gutierrez in Cuernavaca," Miranda was writing down a reminder. "Francisco, you're running out of time. You'll be leaving us in a few weeks."

"Maybe I can stay an extra week," he said in a guiltless tone. *I need to spend some more time down here with Alexi!*

For the next half hour, they reviewed questions that Francisco would discuss with Admiral Azueta.

Back at the faculty housing, Francisco checked his emails. Joel Brenner had written Francisco and informed him that he too would try to contact Roberto Gutierrez. Francisco was starving. He went over to his favorite taco stand, Pancho Villa's. Afterwards, he returned and packed his duffel bag. Francisco went to bed by nine. He had an early flight the next morning.

• • •

The flight to Mexico City on Thursday was uneventful. He sat next to a Tapatio, a native of Guadalajara, who was talking about Brexit. The silver-haired gentleman thought if England broke away from the European Union, then Mexico, China, and other countries would have better access to the overseas markets.

At the Mexican capital, Francisco waited almost three hours for his connecting flight to Zihuatanejo. He grabbed a huevos rancheros breakfast at the San Angel Inn concession at the airport. He had forgotten his Paulo Coelho book back at his apartment. He bought a local newspaper and read about how the United States was trying to intimidate Mexico about trade agreements. *So, what else is new?*

There was an announcement over the airport's loudspeakers. The flight was ready. Francisco couldn't find the gate. An airport staff person who was in a wheelchair gave him directions. The flight took off on time. Francisco was sitting next to two cute little bronze-skinned children that were with their mother. The girl was reading a children's book and the boy had a sort of tablet that he was playing a game on. A snack was served on the one hour plus flight. Francisco asked the mother if he could give the children gum. She nodded affirmatively with a big smile.

"¿Quieren chicle?" Both kids nodded their heads yes. Francisco handed one of the children three sticks of gum.

In less than an hour, the plane began its descent. Francisco saw a beautiful beach and a lagoon before the plane landed. *Wow! I am definitely in paradise. No worries! Be happy!*

He retrieved his duffel bag from baggage claim and went to a counter that sold taxi rides to the downtown area. Francisco purchased a one-way voucher.

The sun was bright, and the weather was hot. He could feel the breeze coming from the shores. The Las Vegas Hotel was located near downtown Zihuatanejo. Francisco checked in and went up to his room on the fifth floor. He unpacked and ascended to the top floor where there was a bar and a swimming pool. As he was sipping his ice cold cerveza, he could see the beaches, the city center, and the surrounding hills. *Life is Good!*

Twenty minutes later he was walking toward the Acopio Restaurant reported to have the best marinated fish tiritas in town.

CHAPTER 42 – THE ADMIRAL

Friday, July 20, 2018
Zihuatanejo

Alexi had boasted to Francisco about how diverse and tasty Mexican cuisines are. Last night's tiritas and this morning's chilaquiles were no exceptions. Now Francisco was in hog heaven.

He had talked to Alexi the night before. The operation that she had performed in Acapulco had been successful and now her patient was recuperating wonderfully. She had decided not to fly to Zihuatanejo because it would take all day. Instead, she would hire a private car to drive her the 150 miles from Acapulco. It would take approximately four hours to get to Zihuatanejo. They would rendezvous at La Casa Que Canta Hotel for their weekend getaway. He could hardly wait.

Francisco took a taxi to La Academia de los Marineros, lugging along his duffel bag. Since it was an official military facility, he was escorted from place to place by a uniformed marine. At the end of a long corridor was the office of retired Admiral Serafino Azueta. To the right of the second-floor passageway, the crescent La Ropa Beach glistened in the early morning sun.

The foul smell of cigar smoke attacked Francisco as he entered the office which had dozens of photos of naval vessels, ship instruments, awards, and certificates.

"Professor Reynoso, welcome to Zihuatanejo," the shortish, silver-haired man with a curled-up moustache, dressed in full military regalia addressed him in Spanish. "Please have a seat. It is such a pleasure to finally meet you. Profesora Rios has told me so much about you."

"The pleasure is mine, admiral," Francisco liked the older gentleman. He reminded him of his grandfather. "Thank you for taking the time to see me."

"No problem at all, professor."

"How was your trip to Portugal?" Francisco was trying to be polite. The Alentejo was on his bucket list to travel to.

"My wife and I had a wonderful time," Admiral Serafino Azueta smiled and started to prattle about the Roman ruins, the Algarve, and the wines. Francisco then realized that the elderly man was a talker who was searching for an audience.

Finally, after ten minutes, Azueta stopped. He pulled out two cigars from his huge wooden desk. "Do you mind if I smoke?" What else could Francisco do but say no. "Would you like one?" Francisco replied that he didn't smoke. Moreover, he hated the smell of cigars. It reminded him of men's public restrooms.

As Admiral Azueta began to light up his cigar, Francisco took the opportunity to start asking his questions. "Admiral, what was it like to be on a Spanish ship in the 1500s."

The admiral began:

"Well, the early Spanish explorers used naos, caravels, and galleons. The naos were cargo ships. The galleons were warships. The crews were usually uneducated drifters. They slept anywhere they could find space on the ship. One third of the crew had night watch duty.

"The sailors could usually count on 1½ pounds of biscuits, a liter of wine, a liter of water, beans, garbanzo beans, rice, salted meat, and cheese as their daily fare. They were furnished with two shirts, two pairs of pants, two jackets, a pair of shoes, and a cape. There were no doctors aboard the ships. A barber usually performed amateur medical duties, including bleeding. The most common disorders were alcohol abuse and combat injuries.

"The crew also had pages, who were between eight and ten years old. They were the gophers for the crew and did menial tasks. Apprentices were under twenty years old and were in training to be sailors.

"The real sailors were responsible for the well-being of the ship, like handling the rigging and sails. They were also expected to be fighters against any enemy. For entertainment the men told stories or played dice . . ."

Francisco was taking copious notes, but he knew that Azueta could talk for days without stopping. Finally, Azueta flicked his cigar and stopped for a minute.

Francisco acted quickly, "admiral, why might a ship have two logs?" He told him about La Florida where the captain had one set of records and the accountant had another.

He started to laugh. "Never underestimate greed, my friend. The Spanish conquistadores went exploring to convert poor heathens and to gain their fortunes. The captain was sworn to the Crown. The Crown received one-fifth of all profits and discoveries. However, the captains did not always report actual cargo or actual profits. That meant more money for Cortes and his cronies . . ."

Francisco should have known; nothing had changed for centuries.

"Professor, did I ever tell you that I was stationed in Coronado, by San Diego, for two years. We did joint operations with the U.S. Navy. We had the best times of our lives . . ."

It was almost two o'clock when the meeting was drawing to a close.

"This has been such a wonderful time, professor," Azueta was catching his second breath. "But before I forget, here is a package that I promised Profesora Rios. They are the ship's logs of the ship Santiago. I have never read them."

Francisco was overwhelmed with the importance of these documents. "Admiral, are these official Spanish or Mexican naval records?" Again, Francisco was thinking of the provenance of the documents. He took the thick envelope from the admiral.

"I don't know," there was a frown on the admiral's brow. "All I know is that a few years back a wealthy family donated them to La Academia. They were found in El Partenón."

"I'm sorry, admiral, I don't understand," Francisco was confused.

"El Partenón. You've heard of it. It's a stone's throw from here. Durazo's mansion that was fashioned after the Greek temples."

Durazo?! Durazo?! Where have I heard that name before? Durazo?! The corrupt Mexican chief of police?! Oh, yes! Roberto Gutierrez's grandfather!

CHAPTER 43 – FAJITAS

Friday, July 20, 2018
Zihuatanejo

Alexi was waiting for him at La Casa Que Canta Hotel which was only a five-minute walk from La Academia de Los Marinos. When he came through the plush lobby, she ran into his arms. The warm embrace lasted at least a minute.

Francisco was overwhelmed by the opulence of the hotel. It looked like a Mexican museum on steroids. Dozens of exotic flowers and sculptures with little Aztec symbols peppered throughout the raspberry-colored stucco lodgings. They walked down two sets of blue and white tiled stairs to a separate cabana room with a view of Zihuatanejo Bay.

He put his duffel bag on the floor. It was nearly four o'clock.

"Get changed and let's walk on the beach," Alexi was feeling energetic.

Moments later Francisco had changed into a polo shirt and lightweight pants. She was wearing white shorts, a purple tank top, and leather sandals. On her head was a wide brimmed white hat that overshadowed her large sunglasses.

She looked him over and noticed his bare feet. "I think we need to go shopping for you tomorrow."

"Sure, I hadn't planned to come to the beach when I was down here." *My gym shorts are a little worn and I don't want to walk around bare-chested. Sure, I'll let her dress me (or undress me),* he imagined.

They walked down a couple of flights of steps. His feet were tender. Little pebbles were not his friends. As they hit the sandy beach, some indigenous women vendors tried to sell them blouses, native jewelry, and baseball caps. Alexi and Francisco politely nodded no. The sand was hot, so they walked closer to the waves breaking onto the beach. There was a big rock offshore that was the resting spot for pelicans and seagulls. The surf pounded incessantly on it, sending up sprays of foamy water.

Alexi took off her sandals. The sand near the water was cooler. The waves eventually grabbed Francisco's pant legs. As they walked along the one-kilometer-long beach, they passed a multileveled, polychromatic resort and other hotels and restaurants. Sandpipers poked their beaks into the sand looking for miniature clams. The couple walked by palm trees and mangroves. At the end of the beach there was a rock-laden barrier that led out to an isolated beach at the point called Las Gatas. There were more vendors and scuba equipment rentals. There were also two parasailing spots where tourists paid money to soar into the skies and shriek with fear. Mexican families hopped upon an elongated raft in the shape and color of a banana, hence the name Señor Banana. Frigatebirds glided a thousand feet above them.

Francisco took several photos of Alexi with his cellphone. In one spot, Francisco asked a young Mexican youth to take their photos with the beach and sun as a backdrop. *Life is good!* He thought.

Halfway back, they stopped at a palapa-covered restaurant that had tables on the beach. It was called Paty's. Juan Pablo, the waiter, informed them it was Happy Hour. Drinks were two for one. Well, that settled that. Francisco ordered two Coronas and Alexi had two Peñafiel mineral waters with limes. They also ordered guacamole and chips.

They looked over the beach and chilled out as the sun started to set. The skies were greyish-blue with fiery reddish orange clouds.

"Alexi, thank you. This place is amazing," Francisco was becoming sentimental.

"Well, thank you for letting me share this with you," she responded with a somber smile.

"I really enjoy your company. Our time together has been wonderful," he didn't want to say anything more. He knew he would be leaving soon.

"I feel the same. I am grateful for the little time we have had together," she was more honest than he. "I wish you could stay a little longer. But, *así es la vida.*"

Juan Pablo came and served the beverages. Francisco's beers were served in a bucket filled with ice. His beers were muertas, friggin' cold. The guacamole came with a plateful of totopos and three types of salsa: spicy, fiery, and dragon's breath. The couple ordered another round of drinks just before the end of Happy Hour and some fish fajitas to share.

The two played footsies underneath the table. He held her hand and rubbed it. *Never had a woman touched his soul like she did. He could stay with her for a long, long time.*

He was making his second trip to the restroom when the food came. The food was served on hot plates. The garlic and ginger aroma of the fish was making their taste buds go into overdrive. They laughed as they filled the handmade tortillas with strips of grilled dorado, black beans, rice, and guacamole.

"You were so right!" Francisco said between chews. "The food down here is so good! I need another stomach!" They both giggled.

Alexi had one and a half fajitas, giving Francisco the other half. He, in essence, had two and a half. He was so full.

A trio of older gentlemen mariachis came by their table and asked if they had any requests. Francisco was in a good mood.

"Alexi, what would you like to hear?"

"'Acá Entre Nos,' por favor."

> *¿Entre nos quiero que sepas la verdad*
> *no te he dejado de adorar allá?*
> *En mi triste soledad me han dado ganas de gritar*
> *salir corriendo y preguntar*
> *que es lo que ha sido de tu vida acá? . . .*

The voices were a little raspy and the music was a little flat, but Alexi held Francisco' hand firmly. She was sending out sizzling vibes. "Okay, your turn."

"Para mí, 'Solamente Una Vez.'"

He reached over and kissed her as the trio sang. It was romantic. They were enamorados. For a third song, she selected 'Sabor a Mí.'"

"See what you are going to miss when you leave, querido?" Alexi was teasing, but in a serious way. "When are you going home?"

"My flight is August 4th," Francisco seemed uncertain. "But maybe I can stay an extra week?"

"Whatever you decide, querido," she replied. *"¡Qué será, será!"*

Juan Pablo came by and asked if they had room for dessert. In unison, both Francisco and Alexi declined.

"In that case, I'll bring the check," said the young man.

The sun was gradually setting. Francisco took some more photos.

Five minutes later, the check was handed to Francisco and at the same time Juan Pablo set two White Russians in front of them. They gave him blanks stares.

"Compliments of the house!" Juan Pablo smiled.

The Kahlua and cream drink was too sweet for Alexi. She gave hers to Francisco.

"We'd better get back to the hotel," Alexi pushed herself close to him. "I hope you saved up your energy for tonight."

CHAPTER 44 – TENTACIONES

Saturday, July 21, 2018
Zihuatanejo

Alexi heard the woodpecker tapping on the wooden support post on their terrace. She jumped into the shower. Meanwhile Francisco was snoring away. The heat of the day had not yet begun. Francisco started to slowly open his eyes. He looked around the room that he had not paid much attention to the night before. It was brightly colored with wicker basket lamps hanging down from the ceiling. The floor was wall-to-wall orange tiles. This was the most elegant hotel that Francisco had ever stayed at.

As Francisco marveled at the luxurious splendor surrounding him on the tastefully appointed room. As he admired the beauty of the beach, the hills, and the sunrise, he couldn't help but wonder what it was like to live here five hundred years ago.

On their way to breakfast, Francisco and Alexi walked past an infinity pool that overlooked a little cove. They sat at an ocean-view table. The first waiter, Alfredo, dressed in α white guayabera with black and gold trim brought them coffee. Francisco requested soy milk and got it. He was so pleased. The waves crashed on the rocks below them. Yellow kiskadee birds were flittering in a tree to the side, chattering to one another.

"Last night was wonderful, querida," Francisco reached over and held her arm. *How can I live without her? She fulfills me emotionally, intellectually, and spiritually. What should I do? What can I do?* Normally, he would be logical and analytical about the situation. But here and now, his heart was taking over.

A second waiter, David, topped off their coffee cups and brought them two pieces of pan dulce.

"Are you ready to order, señorita?" His English was flawless. Alexi and Francisco nodded in the affirmative.

"The egg white omelet. Corn tortillas please."

"And for you, señor?"

"I'll have the enchiladas suizas, por favor."

"Very good. Anything else, señores?"

"A little yogurt with fruit, please," Alexi added. "To share."

David retreated, and Francisco leaned closer to her. "Querida, how did you find this enchanted place?"

Alexi scooted her chair closer to Francisco. "My husband brought me here for our first anniversary in 1996 Unfortunately, it was our last. He died two years later."

"I'm sorry," Francisco was taken aback. *Why is she telling me this? This is some very personal and sad history.*

"I try to come here once a year or every other year," There was a sorrow embedded in her dark brown eyes. "Nicolás was a good man. He would have liked you. And I'm sure that you would have liked him."

"Doesn't it make you sad to come here?"

"Actually, quite the opposite. Nicolás used to say, 'Twenty minutes or twenty years. I don't know how long I'll live. Live in the present. Enjoy today.'"

"Sounds good to me," Francisco shook his head in agreement.

"I've had many good memories here, Francisco," she took his hand. "And now with you, I will have more."

Both Alfredo and David brought the steaming hot food. Alexi splashed a little bit of red salsa over her egg-omelet that was filled with cherry tomatoes, diced red onion, avocado chunks, cilantro, and a few jalapeños. She took a hot tortilla from the basket. At the same time, Francisco was cutting into his enchiladas covered with tomatillo sauce and cortija cheese sprinkles.

"You're easy to be with, Francisco," Alexi said after spooning some yogurt and fruit onto her plate. "You a non-Mexican Mexican." They both laughed.

After breakfast they took a casual twenty-minute walk to downtown Zihuatanejo. Past the town's basketball court in the center of town, there were dozens of shops, bars, and restaurants. Alexi took them to the Boutique Manolo. The men's clothing was elegant. The proprietor, Pedro, had silver hair and a curled-up moustache. He was debonair.

A half-hour later they walked out with a beautiful-lilac colored guayabera, a dark grey "Shawshank Redemption" tee shirt, an orange "Zihuatanejo" iguana tank top, tan walking shorts, navy blue swimming trunks, and some black flip flops. It cost a couple of hundred dollars, but Francisco knew it would cost twice as much in the States. They stopped at a bookstore and Francisco bought Alexi a copy of "Rain of Gold" by Victor Villaseñor. She was happy. They walked back to the hotel hand-in-hand.

In the afternoon, they spent time in the infinity swimming pool overlooking the promontory. They talked and enjoyed the ambience.

"A couple more things about this place," Alexi resumed. "This is the hotel where all the famous people come, especially important Mexicans. A couple of years ago, Luis Miguel rented out the whole place."

"I love his music."

"Me too," Alexi agreed. "In fact, this very pool was in the movie 'When A Man Loves a Woman.' With Andy Garcia and Meg Ryan."

"Really?!"

At four o'clock they climbed back up to their room and showered together.

"Do we have time for a nap, mi querida?" he asked.

She gave Francisco a probing look. "No more than a half hour!"

At a few minutes after six o'clock, they were in the lobby of the hotel. Alexi was dressed to the nines with a black off the shoulder net dress offset by a ruby-colored silk scarf that matched her glossy lipstick. Her black hair was coiffed in a type of French curl that accented her black pearl earrings. She wore stilted four-inch black heels. Francisco's mouth was drooling. *She is so hot!*

Francisco was clean shaven. The newly purchased lilac guayabera contrasted with his black slacks.

"Are you ready for another adventure, querido?" her smile sparkled like a thousand diamonds.

"Sí, mi amor." Francisco replied.

"Let's call a taxi," she suggested.

Francisco nodded and then asked the concierge to call a cab. *Whatever?! It's only up the hill. No more than five minutes. Ten at the most.*

The taxi arrived ten minutes later. The restaurant reservation at Las Tentaciones had been at six, so they were slightly late. The driver asked the destination and three minutes later they were in front of the restaurant. The steep grade of the road leading up to the restaurant would have given a mountain goat a heart attack. Alexi definitely knew the game plan. Francisco gave the driver the equivalent of five dollars.

The couple passed through a two-door wooden portal and were greeted by the host.

"Welcome to Las Tentaciones," the suave and muscular man said. "My name is Salvador. Oh, doctora, it's been such a long time!" Salvador gave her a hug and a kiss on the cheek.

"I think it's been two years, Chava," Alexi replied using his nickname.

"Let's get you seated."

Francisco eyes grew bigger and bigger. This restaurant was high on the hill and overlooked the entire Zihuatanejo Bay. The lights of the city started to sparkle.

"Good evening, my name is Efraín," the tall handsome waiter greeted them. "How are you this evening?"

Five minutes later Alexi was drinking a mineral water and Francisco a sangrita with a shot of Partida reposado tequila. Their table overlooked an infinity water border. Another waiter Oscar lit the candle on their table.

"Alexi, this is the most awesome place I've ever been to!" Francisco was excited. He looked up at the western sky and saw the planet Venus saluting them.

"The most romantic place in the world, I think," Alexi gave him a killer smile.

Efraín came over to take their order but was interrupted by Francisco.

"Efraín, please take a few photos of me and the most beautiful woman in the world," Francisco requested. He was overjoyed. "Several. Can you get the sunset, please?"

Francisco jabbered on for the next half hour. He was so excited. Only when Oscar brought some delicious rolls with sage butter did he stop talking.

"Alexi, I don't know what to say," Francisco was overcome with emotion. He was afraid he was falling in love with her, but he would be going back to Stanford very soon. He didn't want to mislead her.

The first course arrived. It was lobster carpaccio over a carrot and snow pea puree drizzled lightly with a citrus dressing and topped with pistachio bits. The presentation was colorful. They looked out over the bay as the dark green waters met the bluish-grey and pink clouds at sunset.

"Oh, my God, Alexi!" Francisco blurted out. "This is delish!"

Oscar brought Francisco a glass of Casa Madero Chardonnay with the second course. The smell of the arugula, spinach, and fennel salad with bits of turkey, Brie cheese, and figs topped with an anisette dressing overwhelmed their senses. A slight ocean breeze seemed to appear, and the aroma of citronella permeated the air.

"I love figs," Alexi said.

"As much as chocolate?"

"Francisco, are you behaving yourself?"

The third course was a cilantro soup. It went down their throats smoothly.

"I hadn't realized that I like cilantro that much," Francisco commented.

"And it's so healthy," Alexi replied falling into her doctor role.

It was at least twenty minutes until the next course arrived. In the meantime, Alexi and Francisco were resting. They were trying to pace themselves. However, that didn't stop Francisco from eating more bread and butter. Efraín served a rack of lamb with porcini mushrooms lightly crusted with almond bits and topped with a port wine sauce, caramelized shallots, and a side of rosemary and cilantro roasted potatoes. The smells sent Francisco and Alexi to heaven.

The couple was silent as they ate. Only an occasional contented sigh passed between them. Francisco had not even noticed the background music.

"Alexi, I know you won't believe this," Francisco gave a sheepish grin. "But I am full."

"No, I don't believe you!" she teased.

At that moment Salvador, all smiles, came over with two pieces of chocolate cake. "For you, señora, we have made your favorite chocolate cake." He had remembered that she liked chocolate.

"Chava, would you mind if we take these to go?" she gave him a gratified smile. "And the check, please."

CHAPTER 45 – ISMAEL'S JOURNALS

Monday, July 23, 2018
Guadalajara

Francisco was blindly staring past Miranda in her office. He was totally exhausted from the weekend. *I'm not a youngster anymore.* Professor Miranda had asked her secretary Alma to make copies of the records that Francisco had obtained from Admiral Azueta. Additionally, Alma was to scan the documents and send the files to Carlos Erandi in order to bring him up to speed.

"And Alma, please send Francisco and me the scanned files also. It's good to have a backup." Francisco almost forgot to send a copy to Tina. He couldn't think clearly. He could not get Alexi out of his head. His feelings for her were pulling at his heartstrings.

"You've been busy, my friend," Miranda said in seemingly neutral tone. *What was she really saying?* He nodded with an innocent smile. Alma came into the professora's office and gave them each a copy of the notes.

Great timing! He wanted to go back to his apartment and take a nap. "Miranda, what would you say if we ended today's session early? This way we can read the materials and discuss them on Wednesday."

"That makes sense."

"By the way, how is your toe?"

"Fine. The doctor says in two weeks I'll be walking just fine," she was looking down at her foot, exhaling a deep sigh.

"I can't believe the time has gone by so quickly," his eyes started to drift, then he caught himself. "And I still have my last presentation next Tuesday."

"What's your topic?"

"U.S. – Mexico relations."

"That should be interesting with your current president," she gave him a wicked look. "Oh, before I forget, Sol wants to invite you for a few drinks tomorrow night. Very casual. He feels bad about not seeing you."

"Would love to."

"And we want to invite you over for a late lunch on Sunday," Miranda said in a softer tone.
"We invited Alexi also."

"Sounds perfect."

"She really likes you, you know."

• • •

After an hour nap, Francisco picked up his own background notes from the bed stand and began to read:

> At the end of October 1527, the Aztec princess María Del Rosario, and her servant, Inocente, were abducted by Captain Saavedra under the order of the Conquistador, Hernán Cortés. María was the ward of Father Moreno and he was sworn to protect her. Moreno charged his postulant, Diego García, to search for the young woman on behalf of the Catholic Church. The local ship builder Don Romero had refurbished an old ship and stocked it with provisions and trading merchandise in an attempt to rescue the women.

Francisco was still tired and wanted to take another nap, but decided to look at the logs of Ismael, the chronicler for Captain Diego García on the second ship named the Santiago. He saw that the journals were written in Spanish and bore the name of Ismael Gavriel. Francisco had to go to his computer to get background information about Gavriel. He learned that Ismael was born in Granada, Spain in 1491, just before the Spanish Inquisition. His father was Jewish, and his mother was a Moor. The family became Conversos in order to avoid persecution by the fanatic Catholic clergy. Ismael was recruited as a translator by the Spanish royal fleet because of his language proficiencies. He spoke Spanish, Latin, Arabic, and Hebrew fluently, and could get by in Portuguese and French. In November of 1527 he became the translator for Diego Garcia and was assigned to the Santiago that was harbored in Zihuatanejo.

Francisco turned off his laptop and went to lie on top of his bed.

I'm so tired. Can't concentrate. But need to read at least a \few pages of Ismael's logs. His logs are interesting and add new dimensions to the project. I don't know how much value they will be in the long run, but we have to explore all angles.

November 1527
Santiago #2

We had been man days at sea without wind. Our captain decided to order the men to row our ship forward. One of the men, Blas, died from exhaustion. We were demoralized.

Our captain said it was a divine sign that our brother Blas died. "We have been trying to make this voyage without the help of God. We must ask for His assistance. Let us pray."

Captain Diego kneeled and everyone reluctantly followed suit. They prayed for God's assistance. Diego then told the men that there would be no more rowing on this day and that there would be double rum rations in commemoration of Blas. For the rest of the day the ship was motionless. There still was no wind.

The next day the crew resumed rowing. There were no objections. The weather was getter hotter and more humid. Still the wind was negligible. We prayed every day at noon time asking for favorable winds.

One night, Diego and I were talking in our cabin. Diego said that he was beginning to see me as a mentor like Father Moreno.

"Ismael, why does the crew act so ungodly?" he looked quizzically at me "Is it because I am not a priest yet? They are constantly cursing and taking the Lord's name in vain. They steal from one another. What is it?"

"My friend, they have no allegiance to anyone or anything. The oath they made to Spain or God is meaningless. Their god is gold."

"But how can that be? We are on a mission to recover valuable property for the Church. Don't they see this?"

"As long as they think they will make their fortune they will obey you."

Finally, around December 12, clouds appeared to our north. Captain Diego, Bautista, and I met and conferred. The white clouds were a hopeful sign. The sails were still up even though the ship was barely drifting. The night of December 13 was pitch black. No celestial bodies could be seen. The oceans started to swell, and little by little the winds started to pick up. In the early morning lightning could be seen to the northeast. Bautista gave orders to inspect and secure the sails. The first drops of rain felt like pebbles. The crew complained and put on their caps. Then the deluge came. It rocked the Santiago, up and down. The helmsman, Guido Salerno, was having a difficult time keeping us on course. We were at full sail, bouncing on the waters. The winds were now blowing sideways. We were in the middle of a typhoon.

Bautista yelled, "Ease up on the sails!" The crew began to take down the sails. That slowed the ship down. Captain Diego was showing signs of getting seasick, but I gave him more ginger tea.

The storm lasted two days. God had answered our prayers, and then some. Finally, the sun came out and the wind was favorable. We were on course for the Moluccas. However, since Diego had no experience as a captain, we had not taken advantage of the storm to collect rainwater. The physical exertion of the crew's rowing had depleted most of their fresh water. Diego prayed for another storm. The crew was put on half rations.

It was around the winter solstice when an albatross was sighted. Bautista rushed to the deck and scanned the horizon with his brass telescope. He looked first on the port side of the ship. Seeing nothing he moved over to the starboard side. He could make out a wisp of a cloud to the northwest.

"Hard to starboard 45 degrees, Guido!" Bautista yelled to the helmsman. The men were getting excited. Soon we could see three puffs of clouds. Then five.

"Land ahoy!" Bautista shouted. Cries of joy ran through the ship.

By nightfall we were a mile offshore from a large island that seemed to have volcanoes at both ends. We decided to wait until morning to go ashore. We dropped anchor. The next morning a rowboat with five men headed by the second mate Naciso landed on the white sandy beach. There were signals from the beach to the ship communicating that the place was safe. For the remainder of the day, crew members were shuttled back and forth, carrying utensils, sacks, and empty water casks.

Captain Diego could not believe his eyes. This place was beautiful. The crew had procured fruits and firewood. The weather was warm. A white tern flew overhead wondering what these beings were. The cook had grilled bananas over a spit. But just before the crew began their evening meal, Captain Diego called on us to give thanks for landing safely and finding fresh food. Everybody did so. We slept al fresco on the beach but were awakened by a pre-dawn rain. We gathered pots to collect the water, having learned our lesson.

On Christmas Day, we said prayers and had a big feast. There was another double ration of rum. Throughout the next week we hunted and fished. We smoked some wild javelinas and fish. We gathered a couple hundred coconuts and other fruits.

On the last day of 1527, we sailed well-rested and with full provisions from the generous island.

CHAPTER 46 –
ANTHROPOPHAGY

July 23-25, 2018
Guadalajara

Time was going by quickly for Francisco. He managed to accomplish a few errands, but the majority of his time now was consumed with reading and cataloging the Ismael journals.

Francisco did manage to call Alexi to see if she had received the red roses that he had sent her. The pair agreed to get together no later than Friday. She had to perform a minor surgery on Wednesday, so she was not going to be available until later in the week.

As Francisco turned his attentions back to the journals, it occurred to him that the Santiago probably stopped at one of the Hawaiian Islands. They were on the most probable trajectory for the Moluccas. He resumed his reading.

January 1528

These past few weeks, the sailing for the Santiago has been good. The winds and the weather have been favorable. The men are happy. Diego and I have spent a lot of time conversing about religion, philosophy, and history.

February 1528

In February, we decided to be prudent and stock up on provisions. We did not want to chance an errant typhoon or sluggish doldrums. We discovered a set of atolls where we decided to anchor. We selected the one with a volcano. As we came close to a clean beach, several canoes with native men rowed toward us, smiling and yelling in friendly tones. They were olive-skinned and had beards. They had little head bands made from palm fronds. Captain Diego, myself, and three men rowed to shore escorted by our new friends.

On the beach we were greeted by a stocky man with shell beads around his neck. He wore an exotic headdress. He smiled at us and we smiled back. Nobody could understand the other. Captain Diego handed him an official Spanish document written in Latin stating that New Spain was claiming this land. The chief took it, looked at it, and started laughing.

The crew set up camp on the beach. Captain Diego forbade them to take up with the natives. He tried to communicate with the natives about God and Christianity, but the language barrier was too great. However, I did facilitate trading for pigs, goat, chickens, and copra (dried coconut). When the chief was offered gold for the food, he nodded no. I then suggested some of the colorful Aztec textiles. The chief was overjoyed, and the deals were made. The crew ate their fill of crabs and tuna. After about a week, the Santiago set sail in a slightly southern direction.

The crew was relatively happy. However, the rum supply was running low. The men were a little grumpy over the next month but caused no trouble. They all prayed together at noon every day. The rains were moderate most of the time and allowed us to replenish our stock of fresh water, but soon we were out of meat.

April 1528

In early April we approached a large island and weighed anchor. It was late in the afternoon when Bautista sent five crew members to procure some food, preferably meat. The sky was cloudy, and it was very dark. When the five men had not returned to the ship, Bautista signaled the beach by means of a lamp, but there was no response. The chief mate was concerned and recommended to Captain Diego that they send out a second boat in the morning to search for the missing men. Captain Diego spent the night praying for the safety of the absent sailors.

At four bells Bautista was directing three men to prepare to go ashore. The sun had just begun to rise. However, one of the sailors yelled out, "There they are!" Bautista could see the men in the small boat rowing back to the ship doing double time. Then he noticed that there were only three of them. He took out his telescope and saw their faces. They were in a panic. Then he noticed several canoes departing from the beach. The natives were short, skinny, and black-skinned with frizzy hair.

"Gustavo, prepare for battle," Bautista ordered the second mate. The men rushed to the storage room where swords, knives, and other weapons were kept. Since this was a trading vessel, it was not equipped with canons.

A moment later there was a scream behind Bautista from the starboard side of the ship. One of the natives had snuck aboard and clubbed a crew member.

"To starboard!" Bautista shouted. "To arms!" There were only about eight members of the crew, but they ran to the side and started slashing the boarding natives with their swords. After five minutes, all the natives were dead or flailing on deck. Three of the crew were injured.

"Throw them overboard!" Bautista barked. "But stab the heathens first! Make sure they're dead. May the devil take them!"

Meanwhile, the three sailors in the small boat were approaching. They looked fatigued. The pursuing ships were gaining on them. Bautista roared, "Get ready to weigh anchor!"

Captain Diego wanted to assist Bautista, but I waved my head no. Instead, I said, "Let's help get those men aboard and salvage the rowboat." Captain Diego nodded his approval.

The sails were full. The rowboat hit the ship and one of the three sailors threw a rope up to an awaiting crewman. The trio scooted up and over. The anchor was weighed, and the Santiago slowly began to sail. The natives were within a hundred yards of our vessel. Their battle screams were chilling. Some waved spears in the air.

Two hours later the ship was out of harm's way. The three men were in Captain Diego's cabin along with Bautista and myself. They were eating a hearty soup being washed down by rum. They were sullen.

"What happened?" Bautista inquired. "Where are the other two?"

One of the crew members started to cry. Another one took a deep breath and started to explain.

"We landed on the beach. We split up into two groups. Me, Matías, and Tomás in one. João, and Tiago in the other. We were to meet at the boat just before dusk. Matías caught two fowl and Tomás one. I found some green bananas.

"At dusk we went back to the boat. João and Tiago were not there. We waited an hour. Then we smelled smoke and thought we heard yelling. We snuck toward the noise carefully for about a mile. We saw a big bonfire. There were hundreds of small natives dancing up and down. They were singing. Then we saw them." The speaker, Raúl, got choked up and could not speak for a moment.

"The savages were eating them!" Raul cried out.

"Eating what?" Bautista frowned.

"João and Tiago!" snot drooled out of Raul's nose.

CHAPTER 47 – THE MOLUCCAS

July 24, 2018
Guadalajara

Francisco took a lunch break but really didn't have an appetite. He called Alexi for a little cheering up but unfortunately, she was occupied seeing a patient.

He came back to his room and Googled the approximate location of the islands in the journals. The second island could have been the Caroline or the Marshall Islands. The cannibals could have been in New Guinea. Both sets of islands were on the route to the Moluccas.

Francisco paced back and forth in his apartment, trying to clear his head. *Okay, let's get moving! In a few hours some drinks with Sol!* He braced himself. He reached over and picked up Ismael's logs and continued reading.

June 21, 1528
Santiago #2

It was summer solstice and first day of summer when the Santiago sighted a smoking ship at the southern shore of a big green forested island.

"According to my readings, captain," Bautista reported to Captain Diego, "this should be the Moluccas." The captain took out his telescope and scanned the beach. There was a palisade fort near the beach. "It's flying a Spanish flag!" he said.

The news spread aboard ship like wildfire.

"Make ready to drop anchor!" Bautista ordered after getting the nod from Captain Diego. "Captain, I think they are signaling us from the fort." The chief mate was reading the flags.

"What are they saying?"

"We are Spanish! You are welcome ashore. We guarantee you safe passage."

"Have the second mate respond. Tell them that we are coming in peace," Captain Diego hoped that this was not a ploy.

The sun was now overhead and beating down on them. Captain Diego gave the order to make ready with a rowboat. An hour later he was ashore with four of his men, including Monixo.

Captain Diego and his party were greeted by poorly armed soldiers headed by a weathered old Spanish warrior with a long greyish-brown beard.

"Capitán Hernando de Urdaneta at your service, your Holiness," the Spanish commander was responding to the Tau cross around Diego's neck. He had wrongly assumed that Captain Diego was a full-fledged member of the clergy.

Pleasantries were exchanged and everyone made their way toward the palisade fort. Captain Diego observed that it was barren and that de Urdaneta's soldiers looked bedraggled. They went into the galley room where there were long tables and benches. Fresh cut coconuts were given to the guests.

"Captain, I am not a priest," Captain Diego clarified. "I am a postulant. We have been sent here on a mission for the Church."

"Father, you have come at an unfortunate time," de Urdaneta began. "A few years ago, we were shipwrecked on the western shore of this island. We had come from Spain following the eastern route. Right now, we are on the island of Tidore. Our commander, Loaisa, died while we were searching for spices and territories for our Crown. At that time, we numbered 120 strong. The natives were friendly to us and their chief Pattimura moved us to the southern part of the island for our protection. They have fed us, traded with us, and protected us."

"Protected you against whom?" Captain Diego's curiosity had been piqued.

"The Portuguese, of course. They are trying to claim land belonging to the Spanish Crown," de Urdaneta was moved by anger. "They have been building forts on Ternate, the island north of here. They even have a post on the northern point of this island, but it is unmanned. Once a week they come over to our side to assess what we are doing or to see if we are going to attack them. Many of us have been here for too long a time protecting this island from the Portuguese who are like fleas. They are everywhere and are such nuisances."

"Are you planning to attack them, captain?' Diego inquired.

"In March, around the end of the month, La Florida landed here. Commander Saavedra was here. He gave us arms, medicines, and supplies. Those provisions are now gone and we have been barely surviving for two months. We helped him with the repairs to La Florida. While he was here, a Portuguese boat attacked La Florida. Saavedra sank their ship. But, to answer your question, we don't plan to attack them. We couldn't even if we wanted to. More than two-thirds of our men have died, mostly from malaria. We are barely staying alive. But for the grace of God and Chief Pattimura we would be dead."

"Where is La Florida now, captain?" Diego pursued.

"It sailed about nine days ago. They had over eight tons of cloves and other spices to bring back to New Spain."

"Well, what's your plan now, captain?"

"We would have loved to sail with La Florida, but we have sworn an oath to protect Tidore for the Crown. We asked Commander Saavedra to send us reinforcements and supplies. Or better yet send us a ship to take us back to Spain."

"Speaking of ships, why is there a ship carcass out there burning?" Bautista interposed himself into *the conversation. "It resembles Saavedra's Espíritu Santo."*

"It is," said Captain de Urdaneta quickly. "It was torched two days ago, by murderous villains. Some Portuguese sailors who had sailed under the command of Captain Pedro Fuentes de Xérez. They mutinied and murdered."

Suddenly, there was a commotion at the galley door. Everybody turned around to see a person dressed in friar's garb enter.

"Diego?!" the figure asked in astonishment. "Are you Friar Moreno's postulant?"

"Fray Nadal!" Captain Diego remembered him from the Zacatula monastery.

. . .

It was the late afternoon and Sol had a head start at Señor Kaneishi's Bar. He was drinking Sapporo beer. Francisco had joined him after a short second nap. He ordered the same beer.

The Mexican waitresses wore a geisha type kimono with white face powder and red lipstick. One of them came over and asked if they wanted food.

Sol ordered sashimi and tuna carpaccio. The thought of the red flesh almost made Francisco gag. He ordered the chicken teriyaki bento box.

"Francisco, you're almost leaving us," Sol said in a semi-serious manner. "I should take you to another soccer game."

Francisco gave a weak smile.

They talked about soccer and Mexican and U.S. politics. The food came and they ate, Francisco with chopsticks and Sol with a knife and fork.

"You know that Alexi really likes you," he was all too ready to talk about her and Francisco. "You are a good match for her."

"I agree. Too bad I have to go back to Stanford," Francisco tried to be tactful. *Why is this guy in my business? Well, Alexi is his comadre and he has to look out for her.* "I have classes to teach."

"Yes, my friend. I know how important teaching is. And the research. And the publishing," Sol nodded. "Miranda reminds me all the time."

"And I have to finish the project that I have going with Miranda."

"Yes, I understand. And after this project, there will be another one and then another," Sol was trying to make a point. "My friend, what do you want out of life? What will fulfill you? Or who will?"

CHAPTER 48 – THE HUNT

July 24, 2018
Guadalajara

Sol's words kept ringing in Francisco's ears. He barely tasted his food and drink during the remainder of their early evening dinner. He made small talk with Sol and tried very hard to stay focused on their conversations, but his mind and heart were elsewhere.

Shortly after 7 p.m., Francisco begged off, citing all the reading that he still had to complete. He said good night to Sol and thanked him profusely for his hospitality. He hurried back to his lodging.

In the solitude of his room, he allowed himself to feel the full magnitude of his emotions. He was confused, conflicted, and desperately in love. *I need to stop thinking about all of this,* he thought. *I have work to do and it might be the best distraction.* He sat at his desk and began flipping the pages of the journals.

June 21, 1528
Tidore, Moluccas

"Diego!" Friar Nadal asked. "How is Friar Moreno?"

"He's fine."

"In God's name, what brings you here?" Nadal was astounded.

"Friar Moreno sent me here to retrieve some Christian souls," Captain Diego started to explain. Friar Reza is having health issues back home. Friar Moreno had to take care of him. That's why he sent me here on this mission."

"What type of mission?"

"To bring back María Del Rosario and Inocente."

"Why, my son?

"Because they were kidnapped by Commander Saavedra."

"That can't be! I brought them here myself," Nadal was being defensive. "We were told that it would be easier to convert the natives with them," Nadal gave the ecclesiastical pat answer. "They said that María Del Rosario has a gift for languages and could become an interpreter for the church."

"Oh, my God!" Captain de Urdaneta bellowed. "That's not the real reason!"
Everybody looked at him. Captain Diego looked confused.

"Two nights ago, María Del Rosario and her maid servant were kidnapped again. This time we think it was Rodrigo Alves and some of the Portuguese from the Espiritu Santo. The scoundrels must have been colluding with some of the Portuguese here. We think that there are Portuguese spies and collaborators from Ternate amongst us. They're murderers! They killed Milo who was the dearest, sweetest young man who looked after the women. And they assassinated the captain of the Espiritu Santo, Pedro Fuentes de Xérez, and the native guardsman Limahelu."

"But why did they take the women?" Captain Diego was puzzled.

"To trade them as slaves! They're worth a fortune."

There was a loud gasp by the others.

"I don't understand!"

"Many years ago, shipwrecked sailors from Magellan's fleet were captured and sold to the Chinese merchants ships as slaves."

"Where could they have taken them?" Bautista jumped in.

"To Ternate, the Portuguese island north of here."

"How would they get there?"

"Through the jungle," de Urdaneta was exasperated. "The chief's son, Latuheru, probably could guide them. He hates us. He complains to his father about us. He wants to be chief. You see, at the other end of this island there is a Portuguese outpost. The Portuguese have a ship that goes back and forth to Ternate."

"Why didn't you pursue them?" Bautista said in an angry tone.

"The jungle is dangerous. We wouldn't be able to track them. Most of my men couldn't walk a hundred paces. They suffer from malaria and other diseases. I have lost over two-thirds of my men.

"And as you have seen," the captain continued, trying to catch his breath. "Alves' men set fire to the ship. We couldn't pursue them by sea to Ternate."

Captain Diego didn't know what to think or do. Friar Moreno had entrusted him with bringing Maria Del Rosario back. It was a holy mission.

"Fray Nadal, I have a special request," Captain Diego tried to collect his thoughts and asked, "I need you to lead my crew in a prayer of gratitude for having made a safe landing."

"God's Will shall be done," Nadal agreed.

"Captain de Urdaneta, we request shelter and protection in your fort."

"Granted."

In the late afternoon, the crew of the Santiago were all kneeling on the beach with Fray Nadal leading them in prayer. Captain Diego prayed for answers about how to carry out his mission.

As Captain Diego began walking back to the fort with the others, he spotted a small sailboat. "Bautista, get that boat ready to sail as soon as possible. I want Monixo and Iñigo to man the boat. We will sail around the island to the Portuguese outpost. Hopefully we'll arrive before Rodrigo Alves and the women make it through the jungle. Ismael, you are coming with me. Bautista, you're staying here. You'll be in charge."

"Ay-ay, captain."

"Captain de Urdaneta, we need a navigator."

"Yes, sir."

Since it was the summer solstice, they calculated that they had four good hours of sailing before night fall. It was past five o'clock when the sailboat ventured out with these men and the native navigator, Leimana. He was the brother of Limahelu whom Alves and his men had murdered.

• • •

Days before during the abduction, the boatswain Rodrigo Alves had been challenged by the native guard, Limahelu. Alves decided to murder him to protect their plot. And since Alves didn't want to be pursued by sea, he also killed Captain Pedro Fuentes de Xérez. Some of his Portuguese compatriots set the Espiritu Santo on fire.

Alves' new guide, the chief's son, Latuheru, knew the way through the jungle to the Portuguese outpost on the north shore of Tidore. Rodrigo had promised him a reward when they reached their destination. Latuheru and another native easily followed the faint trail that led to the north of the island. However, Rodrigo and his two men were larger in size and the going was tougher. The women also wore garb that easily caught on the underbrush. Nobody had a machete or hatchet, so the going was difficult.

On the second day, Gomes was behind one of the natives. He pushed aside a branch. As the bough quickly whipped around, he felt a sharp pain. He had been bitten by a green python. He tried to scream, but his mouth only foamed. He fell to the ground writhing. The others saw all this and then looked away in horror. In less than five minutes Gomes was motionless.

"Shall we bury him, Rodrigo?" the former cook Gonçalo asked nervously.

"We haven't got time. We don't know what time the Portuguese ship arrives at the outpost."

At first, they proceeded at a quick pace without any breaks. But their water was running low, and Gonçalo was showing signs of chills alternating with a fever. They slowed down to a snail's pace, totally exhausted. At night, they could not sleep with all the mosquitoes buzzing about and the chattering of monkeys in the jungle canopies.

On the morning of the fourth day, they could hear the pounding of the surf. They exited the jungle and could see the Portuguese outpost a half mile down the beach. Rodrigo looked across the strait to Portuguese Ternate. He thought he could detect a ship with one sail departing.

"Okay, let's sit down and rest," Rodrigo bowed his head in a prearranged signal to Gonçalo. The two women saw their native accomplices suddenly fall forward after being stabbed to death.

"That was your reward!" Rodrigo laughed. He wasn't sharing any fortune with heathens. "Let's go!"

Rodrigo's entourage started walking along the northern most point of Spanish Tidore. The outpost looked abandoned. Rodrigo saw that the Portuguese boat was about a quarter of the way across the channel. They were only a few feet from the outpost when several figures appeared out of nowhere.

"Stop and surrender in the name of God!" yelled a young man. Captain Diego and his men had been lying in wait on the beach between the jungle and the Portuguese outpost.

Rodrigo stopped, but Gonçalo inexplicably ran forward with his sword in his hand. Iñigo jumped from Captain Diego's side and easily impaled the ship's former cook, Gonçalo. Rodrigo had no choice but to attack. After only a few seconds, Monixo ran his sword through Rodrigo's right shoulder. The latter fell on his hands onto the sands losing his sword. Monixo came close to the downed man's back but did not press his advantage. Suddenly, Rodrigo swirled around and threw sand with his left hand into Monixo's face and took off running back into the jungle.

Iñigo started to pursue him.

"Let him go, Iñigo," Captain Diego yelled after him. "Let him find his fate in the jungle. May God forgive him."

Then Leimana and I came running from the outpost where we had been hiding.

"Captain, the Portuguese boat is almost here," I warned. "We have to take the women and get out of here! Now!"

CHAPTER 49 – THE SURRENDER

Wednesday, July 25, 2018
Guadalajara

The telephone call came at around 5:30 a.m. It took six rings before Francisco answered. He had been sleeping like a zombie because he had stayed up until two a.m. reading Ismael's papers.

"Amorcito, I'm sorry to wake you up so early," Alexi was speaking in a sorrowful voice. "My abuela Ofelia died. I have to fly out to La Paz tomorrow. I don't know when I'll be back."

"I'm so sorry, mi querida," Francisco was saddened. "Is there anything I can do?"

After a few minutes of trying to console her, Francisco agreed to go with her to La Paz the following day. He told her that whatever she planned was fine with him. He had never been to the southern part of Baja California. He would spend his last few days in Mexico there with her.

He hung up and got three more hours of shut eye, skipping breakfast in order to get to the university campus on time. Fortunately, there was coffee and pan dulce at Professor Rios' office. They chatted casually for a few minutes while Francisco inhaled an oreja and a marranito pan dulce. Back home he would have dipped the pan dulce into his coffee, but here he did not want to appear gauche in front of Miranda.

"The journal reads like a swashbuckling pirate adventure," Miranda smiled. "This Ismael was either writing the truth or had a great imagination."

They talked about how much of the diary of the Santiago could be used in their article. Neither one had finished reading the papers and agreed to postpone any decisions until they had done so.

"The fact that Captain de Urdaneta mentioned La Florida gives us further corroboration with the Saavedra/Duro and Da Napoli accounts," Francisco asserted. Miranda nodded in agreement.

"Francisco, I think we should invite Carlos to one of our meetings next week," Miranda suggested. "Especially, since you will be leaving shortly."

"Sounds like a great idea."

"And you are still willing to do your fourth and last presentation next Thursday?"

"Yes, if the protestors don't burn me at the stake beforehand."

They both laughed.

After their meeting, Francisco hurried back to his room

He was concerned that going to La Paz with Alexi was going to be hard on his schedule. He knew that he couldn't be reading Ismael's materials while Alexi was grieving. Besides, he really wanted to spend some quality time with her before he had to return to Stanford.

Francisco decided to get as much reading done as he could. He continued on the Ismael papers where he had left off:

June 23, 1528
Tidore, Moluccas

After a day and night of sailing back to the Spanish fort against the wind, our rescue party arrived. During that time, Captain Diego wanted desperately to talk to Maria Del Rosario in order to console her, but he dared not to so.

When we arrived at the port, Captain Diego and I jumped out of the small boat first and helped the two woman to the beach. Monixo and Leimana secured the boat.

As we started walking, Leimana pulled fiercely on Monixo's arm. The native was shaking his head in a worried state. Suddenly, a dozen robust soldiers jumped out of the mangroves. They had their swords drawn.

"Surrender," the lead officer yelled. His long reddish-brown beard covered most of his pocked-marked face. He was speaking to them in

Portuguese. Although Captain Diego and his men knew a few words of the soldier's language, it was I who stepped forward and spoke to them in their dialect.

"We have no quarrel with you, my friends," I pleaded. "What do you want with us?"

The officer did not reply. The Spanish prisoners were escorted to the Spanish fort. Captain Diego then noticed that the Portuguese flag was now flying over it. During their short absence, the Portuguese had attacked the Spanish fort and imprisoned all of its inhabitants. As they entered the tiny garrison, they noticed that all the Spanish soldiers and crew were huddled in a corner. There weren't more than forty men. Half of them were lying on the ground writhing with fever and chills.

Captain Diego saw Bautista on one side of de Urdaneta. They were both tied up. Fray Nadal was walking among the prisoners trying to assist and comfort them. The Portuguese officer told me to keep the detainees away from the Spanish.

All the captors left except two who stood guard over the new hostages. Captain Diego and we were thirsty and hungry. The inside of the fort had the miasma of a pigsty. There were flies swarming everywhere in the sweltering heat. A flock of black birds sat cawing on the palisades of the fort waiting for their next meal.

In the afternoon, an older gentleman dressed in black and walking with a limp called for the six captives to assemble in the middle of the fort.

"May I present myself, friar," the wrinkled dark-skinned face seemed friendly. "I am Captain Guy Moura. I am here to take you into custody." He spoke perfect Castellano Spanish.

Captain Diego stepped forward and bowed. "Captain, it is a pleasure to make your acquaintance, but may I ask under what authority do you hold us prisoners?"

"You are like the rest of the Spanish here who surrendered without a struggle. Without even a whimper," Moura smirked. "You are prisoners of war."

"But dear captain, you can see that I am not a soldier. I am just a postulant on a Christian mission," Captain Diego spoke gently.

"But we have captured you here at the Spanish fort. How can we believe you?"

"I am not Spanish, my captain. I am from New Spain. I am Aztec," Captain Diego tried to sound sincere. "And you can ask Fray Nadal to verify my religious station." He pointed to the friar walking among the Spanish prisoners.

"This is very strange! But what is this mission from God?" Captain Moura seemed perplexed.

"The Spanish conquistador kidnapped two Aztec Christian women and was going to sell them into slavery. I was sent by my Order to retrieve their holy souls."

"Oh, my God!" the captain said. "This is such a despicable crime against God. But I believe you."

"God bless you, captain," said Captain Diego solemnly.

CHAPTER 50 – THE PACT

Wednesday, July 25, 2018
Guadalajara

The phone rang. It was about 4:30 in the afternoon. Alexi was calling Francisco.

"Hola."

"How are you, querido?" she asked.

"Fine," he replied as he stretched his cramped neck for a moment. "The question is how are you, amorcito? I can only imagine all the things going through your head."

"I haven't seen most of my relatives in years," she said forlornly. "Everybody probably has grandchildren by now."

"Are we going to bring anything?" Francisco asked. "What about flowers?"

"I think I have everything under control," she replied confidently. "I ordered flowers. They will be at the wake tomorrow night."

They talked about tentative arrangements in La Paz. After the funeral, they would try to hang out for a few days alone. Time was getting short for Francisco.

"Oh, before I forget, we have 1:15 flights to La Paz on Volaris Air," she informed him. "Esteban will pick you up at 10:45. It's about a two-hour flight."

"Anything special I should wear? A coat and tie?"

"No need. It's going to be very, very hot!" she told. "And bring your swimming trunks."

Francisco went back to the table after making himself a cup of hot tea with milk and resumed reading the Ismael papers.

June 24, 1528
Tidore, Moluccas

Captain Moura left us, shaking his head as he walked away. We were escorted to another corner of the fort, away from the other Spanish prisoners. We were given a ration of water, bread, and fruit.

Inocente again approached Captain Diego as she had done on the boat ride. "Oh, holy one, once again thank you for saving our lives!" She had spoken in Nahuatl as she grabbed his shirt sleeve.

"You are welcome, Inocente," Captain Diego looked intently at her and replied in their common native tongue. "It was you who sent me the note with the black pearls. Thanks be to God!"

"Yes, to protect Yepyollotli and me," Inocente nodded. "from the evil foreigners. The Spanish and the Portuguese!"

"Who is Yepyollotli?" Captain Diego was confused.

Inocente explained that her ward's real name was "Cihuatlamacazqui" and that she was a priestess to Coyolxāuqui, the Goddess of the Moon. She had been assigned to be the protectress of Yepyollotli, the 17-year-old daughter of the Aztec chief Cacamatzin.

"But those are Aztec names!"

"Yes, she is an Aztec princess," Inocente explained. "She is promised to Coyolxāuqui."

"I thought you were Christians," Captain Diego had a puzzled look on his face.

"We are," replied Inocente. "But we have made vows to the Aztec gods and we must keep them."

"What vows?"

"Yepyollotli is the promised sacrifice to Coyolxāuqui."

Just then two Portuguese soldiers interrupted Captain Diego. They were there to escort him and myself to Captain de Urdaneta's old office. The others were to remain behind. As the four of us walked, the sun was hot overhead and there was an overpowering stench coming from rotting food, human excrement, and dying bodies.

We entered the office and Captain Moura dismissed the two soldiers. The pair exited and closed the makeshift wooden door.

"Well, gentlemen, I would offer you a glass of wine," the captain began, "but this shithole has less provisions then any favela I have ever seen. No decent food. No Spanish wine even though I prefer our own Portuguese. The men here are one step from death. These Spanish cowards surrendered without an ounce of resistance. If they were my men, I might have them shot for dereliction of duty. But on the other hand, I understand fado, fate. What am I going to do with these unfortunate souls? What am I going to do with you?"

He spoke for a few minutes and then paused. He asked Captain Diego, "What would you do if you were me?"

"My captain, my Spanish is nowhere near as good as yours. I think I understood most of what you said. My native language is Nahuatl," Captain Diego needed time to think. "But Ismael is fluent in many languages, including Portuguese and Spanish. As I have mentioned before, we are not Peninsulares. We were not born in Spain. I think God will show us the way."

"Ah, Captain Diego, you speak like a Jesuit," Moura laughed. "I lived in Salamanca as a child and was destined for the priesthood. The wars came and I was recruited into the Portuguese navy. I have been with them ever since. No wife. No children. It's been a lonely life, but I have faithfully served my king."

They had a friendly conversation sharing stories. Everyone was amazed at the tales that were being told.

"Captain, if I can be so bold and ask a favor," Captain Diego had a serious look. "Would you allow Fray Nadal to say prayers tomorrow for everyone?"

"It would be my duty to do so," Captain Moura replied.

"God bless you!" Captain Diego said.

The next morning the Spanish prisoners, some of Portuguese soldiers, and Captain Diego's party were praying with Friar Nadal. Afterwards, Captain Diego and I discussed our situation.

"Captain Moura is conflicted, Captain Diego," I counseled. "He is foremost a soldier and very loyal to the Portuguese. On the hand, he is a very decent man. And I think a real Christian at heart. He is torn."

"Well, it seems that Moura must fulfill his duty first," Captain Diego replied. "Like I must fulfill my promise to God to return the two women to Friar Moreno. It seems that one of us has to win and the other lose."

"But that is just it, Captain Diego!" I was excited. "What if both parties won?"

In the late afternoon, the same two Portuguese soldiers fetched Captain Diego and me. We were taken to Captain Moura's new office.

"Well, gentlemen, I hope that you are comfortable," Moura was trying to be accommodating. "I thought the religious service was very well received by the men. I think I will have Fray Nadal offer a daily prayer. It will keep the men's spirits up. I apologize for the lack of food, but our supplies are very low. The Spanish have only garbage in their pantries."

"Unfortunately, captain, since these men are your prisoners, you must feed them," Captain Diego was repeating the plan that he and I had worked out. "And of course, the women have special needs."

Captain Moura was getting uncomfortable in his chair. "There is no food here to give. My own men are complaining." He knew that he had said too much.

"Well, maybe your prisoners should be transferred to your fort in Ternate," Captain Diego suggested. "Then they would be your commander's problem and your men would not be wasting their time here."

"My commander would be furious!" Moura's face was reddening. "These prisoners are flea-ridden and are rotting away! They can't be sent there!"

"But it is your duty as a soldier and as a Christian, to provide for them," Captain Diego warned. "You can't set them free."

"Oh, yes, I can!" the captain had fallen for the bait.

In the end, the captain agreed to free the Spanish prisoners on the condition that each would swear an oath not to attack the Portuguese. Any

Portuguese sailor under Captain de Urdaneta or from the Espíritu Santo could depart with us back to New Spain.

Captain Diego had been given permission to leave Tidore with the two women on the Santiago. He was allowed to appoint Bautista as his chief mate and to take most of his old crew. New Spaniards from de Urdaneta's crew on the Espíritu Santo were added. I would, of course, be his right-hand man.

After a week of preparation, the Santiago was ready to sail. Captain Diego met Captain Moura on the beach.

"When do you leave, Captain?" Captain Diego asked Moura, who would be returning to Ternate with a few more Portuguese.

"Tomorrow or the next day," Moura said. "I think the Lord works in mysterious ways. You have been my salvation. I can't imagine being stuck in this dung heap much longer."

"I want to thank you for the extra provisions," Captain Diego said. He had found several dozen bags of spices on the Santiago.

"Don't thank me," Moura said. "Thank Chief Pattimura and Captain de Urdaneta."

Moura also informed Captain Diego that De Urdaneta and Fray Nadal had decided to stay with their men at the Spanish fort. "Godspeed, Captain Diego," Moura shook Captain Diego's hand. "And may God protect you!"

At this point Captain Diego handed Moura a leather bag. It was heavy. Moura frowned as he looked inside. In it were pieces of gold and a black pearl necklace.

"Please accept these as recompense for your kindness."

CHAPTER 51 – HOMEWARD BOUND

Thursday, July 26, 2018
La Paz

The alarm went off at six a.m. Francisco wanted to finish Ismael's notes before he went to La Paz with Alexi. He knew that she would be in mourning and have many family obligations. He felt her pain. He also did not want to be reading or doing work on "their" time. Francisco was leaving soon, and he wanted to make the best of it for both of them. He was really enamored with her.

Francisco picked up the last dozen pages of Ismael's notes and began reading them:

June 26, 1528
Santiago #2

The Santiago left Tidore sailing under favorable winds. Our provisions were meager. We would have to island hop and procure more food and water on the way. Monixo was now in charge of steering the ship. Bautista had the advantage of having the charts that they had used on their westward journey to the Moluccas.

María Del Rosario and Inocente were given the captain's cabin. Captain Diego and I shared other cramped quarters with the Chief Mate Bautista. Captain Diego checked on the women on a daily basis, normally conversing with Inocente.

María Del Rosario always seemed to be kneeling on a cushion in front of the black pearl rosary hanging from the cabin wall. Back on Tidore, she had readily surrendered her black pearl necklace as ransom for herself and the crew.

But today Inocente had gone to see the cook to see if there was any cacao beans or other foods that the two women could eat. Captain Diego knocked on the door as was his custom. He entered and saw María Del Rosario all alone. Normally, she would continue praying when he was in the room. But today was different. She sensed him in the room, and she turned around.

"Good morning, Fray Diego," she spoke in Nahuatl, her black eyes piercing the young man's soul. She bowed her head.

"Good morning, señorita. How is everything?" He was hesitant around her. "Do you need anything?"

"No, thank you," she slowly raised her head. He could see her cinnamon skin and raven hair accented by her ruby lips.

"Señorita, I am not a friar yet," he tried to explain. "I am trying to become one, God willing."

"Thank you for saving us," she said softly. "I remember you from the church in Zacatula. You are a Godsent."

"It wasn't me," he said nervously, remembering the first time he saw her in the church taking Communion. "It was Friar Moreno who sent me." There was a shudder throughout his body.

"Thank God for whomever," she replied.

Thereafter, whenever Captain Diego came into the cabin, both Inocente and María Del Rosario would converse with him and even laugh at times.

A few weeks later, we needed to replenish our supplies. Bautista, Captain Diego, and I discussed what we should do. We did not want to return to the island of the cannibals. Moreover, we feared that the neighboring islands would have similar practices. We set course for south southeast. We spotted land after two days. It seemed to be a land onto itself. We dropped anchor at a white sandy beach. A rowboat was sent out with four sailors. Two were armed. Upon landing, the small group explored the jungle foliage that jutted out to the beach. There were no signs of any inhabitants.

By the next day, the crew from our ship was camped under the banana leaf canopy at the jungle's edge. The water was clear and had the color of aqua blue, like the skies. The sailors easily caught brightly colored fish and harvested shrimp, crabs, and oysters. The men had feasts on the beach every day. They were happy, but there was no rum or wine to be had.

The exploration parties into the jungle found colorful birds singing and squawking amongst the papaya and mango trees. They spotted strange animals that looked like miniature bears. They also saw large hopping creatures with big feet, a long tail, and a small head. Monixo thought they were big rabbits while others argued that they were giant rats.

At night it rained and rained. The shelters were minimally effective, but by morning the intense heat had dried everything. Captain Diego and Bautista had learned their lesson and had a watch posted every night along with big bonfires.

One morning as some of the men were fishing in shallow waters using cutoff fish heads as bait, a couple of long, log shaped creatures slunk slowly toward the sailors. Fortunately, Iriño who had been washing his clothes spotted them.

"Crocodiles!" he cried out. The sailors rushed to shore.

That night the men feasted on grilled crocodile. Moreover, Iriño had skinned the poor beast and was now drying the skin. He was thinking about a new pair of boots.

After restocking the ship with food and fresh water, the Santiago set sail again in a north, northeasterly direction. For the next few days, we spotted hundreds of islands and atolls on the port side. And then one day, the Santiago scraped on a partially submerge coral reef. Monixo inspected the hull of the ship and found only superficial scratches.

Storms began to hit. Monixo did not know if it was the beginning of the rainy season or their northern latitude. The lightness of the ship made it rock back and forth, and side to side.

Captain Diego seemed to visit María Del Rosario more often, inquiring about her status. He lingered longer and longer every day, talking with the young girl. She did not complain. She seemed to like his company. Inocente feigned looking away. She knew that Captain Diego would not mean her any harm.

August 1528

It is now in the middle of August and the Santiago is approaching a set of islands when a commotion started between Monixo and a Spanish sailor named Trinidad Pacheco.

"What's going on?" demanded Herrera, not happy about the feud.

"He says he knows those islands," Monixo pointed to the isles in front of them. "He was with the Espíritu Santo that put in for repairs there."

"Is he sure?"

"Says they spent a month there. Says good place for supplies."

A while later after consulting with Captain Diego, the Santiago made way for the islands. Trinidad was assisting Monixo with the navigation.

The next week was filled with rest and relaxation. There were no inhabitants on the island. The food was plentiful. Trinidad sat around the bonfire each night telling tales about the Espiritu Santo and their docking on this island. During the day he showed them remnants of old rigging, areas where they cut down trees, and good fishing spots they had found.

After three days of solid rain, we set off on our last leg back to Zihuatanejo. During this time Captain Diego spent a lot more time with Maria Del Rosario.

Captain Diego shared with me his confusion about his own personal life and his soul. He prayed every night, but his heart and soul were heavy. One night he started asking me questions.

"Ismael, I have dedicated myself to becoming a friar and serving the King of Spain," Captain Diego began. "But I have witnessed unjust killings and sinful behavior. I have received mercy and kindness from a sworn enemy of Spain. I don't know if I am making the right decision. Is this God's Will?"

"Captain Diego, I see how you look at her. It is only natural. God gives us these feelings," I said softly. "Do not be ashamed. Do not deny them."

Captain Diego was surprised that I had penetrated his inner being. Yes, he felt something for Maria. What was it? Was he was supposed act on it? And if so, how?

"Ismael, have you ever been married?"

"Yes," I closed my eyes and let my head fall downward. I was sad. Captain Diego sensed my sorrow.

"What happened?" Captain Diego asked.

"She was killed by the Spanish Inquisition."

CHAPTER 52 – SABOTAGE

Thursday, July 26, 2018
La Paz

Francisco put down Ismael's papers. He only had a few pages to go. He ran downstairs and rushed through his breakfast. He came back to his room and threw an extra set of underwear into his bag.

He checked his emails and wrote some quick replies. Miranda knew that he was not coming back into town until Monday.

Francisco had just over an hour until Esteban and Alexi would pick him up to take him to the airport. Francisco picked up the last few pages. He continued reading:

September 1528
Santiago #2

Captain Diego and María became closer and closer. She would stop her praying anytime he arrived. Inocente would then leave the cabin.

After about three weeks, Bautista came to Captain Diego with some troubling news. "Monixo says that we are off course," the chief mate informed Captain Diego. "He thinks we are too far north."

"How can this be?" Captain Diego asked. "Tonight, we'll check the stars and the moon. Speak of this to no one."

"Should we change our course?"

"Not yet."

That night Bautista and Captain Diego went on deck and took readings with the sextant. They concluded that we were going more northward than we had planned. They speculated about what could have caused the misdirection. Maybe it was the direction of the wind or the type of ocean current.

The next morning, we met with Monixo who was at the steering wheel and tried to calculate the corrective course. Bautista went over to the wooden binnacle that housed the ship's compass. He flicked it with his middle finger to see if it was stuck. Then he decided to inspect it. He removed it. As he did so, a sack fell to the ground.

"What is this?" cried out Bautista. He opened the bag and found metal shavings. "God in Heaven! These look like iron shavings!" He brought out his dagger and placed it inside the bag. As he pulled it out, hundreds of metal slivers stuck to the knife.

Bautista called out, "someone has tried to sabotage our compass!"

"Why would anyone want to do that?" Captain Diego asked, but no one knew the answer. Monixo and Bautista set the new course. Captain Diego and I discussed the possibility of a complete inspection of the ship but then decided not to. Who knew when the sabotage had occurred? It could have been months ago. Captain Diego told Bautista that we would do nightly reckoning with the sextant.

For the next two weeks, everybody aboard the ship seemed to be getting along. Captain Diego did not notice any grumbling.

Captain Diego and Maria Del Rosario talked more seriously now. She had accepted Captain Diego as her protector. Inocente was often gone, and Maria Del Rosario wanted to speak freely.

"Fray Diego, I do not want be the Aztec princess that must be sacrificed to Coyolxāuqui," she still called him friar.

"Tell me again, who is Coyolxāuqui?" Captain Diego vaguely remembered this name being mentioned by his father, an Aztec scribe.

"She is the Moon goddess," Maria explained. "I was promised to her. So, I must be sacrificed to her."

"But you're a Christian now," Captain Diego was a little disturbed. "We don't allow human sacrifice."

"But didn't Christ die for his people?"

"Yes, but that was different," Captain Diego countered. He didn't know why it was different, and this was one of the things he didn't understand about the Catholic faith. "Father Moreno will be able to explain this better when we get back to Zacatula. He will be very happy to see you again."

"Diego, all I want is to have a family of my own," her black eyes looked directly at him, causing him to blush. Suddenly, she began to cry softly. Captain Diego was astounded to see that as the tears rolled down her cheeks, they turned into black pearls that landed gently on her lap.

How can that be? "You are crying black pearls!" Captain Diego exclaimed.

Maria Del Rosario quickly dried her eyes and said, "Very few people know. Please promise me that you will tell no one. I will share my secret with you. I was a little girl when my mother died. When I cried for her loss, I began crying black pearls. One night my mother came to me in a dream. She told me that crying black pearls was her gift to me. She said that I had to collect them and that someday they would save my life. Please keep my secret safe."

"I promise," Captain Diego replied quietly.

The next day Captain Diego met with Bautista and Monixo. Everything was going smoothly. The Santiago was on course.

On Friday Iriño ran up to Bautista.

"Come quickly!" the sailor prompted the chief mate. "I have found something very suspicious!"

Bautista, with his right hand on the hilt of his sword, followed the sailor to a forward cargo hold.

"Look!" Iriño shouted, pointing to a large spill of tar pitch on the wooden floorboards. "This is dangerous if it catches on fire!"

Bautista stuck his finger into the black resin and brought it back up to his nose. He nodded in agreement with Iriño. He looked around the entire storage area. No barrels seemed spilled over or leaking. The pitch tar was only used to make repairs and plug up holes in the hull.

"Señor, I think I see a footprint near the edge," Iriño pointed out the spot to the chief mate. They both stepped closer. Indeed, there was a barefoot mark. The chief mate went back on deck and ordered a few men to clean up the mess. He did not want the ship accidently or intentionally catching on fire.

"That will be hard to get off his foot," Bautista pondered for the remainder of the day, Bautista went up to every crewman and ordered him to show his feet. He was bewildered.

Iriño was one of the men trusted with bringing food to Maria Del Rosario and Inocente. That afternoon as he was picking up the viands for the women, he noticed tar pitch prints on the galley floor boards.

"Let me see your feet!" screamed Iriño to the old Spanish cook who served under Captain Urdaneta in Tidore.

The eyes of the wizened man opened with fright. He stepped back. He lifted his feet, but there was nothing except regular food grime.

Iriño left with the food and delivered it to the women. Captain Diego and I were present, and he related to us the incident with the black resin. Captain Diego was concerned, and we made our way back to the galley picking up Bautista on the way.

The four of us stood in front of the cook. The old man was physically agitated. None of us had known him before this voyage. He had been one of Captain de Urdaneta's men and wanted to go home.

"Where did these footprints come from?" growled Bautista approaching Gonçalo, the old cook. The man shook his head.

"I don't have time for this!" Bautista shouted as he grabbed the man by the throat. The other three were mortified by the chief mate's behavior but said nothing. Then the cook raised his right arm weakly as he was trying to breath. He pointed to a narrow pantry door where foodstuffs were stored. Iriño threw open the door and in the narrow area there were many more tar pitch prints, a makeshift chamber pot, and a piece of crumbly hard tack.

"Explain this!" yelled Bautista still grasping the cook by the throat.

The old man gasped for air as he was let go. After a minute, he confessed that a Portuguese sailor who had stowed away was going to pay him two pieces of eight to let him hide there.

"Where is the man now?" Bautista barked.

The old man shrugged. He didn't know.

"Where are the coins?"

"He didn't pay me," the man was shaking. "He was going to pay me when we landed."

Bautista shook his head. This man was such a fool.

"Iriño, lock up this traitor," Bautista turned his back. "I haven't decided whether to give him ten lashes or maroon him on the next island.

Nobody said anything as we left the galley. For the remainder of the day, we searched the ship from bow to stern but did not find the stowaway. In the meantime, a young Basque sailor was drafted to be the new cook.

CHAPTER 53 – THE ATTACK

October 1528
Santiago #2

The cold wind was blowing fiercely and pushing Captain Diego off balance as he tried to pull himself steady on the bow.

"Well, Bautista, do you think we can make land within the next seven days?" the captain asked his first mate. Captain Diego knew that if the answer was negative, we would all be dead by the end of the month.

Too many tragedies on this expedition! No food. No water. And moreover, a traitor lurking amongst us. Captain Diego had experienced all of this after he had set sail from the Moluccas. The emaciated crew were mostly Spanish with a few Portuguese thrown in. Now they were all walking skeletons.

"Captain, those black clouds on the horizon bode of another terrible storm," Bautista remarked as the two looked out to the northeast. "I still haven't smelled land yet."

The gale increased and the ship staggered forward. Bautista ordered the sails to be stowed except for the topsails. Iriño was getting pots and pans ready to catch the rainwater. That would be a blessing, thought Diego. How many days from home? He asked himself.

The ocean swells seemed to be getting angrier and angrier. Please, God, deliver my charge to Friar Moreno safe and sound, Diego prayed.

The captain was starving. The crew was on half rations. He was used to it as were his men. The women passengers had been stoic and did not complain.

In the meantime, the helmsman, Monixo, checked the compass and made a two-degree correction northeast to account for the wind. Well, we'll see. Wherever the storm takes us. He checked the sails. They were trimmed. He was prepared to secure the wheel if and when the time came to do so. Monixo pulled his sweater tighter. His whole body ached. He was tired down to the bone.

Diego knew that half the men had scurvy. They were spitting up blood and loose teeth. Their bulging eyes cried out for getting to Mexico on one piece.

Meanwhile, I made my way to see Captain Diego. "Señor, the women are secured," I shouted loudly as the wind picked up and was howling. "The young one is still praying."

"I'm going below to check," the captain quickly pulled away. "Go see if Bautista needs anything."

"Yes, sir."

Captain Diego rushed starboard to his own cabin where the two women had taken refuge. He unlocked his own cabin door and entered the low-beamed room. A young woman was kneeling as usual, facing the black pearl rosary mounted on the wall.

The older woman nodded at Captain Diego but did not speak. "I need to sleep," he told her. "Wake me up in five minutes." He took off his jacket and climbed on top of the bed being still fully clothed.

The ship was listing when he woke up. He had slept two hours. Maria Del Rosario was staring down at him as she sat by his side.

"Why didn't someone wake me?!" Captain Diego was peeved but knew that he had needed the sleep. And he knew that he could never be angry at Maria.

He was getting up when he thought he heard a loud cry from above. He grabbed his jacket and rushed out the door, quickly locking it after him. On deck he saw three sailors carrying a body to the middle of the ship.

"Sir, we lost Omar. He was very weak. Should we have a service for him?" asked one of the crew. "The seas are too rough to do much."

Captain Diego approached the corpse and the crew stepped back with their heads bowed. He said a quick prayer and made the sign of the cross over the dead man.

"Throw him overboard," the captain ordered. "We don't have time to give him a proper service. May God have mercy on his soul."

For the next few hours, the storm pelted the ship without giving quarter. The ship Santiago was turned broadside to the wind and bore the full brunt of the gigantic waves. Bautista was yelling out orders. "Go help the helmsman!" he barked.

Men were slipping and sliding on deck. The waves were washing the deck of anything that was not secure. Monixo, with the help of a crewman, was trying to swing the Santiago starboard to minimize the foamy onslaughts.

The torrential rains were lashing the men. Time and time again a man would slip, only to save himself in a frenzy. The gales were wailing and the ship dipped under the waters and then recovered.

The rigging from one of the masts fell onto the deck crushing a sailor. Another crewman was washed overboard trying to rescue him.

The storm lasted halfway through the night and finally the seas were put to rest by early morning.

Thank you, God, for Your mercy, Captain Diego said a prayer. Hopefully, our crew had caught some rainwater to quench their thirst. Could they survive another week without food? What if it turned out to be more than seven days?! This would be a ghost ship.

After the terrible storm, the Santiago had caught favorable currents and the weather was fair for the next few days.

"Land ahoy!" Monixo yelled out at the top of his lungs. Everybody on ship went to the bow and looked ahead. Squawking seagulls were coming out to greet us. There was yelling and screaming amongst the crew.

"I think we should get close to the shore by midnight and then lay anchor," Bautista informed Monixo. "This night we'll stay aboard and tomorrow we can go ashore. The captain and I will take a reckoning tonight."

The men were overjoyed. In the late evening Captain Diego, Bautista, and I took some celestial readings from the heavens. The chief mate estimated that our latitude was between 24 and 26 degrees and our longitude was 112 degrees west. The Santiago was speeding along in a windward direction and Bautista ordered one of the two sails lowered. It was approaching midnight and the ship was quiet.

"Fire in the galley!" suddenly came a scream. The crew was roused. The flames licked the deck. Bautista was yelling out orders. Should we try to make it to land? Probably not, he thought. Too far. Should we drop anchor and try to put out the fire. Probably not, too risky if we fail.

"Get ready to drop one of the boats over the side!" he commanded. There was total confusion on deck. Some men were trying to pull down the second sail, while others were trying to put out the fire. Sparks drifted up from the galley.

Captain Diego and I ran to his cabin to make sure María Del Rosario and Inocente were safe. We heard a sharp scream and we broke into the quarters. Rodrigo had a knife at María Del Rosario' throat. He saw Captain Diego and me storm in.

"Stay away!" he yelled in Portuguese. "You have cost me my fortune. I'm going to get it back."

Captain Diego tried to rush Rodrigo but received a kick in the balls for his effort. He fell to the ground. He was no match for this ruffian.

"Oh, Diego!" María Del Rosario clenched her black pearl rosary and tried to pull away from Rodrigo. But he yanked her back forcibly. This distraction allowed time for Inocente to charge Rodrigo and jump on his back. Rodrigo whirled around and slashed into Inocente's chest. She staggered and dropped to the floor.

María Del Rosario now had three feet of separation between Rodrigo and herself. Rodrigo slowly moved forward toward her and tried to grab her.

She held the rosary tightly and closed her eyes. She muttered a prayer. Then she opened her eyes and to Rodrigo's surprise, grabbed both of his arms. Her eyes had turned red as she stared at him. Her pearls threw out fiery red bursts toward him. Rodrigo's flesh started to blister and emit steam. Then came the putrid smell of sulphur *emanating from his body. His veins began to bulge. He started to vomit boiling black blood. Rodrigo was writhing in extreme pain. She let go of his arms. Rodrigo tumbled to the ground dying, next to the corpse of Inocente.*

. . .

Thursday, July 26, 2018
La Paz

Francisco was a few minutes late running out of the faculty housing. He had finished Ismael's papers, but was somewhat puzzled by the incomplete records. *Damn!* There were no further records after Rodrigo's attack on María Del Rosario. Francisco felt a combination of shock, anger, and disappointment. *Had Ismael died during the ship's fire? Were some of his papers lost? What happened to Diego and María Del Rosario? He had a hundred questions. If there were no more Ismael papers, the project could not use any of these materials as corroboration.*

¡Qué cabron! Son of a bitch! Really bad luck!

Alexi gave Francisco a big hug and kiss as he slid into the car. Esteban put his luggage into the trunk.

"Did you miss me, amorcito?" she held his head in both of her hands.

He turned toward her and gave her a wet, passionate kiss. All of his troubled thoughts vanished.

At the airport, Esteban let an older baggage handler take the bags to the check-in counter.

"Thank you, Esteban," Alexi said. "See you on Sunday. You have the phone number of the hotel."

They had plenty of time before their flight and decided to eat a light lunch at the Fruty Lonch at the airport. The little restaurant had a dozen colorful Mylar balloons hanging from the ceiling. The smell of Mexican food overwhelmed their senses. She ordered a chicken taco salad and Francisco ordered chiles rellenos.

"Is there anything I should do, mi amor?" asked Francisco. He was concerned about how to act properly at a Mexican wake.

"Just be yourself," she stroked his hand.

The flight took off on time. It was going to be a two-hour flight. Francisco was proud of himself for finishing Ismael's papers, even though he was frustrated that they were incomplete. He could now devote all his attention to Alexi, rather than to his work.

The flight attendant came by and Alexi ordered a mineral water. He ordered a Corona. They were given warm, wet scented cloths to wipe their hands.

"Amorcito, I hope you don't mind," Alexi said innocently enough. "if I read my medical journals. I need to catch up."

"No problem." *So much for quality time,* he thought. He closed his eyes and soon fell asleep, missing a snack.

They landed on time at the Manuel Márquez de León International Airport. There was an hour time zone change. After retrieving their luggage, they went to a small car rental counter outside of baggage claim. Alexi claimed a black Chevy Suburban. She knew that area and drove straight to the Casa Kootenay Hotel on the waterfront in La Paz.

CHAPTER 54 – R.I.P.

Thursday, July 26, 2018
La Paz

The Casa Kootenay Hotel was pure five-star luxury. Francisco and Alexi had a bay view from their room and a comfortable terraza overlooking the hotel pool. The cool breeze floated through their mini suite. There was a fresh bouquet of red and white flowers on the salon table.

"Querido, the wake starts at eight," Alexi was lying next to him on the king size bed that had a colorful indigenous style coverlet. "We should probably leave here about 7:30. We can walk to the cathedral from here."

At about a quarter to seven Alexi started to get ready. She was wearing a black silk pant suit with a lavender scarf complementing her black pearl earrings. Francisco only needed fifteen minutes to change into his burgundy guayabera and black slacks.

They arrived at the church at five minutes after eight. People of all shapes, sizes, and ages greeted Alexi. Aunts, cousins, friends, and neighbors were all present. Most of the people were short and looked indigenous with big black eyes.

"Francisco, I want you to meet my Tía Chucha . . ."

He was overwhelmed by the number of people in attendance. He couldn't remember any one's name or their exact relationship to Alexi.

Padre Porras approached the closed casket, muttered a prayer, and then made the sign of the Cross over the casket that had white lilies laying on top. There was the scent of incense permeating the church as the priest began to say the rosary. The audience joined in the prayer.

After the visitation was over, the audience dispersed. Alexi talked to her aunt and told her that they would see her the following day at the funeral.

As they started walking back to the hotel, Alexi detoured to the right. They walked two blocks and stopped in front of a jewelry store named "Cihuapilli."

"What's this?" Francisco was curious. "What does the name mean?"

"'Princess Jewels is our family-owned business," Alexi pressed herself against Francisco. "It's been here for ages. Are you hungry?"

They walked down to the beach and sat at an outdoor table at La Bestia Restaurant. The waves were pounding softly onto the shore. Alexi had her customary mineral water and lime; Francisco had an ice-cold beer. The moon looked bigger than ever and had a reddish-orange tinge.

They both ordered the grilled fish of the day. It was dorado in a mango salsa. A three-person mariachi group came up to the table.

"Por Mujeres Come Tú" was Francisco's first request.

> *Me estoy acobardando y lo ha notado*
> *Y eso no es muy bueno para mí*
> *Si quiero retenerla entre mis brazos*
> *Será mejor que no me vea sufrir . . .*

He looked deeply into her dark eyes and she reciprocated.

He held her hands tightly. She leaned over and kissed him.

When the trio finished, she asked for "Amorcito Corazón."

> *Amorcito corazón*
> *Yo tengo tentación de un beso*
> *Que se brinda en el calor*
> *De nuestro gran amor, mi amor . . .*

Heat was rising. She took a swig of her water. He inhaled his beer.

"Okay, what song is ours?" she asked him. She half-expected that he would be flabbergasted by her dropping this on him. Instead, he had been thinking about this moment since the day he met her. He knew the answer.

"Señores, 'Sabor a Mí,' please."

Tanto tiempo disfrutamos de este amor
Nuestras almas se acercaron, tanto así
Que yo guardo tu sabor
Pero tú llevas también
Sabor a mí . . .

After the beautiful song was over, Francisco slipped ten dollars into the hand of violinist. With perfect timing, Pepe, the waiter, arrived with their grilled fish dinners. The meal was delicious, but Francisco and Alexi were in an alternative reality.

Pepe came by and collected the empty dishes. "Any desserts?"

Francisco nodded his head no. But Alexi asked for the dessert menu. Pepe brought her one. She perused it.

"We'll take a piece of the chocolate toffee cake to go, please," she said with an attitude. "and the check."

Friday morning came in a blink of an eye. Alexi and Francisco had to sit in the back pews of the church because they had come in five minutes late. Padre Porras had begun the funeral mass. The casket was at the front of the church that was filled with thousands of sweet smelling flower bouquets.

There was singing from a small group of nuns dressed in black, joined in by the mourners. For the gospel, the priest read

The Black Pearl

Psalm 23, "I will fear no evil: for thou art with me; thy rod and thy staff they comfort me . . ."

At Communion time, most of the people took the host. Alexi and Francisco did not. The funeral ended with Padre Porras paying homage to the deceased.

"Señora Ofelia Cruz was blessed with the gift of life for 95 years. Unfortunately, all six of her children predeceased her . . ."

It was almost eleven o'clock when the service was over. As they exited the cathedral, Alexi's oldest aunt, Virgie, came over to greet her. Francisco was introduced.

"Are you going to stay for the reception, mija?" the older women with long silver grey hair asked.

"Of course, tía!" Alexi smiled. No chance of sneaking out now. Alexi felt obligated to stay anyway because Tía Virgie was the organized one of the sisters. She ran the jewelry business for the family.

The parish hall was next door to the cathedral and the food was buffet style. Francisco was not shy and filled his paper plate with a chicken taco, carne asada taco, rice, and beans. Hibiscus agua fresca was the offered beverage. Youngsters swarmed through the hall, running here and there. Alexi sat at a long table with two of her aunts. Tía Amaryllis was there with her two sons, Gordo and Chato. This aunt was the teaser of the family and resided in Rosarito Beach, between Tijuana and Ensenada. Equally as bad, was the other aunt, Tía Armida, who was always telling risqué jokes. Her son Joselito was with her. She lived in Loreto.

The conversation between the aunts and Alexi was fast and furious. To say the tias were nosey would be an understatement.

"He's good looking. Are you thinking about remarrying? You deserve it."

"Are you going to the States?"

"What's your papi chulo like to do for fun?"

An hour later, Alexi and Francisco were walking back to their hotel.

"My aunts are such metiches!"

"I like them," Francisco smiled. "They're kind of cool. I don't think they're busybodies."

"We need to get out of here!" she was shaking her head. "I think I know just the place."

CHAPTER 55 – LUNAR ECLIPSE

Friday, July 27, 2018
Todos Santos

An hour later Francisco and Alexi were speeding through the Sonoran Desert part of Baja California in the Chevy Suburban. The air conditioning was cracked up to maximum. Even with a blackout windshield the sun penetrated the car's interior. They had brought along several liters of bottled water.

"My parents used to bring me down to the beach at Todos Santos when I was a child," Alexi reminisced. "I have good memories."

They had changed out of their funeral garb into shorts and tee shirts, plus one big sun hat for Alexi. It was nearly four o'clock in the afternoon when they finally reached the sandy beach. The azure blue waves were breaking at about three feet. There was a slight offshore breeze. The seagulls and frigatebirds were flying in formations circling overhead.

The couple threw down some oversized towels that they had borrowed from their hotel. The beach was almost isolated. There were a few serious surfers about a half mile to the north.

Francisco and Alexi laid down. The sun was beating down on them. Beads of sweat formed on their bodies.

"Ready for a swim?" she asked, after about ten minutes.

The water was shallow and clear. They waded up to their chests. He gently took her into his arms, and they melted into each other. Passionate kissing. Every once in a while, a wave would try to knock them down. The egret ignored them as it flew over.

They slowly got out of the water and dried themselves off. Their mouths were salty from the sea water. She had brought a book, but it was too difficult to read with the bright light. He closed his eyes and was going to take a nap.

"Are you ready for our walk?" she was telling him, not asking. "There is a little chapel down south of here. I used to play there with my cousins when I was a child."

"Are we going to leave our things here?" he asked.

"Sure, nobody is around," she said nonchalantly. "and there is nothing to take."

Alexi grabbed two one-liter water bottles and put them into her sarape bag. Francisco took it from her and threw it over his shoulder. The pair started walking, hand-in-hand, in a southerly direction down the sandy beach. Francisco could distinguish a promontory about a mile down the beach. It looked like it had a small church on it. They made footprints in the sand as they passed broken seashells, small eviscerated crabs, and pebbles of all shapes, colors, and sizes.

"Francisco, thank you for spending time with me," Alexi looked at him tenderly. "These have been such wonderful times."

"Mi amor, you have been the best," he was getting emotional. "I wish I didn't have to leave you."

"Like I said, twenty minutes or twenty years. Let's just live for the present."

They saw sandpipers squawking at each other as they strolled. The cool water and sand tingled their feet. The salt air seemed to be getting more intense. A hot wind from the west started to pick up. The bluish-green waves started to crest with white foam. Grey clouds started to move in from the horizon. The sun seemed to be turning a reddish orange.

"The weather is changing," Francisco said casually.

"It's always hot," Alexi laughed. "But I hear that there is a lunar eclipse today."

"Maybe that is why the sun is so angry," he laughed.

A flight of black cormorants retreated from the sea. Only one long-nosed curlew persevered looking for its next meal. The wind was getting stronger.

They finally reached the end of the beach and took swigs of water. They sighted the chapel that was atop the little promontory. There were dozens and dozens of slippery stone steps that the pair negotiated upwards. He held her hand to steady her.

The chapel was an old weather-beaten adobe-wooden structure overlooking the crashing waves, ninety feet below. The original exterior color of the chapel was hard to discern. The outside looked like it had been given a Frankenstein makeover.

They sat on a solid piece of stone carved in the form of the ancient Aztec god, Chac Mool. The air was fresh and clean, although a breeze was picking up. They drank more water and ate amaranth snacks. *I should have brought some wine,* he thought.

"I could live here forever," Francisco sighed.

"Me, too," echoed Alexi.

They remained silent and saw the sun set. They could see that the tide was coming in.

"Francisco, it's eight o'clock. Maybe we should go back."

"Sure, but how about five more minutes of paradise?"

She smiled.

"Where is all that moaning coming from?" Francisco noticed the howling starting to increase.

"Some say it is from the empty caverns of the Aztec pyramid that this chapel is built on." Alexi shivered as though she was getting cold. "Others say it is an Aztec man looking for his lost love."

"Maybe we should see the lunar eclipse," Francisco suggested. "I have never seen one before."

"Twenty minutes or twenty years," she nodded her head. "This will be a once in a lifetime experience.

The full moon came into view. The ocean became agitated. Little by little a shadow began to mask the moon.

"This is so cool!" Francisco exclaimed.

Alexi pulled herself closer to him. He noticed her shivering next to him.

"Alexi, you feel cold!" he said. "Let's go inside for a few minutes."

Neither one of them had a jacket. He was only wearing a tee shirt.

Alexi walked into the twenty by thirty dank room and made her way to a dilapidated altar with an old wooden statue of the Virgin Mary. A small amount of light came in from the glassless skylight holes in the walls and ceiling. The paint had peeled off years before. There were no fresh flowers. But Alexi spotted an old votive candle and lit one after three attempts.

"We used to play hide and seek in here," Alexi was smiling as she recalled her childhood days. "Our parents would get so mad at us."

"What is this place called?" Francisco asked curiously.

"La Capilla del Santo Rosario."

They walked around the tiny chapel and noticed the faded-out paintings. They looked like saints, but one could not tell.

"I think there are some stairs over to the right," Alexi grabbed his hand to lead him. "This is where I used to hide."

The room seemed to be getting darker. They could hear the wind howling outside. Alexi led them to an iron gate that led downstairs. They slowly navigated the steps with Alexi holding the candle in front of her. Faint rays of light filtered through the tiny open windows adjacent to the stairwell. Most of the openings were covered with green plastic. The splintery wooden stairs turned into jagged rock stairs. Finally, they reached a small downstairs room that was cluttered with old relics, furniture, and pictures.

"I thought there was a tomb here," Alexi was frowning as she pointed to the back room. "That's what I remember."

Francisco found some old liturgical vessels, a chalice, and some cruets. Alexi found an old rusted altar bell and shook it. It gave off a clunky ring.

They both laughed. "Just trying to wake up the dead," she said.

Francisco and Alexi slowly wandered off in different directions in the room. She kept the candle. He moved about in the semi-darkness.

She opened up some cabinets and some drawers. Dust flew up from old papers. There was a musty smell. Then they heard the sound of thunder from outside the chapel. The room was almost pitch black.

"Mi amor, are you ready to go back?" She yelled out. "I think there may be a storm coming." There seemed to be a slight tremor in her voice.

Her question was met only with silence.

"Francisco, where are you?" Alexi shouted in a frightened voice.

CHAPTER 56 – THE ROSARY

Friday, July 27, 2018
Todos Santos

Francisco was dazed as he sat in a pool of water in a dark cavern with three tiny peep holes on a wall providing the dimmest light. His body was in a crumpled position. His left shoulder was bent forward, and he was experiencing excruciating pain. There was a big gash on his forehead. Hot liquid was trickling down his face. His eyes were blurry, and he faded between consciousness and a stupor. He felt sand under the water. He tried to get up but fell back. His eyes started to adjust to the darkness. His head throbbed. *Where am I? How did I get here? My shoulder is killing me!*

He tried to get up again. He reached out with his right hand to maintain his balance. *Ouch!* He suddenly felt a sharp slash. His hand felt warm as he felt a tinge of pain. Warm liquid was dripping from his hand. Then his ears felt a slight vibrating sensation. A ringing sound came up from the floor beside him. It sounded like a small bell. He closed his eyes to listen better, but instead saw little stars floating before him. The ringing noise was getting louder. Something was swaying in front of him. The ringing suddenly stopped. A yellowish-orange light was curling up in front of him. He could see it was emanating from some sort of crypt. He felt like he was going to pass out.

The light was getting larger and brighter. It was taking shape. It transformed itself into the figure of a naked woman who had sagging breasts and little bells in her hair and cheeks. She wore a feathered headdress. She was now standing in front of Francisco. Even though he was dazed, he recognized her as the Aztec Moon Goddess, Coyolxāuqui.

"You have stolen my sacrifice," the amorphous form said in Nahuatl. "Come to me."

Francisco was frozen with fear. He didn't understand the words. What is this thing? My head is on fire!

He winced as Coyolxāuqui grabbed him by his hair and began pulling him up a gigantic pyramid. His body felt like it had been beaten by a thousand clubs. Finally, he was thrown onto a large basalt table at the top of the pyramid.

"Coyolxāuqui! Coyolxāuqui!" thousands of Aztec natives chanted as the drums beat. "Coyolxāuqui! Give us light!"

What does she want? Oh, the pain! I want to die!

The form approached him. "I need you!" the Moon Goddess said. "You are mine. You will make me whole!

There was a clap of thunder in the background. The loud

noise seemed to break him out of his trance, and he was suddenly back in the chapel cellar. Now the entire chapel and subterranean chambers were shaken with the force of a hurricane. Part of the sandstone wall cracked. Crepuscular light broke through. Francisco was overwhelmed with the sulfur smell that was bubbling beneath his feet. The water was getting warmer.

He thought he could also now smell smoke from above. *Is the chapel on fire? What is happening?*

His head felt dizzy again, and once again he sensed himself being pulled away by the Moon Goddess.

"Coyolxāuqui! Coyolxāuqui! Give us light!" The chanting intensified.

Francisco still could not move away from the Moon Goddess. Her form started to sparkle. Sparks started to fly from her. Then he noticed that the figure had something in her right hand. It was large. It was dark. His mind was spinning, and his head ached, but he tried to see what she was grasping. No, it can't be! I'm not crazy! An obsidian sword?

"She has awoken me!" Coyolxauhqui shouted at Francisco.

"Who?"

"Yepollotli!" the figure hissed. "She was promised to me!"

"But she's dead!" Francisco knew that he wasn't speaking

but somehow was communicating telepathically with this aberration.

"Anyone who shares her blood is in my debt. Her blood belongs to me. That is the curse!"

"I don't know what you mean!" Francisco tried to speak but nothing came out of his mouth.

Coyolxāuqui leaned forward and grabbed Francisco. For such a small creature, she had tremendous strength. She grabbed his right arm with her left hand. She was holding a black obsidian sword.

Somewhere to the right, came a voice out of the darkness.

"Francisco, where are you?" Alexi yelled out nervously. A faint light descended some narrow stairs.

He tried to respond but nothing came out of his mouth.

"Here she comes to fulfill her destiny!" Coyolxāuqui smirked.

Alexi came closer, out of the shadows. "Francisco, Francisco, look what I found in the hidden compartment in the altar!" Alexi shouted out. He could not see the black pearl rosary in her hand.

The Moon Goddess slid in between Francisco and Alexi.

"I need you so I can live. I am your Goddess," the voice of Coyolxāuqui got louder. "I need your sacrifice."

Alexi saw the form and stepped back alarmed. What

sacrifice? What is this creature saying?

"Your heart will make me immortal," Coyolxāuqui continued. "I will drink your blood. You have been a noble sacrifice, Yepyollotli."

Then Alexi saw Francisco in the grasp of Coyolxāuqui. He tried to pull away, jerking Coyolxāuqui away from the oncoming Alexi.

"Run, Alexi," he forced himself to yell.

Coyolxāuqui lifted her obsidian sword.

Francisco did not have the energy to restrain the Moon Goddess. He had no strength left. He saw the blade start to move downward toward him. Instinctively, he grabbed at Coyolxāuqui's arm. She pulled herself free.

The sword was falling halfway through its arc. Suddenly, Coyolxāuqui's right arm was jerked back. There was a swishing sound in the air. "The curse is over!" a determined voice cried out.

Francisco heard a slight gurgling in front of him and then the Moon Goddess dropped the sword. Her severed head fell off. Her body tumbled to the ground and her hands and feet started thrashing about. Francisco was kicked in the face and fell into the water that had started to bubble.

Standing over both Francisco and the corpse was a young Aztec princess who placed the blood splattered black pearl rosary around her own neck.

Smoke was emanating from all sides. Small fires were everywhere. The headless Coyolxāuqui rose and fell like a tethered balloon. The severed head gave a sharp shriek, "Yepyollotli!"

The wall of the subterranean chamber collapsed. Water began rushing in.

A moment later Coyolxāuqui's figure started to shrivel. Her skin slowly dissolved. Soon there was only a skeleton left. It was sinking in the rising hot water. The bones started to sizzle. There was a momentary puff of black smoke. In the next moment, Coyolxāuqui's form had totally disappeared.

"Francisco!" Alexi rushed over to his limp body that was floating in the water. "Wake up!" Alexi struggled to pull him up. He wasn't breathing. She tried to give him CPR but couldn't position his body properly.

Water started rushing into the subterranean space from the beach. Smoke and flames traveled downward from the chapel that was now totally on fire.

Little by little Alexi struggled to drag Francisco's inert body to the opening in the wall where the water was rushing in.

"Mi amor! Don't leave me!" Alexi shouted out. "Wake up! Help! Somebody!"

The floor of the chamber above them collapsed. Old

furniture and relics fell from its ceiling, narrowly missing Francisco and Alexi. Alexi again tried to administer CPR again, but with little success.

Alexi had pinned Francisco against an exterior wall that was still standing, trying to keep him away from the rising waters. She was exhausted and couldn't keep the effort up much longer.

"Amorcito, don't leave me!" Tears started to form in her eyes. "I love you!" The drops were black. They started to harden. As she wiped her eyes, she found black pearls in her hand. At that moment, she lost consciousness.

CHAPTER 57 – E.R.

Saturday July 28, 2018
Guadalajara

Alexi came to and found herself on the beach. She got up on her hands and knees. The eclipse was over. The winds were now gentle, and the seas were calm. She inhaled several times trying to catch her breath. The skies were midnight blue speckled with a thousand stars. There was no moon.

How did I get here? She looked around, trying to get her bearings. There were dark and vague shapes all around. Then she spotted a black outline just about a foot away. She reached out and touched it. She felt wet clothes and cold skin. She slid over and turned the body toward her. "Amorcito! Wake up!" She shook the body. "Don't leave me, Francisco!" She pulled his head upright with her two hands and brought her face close to his. She kissed him. There was no movement.

Alexi was in a trance. She was not thinking. Her cellphone was in the rental car, but luckily, she still had the car keys. Hopefully she could find the car tonight. She closed her eyes and breathed in heavily. *Concentrate!* She took another deep breath. She felt an inner heat within her body. *Concentrate!* She put her mouth over his and blew. She waited and then repeated the CPR procedure. She waited again and repeated the procedure. No response.

She stood up and looked to the south. There seemed to be a small fire around the area of the promontory. She glanced in the opposite direction and could see a few lights. In front of her the luminescence of the waves was of little use. She racked her brain. She couldn't drag him to the car, he was too heavy. Her best bet was to go and find her car. Alexi could telephone the police or somebody to come and rescue Francisco. She felt around and turned his legs. She made a pile of sand under his legs to keep them higher than his heart level. They had no extra clothes, so she had to decide how to keep him warm while she left him. She started to dig around him and began covering him with sand. She needed to find some sticks or rocks to use as markers so she could find him later.

Alexi got up and moved cautiously toward the forest that bordered the beach. She found some old mangrove limbs. Her eyes had adjusted to the darkness. As she came back to Francisco's body, Alexi heard gasping and wheezing. Francisco's body began to quiver. He started to choke. She saw him turn his head. He vomited food and water. He tried to sit up.

"Oh, Francisco, you are alive!" Alexi was overwhelmed. She hugged him and wouldn't let go. *I haven't felt this much love and pain since my husband died!* She thought, *now what is Plan B?* She conducted a superficial examination of Francisco. The gash on this forehead was not a real bleeder, so that was good. He was in pain and he looked blurry-eyed. She didn't know if he could get up and walk yet.

His breathing was shallow but improving by the minute. She was faced with a dilemna. If she left him, he could suffer exposure, shock, or something worse. If they tried to walk, it could cause some permanent damage.

"Can you walk, Francisco?" she asked.

"What happened?" his voice was slightly slurred. At that point she realized that things would not get better if they simply stayed where they were.

"You fell," Alexi replied. "What do you remember?"

"Nothing, really," he answered. Alexi could tell that Francisco was making an effort to recover.

"Do you think you can walk?" Alexi prompted. "We can stop anytime you get tired." *I'm the one who is already exhausted.*

The first hundred meters took them at least ten minutes. "Talk to me, Francisco. You can't go to sleep yet."

"But I'm so wiped out." He sounded weak.

The next hundred meters were not much better, especially when Alexi stubbed her toe on a rock protruding from the sand. She was dying of thirst. They had lost their water bottles back at the chapel. They would be lucky to find the towels that they had left on the beach the prior afternoon.

As they continued gingerly, Alexi thought she could hear sounds up ahead. Francisco was out of it. He was talking to himself and occasionally stopped to vomit. Fortunately, the air was warm, and their clothes had almost completely dried. However, they were still covered with sand from head to toe.

The noises became louder. It sounded like voices.

"¡Auxilio!" Alexi yelled. "¡Ayúdanos!"

The sea breezes were attenuating the calls for help. The pair kept walking at a little quicker pace.

"¡Auxilio!" Alexi cried out again.

The next thing that she knew, a bouncy beam of light was coming toward them. Several minutes later an older fisherman and a young boy were helping them walk. Within an hour they had found their towels and retrieved everything. At the Suburban, Alexi got her bag from under the driver's seat and tried to give the older man named Gregorio five hundred pesos. He tried to decline, but Alexi was finally successful in making the gift. Gregorio had also given her directions to an emergency clinic not far away.

In the Suburban, Alexi cleaned the gash on Francisco's head and right hand with bottled water and hand sanitizer. They then drove to the emergency clinic which was actually an old pink house where the doctor lived. Doctor Morales and Alexi discussed Francisco's condition. He sterilized the head wound and gave Francisco twelve stitches. Dr. Morales examined Francisco's left shoulder and determined he had a broken clavicle. He did not X-ray Francisco's shoulder because it would take too long to get the results. The doctor put him in a sling. As for the hand, he simply dressed it with a bandage.

"How did he injure himself?" Dr. Morales asked Alexi because Francisco was partially incoherent.

"He fell and hit his head."

"Luckily, whatever he hit was flat," the elderly doctor surmised. "If it had been something sharp or a few centimeters higher or lower, it could have been fatal, or he could have lost an eye."

This emergency visit cost the equivalent of fifty dollars with a dozen pain pills thrown in. It was now four a.m. Saturday morning. Alexi's second wind had kicked in. As a medical doctor, she was used to all-nighters.

They drove to La Paz. She was hungry, tired, and wired, but Alexi was a doctor and knew how to remain in control and focused. One step at a time. On the way she called the

Emergency Room at a hospital she knew in La Paz. She gave them all the details and they were ready to receive Francisco when they arrived.

Francisco was disrobed. A male nurse washed his entire body making sure not to disturb the shoulder in a sling and the stitches. An X-ray was made of the collarbone. A neurologist who was on call came in.

By late morning the collarbone fracture was confirmed. The good news was that the doctors found no signs of a concussion. That was a relief to Alexi. The doctors also gave Francisco a tetanus booster and some antibiotics. They said that Francisco would be able to fly back to Guadalajara. They wanted him to take it easy for the next 48 hours. Alexi promised she would monitor him closely.

The next day they took the first flight out. They had wanted to avoid crowds and get back home early.

"Mi amor, thanks for saving my life," Francisco said that night. "Sorry I spoiled our last weekend together."

"You just being here with me tonight is reward enough," she carefully leaned over and kissed him.

CHAPTER 58 – PRISONER IN PARADISE

Sunday, July 29, 2018
Guadalajara

Alexi had called Miranda Sunday night and told her that Francisco would not be able to make his Monday meeting with her. She explained that he had hurt himself.

"Oh, my God! How did he do that?"

"He fell, hit his head, and broke his clavicle." Alexi did not want to divulge the details of the terrifying episode. Since Francisco did not remember the incident, she felt that her simple version of the facts was the best. She wasn't lying. Well, maybe it was a white lie, but oh, well.

"I wanted to have you both over for a little dinner, to celebrate," Miranda was starting to say too much. "I have something important to share. And, of course, we want to show Francisco our gratitude for his visit here. We have enjoyed his company." *But not as much as you have, comadre,* Miranda winked to herself.

. . .

After their arrival at the Guadalajara Airport earlier on Sunday morning, Francisco had accepted Alexi's offer for him to spend the next few days at her house. They had stopped at his faculty housing, and Alexi and Esteban had grabbed some clothes and his computer. She wanted to make sure that he did not suffer any setbacks. At her home, Alexi asked Vera to prepare the large guest bedroom on the first floor. She did not want to subject Francisco to climbing any stairs. It was too hazardous.

Francisco was now able to talk intelligently but still could not recall the chapel incident. She escorted him to the laundry room where Vera had brought a chair. Alexi carefully wrapped a towel around his neck and slowly tilted his head back to a low wash basin and shampooed his hair that was still filthy from the beach sand. She was cautious about not getting the stitches wet or bumping into his shoulder.

Francisco was a good sport and didn't complain. He started to talk. "I see they taught you well in med school."

"I learned this growing up in a one-bedroom house in La Paz," Alexi retorted. "There wasn't much hot water."

Next, she escorted Francisco to the bathtub in the guest room that Vera had filled with bubble bath salts. Alexi disrobed him and he stepped into the tub with her assistance. The color had come back into his cheeks and he was talking cheerfully.

"Mi amorcito," Francisco looked tenderly at her. "You are so perfect."

"You say that now," she was relaxing. "Wait until you see the bill." They both finally laughed.

Afterwards, she redressed the bandage on his hand and helped him change into his jogging clothes. By then, it was lunch time. Vera served them a cocido soup of chicken and vegetables with tortillas. They hadn't eaten in almost 48 hours and had slept very little. Alexi's preference was for her patients to take their antibiotics with food, so she gave Francisco one of his pills. For dessert Vera dished up for them a dollop of Greek yogurt with fresh berries.

The couple talked about the next few days. She told him that he had to rest the next day. He could not meet with Miranda. She would call her comadre that evening to inform her. On Tuesday, he could have light activities. She would rebandage his gash and check out the stitches. It would be a day by day evaluation. She was the doctor, and he was the patient.

"What about my project?" he asked.

"It's on hold," she replied affirmatively. She rolled her eyes. *The educated ones were the worst patients.*

"I'm calling comadre right now," Alexi said. "I'll tell her

about how you feel like . . . Dumbo Dumpsy?"

"Humpty Dumpty!" They both laughed again.

• • •

"I don't think Francisco should go anywhere for a few days, comadre," Alexi said to Miranda. "He suffered a nasty blow to his head. We need to be very careful."

"I understand," Miranda's face seemed to pale. Alexi noticed it.

"How about this, comadre?" Alexi could sense that something was up and that Miranda was disappointed. "Why don't you and Sol and mija come over here tomorrow night for a little get together. Nothing fancy. It would be great to see you. How's Mirasol doing?"

"¡Ay Dios Mio! That girl is driving me crazy!" Miranda said exasperated.

Later that evening Alexi and Francisco sat in the library and drank chamomile tea.

"Francisco, you and I are so much alike," Alexi was holding his right hand. "We're always on the go. Always doing something. Never relaxing."

He nodded in agreement.

"The best and fastest way for you to recuperate is to let go," she said softly, but seriously. "Twenty years from now, probably none of this will matter."

"You're right, mi amor," Francisco knew that she was right. "But it is very difficult for me to do nothing or waste time."

"Trying to get better is not a waste of time," she said. "Tomorrow I want you to go out into the garden and feel life."

At around nine o'clock, she helped Francisco get ready for bed. He could do the basics so there were no problems. She took his temperature and gave him his medication. He was not experiencing any pain.

"You should probably get out of those jogging clothes," she started taking off his pants. He was now just in his chonies. "You can sleep on the side of the bed closest to the bathroom. I'll leave the light on, so you won't crash into anything. Is there anything you need? I'll be leaving early in the morning. Let Vera know if you need anything. She will wake you up at nine if you are not up. She'll take your temperature. You are to obey her under penalty of no chocolate for a whole week."

"You are so cruel," they kissed as she tucked him in.

CHAPTER 59 – CELEBRATION

Monday, July 30, 2018
Guadalajara

Alexi quietly entered the guest bedroom and kissed Francisco goodbye as she set off to work that Monday morning. He was still in a deep slumber. She was grateful that he was making steady progress in his recovery.

Francisco could not turn over on his left side because of the sling. The room was dark as the curtains were drawn. Right at nine o'clock, there was a knock on the guestroom door.

"Buenos Días, Professor Reynoso," Vera sounded so pleasant. "I'm here to take your temperature."

"Adelante, Vera."

She came in and quickly averted her eyes when she saw that he was semi-bare chested under the covers. She took his temperature and nodded that everything was fine. She then gave him a pill with a glass of water.

"¿Cuándo estarás listo para café y desayuno?" She asked when he might be ready for breakfast.

"Treinta minutos, por favor." Francisco was used to

speaking English with Alexi most of the time. Alexi was very proficient in English. But he liked having to practice his Spanish and was always willing to perfect it.

Francisco changed back into some clean jogging clothes and slowly walked to the lonely dining room thirty minutes later. A large cup of coffee with hot milk was set in front of him along with the morning paper, the Mexican Daily News. *How are the Chivas doing?*

Breakfast was brought in. It was cooked oatmeal with sliced fruit and Greek yogurt. Francisco took the last of his antibiotics. He was feeling good. Alexi was right. Relaxing was helpful. But he knew that he had to call Dean Dorothea Chandler at Stanford to apprise her of the situation. It was almost ten-thirty when he finished breakfast. He thanked Vera and went back to the guest room. He turned on the computer and checked his emails.

He then placed a call to Stanford. Dean Chandler was not in yet. Francisco had forgotten about the two-hour time difference. He left a message along with Alexi's home phone number. Francisco was tempted to prepare for his Thursday presentation on U.S.-Mexico relations, but he had promised Alexi that he would take it easy today. No work today.

Francisco was scheduled to fly back to San Francisco on Saturday, just five days away. There were so many loose ends.

His cell phone was fully charged, so he decided to take a few selfies. Was this the "before" or "after" photo? He didn't even want to think about the paperwork he would have to fill out back home: Medical, Workers' Comp, Insurance, . . .?

He was relaxing on the bed when the phone rang. It was Alexi.

"How are you, my love?" she asked.

"Fine. Vera is treating me very well," he was smiling. "I could get used to this."

There was a moment of silence at the other end. "Miranda, Sol, and Mirasol are coming over tonight for a little party, at about seven. I think my comadre has a surprise announcement."

"Sounds good. Will I be able to have a drink?" Francisco knew the answer to that. He would have to appear presentable. It was the culture. "I think I can take a shower by myself. I promise I'll be careful."

Another pause. "Or you can wait for me." Then Francisco could hear the double think. "Just let Vera or Esteban know when you're going to shower."

"No problem."

It was just past noon when Dean Chandler called. Francisco gave her all the gory details. The dean was very astute. She had inherited a hornet's nest, but she was going to share the pain.

"Well, Francisco, what are we going to do?"

"The research project is now on hold, dean. Lots of problems with provenance and corroboration. But we should have a draft article to present to the university by sometime in October. I'm going to need to pick your brain about how to proceed." Francisco knew how to play the game also. Get as many people invested in the project as possible.

"When are you planning to come back?"

"I had planned to return this Saturday, before the accident," Francisco started to exaggerate a little. "But now I'm under a doctor's care and they want me to recuperate completely before they'll release me."

"What about your teaching load? You were going to teach two classes this Fall?"

"Maybe we should cancel them," Francisco knew that she would never go for that.

"Not a good idea," the dean was thinking. "I don't know about starting the classes halfway through the term. Hmm! Here's a thought. Professor Ellison is coming back. He could teach one of your classes. He owes you one for teaching his Caribbean class in the Spring."

Well, at least I can spend a few more weeks down here before I go back. I think Alexi said the broken collarbone would take six weeks to heal. That'll buy me another month.

At around four o'clock Alexi came home. She found Francisco on the bed taking a nap. He awoke and they kissed.

"You're here early," he remarked.

"I wanted to help you shower," she gave him a devilish smile.

He told Alexi about his conversation with the dean, and that he thought he might be able stay another month. She was so overwhelmed that she accidently squeezed his bad shoulder.

• • •

Francisco was starving by the time the Rios arrived. They all sat in the living room. Vera brought in drinks, but only mineral water for Alexi, Mirasol, and Francisco. Then came the appetizers. Totopos with guacamole and queso fundido.

"I'm so glad we could get together. I wanted to share something with the people I love and respect," Miranda was getting tearful. "This week Dean Montoya of our Social Sciences Department announced his retirement."

Francisco remembered Dean Montoya from his presentations. The dean was a nice gentleman.

"Well, they are promoting me to take his place," the tears starting to flow.

"¡Felicidades!" Their glasses clinked in celebration.

The room was full of energy with everyone talking at once. Vera brought in plates with chicken enchiladas, nopales salad, and chayote squash. Mirasol was given a miniature pizza.

"What's this?" Miranda asked her daughter.

"Madrina had a special dish made for me," explained Mirasol. "I'm a vegetarian now. I'm not doing meat anymore."

"¡Ay Dios Mio!" Miranda shook her head and blew out a breath. "Comadre, how you spoil this girl!"

The discussion proceeded to prospective colleges for Mirasol.

"Too bad you're leaving on Saturday, Francisco," Sol was on his second or third reposado tequila. "There's a Chivas game in town."

Alexi then looked around and said, "Francisco is going to stay another month because of his accident," she raised her glass of mineral water. "Doctor's orders."

Everybody laughed. Another round of congratulations.

"Does that mean that you and Francisco are going to be living together?" Mirasol looked at her madrina.

"¡Ay Dios Mio!"

CHAPTER 60 – NIGHTMARES

Tuesday, July 31, 2018
Guadalajara

On Tuesday morning Alexi left the house early. Francisco tossed and turned all night in his sleep. He still couldn't roll over on his side because of the sling. He kept having a recurring nightmare.

The short tunic felt loose around his body as he trudged forward. He was wearing leather sandals on the dusty road. In front of him, a young Aztec princess was being carried in a palanquin by giant warriors. There were hundreds of people on both sides of him cheering and shouting.

Behind him, there were elderly men dressed in long robes, carrying bastons, and chanting. The sun beat down on the multitudes.

He was getting tired. He kept walking. Keeping up with the princess' procession. Where were they going?

Francisco's body started to heat up. He unconsciously threw off the covers. He was thirsty. Beads of sweat bubbled on his forehead. He moaned.

The procession stopped in front of a large pyramid. The palanquin was put down and the Aztec princess was being escorted by several priestesses toward the top. He was pushed forward and then had to wait for several priests to escort him upward. Ten steps. Fifty steps. And finally, 243 steps.

A nobleman with a hummingbird feather headdress and gold earplugs started praying, looking to the heavens. The crowds at the bottom of the pyramid joined in the refrains.

"Oh, mighty god Tlaloc, we are here today to honor you. We are here today to pay you homage. We are here to beg you for rain and a good harvest."

The princess was led to one side of a large stone table that had a rut carved into it.

"Oh, mighty god Tlaloc, we offer you this virgin Aztec princess to join you in the heavens."

She was instructed to bend over the stone table. She obeyed. She laid her head on it. Prayers were said and with lightning speed, an obsidian sword chopped off the young woman's head. Several priests turned her over and excised her bleeding heart. The noble took a bite of it and the crowd roared. Blood ran off the table. The priests took the princess' corpse away.

Francisco had seen the entire ceremony. He was not emotional. His mind was in a different reality. He was not afraid. Other priests took him by the arms and led him to the other side of the stone table.

"Oh, mighty god Tlaloc, we offer you this brave Aztec warrior to join you in the heavens."

More prayers were said. Francisco started to lean forward. As he did, he could hear the whistling sound of a cudgel marked for his head.

Francisco suddenly jerked upward in his bed. He gave a little cry of pain from straining his clavicle. His left eye was throbbing and tearing. He could not see out of it. Slowly and carefully, he staggered over to the bathroom and threw water on his face. He then wet a hand towel and went back to lie on the bed. He threw the wet towel on his face and tried to relax.

He must have gone back to sleep, because the next thing he knew was Vera knocking on the door at nine o'clock and taking his temperature. It was a little lower than usual, but within the normal limits. Francisco did not mention the bad dream or the aching eye to her. *Should I call Alexi? I probably should. But what can she do? She would rush home and wouldn't be able to do anything. Worse yet, she might send me back to the hospital! Let's wait and see. I'll take it easy today. If it happens again, I'll tell her. I don't want to cause any more stress in her life. Am I cursed?*

Francisco took his time getting ready. Alexi called and

asked how he was. He told her that he was fine.

"I've told Esteban to drive you to your apartment to pick up the rest of your belongings," she informed him. "Just tell him what you need."

"Thanks, mi amor."

After breakfast Esteban drove Francisco to the faculty housing. Esteban and the faculty housing night watchman, Jorge, loaded the remaining clothes and possessions (including a bottle of chocolate sauce) into the Lexus. Francisco left envelopes of gratuities for the cook and the night watchman.

Since I am out and about, I should get a haircut. Esteban ran him over to Chester's. Francisco also wanted to buy some wine and food. Now that he was staying with Alexi, he should help with the groceries, especially for the alcohol and sweets that she eschewed. They went to Liverpool's. He bought a case of assorted wines, but no hard liquor.

It was getting close to one o'clock and Francisco was getting hungry.

"Esteban, what is your favorite lunch place?" Alexi's driver was nearly fluent in English.

"Excuse me, señor," Esteban gave him a frowning expression. "I don't understand. You want to eat lunch?"

"Yes, with you," Francisco smiled. "You pick the place."

"What kind of place do you like?"

"Whatever you like."

Twenty minutes later they were eating pozole at a little hole in the wall place called La Casita. Both ordered the medium pork with green salsa and jamaica aguas frescas. The salsa was picante and made one sweat.

Esteban was very uneasy about socializing with Francisco, so he just behaved politely.

"How long have you worked for Dr. Alejandra?"

Esteban then gave his life story about being from Morelia, having been a medic in the military and then getting a job as an ambulance driver for the university hospital in Guadalajara. He knew all the medical staff, and when Dr. Nicolás Mora, Alexi's husband, needed a private driver, he was hired. That was almost twenty-five years ago.

"I really appreciate you looking after me," Francisco said sincerely. "I really like Alexi, Esteban."

"Professor, excuse me for saying this, but she really likes you. I haven't seen her this happy since her husband passed away."

The two were back at Alexi's house by three o'clock, after spending a wonderful afternoon getting to know each other.

Francisco then started to send emails to his Stanford staff and colleagues notifying them that he would probably not be back for the Fall term because of an accident. He attached his selfie for good measure. He wrote a special note to Tina explaining that the article was going to be significantly abbreviated if they didn't find more corroborative materials. He said that he would have the first draft of the paper finished around the first of October. She would do the first edit. He didn't want to interfere with her dissertation writing.

At six o'clock Alexi came home, and they sat in her living room drinking some herbal tea.

"How are you, mi amor?" she asked. She didn't take his temperature.

"Fine," Francisco responded and shared his day with Esteban.

Alexi was close-mouthed about her day. It looked like she just wanted to relax. She had had a stressful few days.

"My mother used to tell me that things happen for a reason, mi querida," Francisco held her hand with his. "Being with you now proves this."

"Your mother was a smart woman," Alexi smiled. "I'm glad she raised you well."

They made idle chatter, getting physically close to each other.

"Querida, I want to always be completely honest with you," he started to say. "I don't want to keep any secrets."

"Thank you, mi amor," Alexi said, waiting for him to

reveal a tragic secret. *Did he have a wife back home?*

They had a light dinner and continued to chat. He couldn't stand not telling her about his terrible morning nightmares. Then he told her about the sweats, the eye pain, and the nightmares.

"Francisco, have you finished taking your antibiotics?"

"Yes."

"Have you stopped taking your pain pills?"

"Yes."

"Have you been constipated the last few days?"

"Yes."

"These are just the side effects of the medication. You're probably fine, but we'll monitor it,"

Alexi responded nonchalantly. She summoned the maid and made a request, "Traiga al señor unas ciruelas pasas guisadas por favor." She ordered him some stewed prunes.

CHAPTER 61 – THE LEGEND

Wednesday, August 1, 2018
Guadalajara

Miranda had asked Francisco to come in early that
Wednesday morning for their normally scheduled meeting.
Carlos Erandi was going to join them later. She had some
thoughts about how to maximize the extended time Francisco
would be spending in Guadalajara. She had been mulling over
some ideas since morning.

On Monday night, Miranda had been feeling overwhelmed.
She was already in shock about Dean Montoya's retirement
and then being selected as his replacement. She was also elated
about the prospect of being a female dean in the Mexican
higher education system. She had had to work harder than her
male colleagues, and now she would have to perform. Right
now, she was feeling responsible for everybody and
everything. Miranda and Alexi had chatted that evening while
the boys (Francisco and Sol) were talking soccer and politics.
Alexi had put on a game face, but Miranda knew her inside out.
Alexi was a doctor and had taken over the responsibility for

Francisco's well-being. She had been granted a reprieve of at least another month with Francisco, *but what about after that? Did Alexi still believe in her "twenty minutes or twenty years" mantra? Her comadre Miranda could visualize all the scenarios. What could she do to support Alexi? What should she do?*

After the Rios drove home that night, Miranda and Sol had a serious conversation in their living room after Mirasol went to bed.

"Pobre Francisco," Sol commented. "He looks like he got run over by a train. Thank God he has Alexi."

"I know, mi corazon. But how long can this last?" Miranda was shaking her head. "I don't want her heart to be broken!"

"But she's a grown woman," he retorted. "She's a doctor. Alexi knows what she is doing.'

"But mi cariño, she is a woman in love. In a case like this, all bets are off."

It was now 9:30 a.m. on Wednesday, and Francisco had just walked in the door of Miranda's office.

She gave him pecks on the cheek carefully avoiding his arm in the sling, and then they sat down at a table. Per her custom, Miranda had coffee and pan dulce available.

"How are feeling, Francisco?" Miranda asked.

"Better."

"The good news is that you don't have to leave on Saturday," Miranda did not need to ask him if he agreed. "First things, first. I suggest that we not have your presentation of U.S.-Mexico relations tomorrow. It provides a logistical challenge, but we can defer it."

Francisco was willing and able to do it but putting it off was a good idea. He knew that Miranda was doing him a favor. "Thank you. We can reschedule it for any time you wish. That's not a problem for me."

A cochinito mysteriously disappeared from the tray of pan dulce.

"Francisco, tell me about your teaching assignment at Stanford for this semester and your other responsibilities," Miranda queried. "I know your system is different than ours, but there must be some similarities."

Francisco explained that he was supposed to teach two classes. He also had research responsibilities which involved publishing an article on the 1527 expedition from Mexico.

"I'm also the faculty advisor for the Stanford Latinx Association, and I have a research assistant named Tina that I supervise . . ."

They continued talking and then took a break. They were expecting Carlos Erandi to join them to continue their discussion about the journal article. He had just arrived.

"Hombre! What happened to you?" Carlos gave Francisco a careful abrazo.

"I really don't know," Francisco replied. "I fell."

For the next hour they discussed the article and all the supporting logs, diaries, and papers.

"Official ship's logs carry more weight than personal journals," Miranda said. "We don't know if any of the personal journals and notes will meet the academic article threshold."

"Well, I can contact Roberto Gutierrez and see what else he wants to sell us," Carlos volunteered.

"That's good! I'll have Tina contact that Brenner guy at Powell's Bookstore," Francisco added. He was getting excited again.

"And I will have someone here at the university check official Spanish records from 1527," Miranda said. "Let's all three of us meet again in two weeks. I'll have my secretary set a time. I understand that we need a first draft finished by the first of October. Francisco, could you please talk to someone at Stanford and see what our options are if we wanted to use the Milo, Diego, and Ismael materials."

"Great idea," Francisco nodded his head. "No problem."

THE PACIFIC EXPEDITIONS 1527-1534

Dates	Cmdr/Capt	Ships	Chron.	Start	Dest
1527	Saavedra Viurco	Florida	Duro	Mexico	Moluccas
1527-34	Saavedra Viurco	Florida	da Napoli	Mexico	Moluccas
1527	de Cardenas	Santiago		Mexico	
	de Xerez	Espiritu Santo		Mexico	Moluccas
		Espiritu Santo	Milo	Mexico	Island #1
1527-28	Diego Garcia	Santiago #2	Diego Garcia	Zacatula	Moluccas
	Diego Garcia	Santiago #2	Ismael Gavriel	Mexico	Moluccas

"I'm not sure," Carlos hesitated. "In some of the papers, there are insinuations that María Del Rosario is the Aztec princess Yepyollotli, the Black Pearl. I was able to do some research at the Archive Office of the Temple of the Moon when I worked this summer at Teotihuacan. Yepyollotli was the daughter of the ruler Cacamatzin. She was being groomed to be the human sacrifice for Coyolxāuqui, the Goddess of the Moon.

"In the Divine Aztec song, Teocuitlatl, the God of the Sun was Huitzilopochtli, the son of Coatlicue (Earth) had a sister, Coyolxāuqui. Coyolxāuqui was the Moon Goddess that the

Aztecs revered and offered human sacrifice to. But the decades and decades of this practice were threatened when Yepyollotli's father was taken hostage by Cortés. Yepyollotli was spared from being sacrificed when she was taken to a convent and converted to Christianity. She wore a black pearl rosary to commemorate her transformation to Catholicism.

"Legend has it that Coyolxāuqui was livid about being deprived of the human sacrifice that was due her when Saavedra abducted Yepyollotli onto his ship. She cursed Yepyollotli who was named María Del Rosario after her conversion. She blamed the Spaniards for robbing her of her promised human sacrifice. Ever since then, the Moon Goddess has been trying to possess the bodies and souls of María Del Rosario' loved ones."

"Has the curse been broken yet?" Miranda was intrigued by the tale.

"We don't even know if it is true," Carlos gave a little laugh.

Francisco didn't say anything. A faint memory was trying to come forward in his mind. *I think this was in my dream!*

It was near one o'clock and stomachs were growling.

"Another thing I discovered," Carlos added, to the chagrin of the other two who wanted to go to leave and go to lunch, "was a misinterpretation of the manifest of goods on the

Espíritu Santo."

"I don't remember anything about this," Miranda frowned.

"Well, we thought the Espíritu Santo was carrying gold and black pearls. That's what the manifest said. And the Spanish Crown required strict accounting," Carlos began.

Francisco wasn't following the significance of this point.

"Well, one of the entries in the cargo manifest was a black pearl."

The others nodded, not understanding what this meant.

"The entry was written in Nahuatl and said 'Yepollotli'"

There were blank looks on the faces of Francisco and Miranda. "Okay?!"

"The Espíritu Santo was not carrying black pearls as part of its cargo," Carlos smiled. "It was transporting María Del Rosario whose Aztec name is 'Yepollotli.' Yepollotli means black pearl in Nahuatl. She was their precious cargo! She was the black pearl! The Aztec princess Yepollotli! And legends say that she was named Black Pearl because her tears hardened into black pearls. Milo's notes allude to this."

Francisco and Miranda looked dumbfounded. They had missed one of the biggest pieces of the puzzle. Fortunately, Carlos had found it.

"And the last thing I found out," Carlos was sensing the other two's impatience. "There is a legend that Yepollotli survived the shipwreck, but Diego did not. It is rumored that the descendants of Yepollotli lived in Baja California and that every September a human voice howls from the sea. It is said to be Diego looking for María Del Rosario. Just rumors and folklore."

Francisco was too exhausted to process the ramifications. He just wanted to eat and take a nap. Finally, they decided to call it quits. But Miranda stopped Francisco before he could leave.

"Francisco, what is the name of your dean at Stanford?" Miranda asked.

"Dorothea Chandler," Francisco was surprised at her question.

"Please give me her contact information."

CHAPTER 62 – THE DAY OF THE DEAD

Thursday, November 2, 2018
Guadalajara

Alexi came home on Friday afternoon from the hospital and immediately went out to the back garden. It was the middle of Fall and the weather was cool. Most of the deciduous plants and trees had begun dropping their leaves. Alexi and Esteban had constructed a three-step ofrenda altar in remembrance of her husband, Nicolás, on this Day of the Dead. Alexi had started this annual ritual after her husband, Dr. Nicolás Mora, had died falling down steps at Teotihuacan in 1996. She had been a young nurse when this tragedy had occurred. They had only been married for three years.

Alexi placed an old portrait photo of Nicolás on the top level. She lit the votive candles and the copal incense that flanked the orange marigolds, pan de muertos, apples, a pitcher of water, sugar skulls, photographs, saltshaker, papel picado, and crucifix that adorned the altar. The scent of the incense stirred her emotions. She was sad. But, on the other hand, she was happy. She was grateful to have had two great loves in her life. Better yet, Francisco was not the jealous type. He was grateful that Nicolás had bequeathed him such a wonderful gift.

A half hour later Francisco arrived. He and Alexi took refreshments in the salon. She had her routine mineral water with lime, and he had a very cold Corona. Vera brought them peanuts to munch on.

"How was your day, mi amor?" he asked, halfway done with his first beer.

"Could have been better," she exhaled slowly. "I had a 62-year-old woman with diabetes and hypertension. She suffered a cardiac attack and was rushed to emergency. We couldn't find her primary physician . . ."

Francisco was always hesitant about asking how her work went. When he did, he was taking the chance that he would be inundated with unlimited descriptions, diagnoses, and prognoses. But he was learning. He liked being around her and was proud of her helping other people.

Vera brought a second beer right on schedule.

"What about you, mi cariño?" Alexi asked.

"Not so good, but it was to be expected," he sounded down, but okay. "The screening committee at Stanford only approved half of our proposed article. The other part was too speculative and did not meet the rigorous standards of the university."

"I know how that works," she agreed. "It's a wonder anything gets approved."

"But, hey, we are still here together!"

"Twenty minutes or twenty years," they clinked glasses.

• • •

Francisco had a guardian angel in Miranda Rios. The newly appointed dean had contacted her Stanford University counterpart to discuss the situation of Professor Francisco Reynoso.

"Dean Chandler, I feel bad that Professor Reynoso can't return to the States to fulfill his university obligations," Miranda Rios was not only intelligent, but she also had street smarts. "On the other hand, we can't let him wither on the vine down here. How can we make this work for both our institutions?"

Dean Chandler immediately formed a sisterhood bond with Miranda. Being a woman in male-dominated academia was a challenge. They talked and brainstormed. A week later they had come to an agreement that was to their mutual benefit.

Francisco was deemed a visiting professor at the University of Guadalajara and he would teach a U.S.-Mexico relations class. He would also teach a hybrid online class on the presidents of Mexico. It would be an onsite class for Mexican students and an online class for Stanford students. This latter class would be given in Spanish.

Francisco was allowed to continue to work on his article with Dean Rios regarding the 1527 expedition from Mexico to the Moluccas. Francisco would also work with Dean Rios and Dean Chandler to establish a privately funded Stanford/University of Guadalajara student exchange program. Professors Segreti and Ellison would take over Francisco's teaching load. And Tina Fang would now be Professor Segreti's teaching assistant.

Alexi and Francisco were ecstatic. Francisco called Dean Chandler as soon as he found out the details.

"Thank you, dean," Francisco had spoken with exuberance. "Things are working out well. I'm even learning a lot. That online classroom platform is a challenge (academic terminology for "pain in the ass")."

"You're welcome," she wished all her problems were so simple. Segreti hadn't been happy about teaching another class but throwing Tina in as his assistant was a winner. Ellison wasn't thrilled either, but he owed Francisco for teaching his Caribbean class. And Tina was just Tina. She had a dissertation to write.

Dean Chandler and Francisco had discussed the problems with the academic article, especially regarding provenance and corroboration.

"Francisco, here is what I have learned," she said with tact. "Every professor wants to discover the Rosetta Stone. But the best practice is to be focused and smart. Keep is simple, Francisco. The editorial committed eats its children for lunch."

They talked about the Stanford/University of Guadalajara project. Francisco reported that the Mexican Stanford Alumni Association and Las Adelitas Foundation were making headway. Some of the Stanford graduates from Mexico were heavy hitters and loved the idea.

"When can I count on you coming back?" she asked in closing.

"I want to say at the beginning of January."

"Sounds good," the dean concluded. "Keep me informed."

• • •

But Miranda was also doing double duty by keeping Francisco around for her comadre and running her department. She needed someone to take up her own teaching load. She decided that Carlos Erandi would be the perfect choice. He would team teach with Francisco, and at the same time Carlos would be enrolled at the University of Guadalajara to earn an advanced degree. He would be provided a teaching stipend, free tuition, and free room and board at the faculty housing. He would only have to be on campus for three or four days each week; he could go back to Guanajuato as he chose. Carlos would be expected to continue working on the academic article. He too was grateful.

CHAPTER 63 – SABOR A MI

Monday, December 24, 2018
Guadalajara

It was pouring rain outside of Alexi's residence. She had set up a fake Christmas tree for Francisco's sake. It was decorated with all sorts of multicolored metal and paper ornaments. They sat next close to each other on the leather couch with a blanket drawn over their laps. Alexi was drinking her hot chamomile tea, and Francisco was sipping some añejo tequila. They were listening to some romantic Mexican boleros. "Somos Novios" was playing.

> *Somos novios*
> *Pues los dos sentimos mutuo amor profundo*
> *Y con eso ya ganamos lo más grande*
> *De este mundo*
> *Nos amamos, nos besamos*
> *Como novios . . .*

Alexi was softly mouthing the words. Francisco was deep in thought. He was conflicted. He was scheduled to leave in just over a week. Alexi had never put any pressure on him. Her "twenty minutes or twenty years" live for today philosophy worked for her. But for Francisco it was another story. He really cared for her. He loved her. But he was a full professor at Stanford with tenure and publications under his belt. He was a well-liked teacher. Francisco had a home in the Bay Area and friends. *How could he leave that? What did Guadalajara have to offer? At best he would be a second-class professor here. He would be earning a pittance. Francisco would have to rely on Alexi.*

Sol also had tried to encourage him to stay around for a little longer. Classes were now over for Francisco. He just wanted to enjoy what little time he had left

"You can always find a teaching job," Sol had said as he was drinking a beer. "Or maybe something else. You won't be making much money. But who cares? You have found a treasure worth more than ten professorships. What do you really want out of life?"

The truth of the matter was that Francisco didn't know or wasn't sure. He had been conditioned to think one way, and this could marginalize his relationship with Alexi.

"There will always be more studies and projects," Sol added. "And more windmills."

Francisco was also feeling petulant because his 1527 Mexican expedition article had again been eviscerated. *What did the committee want?* Professor Segreti had already withdrawn from the project. *Do I really want to spend more time on this article?*

Alexi is the perfect partner, he thought. *What more could I want? Could we move to the States? What could she do? We would have to fix immigration papers. We would have to see if the U.S. has any kind of medical profession reciprocity. Who would take care of her home?* A million questions ran through his mind.

"Mi amor, do you open your presents on Christmas Eve or Christmas morning?" she asked.

He didn't answer. Instead, he reached over and grabbed her. He kissed her tenderly. "Is it too early for chocolate sauce?" he started to lighten up.

"¡Qué malo eres!" she grabbed him. "How about half now, half tomorrow?"

"Sounds like a plan."

"Ready for dinner?"

They slept in on Christmas morning. Alexi had given Vera and Esteban Christmas Day off after giving them some very generous gifts.

Francisco and Alexi had a friendly argument about who would make the coffee. It was decided that she would make the coffee and he would make the eggs.

After a delicious breakfast they retired to the living room. She played some Luis Miguel music.

"Open this one next!" Francisco was excited as he pushed a large, heavy, shiny red package toward her.

With great difficulty and a pair of scissors, Alexi slit open the box. She found a leather-bound, twenty volume set of Alejandro Dumas in Spanish.

"Wow, mi amor!" she planted a wet kiss on his mouth. "With my schedule, this will take me twenty years." She gave him an infectious smile.

Francisco left the room for a minute to refill their coffee cups.

Alexi handed him a small wrapped box and a big red envelope. He opened the package first. It was a pair of gold silk underwear. "And you call me bad," Francisco grinned.

Then Francisco opened the envelope. Inside were two tickets to a Luis Miguel concert. "Oh, my God! This is awesome! I love you!"

"I love you too, mi amor!"

He was emotional. "I want to be with you forever!"

"Me, too!"

"Mi amor, what would you say if I asked you to . . ."

They were interrupted by the loud ringing of the phone. Normally, Vera would be the one to answer it, but she was gone.

Alexi picked up and started chatting. She mouthed that it was Miranda who had just come back from Mexico City where they had visited some of Sol's relatives. After a few minutes, Alexi handed the phone to Francisco. He was surprised.

"Merry Christmas, Francisco!" Miranda greeted him. "I think I might have some good news for you."

"Merry Christmas, Miranda!" Francisco was in a great mood. "How was your trip?"

"Good, except Mirasol got some purple streaks in her hair when she was with her cousins," Miranda sounded exasperated. "¡Ay Dios Mio!"

Francisco eyes moved back and forth. He didn't know what to say.

"Anyway, I was checking the mail. As you know, we've been gone for over a week," Miranda kept going on and on. "Anyway, we got a letter."

"Who?"

"You and me."

"What?!" Francisco was puzzled. "From the Stanford-University of Guadalajara student exchange program. They want you to be its Executive Director for the next 18 months. You would retain your employment status at Stanford half-time with full-retirement benefits. But you would be an independent contractor for the University of Guadalajara portion. You'll have to enroll into the Mexican public health system . . ."

Minutes later after Francisco had hung up with Miranda, he exclaimed, "this is my best Christmas ever!"

"Mine, too!"

"Alexi, will you marry me?" his voice was choking up as he spoke. "And be with me forever?"

"Yes, mi cariño. For twenty minute or twenty years or whatever."

They embraced and then she pushed him away. "We're not quite finished." She handed him a small package.

He unwrapped it. It was a dark blue jewelry box. He opened it and saw it contained two gold bands each mounted with a round black pearl.

"One for you," her eyes twinkled devilishly. "And one for me."

He took the larger ring and tried it on. It fit. Then he took it off and read the inscription engraved on the inside of the ring:

Sabor a Mi
Alexi y Francisco
25.12.18

ABOUT THE AUTHOR

Rocky Barilla lives in the San Francisco Bay Area with his wife, Dolores, and the dozens of avian friends who visit their back yard daily, ranging from hummingbirds (one is named Blanquito) to red-tailed hawks. The couple spend part of the year in the paradise of Zihuatanejo, Mexico.

He was formally educated at the University of Southern California and Stanford University. He also spent two academic quarters in Vienna, Austria. His passions are 19th century French literary fiction, Mexican history, global traveling, studying foreign languages, ceramic painting, and cooking.

Rocky has been actively involved in human rights, social justice, immigration, and multicultural issues, especially those involving Latinos and other people of color. As a state legislator, he was heavily involved in the Oregon State Sanctuary movement in the 1980's.

His books have won several International Latino Book Awards (ILBA) and Latino Books into Movie Awards.

Rocky's mantras are "Life is Good," "Do Good Deeds," and "Be Grateful."

Made in the USA
Columbia, SC
31 October 2022